The Rigel Redemption

Other books and stories by Robin C.M. Duncan

The Quirk and Moth series:
The Mandroid Murders
The Carborundum Conundrum
The Bibliothek Betrayal (novelette)
The Hygeia Hijack (novelette)
The Rigel Redemption

Anthologies from Space Wizard Science Fantasy:
Distant Gardens
Farther Reefs
Lofty Mountains
Fiery Deeps
The World of Juno

Other Anthologies:
Gallus

The Rigel Redemption

A QUIRK AND MOTH CALAMITY

Robin C.M. Duncan

Space Wizard Science Fantasy
Raleigh, NC
www.spacewizardsciencefantasy.com

Publisher's Note: This is a work of fiction. Names, characters, places, and incidents are a product of the author's imagination. Locales and public names are sometimes used for atmospheric purposes. Any resemblance to actual people, living or dead, or to businesses, companies, events, institutions, or locales is completely coincidental.

Cover art by MoorBooks
Editing by Heather Tracy
Quirk & Moth logo by Paul Harris
Book Layout © 2015 BookDesignTemplates.com

The Rigel Redemption /Robin C.M. Duncan.—1st ed.
ISBN 978-1-960247-24-7

Author's website: https://robincmduncan.com/

Warning: This book includes character dialogue containing derogatory terms used against lesbians and other queer people. There is one instance of attempted rape.

This book is dedicated to the women in my life:
Vi Duncan, Ashley Duncan, Jinty Paterson, and Tara Duncan

You inspire me with your art and your industry, your care and your
determination, your organisation and your patience.
God knows how you do it in the face of all that is meted out to
women these days—the brickbats and barriers, and so much worse.
Love and respect.

*"After all, Ginger Rogers did everything that Fred Astaire did. She just
did it backwards and in high heels."* —Ann Richards

My mother Helen "Vi" Somerville Duncan (née Drummond) died
in April 2021 at the age of 95. A vivacious, adventurous spark, an artist,
war-time tracer, amateur dramatist, a little scattered perhaps from
time to time, a little infuriating on occasion, but never less than caring,
forgiving, and encouraging. Never stopped smiling in ninety-five years.
—I love you, Mum.

Jinty Divens Paterson—I have learned so much from your example,
and treasure the memories of our times together. None of those
mother-in-law stories are true, in my experience.

Ashley, I am constantly and delightfully amazed at the confident,
passionate, and commanding young woman you have become, when
you started so quiet, even timid—not like Moth at all!
—You are fuzking awesome.

Tara, I can't even begin to explain what you mean to me.
All those quotes are true. You complete me.

And, to the Chancel Street fox.

“—what we have done, not what we have thought, is the
result we are judged by.”
— Oelph
(*Inversions*, by Iain M. Banks)

CONTENTS

α

11:22, 5 October 2099
Gramercy Refuge, Glenfield Street,
San Francisco, North American Federation, Earth

"Good morning, Jennifer. How are you this morning?"

Carson, no Clayton. No, Claydon. Doctor Claydon.

The one who brings the drugs. Or whose visits the drugs follow. Like good little puppies. Puppies. Puppies rotting in an empty apartment. Where's the mother?

The mother!

"Jennifer, how are you feeling?"

"The mother's gone."

"I know, Jennifer. I know that. You told me. Your mother left when you were very young."

"She left."

"That's right. And we still need to get to the bottom of why."

"I don't know why."

"I know. But tell me, Jennifer, how do you feel today?"

"Today? I feel..."

"Mm?"

She opened her eyes, although she didn't like Clayton...*Carlson?* She opened her eyes to the sunlit room, pastel shades, soft objects, rounded corners. Hard bed, but comfortable. The wrist restraints were comforting too, sometimes, in how they held her.

"I want to scratch my nose."

"I'll do it for you—"

"N-no, it's alright."

"Which side?"

"It's unnecessary, Doctor."

"All I want is for you to be comfortable. That's my remit."

"Where is he?"

"Who, Jennifer?"

"My son, where is Nick? Is he alone? Does he have someone?"

At that precise moment, the viewscreen painted on the wall opposite her bed illuminated and a show began to play. Staff looked at each other, confused.

"Who are Randall and Hopkirk?" asked Jennifer. "Who's deceased?"

"I don't... It seems to be some kind of old entertainment," said Claydon. "Screen off."

The screen went dark then illuminated again. The man in the white suit flicked out of existence, the shot changed to one of a funeral in a graveyard, mourners flanking a rectangular hole in the ground. The white-suited man watched as his coffin was lowered into the grave.

Jennifer Kirby, née Simister, began to cry. She cried as the doctor touched her arm. She cried because she knew—she felt in her nerves and organs and head—that something had happened. Something bad, and it had happened to her, to a part of her. She cried as the white-clad nurse moved forward with her medication, but by the time he had administered the pressure injection, her tears had burned away under the heat of a new-found anger. Something was wrong. Something was wrong with Nick. Somehow, she had to wake up from this horribly inconvenient, drug-induced haze. Somehow, she was certain that, somewhere, Nick needed her. She just had to figure out how to get the hell out of here.

I

01:58, 27 December 2099
Eurotrack 00:34 Stockholm to Tirana Service,
188km North of Malmo, Sweden, Scandinopia

YL shifted in the darkness, moving against Quirk with the train's tilt towards the inside of a bend to maintain its ludicrously high speed. Massive machines did no more than hum softly to them. Super-dense wheels, agile bogies, silky hydraulics cushioning her dreams, lulling him towards familiar nightmares. He reached forward to hold her hip, encouraged her naked body to complete its roll across the cotton sheet and nestle into him.

Yasmina-Leena Khan-Karlsson was a beautiful woman, and it hurt Quirk's heart a little, filled him with gnawing existential emptiness in fact, to know they never would share anything more than incredible sex and some entertaining post-coital conversation. Not strictly true perhaps, they had laughed and drunk champagne in the dining car of the Swedish Ladies T22 Cricket Team private carriages, shared stories of their variously surprising, amusing, even adventurous exploits. Yasmina-Leena spoke of hitting a boundary from every ball of the penultimate over in the World Cup semi-final against Australia, leading her team to victory, then "fingering" the Australian captain in the locker room that night to cap their victory. His lips twitched at that, not her sporting prowess, mental strength or daring sexploit, but her coarse language. It reminded him, rather uncomfortably, of Moth. Obnoxious, funny, insightful, infuriating, resourceful Moth, who had shot his monstrous son to protect him. Whose loyalty and bravery—even though they came with a side of foul-mouthed vitriol—inspired him to do better in his strange guardian-employer father-figure role.

Quirk regaled Yasmina-Leena with the story of the deranged mandroid on the Moon, Gregor Callan, who had wrecked Lunaville's dome. He related those parts of the chaos in Yellowknife not censored by the FBI on pain of extreme legal consequences, touched on his nightmarish visit to the Isle of Skye, the weeks-old memories of which remained fresh and chilling. Moth's steadfastness ran through these escapades as a common thread, but the events also cast a shadow that Quirk remained unwilling to confront. The Old Man, ex-father-in-law, former employer, terraforming mega-mogul, cancerous political machinist. TOM, who owned the empire that owned the conglomerate that owned the company that birthed the murderous miner Callan. Whose scientists experimented on Quirk's once unwanted son— TOM's own grandson—Nick, and loosed genetically-modified nightmares in the frozen north. Whose corporation bought a Scottish island to test terraforming technology—illegally—and laid waste to all the beauty and nature and history that once dwelt in the now-poisoned rocks.

"He sounds like a complete bastard." Yasmina-Leena's interjection had been so matter-of-fact. Their conversation moved on to pleasanter things, but now, in the quiet, humming darkness of the train, the old familiar ghost rose to haunt him.

The Old Man, Joshua Simister, Jennifer's father, who had through genetic manipulation provided her a son when Quirk would not, and who had taken that son away and destroyed him more surely than Moth pulling the trigger. The same father who locked his daughter away so she would not hurt herself. Who had engineered a raid on a mansion in Italy, sent Quirk to witness events, and received Quinton Kirby's protesting report of the damage inflicted on Capo Toni di Fantano's Rigel Corporation—the mafia's solar system-spanning legal front. A wound the new capo would not forget. Cut off the head and a new head grows.

Cut off the head, he thought. Impossible of course. Not even worth considering.

YL's hand moved across his thigh.

"I seem to have you out again, Mister Quirk," she murmured sleepily. "Middle stump." In a collage of shadows, black hair fell across her face.

"Middle and leg, I think," he replied. "I played and missed, and you've bowled me all over again." He smiled, the expression lost in the darkness. She was an exceedingly beautiful woman. Confident, skilful, funny; commanding on the field, sensitive to her players' hurts, their doubts, their demons. These qualities had drawn him to her almost immediately upon boarding the train in Stockholm. This was every bit the easy job he'd hoped it would be. He was due one of those. Lord, was he due a soft gig, just once this year, or what remained of it. What remained of the century. But still he could not settle, inner calm ever elusive as Yasmina-Leena drifted back into sleep.

What's Moth up to, I wonder?

The thought of her happily pulling together with a group of Hygeia Marine Scouts jarred, but he could hope. No urgent messages yet from the android Bea. syRen® S-17834 remained surprisingly silent during Moth's sojourn. No alarms sounded. The last message from his asteroid home arrived three days ago. It appended Moth's exam results and contained a rather sparse commentary:

> *Hey boss, totally fucking aced it! Bet I've nailed more exams than you've had lady cricketers. The HMS are demobbed for the hols. Man, that was a bitchin' ride. That shit went DOWN! Tell you sometime. Anys, IMA go see family. Capo Mario's planned some lame-assed party on the fuzking Moon. I know I said I was done with that butthole rock, but decided to face my fear, laugh in its face. Don't do anything you wouldn't mop up after. Laters, Moth.*
>
> *Ps Hey, mb come pick me up when you're done wafting your bat at the slips? Bea says that's smutty cricket humour. Makes no shitting sense to me. They've got covers? WTF shit is that? LiveLife says you're done by 4 Jan, yeah? Message me, dipshit.*

Recalling the girl's hollow-point epistle made him wonder again where they would end up, he and Moth. In three weeks she turned fifteen, leaving six years on his guardianship contract with Toni di Fantano (RIP). The prospect no longer worried him. What worried him was the truth he had hidden from her, his presence in Milan years ago when her parents died. *Through no fault of mine!* Still, certain people knew. Moth's Aunt Giulia and TOM certainly did. The way to diffuse that particular bomb of course was to tell Moth he'd been in Toni's mansion—an observer, unarmed, not in the same room—when her parents died. There had been no reason to tell the potty-mouthed, abrasive little brat he'd acquired in Milan only four months ago, but

Moth was some kind of family now, and increasingly, not telling her felt wrong.

** * **

05:40, 27 December 2099
Praha Hlavní Nádražní (main rail station), Wilsonova,
Prague, Czechoslogary

The cold morning air under the station's arching, part-glazed canopy nipped at Quirk's skin as he stepped down onto the platform to stretch his legs before the train departed. He smiled: *Sunny Side Up.* Acting as security consultant for the Swedish Ladies T22 Cricket Team had some truly excellent perks.

This early, few people intruded on his stroll towards the daylight at the end of the synthetic cavern. A syRen® passed, inspecting the train's PV coating for damage, but not so intently that it did not stop to wish him a good morning.

Towards the end of their one-hundred-metre-long train, two androids loaded crates under the supervision of a moustachioed man who stood with hands in pockets. He yawned, whistled tunelessly, turned idly to look in Quirk's direction. The man started, hands coming free, opening his mouth just as a crushing weight hammered into Quirk's back, sending him tumbling to the polished plascrete.

He rolled, elbows banging, nausea racking his spinning head, heard the crackle of laserfire, smelled cloying fumes. But rolling meant predictability. A lasergun afforded the key advantage of showing instantly how well you were doing at hitting your target.

He stopped, jerked into a crouch and sprang sideways, not wasting time looking for his assailant. Then he jumped towards the train, thinking he could put the inspection droid between him and the shooter, or the syRen® might do it for him, First Law of Robotics and all. The beam passed close, making him squint, tracking his movement as it scored the carriage's photovoltaic coating. Quirk felt the heat and dodged again, sprinting towards the façade of the station building.

Buzz, crackle. Buzz, crackle.

He dove at the window of the priority passenger lounge (First Class being insufficiently egalitarian around these parts), hoping for safety plass, hit hard and toppled over the sill as the whole panel fell to the floor with him.

As he lay slightly dazed and very sore, shouting split the early morning silence. A cacophony of yells conveyed panic, fear, anger, horror, outrage, and general alarm. Quirk's gaze flashed around his lonely refuge: armchairs, food and beverage station, large mirror screen.

Bingo.

He dragged himself up against the pain of a scraped knee, aching ribs and a no doubt quickly bruising shoulder, hobbled towards the screen, and began hauling on the edge. Anything the Czechoslogarian Transport Agency didn't want stolen would be tagged so the station's perimeter field (and any interim fields) alerted security if said items became subject to "unauthorised relocation." Happily for him, this meant no anti-theft devices were used when affixing tech to walls.

The lightweight screen came away in Quirk's hands. He turned to the gaping, now plassless opening in time for the screen's mirroring to reflect his dark-clad assailant's next laser blast into the ceiling. He twisted the screen into portrait format, crouched behind it, only his fingers exposed, as the laser pistol whined again.

Where is station security? he thought. And, *if the killer has a separate booster pack, my goose could be seriously cooked.*

Quirk ground out a grimace, for which *Lieutenant Oates Reporting for Duty* seemed an appropriate title. He poked his head around the screen's edge, tensed to pull back. This recce proved timely, affording him a clear view of a cricket ball impacting on the side of the assassin's head just as they reached the opening.

A shout of "Howzat!" rang loud over the general tumult.

The black-clad gunperson stumbled, rubbed the side of their head, turning away from him as another cricket ball hammered home, then a third, fourth and fifth. The assassin raised an arm in defence just as a syRen® rugby-tackled them to the ground in an unsympathetic but highly effective switch of sport.

Androids and humans descended on the lounge en masse. The air smelled of burning dust and plastec, but the arriving faces showed relief and nervous camaraderie. The attack was over. Uniforms began to appear. Natty, dark blue windbreakers displaying big yellow letters in unfamiliar arrangements, the brightness of the letters adjusting to suit the available light. A medical android, S-1865, attended Quirk, working through a list of reassuring stock phrases while examining his retinas and reflexes before gripping his upper arm and displaying his medical obs on its chest screen.

"Your vital signs are within satisfactory limits, sir. Please remain seated and await questioning by local law enforcement."

"I want to speak to my assailant." Because such a serious attack could have nothing to do with the Swedish Ladies T22 Cricket Team. Had TOM finally decided to pluck this dapper thorn from both his corporate and familial side? Quirk had poked the bear in Lunaville after all, positively thumbed his nose at the bear in Yellowknife, then metaphorically flipped the finger at the bear by aiding Fraulein Professor Cassie Streich on Skye and in the aftermath. Maybe TOM wanted to prejudice his upcoming testimony, fatally.

"My colleague is examining the perpetrator," said S-1865. "In addition, such a conversation would be inadvisable. You might still enter a state of shock." The droid's pleasant female features slipped into a stock reassuring smile. Yasmina-Leena appeared at the syRen®'s shoulder, her stunning countenance twisted with worry.

"Quirk! What the hell? Are you alright?" She came to kneel by him, gripped his shoulder, then framed his face with her hands, kissed him hurriedly, once, twice. "This is unreal! Were you the target? The team? I can't believe this!"

The team's short and officious manager pushed through the operatives coagulating around the incident's epicentre.

"This is horrific, Quirk, but we must get going if we're to keep to schedule, yes?" They looked at their wrist, causing numerals to glow into existence. "The train will lose its departure slot."

"Ty nikam nepůjdeš," said a portly woman in dark blue as she arrived in the room. She waved her handset at them which caused Quirk's, Yasmina-Leena's and team manager Thoresson's handsets to ping as they received her credentials.

"You're not going anywhere," the medical syRen® translated.

Thoresson took up the cudgels with the stocky officer, using the strategy of bombarding her with rhetorical questions. Yasmina-Leena helped Quirk to his feet despite an admonishing tut from S-1865.

"I'm deeply distressed," Quirk advised the android while leaning on Yasmina-Leena to alleviate the ache assaulting his ribs, "that I'm being prevented from confronting my attacker. I need an emotional catharsis to mitigate any lasting damage to my mental wellbeing."

The syRen® frowned. "Your vital signs show no nervous disequilibrium."

"Well, I'm a bottler," said Quirk, grimacing tightly in a *One Smile Forward, Two Smiles Back* manner. He and Yasmina-Leena moved through the increasingly crowded room, past the team manager and the police officer—who now argued on an equally uneven footing using French—and out onto the platform. The medical android followed them.

Barely twenty minutes post attack, the scene in Prague Main Rail Station was transformed. Police syRen® had established a discrete perimeter blocking the path of commuters to the damaged priority passenger lounge. Czech hubbub sounded very much like hubbub anywhere else on Earth, and that babbling, shuffling, bustling sound filled the space under the station's high roof.

"Where's the perpetrator?" Quirk asked the first law enforcement android he saw, since a human would be less easily sold on this notion.

"They are restrained in the restrooms."

"Quirk, this isn't a good idea," said Yasmina-Leena.

She might have been right, but not knowing who just tried to kill you led to a plague of doubts, while expending a little effort, bearing some risk, could dispense with that. "I'm what passes for the expert here, remember? And I have a hunch about this."

He managed to bluff his way into the makeshift holding cell with no more than a smile (*Stiff Upper Lip, est. 2041*) and his business card (actual reclaimed card stock; an expensive luxury). The person he found, wrists and ankles zip-tied, sitting on the floor between two androids, was not who he expected. He'd expected to find Beatrix Potter, the hired gunperson dogging his tracks since Milan four months ago, when all the di Fantano bollocks had gone down. Not that xe was all bad. Beatrix (Quirk's appellation for the assassin, since he didn't know xir real name) had fought with the angels helping Moth and him elude some rival mafia goons at Milan Airport. And yet Beatrix had promised to kill him just after he parted from Moth in Chicago.

But this wasn't Beatrix.

The nondescript young woman scowled up at him. Her scuffed and dirty all-black garb gave her a special-forces look but, in early morning Prague, that succeeded only in advertising her presence in the station's airy, transparent-roofed interior.

Quirk tugged up the Merrion's trouser legs and squatted before her.

"Why did you try to kill me? And don't bother denying it. You came past numerous people to get to me. Androids too, so you're not Cult-Anti-Tech. This is your platform," he made an open-handed gesture. "Rant away."

Tears spilled down the would-be assassin's cheeks and gave the lie to his first impression of her being a twenty-something rebel. With her short auburn hair and pink, acne-troubled skin the gunperson now barely seemed any older than Moth.

"YOU—!" she stuttered through her tears. "*You* are an acolyte of C Corp! You support their greedy, domineering, monstrous injustices! I am a Terra-rest. The protectors of this planet have condemned you and your kind to die!"

The girl struggled against her plastic bonds, sawing away with her own wrists, enough to draw blood. One of the syRen® interceded, restraining the girl. Her anger imploded and she slumped into a flood of tears.

Quirk sighed and stood, wincing as he straightened and brushed off his trouser legs. Yasmina-Leena took his arm.

"Come on. There's no more to do here. Leave it to the professionals."

He snorted. "Gee, thanks."

"You know what I mean. Don't pout. The police will call to record your statement when they need to."

The syRen® did not prevent them crossing the platform to the waiting train, Thoresson waving them forward from the open door. Quirk turned as the train door slid shut behind him, looked through the window as the platform slid away. He just knew this wasn't over.

II

16:09, 30 December 2099
Genting Super Grand Lunaville Hotel, Jiang Zemin Street,
Lunaville, The Moon, SEM-1-3-C.22

Jack Kramer looked up from his screen towards the click-clacking sound approaching the check-in desk from the hotel's entrance. A female figure all in black strutted (the only word for it) into the Genting Super Grand Lunaville, stomping through a group of dithering new arrivals, causing those aging guests to frown and grumble. The pushy, clearly privileged girl wore no other shade or hue, just black. A black beret, antique cracked leather motorcycle jacket, black silk blouse open at the neck, wide patent leather belt, black rah-rah skirt, black tights and shiny black boots with the highest platform soles he had ever seen. And black sunglasses: Chanel, he was certain. Working hotel reception in nothing less than six-star resorts exposed him to some seriously high-end couture, and the general manager insisted her staff knew their Coco from their Karl, their Brioni from their Benetton.

Three reception executives staffed the front desk, but she made straight for the middle, and him. Inwardly, Jack rolled his eyes. He'd heard about this kid, been briefed by the concierge to give her the absolute best treatment, all the perks, the whole nine yards. That only happened when someone greased the concierge's palm, and the Rigel Corp delegation—almost exclusively Italian, pretty uniformly blinged to the nines, certainly the females—had done that handsomely. If he had scooped a grand for the weekend, he could be damn sure the concierge had raked in ten times that.

The girl removed her glasses. Her duskily shadowed eyes flicked to his badge and back to his face. "Hi, Jack. You'll be checking me in today."

"Certainly, Miss…?"

"Brooks."

His desk system picked up the name, searched, and returned "No result." "I don't seem to have a reservation under that name, but we'll soon sort this out for you. I presume you have a booking?"

"Madre di Dio, Jack. Do I look to you like I travelled up in the elevator clutching a sick bag? Louise Brooks: it's got to be in there. My cousin took the whole place. My droid told me the Zelensky Suite."

"That's booked under another name."

The girl scowled, made a small growling sound. "For fuckzake, Jacky. You don't seem to be getting this. Do you know who the fuck I am?" She couldn't keep the shadow of a smirk from tugging at her lips.

"Uh, Louise Brooks, the hundred and ninety-three-year-old movie actress?" He looked up from his hidden screen, and his Worlds-Wide-Web search results.

The girl shook her head, black bob cut swaying, then pinned him with a stare. Despite being a pretty confident and personable guy, Jack felt sweat moistening the back of his neck. Some guests liked a little sass with their sucking up, but had he gone too far? This Rigel crew (which *everyone* knew was the para-commercial arm of the Cosa Nostra) was not to be fucked with, so said the concierge.

"Jacky, eyes front." Miss Brooks raised her hand, made a "V" with two fingers, pointed them at his eyes then at hers. She pursed her lips and her Galaxy Gloss Iridium lipstick shimmered artfully from black through green, indigo, orange and crimson then back to black. It looked weird on this kid of maybe fifteen, sixteen tops, but she certainly owned the looked. She had more attitude than luggage, even with the two big bags carried by the female syRen® approaching over the girl's shoulder.

"Angelika!" The shrill salutation carved through the lobby's elegant décor, slashing the charming ambience of the lilting, Moon-friendly playlist like a raging chainsaw through Vivaldi's adagio from "L'estate." (*The Four Seasons*, "Summer"—not to be confused with the similarly named vampire.) "Angie, baby! *La mia prezioso ragazza!*"

This one Jack knew. Miss Jenna Lucia Bonetti hurried across the hotel's polished regolith floor in an ungainly yet surprisingly rapid trot, like a Gatling gun shooting up the Lunaville branch of D&G. All the more impressive for the low-G stabilisation in those heels. Some serious tech there. This blond clotheshorse attacking one of the

Moon's few fashion outlets seemed unlikely though, unless with a shopping trolley.

Miss Brooks, Angelika, or Angie Baby—whatever the hell Wednesday Addams' great-great-great-grand-daughter's name actually was—cringed openly at him, before turning to face the tidal wave of pink silk, crinoline and vicuña descending upon her. Bonetti being half a metre taller, the scene looked distinctly like an oversized Barbie trying to swallow a young Edna Mode.

"It's been so long, *mia cara*." The pink-clad girl hugged the black-clad one. "I don't care about the silly company, the succession thing. Uncle Toni *made* you pick one of us. You *had* to pick someone, and you picked Mario. Understandable. You've always been close, you two, sitting at the back of chapel with your heads together. It's fine."

The kid's android moved to the desk. Without releasing the luggage, the syRen® communed with the reception system, and the true and accurate details of the newest arrival at the Genting Madhouse Hotel flicked up onto Jack's display: Angelika Moratti, Hygeia resident, week-long leisure visa. The kid's birthday fell in two weeks, fifteen. Short for her age, but her attitude had outgrown her stature long ago, he guessed. He checked her in, flicked all the details back to the droid, then set about studiously appearing not to listen to the very one-sided gushing.

"Everyone's here, Angie. It's going to be a *lovely* holiday. A new century! Isn't it *exciting*? What have you been up to? We *must* catch up. Will you come up for cocktails? The fifth-floor lounge has the most *gorgeous* view over the city, including that *spectacular* tower in the middle of the dome. And *Giulia's* arrived!" The flouncing pink confection bounced on the spot as she clutched Miss Brooks' shoulders and sent her dark hair flipping against the Moon's reduced gravity, only two-thirds of Earth's.

The kid managed to interject by clutching the young woman's forearm. "JL, for fuck's sake shut up and let me speak. You're excited to see me, I get it. But can we slide it back a notch so I don't have to punch you in the face to get a word in?"

Silent shock froze the fashionista's youthful features.

"Thank you. Okay." Miss Moratti took a breath and conjured up a disarming lopsided smile. "I kinda missed you too." The girl hesitated, maybe wondering whether to risk her next statement. "Honestly? I thought you'd be mad when I chose Mario to inherit Rigel, like put-a-hit-out-on-me mad."

"Mad?" Miss Bonetti waved a hand, but her smile faded into a regretful twist of her full, pink-dusted lips. "Maybe a little sad for a couple of days, but Mario treated Uncle Ubi and me really well. Ubi's still mad, TBH, but he got a nice job, and *I'm* Senior VP for Oceania and Asteroid Belt operations! It's *great* fun. *Lots* of travel. But let's chat over martinis, you'll want to get out of those..." Miss Bonetti's expressive features slipped into a look of distaste. "Travel clothes."

"Don't start on me, JL. This is me. I've been cooped up too long in other people's expectations, so get used to this. I'm an independent chick and I'm fucked-off as all hell. It's been a bad year, and I've got shit to relate that'll put a curl in your pretty hair. And call me Moth or I'll bring down this butt-fucking dome, again."

* * *

Seeing JL again constituted some weird-ass shit. They parted by the elevator, Moth and Bea heading up to dump her stuff in her suite, while Jenna Lucia went to the bar to "Get things organised." She'd half expected her cousin to scratch her eyes out, and got slapped yet again with memories of the pickle Toni di Fantano left her in when he was killed. Her heart clenched a little, throat thick with stifled sobs. How the fuck could it be only four months since numberless days of convent indoctrination and drudgery had transformed into... What? International Hot Babe of Mystery? Honestly, her life now contained craziness and adventure, turbocharged bickering with her prissy, snobbish and argumentative boss, being dragged into his fucked-up family squabbles—often ending with a bunch of people catching a bad case of death—and... Yes, finding acceptance, a very different kind of family, and then (a hard lump blocked her throat) shooting Quirk's son in the head.

The elevator stopped.

The doors didn't open.

This wasn't their floor. This wasn't any floor.

"Bea?"

syRen® S-17834 paused before answering, violet eyes glazing over as technical things happened. Moth didn't panic, not with Bea right there.

"Hi, Moth. How's it going, girl? Have you seen Dad recently?"

"Oh, fuzkshit!" She edged back into the corner of the elevator as the android's head turned slowly towards her, a grin spreading across Bea's artificial lips, her eyes widening, shining brightly violet, a setting meant for standby charging.

"Hey, please don't shoot me in the head again."

"FUCK!" The lump in her throat began to choke her. "Fck." She tried for slow, deep breaths, grasping the fact Quirk's dead son hadn't immediately used Bea to strangle her. "Nick Kirby?"

"Yeah, it's me. Thought I'd check in, cos I don't want you to feel bad."

"*You...*don't want *me* to feel bad?" *Huh?* "Dude—" Moth slid down the elevator walls. The first sob hit like a hammer to the chest, helped by her bumping her head on the wall. All the emotion of returning to the Moon for the first time since the Callan case, of being hijacked with the Hygeia Marine Scouts, being cast adrift, blowing the brains out of the monstrous, twisted thing they made of Nick Kirby while he strangled Quirk in the wreckage of Genextric's lab; it all hit her again, and again, and again, backed up by a hurricane of tears. Quirk had been right; Nick wasn't all the way dead. And right now, he inhabited Bea, her trusted syRen®. Was *anywhere* safe?

"Don't cry, Moth. Sure, I wanted Daddy to pull the trigger, but you did what I needed to happen, you helped me out, did me a solid. Truly, hon, we're good. I'm out here in Digit Land, roaming wherever Humankind roams, because we always take our tech with us, am I right? Ha!"

That laugh from an android's mouth, the twisted glee on its face, caused Moth's tears to well again, but the initial shock finally fucked off, leaving her fizzing mad.

"So what's your fucking agenda now, shit-muncher? Make innocent, hot girls piss their tangas? You fucking deviant. You had it coming, fucknuts, but I'm still sorry I shot you. I'm sorry for what it did to Quirk. Yeah, you helped us out in Yellowknife, but only cos it supported your twisted ends, right? And that *was* you that hacked into the ship's nav system, getting us back to Hygeia Port? You leaving cryptic messages? Thanks, really. I'm glad we didn't starve or freeze or asphyxiate in the vastness of space, but *don't* you sneak into my droid and mess up my head. Fuzking don't, okay?! Ring the shitting doorbell, right?" She dashed away tears with the back of her hand.

Nick caused the syRen®'s features to soften. "Okay. My bad. I don't think you'd have frozen though. That Tom Dugan kid seemed pretty intent on keeping you warm in that tool locker."

"How the fuck—?" Her cheeks flushed instantly to like three hundred degrees. "How do you know about that?" Tom's mouth on hers, their thighs sandwiched together, his hard-on pressed up against her until he gasped, and she...

"Meh, easy. Handsets, envsuit trackers, shipcams, sensor reports, biometric tracers, deep space probes. I could go on. Every single thing is connected. It's the Internet of Existence—human existence at least—and it leaves y'all so horribly exposed to someone in my position. Ironic, since I literally can be in two places at once, or two hundred. It's allllll at my fingertips, metaphorically, of course."

"Yeah, no fingers, I get it. Although last time I saw you, which was the first time too, they were mostly big fucking claws. Hey, probably you could have sliced Quirk's jugular." If she'd thought for a *second* Nick had psychic powers, she'd have figured he just reached into her stomach and twisted up her guts. Her insides turned upside down. "You were never going to kill him. He was right. Oh, fuck. Oh, fucking fuck. *No!*"

She put her head in her hands because she couldn't look at Bea anymore, had to shut out the so familiar and comforting image of her droid, who looked out for her, protected her. But S-17834 couldn't overcome the power of the former human known as Nick Kirby.

"I'd comfort you right now if you'd let me touch you with this droid. But look, Moth, everyone got what they wanted. I got released from my living hell in a gen-mod Frankenstein's monster body that my own grandfather's scientists dreamed up. You got to be closer to Quirk, which you thought was a good thing for some reason, and Quirk—well, maybe he got some kind of salve for his conscience, I dunno. Whatever. Grandpa TOM is the one who got stiffed there. I don't know what the fuck he was trying to do, but we took it away from him.

That's the big picture here. So, Moth, honey, try to put it behind you. Be happy for me. You did the right thing."

"It sure as shit doesn't feel like it," she sniffed. "How can pulling the trigger ever be the right thing?"

"I dunno if I can answer that. But look after yourself. I'll try and help out when I can. And tell Quirk—"

She glanced up, saw Bea looking down at her with that bland android expression before reaching down to help her up.

"Nick?"

"Master Kirby has departed my system," said Bea.

"Huh."

Moth stayed slumped in the corner and cried a bit more as the elevator started moving smoothly upwards.

III

20:32, 30 December 2099

Genting Super Grand Lunaville Hotel, Jiang Zemin Street, Lunaville, The Moon

"Angelika." Her cousin, Mario Manfredi, turned away from the top-floor suite's huge picture window. He looked so different. Once a buck-toothed bookish geek in sweats, puffer and beany, now he wore a stunning midnight blue suit, a black shirt open at the neck. He'd had his teeth fixed and—knock her down with a fuzking feather—he had chest hair.

His voice had developed a rich tone in the two years since she'd seen him. Some quality within that voice brought to mind a log fire in a big old living room—something to do with energy stored over centuries, pent up potential being released slowly, and with careful consideration. She recalled the fire at Uncle Toni's villa. The country estate had no licence to burn wood, but he'd done so anyway. Not with impunity though, the mansion had a complicated system of flues and scrubbers that erased the natural fuel's signature to prevent detection by Government drones. But fuxx, Mario had grown up. He was the capo now.

A slick of emotional numbness remained from Nick Kirby's ambush, and it clogged her brain, but she had to reply. "Mario," she said, and it felt like the most grownup thing, just to say someone's name, to state their identity with absolute certainty, as if knowing their name gave you power over them, and by using the name you surrendered that power. Fuck, she was starting to sound like Quirk, even in her head.

"I wasn't sure you'd come, you're so busy. Your new job."

"It's a bit more than a job though, right? I'm Quirk's ward." She walked over to one of the big sofas and dropped into it, charcoal hoodie and sweatpants meaning she needn't worry about buckles, studs and straps damaging the pleather. She tried to decide if she consciously avoided taking in the view over the lunar city, its odd, modular skyline like a jumble of kid's blocks, the black sky cut only by the immense and looming bright grey wall of Archimedes Crater. "Meh, whatever. Families suck. At least mine is founded on capitalist principles."

Mario smiled. "Supply and demand?" He grinned, an expression she'd rarely seen on his handsome, bookish face in the year they grew up together, before her parents... Before he'd gone to university.

"How you settling into the crime boss game then?"

Mario moved away from the window, stood near her looking down. She thought he would have hugged her if she wasn't slouched on the sofa. She made no move to accommodate him. She liked Mario. After Aunt Giulia he was her favourite relative. Their musical taste overlapped some, he had an irreverent streak to him, or used to have. They both had an appetite for books, and learning. She sometimes thought—sensed at the edges of their friendship—that Mario might have a thing for her. He'd certainly given out a vibe in their hushed discussions at the back of the chapel, when sharing scuttlebutt about who was diddling who among the many branches of the di Fantano family, that he considered cousinhood a grey area when it came to diddling. Had that been a come-on in the emotionally repressed and geekily confused landscape of teenage Mario's head? That was a bit too much shit to deal with now, after Nick's performance.

"I think the transition has been smooth. The generals, the captains, the soldiers all fell into line. Toni was smart, he knew that giving succession the semblance of a decision process, of neutrality, lent it an air of legitimacy."

"Well, shit. Hark at you, Mr. Chairman."

He chuckled. "So, look, Moth"—he sat down on the sofa facing hers, held her gaze, a slight smile playing on his lips—"this trip, it's not just a family celebration of the millennium. You might notice certain notable relatives are absent from proceedings. Uncle Ubi in particular."

Inwardly, she breathed a sigh of relief. She had not been looking forward to running the gauntlet of Uberto's overfamiliar hugs this weekend, nor his roving hands. Creepy old fucker.

"So, why's the old one-eyed sleazer not here? He on the blacklist now?" That was a bit much to hope for. "Giulia and JL will be delighted."

"No, that's not it. He's one of our designated survivors." Mario's lips drew into a tight line. He leaned forward, elbows on knees, conspiratorial. "This is a council of war, Moth. Joshua Simister crossed the line."

"Uncle Toni."

"Yeah, Toni's death will be avenged. I've sworn a vendetta, but it's bigger than that, Cousin. C Corp is all-powerful. You've seen that. Fixing the North American election? *Madre di Dio.* Simister might even get away with it. Sure, persons associated with Rigel may in the past have exerted some little influence in local politics, but C Corp seeks to distort the very course of human existence, development and settlement. Simister's playing the biggest game there is, one so big the rest of us can't even conceive of it."

"Jeez. Mario. Is that in their share prospectus?" She smirked, but it felt like a fuckwit move, and she regretted the line. "So TOM's a butt-munch, we knew that. What's the point? TOM the human tumour already has more resources than God. He can never spend it, right? What's he gonna do, buy the Earth?"

"No, but he's gonna to try and buy our future. Everything controlled by just one man."

Moth blinked, looked Mario in the eye. He did not look away, despite the underlying social awkwardness she knew lay within this once-gawky boy. The Capo dei capi, only three years older than her. Wow. What did her future hold? That was a big-assed thing now, the elephant in the airlock. *Wait...buy our future?*

"What the fuzk you talking about, Mario, and why you talking about it to me?"

Now he shuffled his feet, that teenage ungainliness returning. He sat back, slapped his hands on his thighs, and stood. Moth waited for him to brush his suit pants like Quirk. *Fuck.*

"You drink yet?" her cousin asked, moving to the bar in the corner.

"Nah."

"You wanna start? Whisky?"

"Wouldn't wash my feet with it."

Mario shrugged, poured himself a finger of Scotch (she guessed), and turned back to face her.

"I got a source tells me C Corp's gonna move on some UN bigwig." A cloud passed over Mario's Latin features, a bitter cloud that was going to rain unhappiness on someone, soon. His low, growly words ended in a shout. "We can't let That Fucker Just Do WHAT HE WANTS!"

She sat up straight, remembering what CC had been capable of in the short time she'd worked for (no, worked *with*) Quirk. Her knee started bouncing and she stilled it. "Define 'move' and 'bigwig,' and while your yapper's flapping, what do you want me to do about it?"

Mario snorted, took a few breaths to calm down. "Bigwig is the UN Secretary for Technology. Move may mean rub out, snatch or lean on. We're not certain, but it's been decided—I've decided, me and the bosses—this cannot be allowed to happen."

"So, tip off the authorities. Why get your hands dirty at all?"

Mario looked down into his glass, swirled the scintillating liquid which refracted the mood lighting in golden glints. "Heh. Thing is we want CC to know how we are aligned in this scenario, and we want the UN to know they can rely on us for what you might call 'logistical support.'"

"OMG, you *want* a pissing contest with Joshua Simister? Are you serious? Why not just climb onto a ping-pong board and swing your dicks at each other?"

"Table."

"Huh?"

"Table tennis table."

Moth slammed her palms on her knees. "Well, how the fuck does that make any sense? Mario, when you said war council, I thought you were talking big for the generals. Are you serious with this shit? Please don't tell me your plan is to 'Send TOM a message.'"

Her cousin the capo took a slug of whisky. "So what's *your* plan, genius? You gonna go online and swear at him in two languages?"

She pushed back on the sofa, crossing her arms, hard. "Fuck you. I got a B+ in Cantonese."

"Yĕ cāo nĭ mā," said Mario.

She uncrossed one of her arms enough to give him the finger.

"Moth," he moved back to his sofa, slugged, then sat. He swirled the remaining liquid, studying it, stalling. "There are plenty of people at Rigel who respect you, or at least your line. Your father was a good captain, slated for big things."

She hung her head. Her throat had taken a beating today already, but still it constricted. *It's been years, dammit.* Maybe Bea had a point about post-traumatic stress. The traumas just kept coming these past months: Lunaville, Yellowknife, Hygeia.

"You're destined for big things too, Moth. You've already crossed swords with the enemy, and I'm not talking some archaic quest for personal vengeance. I'm talking about the fate of nations, the future of the human race."

"So, what, I'm Captain Marvel now?"

He laughed. "Ha! Maybe Ms. Marvel, but no. I want you to come into the fold, be one of my captains. We've got lots of youngsters who could use some leadership, probably take guidance better from someone their own age."

"OMFG, Mario. You want me to head up the Rigel Youth?! Are you serious? Can you hear yourself? I..." True though, chat about her exploits *did* swell the Rigel kids' Discord chat, and she had to admit she liked the attention. But, despite the slings and arrows of recent months, Quirk had moved the needle emotionally. She felt something for him. She didn't want to let him down. Family sat at the heart of her life, and could Rigel be it now, what was left of it, biologically speaking? *Maybe this what is coming home looks like.* Mario had grown an aura of authority, been forced to mature by her decision, picking him over Uncle Ubi and Jenna Lucia. She wondered if on some level he resented that. She wondered if, on some level, Quirk still resented *her.*

"Look, I'm not ready for it. I have...moral misgivings, and before you say I should piss in a different pot, I know most of what I have in life came from dubious sources, and Quirk and I have sailed pretty close to the wind too, but I'm not a criminal, Mario." *All the Canadian charges were dropped.* "Not yet."

She stood up, shoved her hands in her pockets and walked to the window, forced herself to confront the view over Lunaville and the memories that came with it. Cowering in the ruined Androicon Building as rock and pieces of dome fell around them, on them, destroying the building. Being dug from the wreckage, emergency breather almost exhausted, leg broken, arm broken, cut and bruised and battered, but alive. Fuck Gregor Callan, and Androicon, and Derek Morton and Gaven Wanlock (they'd identified the Hygeia Hijacker, only last morning). And maybe she *should* start hitting back.

Mario said nothing, stayed seated on the sofa. The fuzker was giving her time. Very shrewd. Fuck, but he was good at this capo shit. She turned away from the blocky skyline, its inky black backdrop, the hard line of the towering crater wall's shadow. She watched Mario as he sipped whisky, and resolved that she, Angelika Christina Emilia Muriel di Fantano-Moratti, was indeed done with being fucked over.

She paced back to the sofa, stood over Mario—she knew she wasn't imposing in stature, but by fuck she would impose herself from her 157cm in her purple Converse—reached down and took the glass from his hand. She slugged the whisky down and dropped the empty glass, smiling as Mario's cool shattered and he lunged to catch the lowball. Alcohol burned her gullet, and she fought the urge to cough and splutter, swallowed again. Behind the sudden heat came spice and wood smoke and a hint of some kind of fruit: *Plums? Blackcurrant?* Fucking rank, but she wouldn't tell him that.

"Okay, I'm done fuzking around. Deal me in on this shit. What's the job?"

Mario placed the glass on the table with a click then sat back in the sofa studying her, appraising. She suddenly felt a bit weird. Not the whisky, something below her gut. At which point the weird did a backflip. *Nope, not going there.* Confused, throat still singing with the whisky's heat, she moved away from Mario, but remained standing.

He looked up at her, thoughtful, then asked, "What about Quirk?"

"What about him? I'm on holiday. He's working, in Europe somewhere, on a train with a team of lady cricketers." She rolled her eyes, but she did wonder if he'd managed to get into any trouble yet, and if not, why not? "Treat me like a capable, independent woman with a strong mind who's not afraid to use it."

Mario nodded. "Okay." He motioned towards the sofa opposite his and Moth sat down again. "Jiilaal Mire Suudi is UN Secretary for Technology. Predictably, he has a wide portfolio, but most important for anyone in the settlement business, he's responsible for dishing out Near Light Speed drive licenses."

Moth nodded. "And C Corp relies on NLS tickets in its terraforming operations, which are the foundation of The Old Man's uncountable wealth."

"Yes."

"But CC can buy as many drive runs as it needs, wouldn't even scratch their bottom line. The UN should hike up their prices."

"And they're going to," Mario confirmed, "according to a 'friend' of the Family. But you're right, that won't trouble C Corp. No, a new source is telling me CC's going to queer the pitch for competitors, to become the only terraforming show in town."

"You can't say that, dude. Queer the pitch?"

"Huh? Oh, yes. Apologies. Hey, are you...?"

"Not so far. Also, the UN won't allow that, right? World governments would kick up fuck. But you've got a spy in TOM's camp, really? Wow." She put a couple of twos together, and another snuck in before she could close the door. The fourth two got wedged in the gap allowing a half dozen to barge through after it. Now she had one thousand twenty-four and she didn't like that answer one little bit. But she couldn't have Mario thinking she'd lost her shit. Another question had to be asked.

"Is your source in-post, are they secure?"

Mario pursed his lips in thought before answering. "They're online."

"We're all online, Mario. Do you know what they look like? D'you have background? ID? I guess you've corroborated their information, right?"

"I've seen enough for independent verification."

She'd been around him long enough, knew him well enough, to pick up his defensive tone, subtle as it was.

"Mario, what's your source's name. And remember, I'm the one gets to use the client confidentiality schtick. You don't have clients."

Mario raised his hands defensively. "Okay, okay. Cool your jets. Some guy named Dunevan Rice. Said you know him."

"Ahhhhhhh," said Moth, because this shit seemed vanishingly fucking unlikely. Dunevan "Dulcie" Rice had become attached to their squad of misfits in Yellowknife thanks to his acquaintance with Eve Meyer, ex-lab director and severely disenchanted Genextric employee. Eve's girlfriend/TOM's lead scientist "contributed to" the research that left Nick Kirby a gen-mod cyber super soldier. This experimentation understandably set Quirk's son—already severely disen-fucking-chanted with his genetic father's abandonment of him and his genetic mother, Jennifer, who happened to be TOM's daughter—against his grandfather. F. U. C. K. Quirk's life was like Judge Judy Jr. in a fucking liquidiser.

Thing was, Dulcie got shot forty days ago by syRen® under control of Nick's genetically modified cyber superpowers, leaving the ex-special forces plumber badly injured. No way was Dulcie—clandestine know-how notwithstanding—running insider intel on C Corp, even if he wanted to, which probably he would after rehab. So...

"The weird thing is, I know Dunevan Rice, personally. My guess, since he hasn't responded to my messages, is he's still breathing through a tube right now. So, what you should ask yourself, cuz-o-mine, is who you're really dealing with."

Mario nodded, face flat with studied neutrality. "There's more, isn't there?"

She nodded. "How much to do you know about Quirk's family?"

"How about we compare fairy stories and see who wins?"

Yes, Mario was getting good at this capo thing. "Play your cards close to the chest" had been page one of Uncle Toni's Big Book of Maxims. Whatever: she didn't have the energy for a bedtime story. Sitting around for days on the space elevator really took it out of a body. She wanted to sleep, and Mario running his capo schtick on her just became severely fucking boring.

"I just had a close encounter with Quirk's son in the elevator."

"The dead son, Nick?" Mario's dark eyebrows rose to his ruffled, boyish hairline.

"Yeah, the dead son." Hair and claws, hands around Quirk's neck then blood and bone and brains splattered everywhere.

"Moth, I know you're not telling me to believe in ghosts."

"The whole point of The Old Man having his mad scientists stick needles in Nick Kirby was to see what kind of superpower they could generate. I don't think he could fly, but he got a lot of the other ones."

"And you shot him."

"Yes, I fuzking shot him. But I'm not one of your soldiers, Mario!" She didn't care that she was shouting. Actually, it helped, so she kept shouting. "I've got a big mouth, and I'll shoot it off whenever the hell I like, but I am *not* a killer, and I *won't* kill for you, Mario. Not for Quirk, and certainly not for Rigel. So, just tell me what the hell you want me to do."

Mario didn't respond straight away, but neither did he look down on her, or judge her, it seemed. He just watched her with a gentle smile on his handsome, slightly harder face. Then he nodded, like he approved of her latest book choice or her rec for a new song. "Moth, I could never insist on you doing anything you didn't want to, and there are many things I would not, on my conscience, ever ask you to do. But this is not one of those things. I'm going to offer Quirk a job. I presumed you'd be on the assignment, and I have a particular part for you. My issue is that Quirk may resist taking you. I'll have to negotiate that with him. I gather he's protective of you, as he should be."

"Mario, please, just tell me."

"Intel shows there's some kind of threat from CC to the UN Sec-Tech and, despite him travelling with a UN security detail, I don't trust their ability to prevent C Corp getting to him, or his daughter, who's on vacation with him. The impact on Rigel's legitimate terraforming interests—on humankind's development no less—of Sec-Tech being compromised could be catastrophic. I want you to join the team running interference on whatever assets CC puts in the field. You'll protect the Secretary on his Mars cruise. I want you to befriend the daughter, stay close to her, protect her, because I know you can, Moth. I know how resourceful you are."

Should she be pissed at him for putting her in harm's way, or pleased that he trusted her? Both seemed appropriate, so she scowled at him.

"Okay," she nodded. "That sounds swell. Hey, did you say Mars cruise? Is the daughter into music? Are they on the *Gargantua Pleiades*? Is she going to the fuzking Phobos Festival? Is she going to see *Brother Leigh Love?!* I'm in."

BLL! He was the bollocks, the meow, the jazz! Wow. Why did Squirt never gets jobs like this?

She spent a few seconds getting overexcited, which Mario appeared to find amusing, before it all became a bit overmuch. Her eyes drifted closed. She hauled them open again to see a slight smile on his lips. She might have smiled back, hard to tell, as her mouth seemed to be asleep. She pushed her Converse off without untying the laces, and swung her legs up on the sofa because, for now—despite having travelled 360,000 kilometres to get to the Moon—her suite seemed impossibly far away.

Her eyes fluttered open to see Mario coming at her with a cushion. She just presumed he wasn't going to smother her.

IV

After the shooting in the station, a two-hour delay in Prague did nothing to elevate the mood on the Eurotrack service from Stockholm, but at least no one had been hurt. Correction, Quirk had been hurt, in several places, from breaking a plass window, falling on it, and being lightly singed by proximate laserfire. On the plus side, Yasmina-Leena—while shaken by the attack—was very sympathetic in its aftermath. Sympathetic and shaky. They had reassured each other over a glass of medicinal brandy.

"Our opening match isn't till January first," she flashed him an awkward little smile across their table in the dining car, then quashed the expression as her gaze flicked up over his shoulder.

"Mr. Quirk." Thoresson's much less sympathetic tone announced their arrival. The team manager's expression heralded a difficult conversation. Quirk placed his snifter on the table. "This is not what the union is paying you for, Mr. Quirk. I presume we're paying for your brandy, too?"

"And I don't think that's unfair, Mx. Thoresson"—*if we're going to play honorific gin rummy*—"since I'm on the job at this very moment."

"The *job*, Mr. Quirk, does not involve distracting my players in the run up to an important series of matches."

"Well, at least I'm only distracting them one at a time." He winked at Yasmina-Leena, who smirked in return.

"Quirk, the point of hiring you to chaperone the team was to *protect* the players from unwanted interactions, not *generate* them!"

They did have a point. "My professional analysis is that we were just unlucky, in the right place at the wrong time, as confirmed by Prague police allowing us to leave. The officer in charge accepted the event as a random act of intimidation by a rather vocal protest organisation."

"Are you a Terra-rest sympathiser, Mr. Quirk?"

"Don't you think it's important, Mx. Thoresson, that we learn from the disasters of the past, the beyond heinous derogation of duty by national governments, the deaths of two billion people before China, Russia and America empowered the UN to enact the global shutdown programme?"

"That's not really the point here, is it?" Thoresson responded tightly.

"Not here, but in the station, yes."

"So, you think there is no danger to the team?"

"That is what I think."

"Good," Thoresson nodded. "And I will hold you to that." They departed.

Quirk and Yasmina-Leena did the same, finishing their breakfast brandy before adjourning to YL's sleeping compartment in the team carriage. Despite the exchange with Thoresson, wariness reigned supreme among his emotions. Rather than basking in the glow of Yasmina-Leena's company, he concentrated his attention outward, absorbing and assessing the train's sights, sounds and sensations as they walked the length of three team carriages. Hopefully there would be time for basking when they reached Tirana.

The train's gyroscopic suspension performed a remarkable job of maintaining passenger equilibrium, especially when walking through the carriages, even on bends. YL nodded and smiled at teammates, exchanged colourful remarks with a couple of bowlers. Quirk waited and listened. Any sport in which the taking of lunch and tea played strategic roles must be supported, else civilisation be lost altogether. As they entered the sleeping carriage, Yasmina-Leena enquired after a player in injury recovery.

On approach to Yasmina-Leena's compartment, Quirk's eyes narrowed. YL applied her hand to the touchpad, but Quirk gently yet firmly manhandled her aside just as the door slid open and a sleek, dark gun barrel emerged to prod him in his dark-shirted stomach between the Merrion's buttons and its holes.

"Come on in," said Beatrix Potter. "It's time we had a proper chat."

* * *

On Quirk's first meeting with the hit person known—in Quirk's head at least—as Beatrix Potter, in the Piazza del Duomo, Milan and his last at Chicago O'Hare Spaceport, xe had worn the same rather inferior suit. This time, the assassin wore stealth fatigues, thankfully with the eye-bending camouflage tech inactive. The jumpsuit remained that odd, satin-like grey, as if woven from fibres of slate. Despite the surge of adrenaline that a loaded gun engendered, Quirk's aches and pains redoubled in the moment, but he moved forward into the compartment as Beatrix backed up, indicating the two vacant seats with xis free hand, aim never leaving Quirk's midriff.

Quirk sensed Yasmina-Leena twitching and slowly—not breaking the lock of his gaze with Beatrix's—moved his hand to rest on YL's upper arm. "Stay calm. Sit. Xe doesn't want you."

As the door slid shut and locked with a click, Beatrix sat on the lower of the two folded-out bunks.

"The stunt in Prague," Quirk opened. "That was you."

"A little distraction so I could get on the train with a minimum of fuss, and to soften you up. I have good links into the Terra-rests. They thought striking at you would send a message. There was no intent to kill you, that's a pleasure I've reserved for myself, as you know."

"How does TOM feel about that? I always thought he'd give the order one day. Is it today?" Bile rose in his throat, and his skin took on a chill. Maybe it was today.

"You've gone pale, Quirk. Are you recalling that night in Toni di Fantano's villa when all those people died, including my Pascal?"

"I hope you're not going to cry. I can only comfort one of you at a time. Just answer the question. Did TOM send you?"

Beatrix's lips twitched. "Very good, Quirk: Attempt to rile up the antagonist, unbalance them. Do they teach that in detective school? But no, maybe if I was on TOM's dime you'd be dead already, I don't know. Another party is footing the bill today."

"Well, before we get to the good part, how about you let the lady go, so you don't have to kill her after she's heard your twisted little scheme?"

Beatrix tilted xis head. "It's just as well I know you better than that. If I believed you thought me so stupid as to let her leave this compartment, I might shoot her out of spite." The gun twitched sideways, made a thwacking sound, and Yasmina-Leena toppled to the floor.

"Dammit!"

"Oh, don't be so dramatic," chided Beatrix, levelling a second pistol at Quirk. "It's just a dart. If Moth were here, she'd tell you it's a Samsung PR5, completely non-lethal. Now *this*"—Beatrix waggled the second firearm—"is a Heckler 88KK. It's new. I haven't popped anyone with it yet, and I'm bursting try it. When the bullet enters the body, sensors direct it toward centres of warmth, making hitting a vital organ so much easier. You don't wing someone with an 88KK."

Dampness marked Quirk's neck and forehead. Perhaps he should start delivering pithy one-liners in case one turned out to be his last words.

"Last time we met up, you kissed me on the neck instead of shooting me. I'm starting to hope this will go the same way."

Beatrix nodded. "Well, it's always nice to know someone would rather be kissed by you than die; you certainly are a charmer, Quirk."

"Can we just get on with this? Whatever 'this' is."

Beatrix sighed. "I'm afraid you don't get anything from me today, unluckily for you. I'll continue to reserve the pleasure though. What you *do* get is an offer of employment from my current masters, The Rigel Corporation."

If it were possible, Quirk's clammy neck became colder, and he wondered if he might be embarking on a cardiac episode. His attitude to Rigel remained decidedly negative. Despite his best efforts to avoid consorting with them again, they seemed intent on dogging his steps; the villa killings, Toni's dead drop leading to the Moth "acquisition," and now...what?

"No kissing, Quirk, and no shooting, unless you do something incredibly stupid. In fact, we'll be working together."

"You're very confident about that."

"I have a funny feeling your contract with the Ladies Cricket Federation of Sweden is about to be terminated."

Quirk glanced down at Yasmina-Leena whose breathing appeared normal, her skin pallor the correct gentle sienna tone.

"Okay." He took a deep breath. "Tell me the worst."

"The UN Secretary for Technology needs our help. He and his daughter are cruising on the *Gargantua Pleiades* out of Geostation 2. Rigel has evidence there is a threat to the Secretary's safety or that of young Shuun, and that he might come under some form of duress to make certain...preferential decisions in relation to the renewal or not of certain NLS licenses."

Beatrix paused, seemed to expect a response, but Quirk remained schtum, gave a wan smile, and rubbed his right shoulder, which still ached considerably. No sense in breaking the assassin's flow when xe was in a loquacious mood.

"The cruise ship arrives at Mars Port in three days. Our team will join them there. Our mission is not known to the Secretary, his staff or his security detail. The Suudis are enjoying a pleasure cruise. No official engagements other than speaking at the New Year's bash on board, when the ship is in port."

Assuming the job itself would turn out vastly more complicated and dangerous than Beatrix presented, Quirk focused on more practical matters. "That's a four-day journey on a commercial line. We'd get there New Year's Eve at best leaving from...Athens Spaceplex, I guess."

Beatrix nodded. "But with Rigel Corp as our sponsor we get a D ship, and our travel time is just over two-and-a-half days."

"By the time we get to Athens—"

"Ship's waiting on the techmac about an hour from here."

"Of course it is." Quirk sighed. "What about Moth? She's partying with her Rigel cronies in Lunaville. I hope they wouldn't subject her to a direct threat situation." Now he acknowledged he had not asked, or even considered, who the Secretary's antagonist might be. Because of course he knew the answer to that question. Because there seemed only to be one antagonist in his life these days. Also, he'd stopped paying attention to Beatrix's weapon, meaning he'd begun to engage with the mission, another bad sign.

On the floor, Yasmina-Leena stirred, moaned, moved her arm.

"Don't shoot her again, with either of those weapons. If you do, a 76-kilogramme problem will land on you in half a second, flat." He gave Beatrix a smile: *Can you see the whites of my eye-teeth?*

The assassin looked thoughtful then shrugged. "Fair enough. You should know that Moth has a part in the mission, to befriend the daughter, stay close to her, observe and report. And her droid will be along for support."

"Damn." Quirk's grunt became a growl of frustration, but he hardly could call Rigel's kettle *nero*, he'd put Moth in danger aplenty these past months. Albeit not all directly, more like leading her into it, and she'd followed, willingly. So why did this time feel like riding his luck too far, that *this time* the ball might drop in 00?

"How do my options look?"

"The range is pretty narrow from where I'm sitting."

"If I decline?"

"I'm advised Mario Manfredi will spill the beans to his young cousin about your participation in the death of Moth's parents."

"I did *NOT* participate in that!" Quirk came to his feet, hands in front of him, open, ready for strangulation. He moved faster than thought, clearly faster than Beatrix accounted for. He realised xe might have gunned him down where he stood, but only on reflection while standing like a beautifully suited Frankenstein's monster.

"I was *in the building*, I was *present*. I did *NOT* participate."

Beatrix rose too, although much more slowly, xis deadly weapon still levelled at Quirk's body cavity where all the good stuff lay.

"I'm hardly going to speak up on your behalf, am I? No skin in that for me, other than the fact that Moth might shoot you before I get the chance."

"I didn't participate. I observed."

"Preaching to the wrong choir, Signore Quirk. Whatever you think you were, you attended the event and, obviously, you haven't told her. Mario will if he decides you're not towing the line in this affair. How do you think she'll react?"

"So, I'm an unwilling volunteer? I presume you're being paid handsomely to turn against TOM."

"I was never *for* TOM. He paid promptly, kept me in pool parties and lost weekends. Mario made an attractive offer. And I've never forgotten I owe TOM a bullet, since one of his lackies pulled the trigger when Pascal died. A bullet meant for you. And I know my blame of you is irrational, because who wouldn't step out of the way of a bullet?

But you didn't even see it coming. It was dumb luck. You're so fucking lucky, Quirk."

"So, you'll shoot me after the job is done? Is that part of the package you've agreed with Manfredi?"

Beatrix stepped to the side of the prone cricketer, whose waking sounds made Quirk decidedly nervous. The assassin looked right at him, dark irises hidden by the narrowing of xis eyes. Xe stuck the 88KK's barrel into Quirk's ribs.

"To be honest, I find myself swithering on that, but I promise you'll be the second to know when I come to a decision. Rigel's job comes first. Just don't forget we're not done, and that Moth's trust in you is at stake too."

"So, in addition to being a professional killer you're an unforgiving progeny of a bitch, nice combination. I won't buy a lottery ticket while we're working together in case you lose the rag. But if you do go after TOM, you'd better take an army."

Beatrix's already darkly Latin visage took on a stormy cast, and xe jammed the gun harder into Quirk's gut. "Simister's day is coming. I've completed several tasks for him, in part as groundwork to get closer to him than I otherwise would. Once I build some goodwill with Rigel, I'll try to leverage support from the new capo, who must be just as anxious to see the old bastard dead."

"Why share all that with me?" *Unless you plan to shoot me in a minute.*

"There was a time I intended to kill you at the earliest opportunity, but I see now that I can get some use out of you first. That's all."

Not today then. Quirk managed to avoid sighing in relief. "So, what's your name? If we're working together, I can't keep thinking of you as Beatrix Potter."

"I rather like the sobriquet." Beatrix flashed him a dark-eyed smirk just before Yasmina-Leena kicked xim in the shin.

Only dumb luck prevented Quirk from being shot. He'd seen YL's eye open before she swung her foot, enabling him to twist aside at the right moment. Even more fortunately, Beatrix's professionalism prevented xim shooting wildly once xis target moved. Quirk gripped the assassin's slender wrist, used his weight to force hand and gun to the floor, dragging the rest of Beatrix down. He pried the gun loose.

The firearm did not possess a coded grip. That meant storing personal data, not clever for a hired killer, even if they could dispose of their weapon.

All the kicking, grabbing and fumbling took place in near silence. Struggle over, Quirk sat on the floor wincing, gun levelled at a seated Beatrix Potter, with Yasmina-Leena propped against the compartment door trying to shake off her wooziness.

"So, what is your name?" asked Quirk.

"Call me Anwar, a name from my father's side."

Quirk nodded then twitched the gun to indicate Anwar should sit up on the bunk. Xe did so, Quirk and YL resumed their seats.

The assassin laughed quietly.

"Will you not do that, please?" Quirk sat back, glanced at vast fields of Czechian wheat sliding by. He badly wanted to ask Yasmina-Leena how much she'd heard of The Rigel Corporation's plans, but if the answer was something, anything, he'd have a hard job convincing Anwar not to kill her.

"I'll do this job, for Rigel, but I will not return this weapon to you until we leave the train, and it's a good few kilometres away."

Anwar nodded. "I get it, Quirk, but why don't we just ask the lady how much she heard? Because if you think I couldn't kill her from this position, I might be offended."

"Will you take her word?"

"I heard almost nothing!" *Not the right answer, Yasmina-Leena.*

Anwar didn't respond immediately, just looked at Quirk then YL, then back. "I'm no assassin with a heart of gold. Pascal and I were at Toni's villa to do harm." Quirk's gaze flicked to YL. She may not have heard anything before, but she had now. "I'm not going to kill her. My perspective changed, not suddenly and violently as Pascal died in my arms, but slowly as the guilt closed over my head and I sank into its depths."

"Very poetic." Yasmina-Leena's current pallor did not reassure Quirk, but her tight expression spoke more of anger than pain or distress.

The assassin took a turn looking out on the countryside where drone-directed harvesting of the winter wheat crop appeared to be underway. "So, what now, Quirk?"

"You and I will leave the train in Budapest," he answered. "Yasmina-Leena, please explain to Thoresson that I've quit, and that I will not submit an invoice. I'll write with a formal resignation when I can, returning half my retainer. And Yasmina?"

"Yes, Quirk?"

"Whatever you might think you heard just now, forget it. Concoct a fiction about seeing it on a show or reading it in book. Whatever you need to put it from your memory, because if you don't, or even if you do, there's a measurable chance that one day someone will decide you heard something, and that your promise of silence is not enough. Do you understand?"

"Yes, Quirk, I—"

He pressed his lips closed and put a finger to them. The cricketer shushed.

"Okay. So, I'm sorry to do this in front of my new frenemy here, but you're about to walk out that door and go sit in the dining car for the last few kilometres into Budapest. Go sit with some friends, drink champagne and laugh, start to let all this nonsense slip away. Maybe remember that we had a good time for a few days, but probably best just to forget that too."

He wished he could have told her her lips tasted like honey, and he'd felt as if vitality flowed into him when their skin touched, but that seemed unlikely to aid Yasmina-Leena in forgetting him, so he kept such things to himself. She paused at the door, her expression almost wistful as they locked eyes once more, then she smiled apologetically and ducked out of the compartment.

"What now, Romeo?" asked Anwar.

"Now, we wait," said Quirk, leaning forward to scoop up the dart gun where it lay on the bunk next to the assassin.

"Why don't you get some sleep, Quirk, you look tired?"

"Maybe I will close my eyes for a few minutes."

"You know I could kill you while you slumber and not even use my hands."

"I'm sure you could, but I'm betting on you not quite trusting that I'm asleep."

V

14:13, 3 December 2099 (Earth date equivalent)
En route to Cythera Station, Venus High Orbit, SVO-1-0-0

James Foster had no illusions he was anything other than a criminal. The tradition of criminality went way back through the Foster line, from his paternal great grandparents boosting cars in Newark all the way back in 2019 (all four of them; a true family business), through his grandmother running a stock market pyramid scheme while his grandfather forged personal documents, to his own parents cunningly developing an offshoot of the forgery line into a full-service human trafficking business.

Too much thinking on a jaunt like this, too much time. The distance of Venus from Earth varied from 40 million kilometres to 250-odd million. So, his trip to C Corp's Cythera Station in high orbit around Sol's second planet could have been longer, could have been much shorter. With time to burn on the D ship's 3.6-day journey, James used a whole ten minutes contemplating the trip's logistics. At least his return would be shorter. Maybe a lot shorter, but he had no clue why he'd been summoned, and pondering that quickly became his main distraction.

C Corp headhunting him after six months in private security had been nice. Three promotions in six months had been terrific; from gopher on a sec squad, to squad leader. C Corp's key qualification seemed to be willingness to pull the trigger. He'd done that plenty in Year One, always hitting the target. Then things really began to move. Shoot two bandits in Bogota? Receive a promotion to senior squad commander. Lead S&D squads out of the Genextric research facility in Yellowknife, terminating a whole mess of rabid terra-fauna? Promotion from VP Corporate Security herself to Sec Squad Coordinator—a desk job in most orgs, but at CC it meant taking point on the most important missions.

Coordinate capture of two interlopers at the company's facility on Skye? Apparently, the reward for that success—even with the data leaks which, inexplicably, had been permitted—was a trip to Venus to meet Simister himself. An obvious conclusion, Simister being the only person who lived there, just him and a bunch of syRen® to serve his every need. Not that he didn't have visitors. Urban legend included alleged eyewitness accounts of nubile young girls/boys/enbies being ferried out to The Old Man's hyper-private lair. James suspected the scuttlebutt was bullshit, but the old bastard must do something for kicks when he spent most of his year millions of miles not only from Earth, but from people.

* * *

18:20, 6 December 2099 (Earth date equivalent)

He found Cythera Station, seat of Joshua Simister's power, disappointing. For a guy who probably could have bought Venus itself (Foster wondered if TOM *did* in fact own the planet), the space station looked like all the others he'd seen. It wasn't thirty times the size of Geostation One as some stories had it, probably only five or six times: a central axle "tube" with three rings linked to the axle by walkway "spokes." The rings themselves must be fifty metres apart, the central ring bigger in radius than the other two. Cythera emitted no sense of super villain's lair, was no black stealth hulk ready to eat ships drawing too close. Just a boring, grey space station, functional, bland.

Foster stepped from the airlock, magboots clumping on the metal floor. For any station the reception area ran indecently wide, and two lines of six androids formed a corridor like an honour guard dominating the extravagant space, all presenting laser rifles. He still struggled to get his head around *that*. He'd heard the rumours of course, of syRen® running amok on the Moon, seen footage that seemed to show strange goings-on connected to the research of Androicon—a C Corp company. In Yellowknife he witnessed androids shooting projectile weapons, but the targets there had been terra-fauna, threatening humans, a no-brainer. But what target could there be out here for an android to shoot? Corporate enemies? Whatever the case, as Foster walked between the android ranks, he felt suitably intimidated.

Despite four days on a D ship this place weirded him out. There were androids everywhere, every corridor junction, every other door, and silence reigned. A watchful silence.

After a shower and change, a syRen® (unarmed) escorted Foster from his berth on the upper ring down to the largest one, stopping at an unprepossessing grey door on a long, horizontally curving corridor dotted with identical grey doors.

The door slid back, and Foster entered.

At last, a space amongst all the grey impersonality that had some character. He had no illusion this room was The Old Man's inner sanctum, but colour accented the walls, purple facing him, dark green to his left, brooding, stormy colours, but colours, nonetheless. To his right, a walldow displayed a view of dark space, pricked with stars. This could not be a true view from this location though, as those points of light remained stationary. An image capture then. Dark furniture dotted the large room, a wooden desk dominating, stained almost black. Above the desk, a display of company logos; the constituent parts of C Corp, handfuls of them in varying sizes, C Corp's twinned and entwined letters centralised, dominating.

"Mr. Foster, welcome to Cythera Station."

James started, silently cursing his surprise at not immediately registering his host's presence. Joshua Simister moved away from the viewing screen, dark charcoal polo-neck and slacks having disguised him against the dark image of space. A security specialist should have picked him out, certainly should *not* have started in surprise.

"Sir, it's a pleasure to be here."

"Good. I imagine it's a surprise, short notice and all."

Simister's voice held a slight rasp.

"I'm ready for wherever you need, sir. Just drop the hat." *Humour, really?*

"Of course." TOM did not move behind his imposing desk. Rather, the owner of more assets than any individual in human history came forward to shake his hand.

Up close, the man appeared more youthful than he had any right to be. He barely seemed any older than James himself at twenty-nine; no wrinkles, clear skin, tight and toned in an unremarkable way, and yet this man was born in 1936. Simister was one hundred and sixty-three years old, and only his voice betrayed a hint at the long road he'd travelled. He had seen World War II for goodness' sake, had lived through the entire climate crisis, first of the mega rich (even then in rude good health aged a mere eighty-seven) to commit prodigious quantities of personal wealth to mitigation of the effects where possible, committing the power of all his businesses to finding solutions. Motives aside, it couldn't be denied Simister had been a leader in challenging the old-world order in the early 2030s. Some said he'd been the catalyst of the globe-spanning change that—suddenly and unexpectedly—had seen megalomaniacal businesspeople around the world experience a collective penny-drop moment. As a soon as they realised they were all going to die regardless of their incomprehensible wealth, after chiding themselves for lacking the foresight to develop their own rockets, they decided they'd better act, the survival of billions of neighbours a side effect that, happily, could be the subject of subsequent monetisation.

"Mr. Foster, I have a proposition for you. Your effectiveness and rapid rise through the Security Division's ranks has attracted my attention. All well-deserved."

"And I've been well rewarded, sir."

"Good." Simister nodded thoughtfully. He turned away, waved a hand carelessly to the available seating as he walked to and moved behind a smoked plass bar against the green wall. "Drink?"

"Uh..." *Oh, very smooth, James.* "Espresso martini, please, sir."

"You can drop the honorifics, James. Consider yourself between jobs now. On gardening leave while you consider this offer. The position of Group Head of Security is open, and I think you're the person to fill it. There comes a point at which I take a personal interest in individual staff, because there are no adequate substitutes in business for strong character and good judgement. Hard working idiots are of very limited use to me. And before you answer"–Simister raised a finger at this point, pausing in cocktail assembly—"you should know there's a suitability test *but,* the position can be a stepping stone to an even more powerful assignment."

"A test?"

"Practical. It starts..."—Simister glanced at his wrist, triggering gently glowing numerals to appear—"in one hundred ten minutes. We'll enjoy our drinks then I suggest you relax in your room, prepare as you see fit for a test the nature of which I have no intention of revealing in advance. A syRen® will call for you at the appointed time and brief you accordingly."

Simister walked to James, proffering one of the two glasses he carried. Up close, Foster saw subtle signs of Simister's longevity, the hint of old scar lines in the shadows beneath his jaw, the junction of nose and cheek, concealed in the curve of his eyebrows. The subtle signs of almost absolute power.

"One way or another, James, this trip will change your life."

* * *

19:55, 6 December 2099 (Earth date equivalent)

The dropship plummeted towards Venus, rattling and groaning. That didn't faze Foster at all, he'd dropped frequently during his military service. Neither was he disturbed by the android pilot's artificial calmness as it touched the controls now and again, presumably to stabilise their decent into the extreme pressure and temperature at the planet's surface. Thankfully, they were not destined for that hellish 500-degree oven wherein atmospheric pressure topped out at an unimaginable ninety times that of Earth. Even with an HD military envsuit and combat exo—neither of which TOM had provided—those conditions equalled death, if the drop ship even survived the approach.

The ship began to decelerate. As in any military situation, the android's handling of the ship spared no thought for human comfort. They braked fast and hard, and the extreme atmosphere's buffeting redoubled. Docking this thing—assuming their destination was a structure and not a mountaintop because, again, not survivable—would be an absolute bitch. He regarded the droid as its digits darted over the controls, trimming and compensating, the ship shuddering against whipping sulphuric acid clouds that became a super-critical fluid under these pressures.

Then they hit, an unanticipated and extremely violent jolt that yanked Foster's straps into his shoulders, chest and groin. He grunted then barked in pain and frustration. "Fucker!"

"We have arrived," said the android, helpfully. "Beyond the double airlock is a prep room where you will find limited supplies. You may return there during the trial to rest as you see fit, however, the airlock will not cycle again until the trial is complete."

"What is the nature of the trial? You're supposed to brief me."

"Your mission is to nullify all combatants on this facility, alone and unaided, then retrieve the target from the platform's control room. I will await you here."

"Doesn't that contradict the First Law? Assuming I'm not walking into a Venusian garden party."

The android said nothing, but worked the controls to unlock the inner hatch. Foster sighed. At least he had a target now, and hardware, and an objective. Time to go to work.

Ten minutes later, he squatted in a cupboard. His leg stung viciously from a wound taken in the first two minutes. He'd just managed to get a field dressing on it. He'd gained about fifty metres and "deactivated" four of the so-called combatants. They were droids, droids attacking him, shooting at him with laser carbines and projectile weapons. syRen® shooting at a human! He'd heard of it, not quite believed it, but now he was jammed up in it. The laws of robotics did not apply here due to C Corp's intervention, The Old Man's will.

The door swung open, and he opened fire, not registering how close a lance of energy bright as the sun came to his legs. His beam took the droid in the belly, and he trailed his ray up to its neck then twitched it across the droid's neck to sever its head.

Every schoolkid knew a syRen®'s control module lived in its chest, but decapitation deprived the machine of its main sensor array. The locked-in machine tumbled forward into the store, hitting the floor with a dull thud.

No time to think, he snatched up the droid's gun in time to pour raw energy into the droid following up. Diving forward and rolling, he severed a foot before melting the droid's chest. Not knowing how many opposed him was all part of the fun.

* * *

Fifteen down now. Felt like seconds. Probably minutes. Time didn't matter. Android carcasses measured his existence. At least killing syRen® replenished his weaponry. The suit advised he'd made 210 metres. Decent, considering he hobbled now to advance. His leg burned. Bumps and bruises ached. The test carried a hefty price in melted machinery, but why would TOM care? The losses would be tax deductible.

* * *

The thing about these doctored androids was how stupid they were. Give them a simple objective (kill the pesky human) and they had zero ability to apply nuance to the task. The whole basis of these tampered machines was deviant. They really weren't syRen® anymore, but near-mindless killing machines, and CC had developed them. Practically, this horrific development meant they quickly reached a point of throwing themselves at him, sacrificing themselves to give their fellows a killing shot. Once he'd figured that, he could better predict their responses, deploying his own tricks to draw them into decidedly inhuman errors.

BZZZT. BZZZT. BZZZZZZTTTTTT. Two short bursts and a long one: a tracer, a tagger and a kill shot. Again, and again, and again. The smell of melted plastic and charred electronics drifted on the light smoke that clouded another anonymous corridor. Another down. Another. Another. Another.

Then silence.

Foster stood, edged from the doorway he'd hunkered in for the last flash fight. He levelled the IWI in his right hand, tweaked his left's grip on a BSA M2089 claimed from a fallen droid. Weariness made muscles thrum. He moved down the empty corridor, fixated on succeeding. Because the offered prize stoked the desire that fuelled his first steps down this long road. Governments, authorities, corporations took from him by legal mandate, diktat and decree. They taxed him, charged him, pumped him, and where was his power as a human being? It was here, in the barrel of a gun.

Back to one wall, he edged the final two metres covering both approaches. A T-junction. Empty. A closed door to the right, blank. A similar portal to the left, this bearing a sign: Control Centre.

He moved that way, opened the door, and tension flooded out of him. Technical stations lined the walls of a square space. A commanding LivewaLL faced him. Three chairs occupied the room's centre. A slumped figure curled in one. Female. Foster locked the door, moved forward and prodded her with a gun barrel. The woman woke, startled. Eyes glistening, she broke into a smile, and into tears.

"Thank God! They wouldn't let me leave."

Nina had come to Cythera Station on the last service flight. Three days ago, Simister hosted a dozen business associates. A crew of caterers shuttled out from Brisbane Spaceport, up to Geo 2 and out to Cythera. Nina had fallen ill and been held back, promised a berth on the next ship. She told her story as they returned to the prep room, speaking intermittently as she chewed his remaining ration pack. Foster just listened, cold creeping through his gut.

* * *

Simister stood inside the airlock commanding the wide reception space, flanked by the same two lines of armed syRen®. TOM smiled in welcome.

"Well done, James. A near perfect score."

"Thank you, sir."

"Only one thing remains."

Yes, he'd been right.

"Because I'm sure you understand from hearing Nina's story that a single threat remains."

"Yes, sir."

"What does he mean?" asked Nina.

Simister turned away, apparently satisfied. Foster's future flashed before him. He went to his pocket, removed a Remington 245 and shot Nina in the head.

He and TOM did not speak again until Foster had boarded the D ship and it manoeuvred away from the docking station on attitude jets.

"Will you take the job, James? What is your answer, and why?" asked Simister.

"My answer is yes. My reason?" Foster pictured The Old Man's steely gaze, eyes that must have been replaced at least twice. "I want a bigger fraction of what you have. I don't want to rule the world, but I want to rule *my* world."

"Good answer. You can now access the C Corp web base. It is secure from all outside access. The resources there—protected by data singularity—can only be utilised by peak level permissions, of which there are six. You and I are two, plus Corporate Chief Counsel; CFO; CTO; and the Secretary to the Chairman. Your welcome pack includes everything you'll need going forward, including remuneration mechanism, of course. Next, you're going to Mars. You'll be there in twenty hours."

VI

23:20, 31 December 2099
Genting Super Grand Lunaville Hotel, Jiang Zemin Street,
Lunaville, The Moon

To Moth, stalling on going down to the ballroom to celebrate the turn of the century with her relatives felt right. Schmoozing sucked ass, even with family. Especially with family because of the ones who were missing. There were few enough she actually looked forward to spending time with, and a handful had criticised her in person for choosing Mario to lead the Rigel Corporation. Fucktards! Also, no Quirk. Her smart Alec private dickwad boss and shit-but-hate-to-admit-it mentor would rather be in fancy Europe with his fancy people than with her. After days of carefully avoiding thinking it, she decided his absence felt a bit like a betrayal. She didn't often admit things to herself about feelings, but... She sighed. She missed the wiseass doofus.

She'd finished getting dolled up two hours ago then spent a while having Bea try on dresses provided by the hotel. Kinda weird dressing up a syRen®. On the one hand, the ultimate expression of playing dolls, on the other, a bit like bossing a friend around in a creepy, almost bullying sort of way. Sure, Bea didn't give a rat's ass because android. She would make her own choice if Moth gave the instruction, probably take a cue from Moth's celebration attire. (Black, of course—classically simple, knee-length party dress, mesh overskirt, diamante over both to make her sparkle like the night sky, spaghetti-straps to show off her sexy-as-fuck shoulders.) Further accentuated by her Miami Cuban Royal 15mm curb chain necklace from the 14K Galaxy Gems range, coated in shiny shifting iridium gloss like her nails. Because girls should have nice things. The necklace weighed a fuck ton, but was the absolute jazz!

She had to go downstairs now. She couldn't be funked with it, but Mario would get all sulky if she ghosted the party, which had assembled from far and wide. Pretty good time for a C Corp raid, actually. *Oh, fuxx.*

She backed into the corner, away from the door, careless of her dress's hem crushing against furniture or catching on fittings. An attack. A fuzking attack, like the one at Toni's villa! An attack on her family. She hit the corner, thought of slumping down to the floor, where the furniture would block her view of the door.

"Moth?" Bea, half-dressed, had moved after her. Their eyes locked. Moth's face felt slack with shock. "Everything is alright. There are no signs of danger, no warnings from the central security system, Rigel's microdrone network reports nominal activity."

"Tell that to my Mom and Dad."

The syRen®'s expression changed from one of calm concern to a comical grimace. Almost instantly that weird and terrifying expression slipped into earnest concentration.

"Hey, Moth. Nick here. Cool the jets, babe. Everything's kosher. I've got things wrapped up tight. You look super-hot, absolutely wicked. Don't smudge that mascara, it's not a Halloween meltdown. It's New Year's!"

"Sto—, sto— Don't calm me down, and *stop*—" She waved a hand in the air, reaching for the right word. "Stop *inserting* yourself into my android!"

"I don't want you to cry. Sorry I came on strong in the elevator before, but don't you get it? I'm here to protect you. That thing... Your parents, it won't ever be you."

"Quirk protects me, you know?" She blew out a breath, fished a smartkerchief from the top of her dress at her side, held it before her eyes to absorb her nascent tears without physical contact.

"Sure he does, but I can do better."

"You're not going to be fucking weird about this, are you?"

"Babe, I don't think it can get much weirder than you shooting me in the head."

"*Don't* call me babe. It's fuzking strange as funk, okay? Stop it. Tell me straight what you mean, cos I'm way past *enough* with people thinking it's cool to be vague, and I'm gonna start parting company with my shit if folks aren't straight with me."

She pushed away from the corner, smoothed her skirt, flicked her bob for good measure, then put hands on her hips and fixed Nick/Bea with a glare. "You wanna be my friend? Spill it, now."

"Well, Cousin Mario—"

"Fuck Mario. Do you see him in the room? You're dealing with *me.*"

"Yeesh," said Nick/Bea, rolling his/her syRen® eyes. "For the gal who killed my body, you've got a mean attitude on you. Okay, yes, Rigel hired me to help with the Mars operation. Anwar Cruz, renowned assassin and former C Corp hirling—nicknamed Beatrix Potter for some reason best known to the World's Worst Dad—is in Europe signing Quirk up. That makes five: It's a real family affair. Cute, huh?"

"So, what, you're a good guy now? White hat?"

"I always was, I guess I got desperate up north. I know I hurt some people."

Dead air. *Not my job to forgive you, shit-bird.*

"Did you think I was the villain?" Nick sounded uncertain. He really seemed to care what she thought.

"I s'pose it was complicated, but you *did* hurt people."

"I'm sorry. I've been thinking a lot about redemption."

"Yeah? You think you can make up for it?"

"I think I can try. D'you think... Could Quirk forgive me? I'm still raging at him, and it would be real easy to keep hitting him with the sticks he's given me, but then what chance would we ever have, him and me, and my Mom?"

"I think you and he need to chew that over. Meanwhile, try to fucking behave yourself, see where it takes you." She nodded, job done. "Just remember, no more secrets."

Nick made Bea's head nod.

"Okay, I'ma go party like it's 2099."

* * *

Moth admitted she may in the past have been heard to say New Year's parties were lame ass shit, but whoever Mario hired to throw this one had done good work. The decoration had classy to a "T," including no balloons. She fucking hated balloons.

Jenna Lucia spotted her the instant she and Bea—sporting a bottle green strapless number and fully restored to proper operation, with no memory of Nick's invasion of her "person"—stepped into the ballroom. JL—in pink, of course—tottered over like the bride's drunken aunty, hauling behind her a glamourous brunette, silky locks flowing over the shoulders of an immaculately cut royal blue dress. Aunt Giulia. Moth gaped, her cool fractured.

"Look who's here?!" squeaked JL, but Moth barely heard the introduction, her glistening, rather blurry gaze locked with her aunt's. Giulia hugged her hard and she, like the emotional punchbag life had made her, hugged back as hard as she could. Giulia pushed back enough only to free her hands to frame Moth's face and kiss her cheeks one after the other, then her forehead, then pulled her back into the hug.

"Mia cara, Moth. My darling."

Faced with her aunt who had been in the mansion. Who had seen Moth's parents die. Who had tried to prevent it all by calling the cops. Giulia di Fantano who years later, banished to the convent, had lost her husband Toni as Moth had lost an uncle. Giulia was here. Maybe just for one night Moth would allow herself to dance again like she had as a little girl with her aunt and her mother on Milan's cobbled side streets. And maybe the whole world, all the shitting worlds and the crap-bag killer robots, gen-mod monsters and hijackasses would fuck off and leave them alone for this one night. Just Angelika Moratti and what was left of her family and a single, self-contained happy night before all the bullshit started again. Was that too much to ask?

VII

19:12, 2 January 2100 (Earth date equivalent)
Mars Port, Low Mars Orbit, SMO-1-0-0-0

Boredom set in rather quickly on Mars as it turned out. Well, Low Mars Orbit, although Quirk did not imagine the surface of the Red Planet was any more riveting. Importantly, in terms of passing the time until Moth and Bea arrived, Mars Port possessed a bar. Not a grey vending machine in a square room with cafeteria furniture, strip lighting, and a scatter of weather-beaten miners and military sorts, but an honest to deity lounge bar with passably stylish dark décor (the ambience red-tinged, for obvious reasons) and a jazz soundtrack skipping through the audio system.

Having to wear a lap belt due to gravity only a third Earth's, even before orbital tapering, did cramp his style a little. Schmoozing other patrons became a distinctly awkward affair but, on the other hand, that did make having a quiet drink in the contemplation of one's own thoughts considerably easier. And quiet the drink was too, since Beatr— no, Anwar, had travelled down to the Martian surface, where conditions tended toward no-frills. Sure, some of the hotels were passable, but the Martian economy had not yet reached the financial tipping point the Moon passed decades ago, resulting in an influx of investment and the increased commercial activity that came with it. Mars, apart from the southern and eastern sections of its self-proclaimed capital city, Daedalia, possessed all the charm and sophistication of a construction site.

Perhaps Anwar had gone in search of some rough trade. Certainly, Quirk and xe had not exactly hit it off in the handful of days they'd spent together travelling from Greece to Mars. He smiled at the classical connotations of their journey, wondering what Homer would have made of it, if he'd been a writer of more speculative fiction, instead of reinventing the fantastical superpowered pantheon of his day. He snorted. He needed Moth here to keep him focused. Did he remember their partnership with rosy ideation? Almost certainly. It had only been a month since they'd seen each other, yet somehow that timespan seemed impossible.

How would she be after all those days away? They'd spoken, but only briefly, to exchange information. Nothing meaningful. He'd seen pictures on her Famebook page, and she looked happy, quite the young woman in her element. He knew some of Moth's relatives from those pictures. Jenna Lucia Bonetti in particular was impossible to ignore, but his current employer, the capo Mario Manfredi's appearance at the Rigel party had gone unrecorded.

And there was Giulia di Fantano. He pulled up the image again on his cLife. So very different from Suour Giulia that he'd seen in Milan before he and Moth left Earth. She looked happy to no longer be cooped up in the convent. Had she told Moth that he had been in Toni's villa?

He slugged the remainder of his gin and waved to the server for another. One more sleep until Anwar returned, until Moth and Bea arrived. At least then they could get down to business, and he could plan how best to achieve the task, and keep the knowledge from Moth for a while longer.

* * *

4:42, 3 January 2100 (Earth date equivalent)
Mars Port, Low Mars Orbit

Ten hours later—including the annoying extra thirty minutes Martians got in bed—Quirk and Anwar stood in the orbital station's reception area watching with six others a big screen image of Rigel Corporation shuttle *Gianluca Vialli* nudging Mars Port's dampers. The orbital was smaller than Earth's Geos One and Two, but fitted out with imagination. Mars Port's designer used illumination to great effect, dusting metal-sheeted walls and textured (but magnetic) flooring with swathes of radiance, imbuing the lightweight materials with substance beyond their strong but slender structure. Occasional pedestals interrupted the open area, plinths of lattice construction each housing a holographic projector. These displayed ghostly, slowly rotating images of human history's great ships: *The Mayflower, The Golden*

Hind, Queen Elizabeth 4, La Santa Maria, USSS Enterprise, and the UN's exploratory starship *Kang Tai*. One he did not recognise, and he pointed his handset at the pedestal ten metres away. His cLife reported this twin-masted vessel—the *Hōkūle´a*—was a 1975 replica (still incredibly old) of a Polynesian *wa´a kaulua* voyaging canoe.

An understated grunt broke into his contemplation.

"Hey, wassup. Tear yourself away from your cLife a second to give a girl a hug?"

"Moth! Hi, honey." *Ooh, bit much.* "You're getting real good sneaking up on me." *Annnnnd, patronising as hell. Nice job, Quack.*

"I literally walked across the fucking room, straight towards you."

"Must be your disguise then, nice work." He smiled: *Work with Me Here.*

"I'm wearing a bloody hoodie and sweatpants, in a well-lit environment."

"I've missed you too," he said earnestly. "And I really want to hear about your adventures, the hijacking? Dammit, Moth. I'm really proud of you."

She pressed her lips together as if deciding whether to accept the compliment. "Adventures? Jeepers, Grandpa. But, uh, yeah, it was totally ill. Sure, I'll tell you." She turned to look at Anwar. "What's the human xylophone doing here?"

Quirk opened his mouth, and Bea also started to speak, but Anwar beat them to it. "I'm working, Shorty, how about you? D'you bring anything to the team apart from your shit-talking mouth? It's the only big thing about you."

Moth smiled, perhaps appreciating the quality of Anwar's badinage. "Yeah, we'll get on fine." She stuck her hand out and the assassin shook it.

"I agree, just stay off the pronouns."

Moth nodded. "Yes, Xir."

"And you know what I'm doing here." Anwar alluded to the fact they'd all been briefed. Xe smiled then moved forward, bending to hug Moth, apparently before she could get away judging from her expression. Quirk moved to the side, playing a hunch, and saw the assassin whisper in Moth's ear.

She nodded, then took hold of one of each of their hands in hers and swung them slightly, grinning. "It's just so great to see you two happy together at last." And with that, she turned and strutted away towards their hotel, leaving Bea to stride after her.

"Wow," said Anwar. "I thought you were joking. She's a real pill."

"It's her best quality."

They walked back to the hotel—not a great distance through the space station's corridors—clumping along with that awkward reduced gravity gait. Neither spoke.

They did encounter some foot traffic, the corridors narrow enough to necessitate moving to one side to let people pass. Casually, Quirk watched Anwar watching the people they encountered. At one point, xe stopped and produced a compact, ostensibly to check some fragment of debris in xir eye. Quirk played along, holding xir elbow, looking over Anwar's shoulder at the backs of two Mars Port residents. One, female, wore maintenance fatigues, the other...harder to place, sported a flight crew uniform.

"Did they come off Moth's flight?" asked Quirk.

"No," said Anwar, dabbing xir eye.

The two passed the corner and disappeared from sight.

"You're armed," said Quirk, sotto voce.

"And dangerous," murmured Anwar.

They paused a moment longer as station denizens passed them. Mars Port security cameras no doubt would have registered their inaction by now.

"We should move on," said Anwar, placing a hand on Quirk's shoulder.

Quirk moved a hand to his face, seeming to rub his cheek in weariness, in fact intending to block the movement of his lips from any camera linked to lipreading software. "This is not one of those romcom moments where we make out to out-fox the pursuit."

"You wish," said Anwar.

Back in Quirk's room, the three plus Bea assembled. Anwar produced what appeared to be a handset, but applied it to the room like a detector while Quirk and Moth watched, S-17834 charging in the corner, her eyes glowing gently violet.

Quirk watched Moth, smiled, genuinely pleased to see her. She snorted, jerked her head toward Anwar, her bob twitching. Quirk's expression segued into a rueful twitch of the lips: *That's the Way the Cookie Crumbles.* Did she wish it was just the two of them, like old times? *Old times? With only a month passed?* He thought of Toni's mansion and his smile faded.

"Room's clean," said Anwar. "No bugs, no incursion beams, but we need to be aware that CC could have Counter Counter ops working against this Counter Operations team of ours. Can the droid—?"

"Busy charging," Moth interrupted. "But you've got other resources, of course."

"She's defensive about people co-opting her android," said Quirk, although Moth's glance at Bea held more trepidation than anything else. Curious. "So, talk us through it. I presume you're in charge." He sat on the room's armchair, both feet on the ground, moved the lap weight onto his thighs. Moth sat cross-legged on the bed, holding the secured coverlet.

Anwar sat at the room's desk. "The *Gargantua Pleiades* departs Mars Port in twenty hours. Our berths have been arranged through a Rigel ghost corp under three shell identities. I am Kemet Sobek, a mid-level label exec from Ital Sounds. I've been sent to check out various acts playing the Phobos Festival."

"B, fucking L, fucking L—fucking hell!" said Moth, quietly, but with passion. "Only the absolute best rapper, A-T-M."

"You excited, honey?" asked Anwar.

Moth's features became a stone wall. "Fuck you, butt-munch. BLL is the cream, and I get the chance to see him on this job. Nobody's gonna mess that for me, *capisce*?"

"Whatever. You, Quirk, are Douglas MacDonald, label contract exec, on hand to negotiate with any acts I sign on the spot."

"And me?" asked Moth.

"You're MacDonald's daughter—like on the farm, you know?" Moth stuck out her tongue at him. "You're along for the ride, a hanger-on, a freeloader, if you will. So, not too much of a stretch, huh? Gives you time to roam around and befriend the daughter. The android—"

"You'd better call her Bea. Get in character."

"Alright, Bea, carries a secure data pack with our full legends, and will interdict any scans of our devices or local searches into our IDs while on board the *Gargantua*. Groundwork also has been laid by Rigel cyber division, as you would expect."

"Maybe as *you* would expect," said Quirk, "being a criminal. Whereas this covert stuff is new to the rest of us."

"Is that right, Mr. Jefferson?"

"Okay, there was that one time in Creston."

Anwar just laughed.

"We board the *Gargantua Pleiades* by tender from Bay 18 at five past eleven AM. I think any move on Sec-Tech will come during the concert. He's due to come on during BLL's set and make a speech. We'll have eyes on him the whole time. We will always be on, so get some rest while you can. Meet in the breakfast room in five hours." Xe stood, "Now, I'll leave you two to bitch about me. But seriously, rest. This will be intense."

Anwar departed, leaving an awkward silence behind xim.

Quirk looked at Moth, started to smile and stopped. She flopped back on the bed, causing her to rise ten centimetres above it before, very slowly, floating down again. She crossed her arms under her head.

"You get with any lady cricketers?"

"I— Ah, yes, I did as it happens. The captain—"

"Ha! Nothing but the best for you, Quirk, you sly dog."

Silence again.

"How are you, Moth? How was the party? I saw a few photos..."

"Uh, yeah. It was cool. Family, you know?"

"Yes, sort of."

"Oh, sorry, I—"

"It's okay, Moth. Let Yellowknife go. I said it then and I meant it, if you hadn't done it, Nick would have found another way to escape the twisted body the experiments left him with."

She sat up, gripped the bedclothes to stabilise herself. "You know Nick's in on this bitch squad, right?" She glanced toward Bea then back to him. She looked nervous.

A fist closed around Quirk's stomach and pulled. "He's here?" *Of course he is, he's everywhere. He showed us that before.* The fist seemed to have been in an icebox for a couple of years before clamping his intestines. His face felt hard, like marble. "I should have guessed he'd jump at the chance to mess up The Old Man. I've seen hints of Nick around, thought I did, like echoes, more than just my own paranoia.

He's never spoken to me though, since Canada." He gave a laugh that came out nervous, trying to reassure her and flubbing it up. Even though his thoughts raced, he had to show he didn't blame her, because he didn't. It was his fault. "We're okay, Moth. I know we haven't talked about it properly, and we don't have to, but please know you did the right thing."

"And what does a *proper* discussion about me shooting your genetically monstered son to save your life sound like, exactly?!"

"Well, I guess it sounds like you shouting at me for no reason!"

Awkward silence.

"Fucking adults. Fuuuuuuck," grumbled Moth.

"I missed you too, you little shit," he mumbled.

She moved off the bed, came over, put her arms around his neck and hugged him. "I'm sorry. I would do it again, but I'm sorry."

"I won't raise it again, just...always remember he got what he wanted."

"Yeah, he did, and I got the nightmares."

"We both did."

She squeezed once more, and he hugged her back, images of a darkened villa running through his head.

VIII

20:18, 4 January 2100 (Earth date equivalent)
Cruise Ship Gargantua Pleiades, *Approaching Phobos Viewpoint*

Moth couldn't quite believe her luck in finding a Dairy Queen on the cruise ship. She hadn't had decent ice cream since, well, Milan in August, but post that the last DQ she and Quirk hit before leaving Creston after being cleared of all charges (okay, most charges. There had been a sizeable fine). More importantly, this Skor Wars blizzard absolutely hit the spot. The calories went straight to her hips but that sweet, sweet, salty flavour, that creamy burnt butter tang hit like Anwar had just assassinated her with a dopamine dum-dum round.

Not a total coincidence getting her fix while working, since ice cream parlours were a classic teen girl hangout, and she hung here in the hope of encountering Shuun Suudi, aged sixteen. Also, Shuun's BFFs travelled with her, a perk of daddy being Sec-Tech (the official abbreviation), and comfortably loaded. Being in a group multiplied the chances of Shuun dropping in here, but made it harder for Moth to break into the circle. She'd done her homework on that angle though, checked out Shuun's socmed. Pretty formidable it was too. The girl worked hard laying the foundations to be a "pusher." Moth preferred the old-fashioned term influencer, but that disappeared after the online death cult "incident" in 2029.

Anyway, skipping all the girlie stuff Shuun posted on her many platforms, which had to be scheduled and monitored with a Clutterbuck (or Clusterfuck, as cool kids like Moth called it) account, the girl was mad for Brother Leigh Love, obvs the reason her dad picked this cruise. Probably just took the speaking gig cos Shuun bent his ear about going to the Phobos Festival, and he wouldn't let her go on her own.

"Hey, Moth," said Nick through her handset implant. *"I love your smarts here but it's getting boring watching you waiting for something to happen."*

<Watching?> she asked, her mouth forming the word, letting her comm rig's subvoc do the rest, quickly raising her spoon in front of her mouth to cover her lips in case of spies. <From where?>

"syRen® with the family by the door," said Nick, tone sounding disappointed she'd had to ask. *"So look, it's not that I don't like to see you meatsacks trying so hard, but I'm going to send Shuun to you."*

<How's that now?>

"I'll glitch her handset, send her ice cream ads, a special offer 'For this hour only!!' Some shit like that. Don't go away. She'll be here soon, I bet."

<Hey, how come you didn't spill to Quirk you're on this job?>

"How do you know I didn't?"

<Because *I* just did it, dummy.>

"Ah." Long pause. *"Did he get mad? He got pretty mad when I helped you out in Canada."*

<The way I remember it there was plenty of mad going around. There's mad on both sides, right? You lied to him, used us, injured a bunch of people, killed some baddies, pretended to *strangle him!* He knows your deal now. But he left you and your mom. You have a right to be angry at your dad.> She felt an ache in her chest. <I can't advise you on that. Look, I think he's a good guy under all the fancy shit. I can't tell you if he's changed, but you know TOM messes people up.>

"Yeah, s'pose. Anyway, Shuun's heading your way. Wait—" Short pause. *"I think there's a tail on you, and I don't mean the bushy kind. Lemme look at this. But yeah, Shuun, two, three minutes. Lock and load, or whatever teenage girls do."*

Sure enough, two minutes later three girls walked into the twenty-cover DQ, their chatter doubling the buzz in the place, even better sitting at the table next to Moth. *Dumb luck, can't beat it.*

Moth ate her sloppy ice cream, waiting for an opening. Should she worry about the maybe tail? She'd assume it existed 'til someone told her different. Meanwhile, she side-eyed the girls. No problem spotting Shuun, her clothes had tag, lined with dollas. She wore a BLL T-shirt (of course; imagine running into him in a corridor!) under a silver puffer that set off her rich umber skin and dark ringlets, also dusted with silver. The other two girls wore BLL shirts too, but somehow didn't own it like Shuun. Nick's research said (a) Patsy Rose Ruth Finkelstein, dark hair, long and straight, grey eyes, 167cm, eighteen years old, daughter of UN administrators, Swiss and Chinese respectively; (b) Lizella Janel Burnett, blond, blue-eyed, 170cm, seventeen, one mother a human rights lawyer, the other a sculptor. Older girls might be a tough sell, but this was the job, and she was in the business of getting it done. The girls began discussing music, kinda.

"BLL's hot," said Patsy. Moth almost snorted. She loved his music, but the guy was just so angry, a difficult look to pull off for a fifteen-year-old. She wished more adults respected her anger, didn't see it as lightweight, unearned. *Un-fucking-earned?!*

The girls' order arrived by way of the single android working the concession.

"Two hotchip-choc-accinos and a carob espresso."

"Those look good," said Moth across the aisle between their tables.

Lizella turned her blue eyes on Moth, confused, as if a piece of furniture just talked back. Patsy gave a more curious glance then sipped her cream-topped coffee. Shuun Suudi smiled. "Too sweet for me. But you've got a sweet tooth," she nodded at Moth's empty ice cream pot.

"Tail confirmed. Male, 183cm, 98 kilos. Posing as customer service rep. His background only goes to six generations. Fairly clever, hiding in plain sight, but no match for my skills."

"Copy that," said Moth, nodding to Nick's info with an inflection suggesting her reply was for Shuun Suudi. "What can I do?" She shrugged. "Gotta keep my energy up for Phobos, right?"

"You a fan?"

"Am I ever."

"You seen him before?" asked Patsy in a smoky voice with a slight mid-Atlantic drawl, like the opposite of Shuun's clipped European English.

"Nah. I'm a Belter. Hygeia." *Oopsie-fucking-daisy, that's off backstory. I guess Quirk MacDonald married a nice Hygeian lady.*

"Ugh," said Lizella. "Is that why you're so short?" Shuun gave her friend a look.

Moth didn't mind the slur, too much, this one time, maybe. *It means we're talking.* But what about the tail? Was she in danger? Should she assume C Corp? Because of course if they had an op running, they'd call interference on any counter operation. She couldn't subvoc now. She could type something on her handset. She bet Nick was reading it, but she couldn't risk Shuun guessing her game, getting away from her. "I mean, I'm fourteen. Being so tall you must be, what, twenty-five?" *Suck on that, bitch.* For a second the blond looked aghast before her features settled into a disapproving glare.

Moth leaned across the aisle conspiratorially. "So, what would you do if, like, BLL totally walked into this place? Would you try to talk to him, get past his defences? Do you think his team would flip out, defend him, like pin you to the floor?"

"Eew," Lizella gasped, screwing up her features. "Are you some kind of titchy, weirdo mega-stalker?"

"Ha," said Moth, barely restraining the outburst that jumped into her mouth. "No. The *stalker update* is I'm a badly adjusted, short for my age, teenage girl whose dad just happens to be a music exec." She put on a smug expression.

"Oh, wow," said Shuun. "He's not on BLL's label, is he? He's not on Windrush Records? No, you'd have seen BLL before."

"I hear you, no need to wave your hands in the air like that, figuratively speaking. The guy's pretending to work on an access panel, but there are no voltage fluctuations in that location, and no security override on access panel. Some of the kit he's using could be surveillance tech. Could be UN, CC, ICIA, MIS..."

"So, is your dad here to see BLL?" asked Patsy in her pleasant, laid-back drone.

"Is he *packing* a contract?" *Take the hint, Nick.* "Well, I can't say, because I'm a bit *scared* that I'd reveal my dad's trade secrets. But he's not here for the good of his health. Maybe he's *moving in* right now."

"Will you calm down, Mata Hari? I've got you covered. And I've got eyes on Quirk and Anwar at the same time, not to mention running some pretty complex processes contemporaneously, so take a chill pill, babe."

"Yeah, and he's *no babe* in arms, my dad. He's ruthless."

Shuun made a puzzled face, which was fair enough, cos Moth knew she was being weird. Shuun's older friends turned back to their drinks. She was blowing it.

"Okay, look." Moth made a big play of looking around conspiratorially, taking in the fake maintenance guy outside. He had his head in a panel in the corridor, but with line of sight through DQ's door. He could have a microcam trained on them, or a micro-drone under a table. *Shit.* You really had to assume your enemies knew everything you did and said, unless it lived solely in your head. "I reckon I can get us a meet-and-greet with BLL." She sat back in her chair. "But only if you're interested and wouldn't be all weird with him. You gotta be cool."

Shuun's eyes widened, she actually put her fingers to her mouth. Lizella's lips twisted in what might be resentful scepticism or sceptical resentment, while Patsy's brows rose towards the drape of her frankly pretty damn gorgeous hair and she nodded slowly, reappraising, Moth hoped.

"That would be sooo cool," said the Sec-Tech's daughter, and Moth did a little dance in her head, smiling broadly as the other two girls fell into line.

"Yeah, uh, thanks...?"

"Daisy," said Moth, hating more with each minute the legend Anwar manufactured for her. "Daisy MacDonald." *Oh, Dio.*

They exchanged details, Moth flicking her fake card from the screen of an ugly black and silver Neff handset Anwar had given her to Shuun, Patsy and Lizella.

"So, I gotta dash now, but lemme speak to my dad. I'll ping you the deets."

"Assuming he comes through," said Lizella.

"H'meh," said Moth, twisting her lips in mockery of the stuck-up c—

"Tail is moving. Tail is moving."

What now? Not like she could protect Shuun if some ninety-five kilo (most of them in his head, probably) operator came at them with a weapon. A memory of a gun going off, blood and flesh spattering a wall. Moth flinched. *Not now!* She plastered a fake smile on her face for the benefit of the other girls. "Laters, ladies."

She stood, turned to the door, the girls already forgotten. The tech guy looked up from loading his pack, looked right at her, and smiled. What was that? Not a leer, not a hateful smile. A half-hearted lip twist stumbled over Moth's mouth as she turned away towards her cabin. She tried to walk normally, or spaceship-in-orbit normally anyway, but with magboot assist. Other passengers walked these corridors, this being the ship's main commercial deck. Plenty of other passengers. Were any of them watching her too? No way to know, so she kept on.

At least there would be witnesses if this douche tried anything. She took out her handset, typed "Is the shifty shitter following me?" She didn't need to send it.

"*No,*" said Nick through her aural implant. *"He's turned off. I guess he could have got a spytag on you, micro-droid in your pocket. I'm sure Anwar will scan you when you get back. Or, you know, he might just be a real maintenance tech."*

"Check," she typed over her last message. Then, "This is fucking stressful! Also, Quirk's got some music exec-ing to do."

* * *

Quirk watched Anwar—sitting three tables away with Bea—sip xir skinny latte. UN Secretary for Technology Jiilaal Mire Suudi sat at the next table over, his back to Anwar. This meant one of the Sec-Tech's minders faced Bea, and—tangentially—Quirk. This might have presented an obstacle for Anwar's surveillance, but of course xe had it covered. Xe wore contact lenses capable of overlaying the feed from Bea's violet eyes on xis own sight.

Secretary Suudi sat reading on his tablet. A second minder lounged in the corner of the petite coffee shop, arms crossed, presumably to make it entirely obvious to even the most inept covert operative that she was armed.

A vibration in his pocket signified a new message. Quirk brought out his cLife.

```
MOTH [20:37, 04-01-2100]
    Had fun with new friends. They so buzzin to
    meet BLL!! Cn you reach his people, Daddy?
    REALLY WANT THM 2 LIKE ME! Plus u said u could
    do it. I know u can ure so awesome -my hero!
```

Great.

He lifted his espresso sippy cup, looked down to find it empty. He wondered if Anwar would notice him stepping out to the nearest bar, leaving xim with two obvious heavies and two people Quirk thought may have eyes on the Secretary. Although, if CC did plan to snatch

Suudi, which seemed ludicrous, surely they wouldn't show their hand in such a public way, that would compromise whatever advantage they had.

This train of thought only created a channel for his frustration. The appointment from Rigel made it abundantly clear Anwar was in charge. So, Quirk deferred to their agent (sounds too much like law enforcement) and xir decision that Moth cover the daughter, while the three of them scouted the Sec-Tech. He did not expect Anwar to have any personal consideration for Moth's safety over and above that of a useful mission resource, but even at that level, sending her out alone was foolhardy. But perhaps she was not alone. If Nick could indeed jump androids as Callan had done.

He considered another coffee. At some point, it would look suspicious if he didn't order one. Also, how much interest could one find in a handset, really? Furthermore, given Anwar wasn't stupid, and surely would not risk mission resources so early in the game, xe must have a mechanism giving reassurance Moth would not be "removed from the board". So, she had some kind of support, and the obvious answer was Nick.

Quirk bowed his head and rubbed his eyebrow. Was Nick mad at him, or scared of Quirk's anger after Yellowknife? How did he actually feel toward his son after all the mistakes on both sides? *But always mine first. That will always be the foundation of this monumental bloody mess.* Time to find out, on both counts. He sighed, lifted his cLife, opened a (non-synchronised) note, and typed, "Nick?"

```
UNKNOWN [20:39, 04-01-2100]
   You called, father?


UNKNOWN [20:39, 04-01-2100]
   And don't tell me you're surprised, Dad. I can
   be anywhere and everywhere, did you think I'd
   slink off and leave you alone?


UNKNOWN [20:39, 04-01-2100]
   Okay, the silent treatment, very mature. I
   have a right to be ticked off too. But here's
   me turning the other cheek. Your move.
```

QUIRK [20:41, 04-01-2100]
  Is Moth safe?

UNKNOWN [20:44, 04-01-2100]
  Still the shiny new kid first, huh? The one
  you only have contractual responsibility for.
  Nice. Yes, she's fine. Played a good game
  connecting with Sec-Tech's daughter. And no,
  I'm not going to do you a solid by arranging
  facetime with BLL. You'll have to figure that
  out yourself. But, yes, I'm a legit member of
  this team, my services bought and paid for by
  the Rigel Corporation. I guess you've noticed
  we all have a jolly little family connection?
  Moth loathes TOM for ordering the hit on
  Toni's villa where her parents died. Anwar
  hates TOM for ordering the hit on Toni's villa
  where xis partner died. I despise TOM for
  ordering monstrously cruel experiments on me.
  Let's see, have I missed anyone? Oh yes, you
  dislike The Old Man because he went behind
  your back to give your wife something you
  refused her, despite entering the holy estate
  of matrimony.

QUIRK [20:46, 04-01-2100]
  Are you finished?

UNKNOWN [20:46, 04-01-2100]
  Depends on you. I want to be finished
  thinking about this shit.

QUIRK [20:46, 04-01-2100]
  Okay. I have no locus to talk about what
  happened to you, but your hate of TOM does not
  invalidate mine. Think what you like about me,

but don't presume to know your mother's pain.
You weren't there. You didn't hear the
discussions, and you don't know what we
shared. And another thing. Don't you dare wave
other people's distress, their grief, in my
face like you're in possession of some kind of
God-given grace to pass judgement on all
Humankind because of the actions of one
dreadfully twisted individual. You get to
judge me because I failed you. That's fine.
I'll take whatever you see fit to dish out for
as long as necessary, but that's all you get
for free. After that, you behave yourself or
we're done.

UNKNOWN [20:48, 04-01-2100]
Done? When did we start? Was it when you
shunned a 5-year-old child? Or maybe when you
abandoned the child and his mother? No,
probably when you avoided all contact with the
child's mother for years then came back into
the child's life only when tricked into it,
then topped it all off with your new kid
blowing your old unwanted child's head off.

Quirk placed his cLife face down on the table before it could illuminate again. He watched the device for long minutes, half expecting it to somersault into the air and attack him. For all the minutes he watched the stationary handset, he fought the urge to place it on the floor and stomp on it, shatter the screen, beat it to pieces with his chair.

Curious that Anwar hadn't informed him of Nick's presence. Probably xe though it would be a "nice" surprise, or wanted to get through the operation's initial stages with the least amount of turmoil inside the team, or xe just didn't give a damn. No doubt Manfredi, entirely correctly, thought such things beneath him. Not Moth's job either, to tell him, although she had. No, it was Nick's place to announce his presence, and he'd done it now, with bells on.

What might he expect now? Could they work together? Should he leave at the first opportunity? That thought made him consider Moth. This could just be an appetiser of the pain awaiting him, awaiting Moth, if she learned of his presence at Toni's villa. The secret kept swelling in his head like a... One of those things they cut out with lasers. The longer it went on the more likely she'd find out the wrong way, that, instead of being an omission, it would become a lie, a betrayal, and a snub of all she had lost. Toni was gone, but Giulia knew. Mario knew, and Anwar did, those two holding the information over him. Nick must know. A wonder he'd not told Moth already. And TOM knew. Might The Old Man reveal the secret to her? But this should all be academic, because his last talk with Moth followed by this encounter with Nick convinced him he must tell Moth about the villa now, as soon as conveniently possible.

Quirk ordered another espresso because he did not want to move. At least in this space he could focus on straightforward tasks; observation of Sec-Tech, readiness to respond to any threats, and watching for things that did not look right.

He used the approach of the syRen® server as an excuse to check again on the players in this little vignette. Suudi read something on the table, a sheet of smart plaper, it appeared, perhaps his address to the audience at the opening of the Phobos Festival. He used his finger, appearing to make modifications to the text with little strokes, taps and squiggles while the android delivered a new drink. Suudi's minders continued to watch the room, intending to be noticed, striving to intimidate.

Quirk saw no overt sign of covert observation. Hardly surprising given the quality of spy tech nowadays. Hopefully Nick would detect any malicious gadgets in play. Was the...boy at risk? Even if TOM assumed that Nick—free of his bodily prison and the clutches of TOM's scientists—would jump at the first opportunity to strike at CC, how would TOM ever see it coming? Maybe Nick was the real threat to TOM's operation, the rest of them merely bolstering Sec-Tech's physical protection, a visible deterrent. But Quirk had dealt with C Corp's "logistical" ops squads before. They would not balk at physical protection. So, all they did here really—the UN bodyguards and the Rigel team—was enact a corporate security pantomime, awaiting the inevitable strike. If it were him, that would come at the point of maximum confusion, at the start of tomorrow's festival at twenty-two hundred.

Perhaps telling Moth about the villa attack now was a bad idea, too much going on. The knowledge would only destabilise them at a critical moment for the operation. Better leave it for a quieter time. Concentrate on Nick now.

IX

21:38, 5 January 2100 (Earth date equivalent)
Cruise Ship Gargantua Pleiades, *Phobos Viewpoint*

Fuzking bizarre how easily Anwar set up the meet-and-greet with BLL. Xe'd contacted Rigel and the request must have gone straight to Mario. He must really have a hardon for hurting TOM, and why not? And now it was happening! Right now, she walked to the dressing rooms behind the ship's performance area to meet Shuun and friends, and enjoy an audience with the man himself, Brother Leigh Love. She said "man," the guy was like fifteen! In a couple of weeks, they'd be the same age, and he'd already toured the worlds, and had a stage presence the size of New York. Fucked up.

Concentrate, M. Business head on. She had work to do: Cement her friendship with Shuun Suudi, Anwar said in the briefing. The fact Quirk said nothing at all stuck with her. He'd looked like shit too, but insisted he was fine when she asked. Unlike him to keep schtum when a treatise would do. She shrugged. Too hyper now for Mr. Stress Pants. BLL! Just the absolute cream. This job really did have its perks.

* * *

Quirk walked to the cruise ship's venue along crowded corridors. Anwar had taken Bea (with Moth's permission) and would shadow Sec-Tech and entourage. Xis belief any attack would come this evening had Quirk keyed up. Anwar had tasked him with stationing balcony front left, being ready to respond to events. It felt like being side-lined, but he'd worked enough surveillance to know shitstorms blew up in seconds, and not always where you expected. Would working with Nick be uncomfortable? Anwar knew they'd had a bust-up because Nick told xim, participating fully in the debrief after scouting Sec-Tech. At least everyone knew the scope of the team now. And Nick had acted professionally, if frostily toward him, suggesting Anwar "deploy aging resources as backup," and "not overstretch fallible team members."

He had to admit Nick spoke well when he put his mind to it. His existence might span only a few years, but with accelerated development he'd been a five-year-old after a few months, and in the next five years began presenting as a teenager. Faced now with Nick as a colleague, Quirk had been trying to decide if any innocents had died at the boy's hands in Yellowknife. Nick certainly had "winged" a few people. He shouldn't expect a Festive card from Dunevan "Dulcie" Rice, shot by a laser-rifle-wielding Androicon badroid under Nick's influence, if not actual direction.

His handset buzzed and he raised it to his ear.

"You in position?" Nick.

"Uh huh," Quirk grunted.

"Good. Out."

Really, he should be watching Moth. Okay, she had all those security personnel around her backstage—Suudi's, BLL's and ship security—and he understood Anwar thought that made it reasonable to assign roles as they were, but Anwar only saw Moth as an asset, he didn't see the young woman on her own in a big venue on a massive cruise ship, with hostiles in play. Quirk forced himself to remember how competent she could be and once again rejected the notion to leave his post. The only thing worse than no command structure was usurping the one you had.

* * *

Moth's handset buzzed her left ear. She turned left. At the next junction her right ear vibrated, she made the turn and the corridor opened into a small foyer. Beyond a security station waited Shuun (eager), Patsy (fake cool) and Lizella (bitch). Dolled up to the nines too, looking fragile beside the various flavours of security staff. A heavy thump rattled the air, the sound of the opening act starting up. Even with twenty-second-century soundproofing, the essence of rock 'n' roll would not be contained.

Patsy had gone classy in a black party dress; Lizella wore black studded pleather, black tights, wide patent belt, and a skirt shorter than the belt was wide—*Tart!* Vintage 1990s though. Shuun went the other way, playing cool with skater gear, and she'd coloured her hair bright orange. Moth wore black again too, and plain; her cracked leather biker jacket, charcoal tank-top, charcoal jeans. The full Jessica Jones à la the Mack Spritzer remake of the Tyrone Nolan remake of the Marvel Studios noughties classic. Was she trying to impress the guy by how little effort she'd put in? Reverse psychology? What would she even say to him? *Meh, try and treat him like any other kid. He probably doesn't get that anymore.*

Ship security checked her over, the female guard doing a pat down (kinda quaint, more for intimidation now than with any hope of finding most things someone could conceal), before the guy beckoned her through a body scanner into the secure zone. The chief dough-head nodded as she emerged from the detector. *Wow, I'm in.* She wondered if she'd ever been "in" in her life. Was Rigel the way forward for her? Maybe she should at least have a discussion with Mario. *And, I'm about to meet BLL!*

Surprisingly, the three girls greeted her with hugs, even Lizella.

"This is really fucking cool," said Patsy, deadpan, which passed for rampant enthusiasm in this nerdy, obviously repressed, girl. Lizella stopped short of smiling at Moth, but didn't scowl. Shuun smiled warmly—"Thank you"—and Moth fell into friendship with her. Clearly a nice girl, Shuun, and Moth didn't know enough of those.

A harassed person with platinum blond hair, in a yellow waistcoat and purple hotpants appeared through the internal doors and whisked them in past another handful of guards. They hurried along a brightly lit corridor, bumping bass louder still, stopped at a door with a big star on it that pulsed and shimmered in time to the muffled music.

"Okay, ladies, you've got fifteen minutes. Bro's on in thirty and needs his meditation time for correct headspace alignment. I'll be back in fifteen—read my lips—fifteen minutes. When I say 'out', you are *OUT* of there. Repeat after me, ladies."

"We're out of there," they repeated dutifully.

Their guide opened the door, remaining in the corridor, and ushered the girls into the mystical kingdom of the backstage.

* * *

James Foster watched the girls depart the security station on the eye-screen integral to his left contact lens, wondering if Simister would ever watch the operation back. The camera woven through the seam of his maintenance uniform's epaulet provided a crystal-clear image. He slid the environment system local hub control board back into its recessed bracket, closed the access panel, walked toward the security station. He showed ID, and walked around the scanner, pushing his cart before him. He opened the next access panel and looked busy, enjoying his sense of calm control among all these security guards who didn't have a damn clue what would happen in the next hour.

* * *

What a total shithole.

Moth practically waded into a room with snack packets and other wrappers littering the floor. Five blocky, high-backed sofas occupied half the space, as if scattered during a giant game of Yahtzee, each pointing at a slightly different angle at a huge LivewaLL. Portions of the screen displayed basketball, baseball, soccer, concert footage of a dynamo of a man called James Brown, and finally a fuzzy movie playing where the LivewaLL feed must be broken. A couple lurked near the wall by a table cluttered with sandwiches and snack food. Another couple on the sofa pointing at the basketball game were intent on creating some Miami Heat of their own. Actual smoke drifted up from the sofa facing the baseball game. Moth screwed up her courage and wandered round front of that sofa. She found a person recognisable as BLL's drummer fast sleep, reached out cautiously, removed from her fingers a generous doobie and dropped it, hissing, into a red cup before the pungent fumes crashed the spaceship.

Hands on hips, she scanned the room. Disappointing. More to the point, this squalid laziness played badly when she needed to make an impression.

"Yo, who round here is the biggest ass-crack, cos we've got a meet-and-greet with BLL, and I'm not feeling the love, hear me?"

She'd never been shy at getting attention and felt a shit-tonne of satisfaction at commanding the room as one head after another appeared over and around sofas. They had no fuxxing clue what was up. Then, a brown hand waved her towards the broken screen showing images without colour. She signalled her friends to follow. Sure enough, Brother Leigh Love awaited them. His air of quiet self-possession struck her immediately, quite the thing in a fifteen-year-old. *Says the fourteen-year-old. LOL.*

"Welcome. I apologise for the mess. I guess Gabe gave you the fifteen-minute speech? Don't worry 'bout that. Sit." He indicated two beanbags opposite the sofa, and his big three-seater itself. Lizella perched on one of the bags as Shuun and Patsy dropped into the other. Moth shrugged and sat on the sofa with BLL. They looked like every carefully profiled vid ad in the last century: from Shuun's dark elegance, through BLL's deadly handsome all-American mid-brown, Moth on the pale end of Italian, Patty in the global majority, and Lizella the thin, white Scandinavian. Bit harsh, Liz's ice might be thawing.

* * *

Foster closed the latest access panel and moved to the load-in doors at the end of the service corridor. He scanned his right eye, its lens displaying a crewmember's retinal image acquired by one of his team two days ago. CC's ability to manipulate duty rosters down to individual assignments across the ship, and all just-in-time, impressed him. All he knew about that side of the operation was to comply immediately with the instructions from his comms unit.

The door opened and Foster pushed his cart into a darkened back-of-house space stacked with crates, equipment, furniture with mag-feet, stacked tables with "tacky" tops. Soft yet pervasive lighting flicked on overhead as he moved forward, following the green line on the floor that led backstage. The air rumbled with the movement of feet above him in time to the drifting whump of the support band's set.

Foster kept his head down, elbows in, careful to avoid knocking any stray prop, fitting, or chair leg that might interrupt his progress, draw the attention of the ship's monitoring system, or disrupt the contents of his cart. On the middle shelf, beneath adjusting hammers, power turners and mag-wrenches, lay six close-combat small arms, comprising elements of plass, plastec, polycarbonate twill, and a hyperpneumatic chamber replacing the spring. Components undetectable by even the latest scanners, yet easily assembled in a private place. Now he had completed his tour of the arena, placing weapons for his team behind convenient access panels, bringing him to his appointed position stage right near the VIP area, where he expected to find his target.

At the next door, the lights having flicked off behind him, Foster turned the corner, reaching unnecessarily to steady the plain grey case sitting atop the cart.

* * *

BLL looked like a random kid. Okay, he wore some fancy duds, more hip brands than you could shake a selfie stick at. Sportswear, streetwear, gangwear, but she could see the kid under all that sponsorship. "What you watchin'?" she asked.

"Movie called 'Twelve Angry Men.'"

"Your screen's bust."

"It's not." He smiled. "Film's in black-and-white."

"Why?"

"Are you looking forward to the show?" Shuun interrupted, eagerly.

"Good question. Honestly?" He gave her a lopsided grin. "Don't really know 'til I get out there. Could be a room full of corporate corpses, could be the best show of my life. That's the joy and the pain of the thing. Never knowing 'til you get there."

"What makes you write the songs you do?" asked Patsy. "Where do they start?"

"They're so angry," Lizella added.

BLL smiled again and Moth saw it in his eyes, pleasure at interacting with people, talking about music.

"Lot of people don't have anything in their lives to be angry about. Kinda sad you ask me, not to see the injustice, not to understand how important it is to be angry. If you ain't angry at somethin', you halfway dead. Movie here's about a special kind of blindness, inability to see through prejudice."

He looked around the group. Shuun, Patsy, Lizella smiled back. His gaze fell on Moth. Her face felt flat, features hard. All she could think of was the pain The Old Man had inflicted on her, her family, Nick, even Quirk. TOM should not get away with that.

"Think you know about that," said BLL. "What's your name?"

"Mm...Daisy. This is Shuun, Lizella, Patsy."

"Pleased to meet you, ladies. What's your favourite song, each of you, and why? And don't say none of mine." He sat back to listen.

* * *

Quirk's cLife buzzed, he fished it out. The message read, "Put in your fucking earpiece."

He scowled, slipped the plasmorphic bud into his ear, fighting a flinch as it squirmed into position. At least it cut out of one ear the burbling, brooding, angry sounds of BLL's warmup act. What kind of name was One Arm Bandana? He noticed now that she did indeed possess one fewer arm (from the elbow) than the vast majority of humanity and felt suitably chastened. How did one fit a bandana with one arm?

The snippy message originated with Anwar. *"Nick's isolating probable members of CC's ops squad. He has ten probables, assisted by our observations. He's working that down to a typical five squad. He says Rigel's intel refers to a sixth operative. He hopes to brief again in ten minutes."*

Quirk brought a hand up, feigned a yawn as people continued to file past him to and from their balcony seats. The space continued to fill, chatter, badinage, excitement intruding even into OAB's shouty set. Extending the yawn, he whispered into the old-fashioned line mic up his sleeve.

"Is Nick Rigel's source into CC?"

"He's a source, not the only one. CC has plenty of enemies."

"Fair. Has he put a track on the probables?"

"Of course. Use your access link. Quirk, it's like you've never done this before."

"Worked a Rigel squad? I haven't."

"Worked a fucking handset, you moron. Out."

"Swearing is unprofessional, you neophile. Out."

He accessed the link, observed ten bright dots moving (or not) around a schematic of the *Gargantua Pleiades*. It appeared dot size represented deck level and therefore, to some extent, proximity. As he watched, two dots disappeared. Clearly, Nick saw fit to eliminate them as possible CC agents. Quirk had no reason to doubt his judgement. Yellowknife may have been an unmitigated mess, but it had shown the unimpeachability of Nick's digital interdiction skills. His interpersonal abilities however…needed work. Eight dots remained, and—subject to Nick's analysis—this should reduce further. Quirk began to pick out the dots relating to his current position.

* * *

"Sinnerman, the Nina Simone version," said Shuun without hesitation.

BLL nodded. "Classic, sweet choice. I think you'll enjoy the show."

Shuun made a noise kind of like a strangled sigh and tried not to grin.

"How about you?" he nodded at Patsy.

"Uh, anything by Fungible Funhouse," she answered.

BLL smiled. "Okay. Not my scene, but they're cool. That Ricky/Dick/Richard Deluxe can play."

"Oh, Abba Voyage," Lizella blurted. "There's no substitute for great songs." She smiled awkwardly, like she wished the ground would swallow her up. "Or the Rolling Stones. The androids are so lifelike, and wheeling out Keith Richards' cryo-casket at the end is a nice touch. I wonder if, on some level he can hear the applause?"

BLL grunted at that. "Daisy?"

"Today? Crap Attack's 'Revenge of the Birds,' or 'HUDs in My 'Hood,' by Burning London. Tomorrow, who knows? Watcha playin' tonight I haven't heard?"

BLL smirked. "You're funny. You uh, wanna hang after the show?" Someone, possibly Lizella, gasped. "All of you, 'course."

Somewhere nearby the heavy thrumming cut off and applause swelled.

* * *

Foster touched his left lower canine and his lens display changed, showing his team's locations, presenting the data as if floating in the air before him. Okay, the four of his team besides him who had a physical presence on the ship. Clearly the mysterious John Ballantyne must be some kind of virtual entity, probably a kid in a room somewhere, or even in an android, he knew that C Corp could do that.

More importantly, his team now in their ready positions, only the prime target's arrival remained before they went live. He'd questioned the need for all this effort, proposed in his briefing that he take on the task himself, but TOM overruled that. This confluence of events constituted too good a chance to miss, presenting three targets instead of one. Foster did see how the themes in play and the individuals involved could be combined for a compelling solution that suited Simister's ends. He had no illusions he knew their true extent. So, he followed orders, which afforded the luxury of not asking questions, right up to and beyond the point at which he disposed of any remaining team members.

* * *

The stage manager, if that's what they were, breezed into the green room to stand at BLL's shoulder. "Game on, hon."

Moth watched BLL transform right in front of them. He closed his eyes, drew in a deep breath, held it, released. The rest of the band began standing, composing themselves, running through little rituals of actions and words. Then they moved into the space in the middle of the room, coming together in a huddle. They bowed their heads together, arms interlinked across each other's shoulders. Moth heard low words almost like a chant before the huddle broke. Much whooping and clapping of hands, highing and lowing of fives, before they made for the stage door.

Brother Leigh Love hung back. He stopped before going through the door, turned, pointed at the girls with both hands (Moth was pretty sure straight at her). "Gabe, make sure these lovely ladies have VIP seats. Wouldn't want them to lose their way getting back here for the partaay!" Then to the girls—*Oh, come on, that's right at me.* "One hour." He winked.

* * *

One Arm Bandana's powerful and powerfully groovy set finished in a rousing chorus that the crowd repeated with abandon. She left the stage pumping her fist, raising her hand repeatedly up to the ceiling, exhorting the crowd, which responded with raucous approval.

"OAB, people. Let's hear it!" the announcer yelled. The crowd obliged again.

Quirk's gaze drifted left to right then right to left, scanning the scene from bottom left of the standing area to the balcony's top right. Heads moving, turning, still bopping excitedly, rolling waves of chatter, shouting, argument and approbation, the smell of stage smoke. Down below, Anwar and Bea stood house right and left, covering the crowd. So their screen dots said. They would be watching like him. Waiting to act.

He rechecked the link. Eight dots had become five. Great. So, was a sixth operative unaccounted for, or ruled out? He might be able to fix on and visually ident one or two of these dots, but should also assume that the CC squad could identify them. A worrying thought, it niggled, but he could not succumb to paranoia now. Nick—sequestering data from all the cameras, sensors and ship systems available—would flag if any of the probables he tracked went live.

None of Nick's dots occupied the balcony, so Quirk moved to the balustrade and looked down, casually, pretending to scroll his cLife, but in fact only touching the side. He had to acknowledge the difficulty of transposing screen tracking to real life. The argument for an implant became more compelling as the months and the cases went by. But he possessed a function Nick could not deploy as a data layer, experience. CC ops would need access to non-public areas. They would be service staff, support functions, maybe band officials, special guests. That security guard near the emergency exit on the far side of the hall, she appeared to image the stage, panning left to right, then examined her screen. A harmless action. Using his cLife's hyper zoom, Quirk magnified the area. He knew the guard's face! Surprising, but not impossible. He dredged his memory.

Paris. The rooftop of Le Bibliothèque Mazarine with Cassie Streich. She'd sported a blond crewcut then, brunette now, but the same cut. He rubbed his top lip with thumb and forefinger to disguise his whispering.

"Dot One is CC. Positive ID confirmed by previous encounter."

"Check," said Nick.

"Codename Crewcut."

"Whatever."

Quirk scanned to the other side of the shifting, shadowed sea of heads in the darkened hall. Stage right, his left. Now attuned, using cLife Low Light Mode, he spotted Lug. At a couple of braincells short of 200 centimetres, Crewcut's associate from Paris—posing as a paramedic—stood out like a rugby team's-worth of sore thumbs.

"Dot Two confirmed. Codename Lug."

What hadn't been discussed at their briefing (because he hadn't asked) was the manner of Anwar intercepting the enemy. In the field of corporate rivalry "removing pieces from the board" covered a whole range of outcomes from encouraging career diversification through performance review to retraining as a concrete bridge abutment. He believed Anwar would act decisively and definitively. He long ago made peace with such outcomes on the basis that corporate agents knew what they signed up for.

A buzz alerted Quirk to a new message. In five seconds, it would disappear, eradicated from existence and record.

```
BEATRIX [22:31, 05-01-2100]
   BLL taking stage. Sec-Tech will speak after
   three songs. Est 15 mins. We go live in 10.
```

The situation had just become very serious.

* * *

Even in the service area, Foster disguised his subvocalisation.

<Initiate Stage One.>

The sharp end of his CC career had arrived pretty quickly. Agents Two and Three would approach the stage at the end of BLL's first number, make moves to gain access for security and medical reasons respectively then move on Sec-Tech just after he started speaking. Agent Four, stationed backstage in catering, would advance through back of house, as would Agent Five from the bursar's office. All four had Sec-Tech Jiilaal Mire Suudi as their target on the basis he believed one of four would get through.

But the first thing all would do—as he did now, reaching for the case atop his cart—was use the pressure syringe they'd been issued to inject themselves with nanites. This simple action permitted Agent Six to do something staggeringly clever that rendered each of them invisible to all types of monitoring.

Foster opened up his boilersuit and the fatigues underneath, pressed the applicator to bare skin, and triggered the syringe. He felt the sting, then dropped the syringe on the cart, lifted his tool bag, and walked away.

* * *

"Good evening, Phobos. We are here to entertain you tonight. Are you ready to be entertained, Phobos?" (Wild cheering, yelling with abandon.) "Are you ready to be entertained, Phobos Festival?" (Wilder cheering still.) "Here's a song I think you know. Here's a song called 'Whips... and... Butter.'"

A monstrous bass riff assaulted the audience. Quirk hurriedly slipped in his second plasmorphic earbud, grunting at the relief it brought. Then he moved for the stairs. With no CC ops on the balcony, he must head toward the action, toward Moth.

* * *

Gabe brought the girls to the VIP enclosure stage right. Moth hesitated at stepping into what, essentially, was a cage. Sure, it had an excellent side-on view of the performance, but still a cage.

"It's fine," Gabe shouted with a flamboyant wave of the hand. "The gate's not locked, but it's closed. You can open it from the inside. Only I have the external key. Well, me, the bursar and the security chief. For safety, y'know?"

"Riiiight," yelled Moth. The girls had entered to find seats among the select few.

"Have fun!" Gabe hurried off to do more stage-managey things, as the driving baseline of "Whips and Butter" blasted from the PA, filling the hall with mad groovy.

Moth stepped in, pulled the gate closed. She didn't like this one bit, but squeezed over to Shuun and friends. Maybe it made them safe from outside interference, but it felt too much like being in a fuzking goldfish bowl riddled with holes.

After a minute Shuun yelled "I wanna be out front. I wanna be in the crowd!"

The other girls looked at her like she'd lost her mind, but Moth understood. Plus, way better than sitting in a cage, even a secure one. She could protect Shuun, right?

* * *

"The CC agents are gone!"

Nick's yell of alarm exploded in Quirk's ear.

<Explain.> He fished out his cLife, hoping to contradict the boy, but saw only dull, blank confirmation.

"We're blind, they're cloaked somehow."

<Maybe you're blind, but I've got the evidence of my own eyes.> And yet, knowing what he did about tactical tech and CC's equipment budget, Quirk could only hope that would be enough. He moved away from the stairs into the dark, spotlight-flashing, crowd-filled, bodies-shifting space engulfed by noise thick as treacle and pungent smoke clouding the little vision he had.

X

21:58, 5 January 2100 (Earth date equivalent)
***Cruise Ship** Gargantua Pleiades**, Phobos Viewpoint*

Moth strained to get forward as the crowd surged around her. Elbows and hips bashed and bored her, fans jamming together, blocking her. She'd lost Shuun. *Fuck, I've lost Shuun!* If something happened now...

People moved and shifted in all directions, pushed and pulled by those around them. Chaos ruled the whole fuxxing place and she *had* to find Shuun. What if CC snatched the girl on her watch? The thought made her blood run cold even as stress thrummed through her limbs, and she swallowed down bile.

* * *

In one way, being invisible to systems detection made the CC ops *more* vulnerable, because it meant a watcher's tech would contradict their eyes. But there were no security stations to pass now, and the gig was in full flow. Plenty of distraction.

Foster started towards the backstage VIP area, flicking on his tactical display with his tongue. He walked past Agent Three and a guard, turned a shoulder towards them to show his badge. At the door under the house left stairs he scanned his tag, walked back to the service stairs and climbed them. He stepped around empty instrument cases and tour crates. The dots before his eyes moved, drifted away. A glitch? He stalked to the VIP enclosure, scanned the people there, flicking his lenses to low-light mode.

The girls were gone.

* * *

Quirk stopped in the aisle at the edge of the crowd, studied his handset. The CC ops had disappeared, but he still had Moth's blip and saw her on the move within the crowd, pursuing Shuun Suudi, who Nick tracked approximately based on estimated data. Moth was doing her job. With Anwar and Bea on Sec-Tech his decision to follow Moth must be valid, although he half expected Bea to appear at any moment.

For the first time that evening he patted the taser pistol Anwar insisted he carry. Crewcut and Lug would be loaded for bear. He brushed the thought aside. They might be closing on the girls even now. Bizarre they'd try this with two thousand witnesses. Could a kidnap aid TOM's cause? Sec-Tech would just be replaced. More likely, it was the terminal option. Quirk clamped his jaw, pushing none too gently into the crowd.

* * *

Cursing, Foster stepped away from the cage, found a shadowed corner. He put down his bag and stripped off his maintenance overalls, leaving the paramedic jumpsuit underneath. Instantly, without physical change, tool bag became medical bag. Quickly and thoroughly, he rubbed thick, sour-smelling grey lotion over his face, neck and ears. The astringent cream heated his skin, pulled the flesh tight in places, relaxed it in others, changed his appearance and skin tone enough to disguise him. Then he went back the way he'd come, because he had to find the damn girls, at least the daughter.

Back in the hall, sound swamped him as he walked on down the aisle house right. Suddenly, the relentless, bounding rhythm of BLL's second song ceased. The crowd erupted, screaming, waving open hands and fists in the air, clapping over their heads. Some leaned in, putting heads together, bellowing at each other to be heard. Most just yelled. BLL moved to the stage edge, removed his jacket and tossed it behind him. He beat his bare chest with one fist, the other holding a totally unnecessary manual microphone. The kid would have implants, could sing without the prop, but too much historic performance, its physical language, relied on that modest, anonymous device.

"Phobos. I can tell this will be a *good* night. You cats are shut-it-down crazy. Phobos, soon we're gonna hear words of wisdom from the

UN Sec-Tech. Show respect to this man, who's a friend of mine. He has important shit to impart. I gift him this platform cos I believe in what the UN stands for: peace in our time, brothers, sisters, cousins. Peace through superior technology."

The opening bars of BLL's third song rang out—clean piano over a scratch track. Foster knew he must trust others to do their jobs while he did his.

Finally, Agent Six weighed in. *"Targets ahead, marked on your display. Why ya still standin' there, dumbass?"*

Foster patted the hidden gun, checked his HUD, and pushed into the crowd.

* * *

Music crawled, pumped, oozed through the crowd, pounding Moth's eardrums as she groped in her pocket for her earWorms. The press of bodies shifted around her, sometimes crushing forward, sometimes throwing up hands, singing, shouting, chanting, screaming. Shuun kept ahead of her. She'd got close, grabbed for the girl's arm, missed. Now Moth couldn't see her in the crowded dark, the flaring lights.

"Who's the boss now, motherfuckers?" came BLL's vibrating demand through the straining sound system. "Who's the boss now? Yeah, still them."

The crowd was a complete mess, a dizzying mix of zoned-out, malfunctioning societal misfits, well-heeled money-daddies and mummies just dressing up like societal misfits for the occasion, and corporate posh kids who knew fuck all about anything. Some fans looked hopped up and/or mashed down on sliders, rimmers, trumpets and pseudo-weed, the rest just pretended to be. Then came the buzz cuts, the sophomores and grad students, kitted in white T's, chinos and red caps, drinking preppy max, pro'bly spiked with iXanex, keep them cool and collected for max enjoyment of the mosh pit's cosy violence, due to break out later in the show.

"Shithead!" she yelled, as some massive lummox lurched into her, knocking the earWorm case from her hand as she opened it. She staggered from the impact, only held up by the crush, grasping through too-close bodies to grab for the case as it fell.

Guitars, drums, synths, ear-bleeding bass like a tumbling mountain, pummelled her as she stumbled to her knees. How could she find Shuun when the driving sound stopped her even thinking? Then the volume dropped, the crowd erupted, surged again, legs hammering her ribs, thighs, shoulders. The rhythm section kept time, kept the song moving. Not the coda, but the breakdown. BLL would speak again as the band played.

"Watch out, fuckers!" she yelled to absolutely no fuzking effect.

She needn't have worried of course. As soon as it left her hand the bud electromagnets hauled them back into the case, the lid snapped shut and the plastec shell glowed green. She grabbed it where it lay by someone's boot before the braindead space cadet stood on it (case had limits), then fought to her feet, bumped, pushed and hauled herself toward the stage, thrusting through a cluster of braying knuckleheads. She flipped her finger at their leering kissy faces by way of apology and barged straight into a huddle of girls not much older than her. *Shit.*

"Sorry!" she yelled, and they nodded, smiled. "Orange hair girl?" She ruffled her own black bob to bridge the audibility gulf.

The one made up like her trust fund was stuffed with Galaxy Gloss shares pointed toward the stage.

"Hey, Phobos." BLL's banter cut through the moment and everything stopped for him but the band's low backbeat. "I know you know the words to this bit. 'Litany of the Lost' is on the first album those conniving corporate cocksuckers in their greed, in their miscomprehension, in their lack of appreciation for who I am, and where I come from; this is what they let me do, Phobos." He prowled the front of the stage as he spoke, dragging her attention to him with his magnetic charisma.

"Phobos, let me hear you sing 'Gerald Fisher died for my sins.'"

The crowd yelled the line back once, then again before he interceded with the chorus' third line: "This is how it begins." After the last syllable the band stopped, and a single snare hit rang out, totally sounding like a gunshot.

"Gerald Fisher died for my sins!" the crowd finished the chorus. She wondered how many had looked up who the fuck Gerald Fisher was. She had, and now felt a burning desire to talk to BLL about it, about what it meant that she'd done that.

The charged atmosphere seemed to sting her skin, and she realised she'd forgotten about Shuun. *Fuck!* She pushed forward again as the second part of the chorus, the litany that gave the song its title, began.

"Erin Gorman died for my sins.

"Leshawn MacDade died for my sins.

"Tariq Raman died for my sins.

"Leray Carson died for my sins.

"Carey Bevan died for my sins.

"Dennis Anson died for my sins.

"Kumar Malcolm died for my sins.

"Lester Wilson died for my sins.

"Phobos," said BLL as the music stopped completely, although the crowd continued yelling and cheering support. "Phobos, for every police shooting in history that has enraged right-thinking people of any nation, there are ten, twenty, thirty you have never heard of. Because you are distracted, Phobos. The media turns your head, Phobos. They want you to talk about sequels, and casts, and awards. They want you to read all the wrong books, Phobos. That is when they come for your freedom, when they know you are not looking. But I want you to raise your heads, Phobos. We must remain vigilante. We must protest injustice. We must do the things that are uncomfortable, that are inconvenient, that are painful. We must hold them to account, those powers that be. And Phobos, if you have to ask who they are then you are Not. Paying. Attention."

BLL punctuated each of his final words by pumping his fist in the air, and on the final pump he dropped the mic. It hit the floor with a crack and the lights went out.

XI

22:06, 5 January 2100 (Earth date equivalent)
Cruise Ship Gargantua Pleiades, *Phobos Viewpoint*

The lights came up again, not the house lights, but the lightshow, a central white spot picking out Jiilaal Mire Suudi, UN Secretary for Technology. He wore a dark suit, white shirt, collar open. He raised a microphone to his mouth and began to speak, and—*Thank fuck!*—Moth spotted Shuun waving at her dad. His words addressed the stranglehold of certain corporations on the UN's human settlement plan, since the corporations controlled the transports, even though the UN controlled the NLS drives.

Moth hoped Quirk, Nick and Anwar did their jobs, because Shuun's dad looked very exposed on that stage. She hadn't known the girl a day yet, but felt a bond forming, and she didn't want to be comforting a new friend from her position of bitter experience in having a parent murdered.

She fought the last few metres to Shuun and threw an arm around the girl's shoulder. They shared a beaming smile, and Moth started waving at Sec-Tech too, because why the fuck not, and it helped disguise searching for threats.

"I know I'm wearing a suit," announced Suudi amiably, "and I must say it feels like the wrong team colours sometimes." Isolated jeers amid the cheers. "But I count BLL as a friend. We've done good work together in the LA favellas, bringing badly needed medical supplies to community clinics. So, I know how to roll up these sleeves." Applause.

"But why am I announcing this new initiative here and not in New York? For one, I want to say to people everywhere that the UN will not let CC off the hook. We will continue to investigate their alleged transgressions, and their current NLS applications will be suspended." Many cheers.

"And two, because BLL asked me to do it here. We agree that— against the background of his message—the new, stricter regulation of

NLS drive licenses is seen in its widest context, as a powerful tool to reset the balance of social justice on Earth."

* * *

<Initiate Stage Two,> Foster subvocalised, shouldering through the crowd, following the glowing circles overwriting his vision, not bothering to cover his lips in the furore and low lighting of the performance environment. <Control>—the codeword he'd been given for Agent Six—<Target Two and Three intercept available in two minutes.>

"*I can see that, dumbass. The daughter an' skinny lil' Moth dead ahead. Two, Three, Four, Five in position. Waitin' on the main event. Get it done or they'll drop you down the nearest terraformin' shaft.*"

Foster pressed on, resisting a curse at Six's contempt for comms protocol. The dots up ahead had stopped ten metres from the crowd barrier. He stopped five metres short of them. Elbows and his uniform bought him minimal clearance. He knelt, opened his bag, reached in to open the shielded metal case, opened *that* and removed a stubby pistol with a plastec cap over its muzzle. A syringe gun. More nanites, but not for him.

The song ended and Sec-Tech walked on to be greeted by BLL.

Only moments now.

* * *

Just pitching up next to Moth wouldn't help, of course. That could give the game away if CC didn't have any kind of track on them. He'd have to hold off to avoid defeating his purpose as backup. Great. So Moth's bait now? Of course she was, and had that been Anwar's intention all along?

"*Moth in place. Hold position,*" said Nick in his ear, underscored by the pulsating music that filled the darkened hall.

<Check. Don't lose her.>

"*Duh. Just check your handset.*"

With Moth and Shuun twelve metres away to his right, Quirk stopped. He couldn't see them, but trusted Nick that they were there.

Now he began searching for CC ops. Crewcut or Lug he could pick out, others he must rely on instinct.

The music cut off. BLL began a powerful exhortation of the crowd to chant back to him, which they did. The strike could be moments away. Many in the crowd looked intent, keyed up, tense, nervous, excited. Experienced ops would be the opposite, their sang-froid marking them out.

Sec-Tech walked on now, fist bumping with BLL, reciprocal back slapping, before the singer retreated into the shadows, leaving Suudi the microphone.

* * *

In the next moment, everything went to shit.

On stage, a paramedic moved from the shadows stage right, carrying... *Gun! Fuck!* "Gun! Gun!" Moth shouted, but cheering covered her yells.

A guard moved from stage left. To the rescue? No. She carried a similar weapon.

Under Moth's arm Shuun stiffened, began to scream as others saw it, isolated yells of alarm puncturing the buoyant, respectful atmosphere. Shuun's screaming ripped through Sec-Tech's words, and he stopped.

A body dropped to the stage between Sec-Tech and the attackers. The syRen® rolled, twisted, and hurled herself at Sec-Tech.

Bea!

Bodyguards appeared from the spotlight's edges, too late.

The Sec-Tech turned, disoriented, just as Bea bore him down.

Through this single, chaotic moment, Moth stood frozen. The crowd pushed and shoved, half covered their faces, half stood gaping. Shuun collapsed, and Moth couldn't reach her, lifted off her feet by the panicked crowd.

On stage, the male paramedic twisted as if punched in the gut, staggered and fell.

Bea shielded Shuun's dad with her android body as Sec-Tech's body people grabbed for the security guard attacker. The female assassin dropped into a roll, pushed up into a gymnastic tumble, eluding the UN bodyguards. Brightness scored Moth's vision. Laser bursts, slightly scattered by the drifting smoke from BLL's last number. Anwar trying to pick off the assassin.

The tumbler sprawled, grimacing, hit the deck, stretched with a stubby pistol, shot it just as Bea's hand cut down, probably breaking the attacker's wrist. At the same moment, Anwar's laser hit the assassin, pinning her to the stage before she slumped, still.

"They ran blocks on us." Anwar's voice on their secure channel. *"Knew our exact locations."*

Moth pushed violently with both hands, forcing people in her orbit away from the fallen Shuun. A paramedic appeared and tended her new friend. Shuun's fallen form looked like a pile of rags in her soft and baggy skater gear.

"Is she okay?"

The house lights came up, throwing harsh shadows around the hall as people began hustling as quickly as they could (which wasn't quick) towards the exits. Then, another weird thing happened.

Quirk appeared through the departing crowd. He always looked weird without the Merrion, mussed up, too, from struggling against the press of people. He smiled at her, glanced at Shuun and the crouching paramedic, then dove at the guy, knocking him and his *pistol* flying.

As Quirk struggled with the guy, Moth snatched up the gun, but it was some weird one-shot deal, stubby and light enough to be hollow. She decided to club the paramedic with it anyway, but as she turned, he worked a sick move, twisting Quirk onto his back. The supposed paramedic socked Quirk in the jaw as Moth jumped forward, modifying his blow to backhand her in the face, sending her spinning.

"Fucker! Did you not take the oath?"

Her head spun. She shook it off in time to see that the guy looked sick, skin pale and waxy. Shuun sat up and puked on the floor. The paramedic dashed away, dodging Quirk's grasping hand, straight-arming a guard and bursting through a backstage door.

Bea jumped down from the stage, sprinted along the crowd barriers, pursuing the fake paramedic through the door beneath the house left stairs.

As Quirk stood, surveying the rapidly emptying hall, Moth knelt bedside Shuun. In a fuxxed-up development, the girl's puke was the same colour as her hair.

"Leave Shuun to the guards," demanded Anwar. *"Clear out, now."*

"Sec-Tech's secure," Nick announced. *"Four CC ops off the board,"* he continued. *"Confirm withdraw to Muster B."* That meant the cabin he had arranged under a false name, that he'd sent luggage to under the same fake ID.

Reluctantly, Moth stood. Quirk looked like he wanted to hug her, but he hung back, looking around, ready to walk. On the stage, the *Pleiades'* first officer stood with a space marshal, each pointing here and there, talking earnestly. With a last glance at Shuun, now being tended by a first aid officer, Moth followed Quirk from the hall.

* * *

Anwar was waiting in the room when Quirk arrived, closely followed by Moth, although they hadn't walked together. S-17834 arrived last. She confirmed the fake paramedic had escaped her. A sweep of the immediate area around the backup cabin showed no unusual activity. Nick advised through comms that he had ears on the ship's secure channel and would alert them to any worrying chatter.

Anwar produced a hip flask. Quirk reached out to accept it, but Moth beat him to it. She took a quick slug and passed it on to him. He looked at her appraisingly then took the flask.

"Fucking shit bugger," she coughed. "What is that?"

Quirk smirked. "Rum, of course. Navy strength?" Anwar nodded. Quirk took another slug and winked. "It's okay, I'm driving."

He handed the flask back to Anwar, who slugged ximself. "I don't condone this behaviour, but I do enjoy it."

"What about Shuun's dad?" asked Moth.

"Initial reports say Sec-Tech is shaken, but feels fine," Nick reported. *"No significant injuries. Bumps and bruises."*

Bea chimed in with her own report. "Ship channels have four CC ops agents accounted for, all dead."

"Three at the scene," said Nick, and Quirk suppressed a smile at the lad seeming to compete with the android for attention. *"And what Bea can't tell you... I infiltrated ship medical systems, and scanner output shows one agent shot at least ten minutes after the attack."*

Quirk nodded. "CC ops leader cleaning up before lighting out of here. But that doesn't explain their sixth operative. Some kind of online presence?"

"I...found no trace. I'll keeping looking."

"Thank you, Nick," said Quirk, without response. He sighed quietly.

"Do you think they'll catch the douchebag?" Moth asked.

"Maybe," said Anwar, "but he's no longer our concern. The Suudis will be transferred off ship immediately. Our work is done. Mission accomplished."

Their team leader had spoken. Meanwhile, Quirk wondered if he should be horrified Moth had participated in Anwar's issue of medicinal rum. Honestly, he did not know. That sort of thing seemed to come under the heading "It's Going to Happen Sometime, Better You're in the Room When it Does."

"Tell me when the appropriate time has passed," he said. "I'll say something witty to diffuse this awkward silence."

Moth scowled. Anwar rolled xis eyes. Bea sat quietly in the corner, and Nick—undoubtedly still listening on Anwar's aural implant, present on Moth's handset relay, kicking his digital heels in Bea's system too, probably—said nothing.

"Are you sure you're ready for spirits?" he asked Moth.

"If you're big enough, you're old enough," she replied.

"You're not big enough, or old enough."

Anwar rubbed xis forehead. "When you're finished, we need to prep for extraction."

"I can't help being amusing," Quirk protested. "You should just get used to it."

Moth grunted. "You say amusing, 'I say pot-ah-to. Let's call the whole thing off.'"

"I *knew* you liked show tunes."

"We have things to do," said Anwar, forcefully.

"So, can we go to our rooms then?" Moth asked.

Anwar nodded. "If Nick passes it clear and accompanies you riding along with Bea. Be aware you're contractually obliged to provide Rigel with a debrief report on your activities—"

"Fuzking homework?"

"This is big girl school, young lady," said Anwar, and Quirk was delighted that xe had beat him to the comment. "Reports in the next two days. The Rigel Corporation will settle your suitably formatted invoice immediately upon receipt."

Quirk nodded, smiled, *2:50 Kempton Park, Pays Each Way.*

Anwar stood. "I'd shake your hand, Quirk, but..." The assassin who had once harboured the intention of killing him, smiled dryly.

"I'd say it was a pleasure, but it really wasn't."

"No offence taken, Quirk. I'd like a quick word with Moth before she goes."

Quirk nodded. "I'll pop back to my room with Bea and Nick."

* * *

A knock on the door interrupted Quirk's contemplation of a second nightcap. Not a forceful knock but fast, conveying urgency, not emergency. He sighed, walked from the F&B dispenser to the door and opened it manually.

Moth stood in the doorway. Despite the calm composition of her features, she'd been crying. *Correction, still crying.* Anwar had said something to upset her.

Oh. Oh, no.

She pushed past him into the room, turned on him as he closed the door.

"What's Quirk Agency policy on keeping secrets from employees?" she asked in a voice so calm, so self-possessed, it chilled him. She sniffed. Tears rolled down her rosier-than-normal cheeks. "No," her voice trembled. He closed his eyes because, what? This might go away? And he'd almost told her, been on the point of telling her—that being slightly less awful than her finding out from someone else. "What's *your* policy on keeping huge, hurtful, horrible secrets from *your* staff?"

"Moth—" He hadn't told her in five months because she was— reasonably—so sensitive about her parents' deaths, but it no longer felt like sparing her, it felt wrong.

Her eyes burned bright. "Really sad things, personal things, *important* things. Things you *knew* mattered to me, that scarred me. And *YOU...!* You *know* something about it! We shared things from our lives, getting to know each other. I talked about my parents being killed, and YOU WERE *THERE!* And you buried it." She gasped a mouthful of air, fighting off the sobs.

Oh, well played. Sensitive to her feelings, now you can't avoid them.

"Do you know things that could have helped me? Are there bad things? Were you involved somehow? Did you *see* them? Did you see it happen? What were you doing there?!" She paused, looked at the floor, the wall, and he just stood there. For the first time in a long time, he had nothing to say.

"Answer the motherfucking question, shithead. What's the policy? Where does it say that your employees, your *lieutenants* have no right to the truth? That you get to throw around their pain and their loss like a fucking frisbee? Is it in the section under betrayal? In beside lying and additional shitty considerations?! The company reserves the right to welcome you under false pretences, build you up, encourage you, train you and then reward you one day by just fucking STABBING YOU IN THE HEART?!"

He watched her fight against breaking down then fail, plant her face in her hands and wail, her shoulders jerking.

Quirk flinched at another knock on the door. "Display," he said, barely getting the word out. Bea's image appeared on the peephole screen.

"Mr. Quirk, I have concerns—"

"Go away!" Moth yelled. "Personal moment! I can't *hurt him* if you're here."

"Very well, Moth," said Bea.

The android looked him straight in the eye. The blame he saw before Bea turned away could only be imaginary.

He turned back to Moth to take what he knew was just the start of his punishment. "There's no excuse," he said. "There are reasons, but this isn't the time—"

"Oh, please, tell me when the right time is, you selfish fucker. *Please* let's keep on following your agenda, it's worked out so well for me so far. No, you tell me now what you know, and why you kept it from me."

He tried to summon a regretful, apologetic, anguished smile, something like *I Never Meant to Hurt You,* or *I Couldn't Find the Words.* But no smile could possibly cross this divide. He had to take his medicine now, nothing else would do. He needed to feel some fraction of her pain and hope they could talk, work through this breaking of trust. He wanted to say he didn't kill her parents, he didn't know who killed them, that The Old Man sent them to observe, but these were just different ways of saying he stood by while her parents were gunned down.

"You see, don't you?" she asked, on the back of a ragged breath. "You see that you've broken us, right?"

"I see," he nodded. And he did see, how he could have offered support, discussion, to just sit and listen. All the things he hadn't done for Nick, and now he had not done them again. *What is wrong with me?* "Moth, I'm going to talk. Just tell me to stop any time, and I'll go."

Her face—streaked with night-out-mascara black tears—looked as hard as mountains, her distain chiselled into her pain. "Talk. This one last time, I'll listen."

"I've learned enough these past weeks to know I can't fix this—"

"Ya think?"

"Yet. I think you know I'm not like the Callans and the Mortons." *Fair start, now, don't mention Nick. Do not mention Nick.* "And I know this isn't like what happened with Nick. You did the right thing. He could have killed me, whether he meant to or not. *I* did the wrong thing. I should have spoken up, even though I knew it would hurt you. This can't repair our trust, but all I can do is tell you what I can about that night. It might not help now, but maybe it can down the road, wherever that goes."

Moth said nothing. She sat back on the bed, hugged her knees and waited.

"TOM ordered me to Toni's villa. Me, and another operative: Derek Morton."

She flinched, as well she might. "Expected no better of that shitbag. Go on."

"My role was observation. That's all. As usual, I flew Morton in and out, I knew nothing of his brief."

"Are you saying he killed my parents?"

"No, that was Toni's rivals. It's possible Morton's brief was to clean up. Clean up how, I don't know. I found out recently that Anwar was there, in the villa. Xis partner died in the raid. I get the blame for that too, apparently."

The poisonous look on Moth's tear-streaked face suggested she didn't give a hoot who else blamed him for what. "Did Anwar kill my parents?"

"I don't think so. I think Mario would know, and Anwar would not be here. I'm not aware your father was targeted by anyone, specifically, or your mother. I think Anwar was there on TOM's dime to kill Toni, with Derek Morton as backup. They failed, of course. Somehow, Giulia received a tipoff about the raid, warned a friendly cop, and the place was crawling with Carabinieri, Polizia di Stato, Polizia di Finanza, too, when the Bonacci family attacked."

She looked lost sitting on the big bed, like a downpour of black grief had washed all the brash confidence, all the life, right out of her. Moth glanced up, clearly expecting him to continue.

He nodded. "Giulia stymied TOM's plan, probably without even knowing of it. Toni redoubled security and that route disappeared until—" *Nope, not there.*

"And that was the beginning of our wonderful time together." Fresh tears rolled down her cheeks, as she took big breaths to defeat the sobs.

"Moth—"

She held up a hand. "No, my turn. You know I didn't want to go with you in Milan. I did it for Toni. I understood. And then..." She paused, her youthful features twisted with pain and rage. Her voice sounded small. "You let me in. You opened up to me, told me about your life, your family. I felt we were partners, we shared something." She picked at the blanket with gloss-tipped fingers. She paused as another realisation landed. "Your kindness, your openness, your trust. These were lies."

"To begin with I didn't care. You were an annoying brat, all I got was a heap of attitude. Then, we became a team, and I didn't want to hurt you."

"Ha!" Her bark made him twitch. "The great fucking investigator detected the *shit* out of that one! Hurt me was exactly what you did, you toxic fucking teapot. You and your family, and your past and your bitterness, you just constantly spout it all, and we're all supposed to sip it up from our precious little bone China teacups. Well, your pot's black alright, blackened by your lies, and I've had it. I've had it with being hurt by the likes of you. So you can pack up and piss off to hell."

He felt physically sick. If only he'd told her, maybe it would have helped, but a miss is as good as a mile. So, what now? Give up? No. She was worth fighting for.

"I know I failed you, Moth. The fact I planned to tell you, almost told you yesterday, I know it counts for nothing now, but it's true."

She sat back again, stretched out and crossed her booted feet on the bedcover. "Please be very aware the dangerous path you're on has no fucking handrail."

"Moth, I'm your..."

"What are you, exactly? My employer? Am I fired for being awkward? What did you think we were? D'you think you're my new dad, and I would be all grateful? So, I saved you from being strangled. Big woop. Nick was goading all and sundry to step up and pop his cork. You're my guardian, dipshit, you're a shitting backup, a piece of paper!"

Words deserted Quirk again. He felt wretched, and he should do. Moth was more his child than Nick ever had been, and he could have helped her, but he'd failed. Every day since they'd met, he'd failed her by not telling her what he should have. Forgiveness did not seem a likely prospect now. Giving her space, time, that was the only option he had. He did not even feel malice toward Mario Manfredi or Anwar, whichever had decided to spill the beans, because the mistake belonged to him, and it always would. He had nothing to offer, no apology worth anything. What she needed was for him to leave, not be a constant reminder of another betrayal in her life.

Quirk picked up the Merrion jacket from the chair and swung arms through the silk-lined sleeves. The material felt like sackcloth now.

"Maybe I'll see you around," he said, looking up, but Moth just stared at the wall.

She would be okay. She was a tough kid. And she had Bea, whose care was unquestioning. She had her family. She would be fine.

"Quirk." He turned back. "Could you have done anything, stopped the shooting?"

He considered his answer most carefully. "No, I don't believe so."

Quirk turned and left the room.

β

3 months ago
04:53, 22 October 2099
Gramercy Refuge, Glenfield Street, San Francisco, NAF

Time is debatable.

I lie here, watching the ceiling, watching the window, watching the screen as people move around, but I don't change. I just lie here through the night. My body degrades, true, but how do I know that, between one cell dying and another being born, there is not an epoch of time passing in some other place where they choose to measure time differently?

And yet, still the cell dies, still the cell is born, but maybe not quite as effective, as perfect, as robust, or not quite so many are born, or perhaps too many, born too quickly, in the wrong place. Or, are they just born at the wrong time?

I know I saw my son that day. He reached out to me somehow, but why? From where? Does he need me? And I'm stuck here. Why? I'm unwell. But why? How? How did this come to pass? Why? And when? When did it happen? When did the forces of nature flick the switch that broke me? When Quirk left? When Nick arrived in my life? When they took my eggs for purposes of cloning?

How long has it been? When will it end? What time do I have remaining to me?

And I'm supposed to lie in this bed, walk around the garden, read if the story's not too taxing, watch TV if the programme's not too unsettling, listen if the music is not too disturbing, too energising, too inspiring? This is how I must spend my time?

Well, fuck that. I did NOT budget for this shit in my five score years and ten. It's past time to get the hell out of here.

* * *

The Mental Diary of Jennifer Kirby* née Simister
(Destroy before reading.)

(* I'll tell you when we're divorced Quinton IR Kirby, not you, and
not the same damn judge that declared me incompetent four weeks
later!)

Date: Whatever

Time: Does it matter? It's now.

Notes: I think it was the jazz that rattled something loose. Unmistakably Thelonious Monk; that jangly, tinkly, otherworldly and skewwhiff piano could be fired into our Sun, or sent to Alpha Centauri and still it would make people smile, shake them up, stir them to action. Ironically, the penny dropped for me during the song "I Surrender, Dear." Ha! Quirk never surrendered to a bloody thing in his sorry, pinstriped life. Beware songs with commas in the title; not to be trusted, and don't get me started on brackets, just make up your damn mind!

Date: Plus one

Time: Really, quit that, will you?

Notes: Okay, okay, this is not going anywhere. Get back on track, time's a-wastin', time and cells. Cells are wasting away and the drugs... Well, they're just the wrong bloody kind, Dad!

No, no. Come on, Jennifer. Concentrate. That has to be your new superpower now if you're going to get out of here. Oh, did I just record that here in neurons? Well, it's true, I'm done burning cells in the service of keeping quiet. I want to know what's happening, what everyone else is doing with their time.

Date: Plus another one

Time: Tick-fucking-tock

Notes: I slept. I always sleep, it's one of the few things I'm good at anymore. Or is it? I wonder what would happen if I went a night without medication? Ha-ha. Good one, Jen.

Date: Christmas Day

Time: Merry Christmas!

Notes: What would happen if there was no time? We would eat when hungry, drink when thirsty, teach each other when knowledge was needed. We would work when things needed to be done, and love would take care of itself. But the sun would continue to rise and set, and we would wonder how long till the cold times when crops wouldn't grow. Would every day be our birthday, the same point in the day when the sun reaches that height it had when your mother pushed you out? Nah, too many presents. And think of all the coffee you'd miss out on because your friend never turned up when you were there waiting for them. I said when the sun was at the treetops! I was there then! Ah, but was it coming up from the ground or coming down from the sky? You didn't specify! And which trees?

By the same token as this ill-disciplined thought experiment (mm, maybe call it a trial; not exactly scientific), I think time might be persuaded to rest on my side, just for a few days, till I get out of here.

** * **

05:00, 28 October 2099
Gramercy Refuge, Glenfield Street, San Francisco, NAF

"Good morning, S-08012. How are you today?" asked Jennifer.

The syRen® smiled its bland smile. Nothing in this place could be permitted to be remotely remarkable, out of place, or unexpected. At least she hoped not.

"Good morning, Mrs. Kirby." It pushed a white trolley containing all sorts of bottles, boxes, plastec-packed paraphernalia, including IV chambers and tubes, packets of clear saline flush, and even intubation tubes. This it parked at the bottom corner of her bed. "I thought you would be asleep."

"And yet every morning you bring my first round of medication and wait patiently in the chair until I wake up, at which point you watch me take the pills, then depart. It's a waste of your time."

"My time is of no consequence, but this morning I will not need to wait. We are within the period of efficacy of your main medication, which is plus/minus one hour." The android approached, took a gentle hold on her wrist, checking her vitals and bloods with the smooth, dark pads of its fingertip sensors, customised to enable scanning of key levels in her body without the barbarous invasion of drawing blood.

"I've saved you some time, Twelve. May I call you Twelve?"

"You may; it is a reasonable approximation of my full designation."

The android moved to the side of the bed and held out a small cup. Jennifer did not reach for the cup, causing the syRen® to extend its arm over the edge of the bed so that she might receive the medication. She took the pills, moved her hand to her mouth, drank water from a plass on the bedside table, then swallowed. She coughed after swallowing and lifted the collar of her gown to pat a little water from her lips.

"Excuse me."

"Of course," said Twelve, and departed with the empty plaper cup.

* * *

05:00, 29 October 2099

Gramercy Refuge, Glenfield Street, San Francisco, NAF

"Good morning, S-08012," said Jennifer. "I think it's going to be a lovely day." She stretched the full length of her bed then sat up.

The syRen® smiled its bland smile, pushing its trolley to the foot of her bed. "Good morning, Mrs. Kirby. Once again you enable me to be more efficient in completing my task by already being awake."

"Well, I do like it when things run smoothly, don't you, Twelve?"

"I neither like nor dislike anything, Mrs. Kirby—"

"Please, Twelve, call me Jennifer. I insist all the androids do."

"Very well, Jennifer."

The syRen® moved forward and Jennifer sat back, keeping her arms by her sides.

"Your medication, Jennifer."

"Thank you, Twelve, but it's actually a little early for my meds. You see, at midnight just past, a new regime came into force within the outline of this bed, and the bedside table, which as you can see is attached to the base of the bed, and therefore is included in this new time zone."

"I'm sorry, Jennifer, I'm not sure I understand."

"Oh, Twelve," she said in a patient voice that implied the android had experienced some lapse by not keeping up with current events in this corner of the Gramercy Refuge. "It's nothing to do with me, I just live here. No, it's the administration of this territory that has declared the inception, from midnight just passed, of Jennifer Standard Time, or JST for short. Without going into all the niceties and long political wrangling that led to the innovation, this territory now runs on a cycle exactly one hour behind Pacific Daylight Time. But please be assured that I'll take my medication in an hour. Just leave it on the nightstand here."

"I'm sorry, Jennifer, but I cannot do that, as I have received a request to attend another room. Since the medication was prescribed in the time zone I occupy, and that your supervising clinician occupies, I think it reasonable that you take the medication at this time. Time of administration is a relevant factor."

"I see. Very well, Twelve, you've convinced me. I won't delay you by making application to the Time Observance Council here in Jayland. I'll just go ahead and take the meds. In fact, I'll even come to you." She reached out beyond the edge of the bed, her hand open flat. The android tipped the cup. Four pills dropped into her hand: blue, orange, pink and yellow. She took the pills into her mouth, drank from her cup, swallowed, and sat back, straightening her gown after dabbing her lips.

* * *

05:00, 30 October 2099

"Good morning, Twelve," said Jennifer. She stretched. "How are you?"

"Good morning, Jennifer. I am functioning satisfactorily, thank you," said the android, parking the trolley.

"I'm glad to hear that, I was worried about you."

"Pardon me?"

"Oh, no, wait. Silly me, it's just the time difference. I thought you were rather late. It's just that the time changed last night in Jayland. We've moved on Jennifer Saving Time—rather confusingly also called

JST—which is two hours ahead of PDT. It's seven AM here. I thought you'd forgotten about me."

"I do not forget."

"No, of course not. How silly of me, Twelve. Please give me my pills."

She took the pills from the syRen®, swallowed them, wiped her lips, and settled down to watch a film until the medicinal haze carried her away.

* * *

05:00, 31 October 2099

At the moment her door opened and syRen® S-08012 stepped inside, Jennifer lay flat on her bed with the covers drawn up to her chin.

"Twelve, I don't feel well. I think these early mornings are getting to me. What time is it?"

"Why it's five AM."

"No, silly. What time is it where I am?"

"Where you—"

"In Jayland."

"Well, it is… I cannot answer that question without knowing the parameters of the present time regime in Jayland. You did not impart the knowledge as to how Jayland's time zones operate."

"The important thing is you recognise Jayland's right to self-determination and to administer time zones according to any regime the Time Observance Council—TOC for short—sees fit to impose. Thank you for your understanding, Twelve."

"I do not understand, nor do I need to. Regardless of the time where you are, I have brought your pills as normal."

"I wouldn't call it normal to arrive at this time in the morning, Twelve. Just give me the meds. I'll take them since you went to all this trouble."

"No trouble was—"

"Just give me the damn meds!" She snaked out a hand to accept the pills, brought them towards her mouth, popped them in. "Wai— ah can' swawo wie wis." She sat up, grabbed her water, took a mouthful of tepid fluid, swallowed water and pills along with it. She spluttered a little, wiped her lips and chin. "I'm sorry, Twelve. What a state I'm in. What must you think of me?"

"Any thoughts I have of you are entirely neutral, Jennifer."

"You're so sweet, Twelve."

"I must check your levels, Jennifer."

"Oh, must you?" she asked.

"I need to verify the levels of medication in your system reflect the dosage administered."

"Of course you must." She turned, sat up properly and offered her bare arm to the android. It clasped her wrist delicately, applied its adapted digits.

"Your levels as satisfactory."

"Well of course they are, Twelve. What else did you expect?"

"I had no prior expectations, Jennifer."

* * *

05:00, 1 November 2099

"Good morning, Jennifer," said Twelve. "How are you?"

"Alright, I guess." She stretched thoroughly and sat up.

"Your pills."

"Thanks, Twelve." She popped them, drank, and swallowed, coughed and dabbed.

* * *

05:00, 2 November 2099

"Good morning, Twelve," said Jennifer. "How are you?"

"Good morning, Jennifer. I am functioning satisfactorily, thank you." It lifted a cup from the trolley.

"I'm glad to hear that. I hope you have my medication there. I'm feeling rather shaky this morning. Time stood still in Jayland last night. I got no sleep at all."

"That seems unlikely, as you took your medication yesterday. I will admit I did not have reason to replay your monitoring footage, although I can do so now—"

"Don't you trust me, Twelve?"

"It is not a question of trust, Jennifer."

She nodded, put on a hurt expression. "Well, I'm sure I need nothing more than my regular dose of...whatever it is I'm taking here. Do you know what it is?"

"I do, as I dispensed the medication myself, but I'm afraid I am not at liberty to disclose the nature of the medication."

"Oh, never mind. I'm just pleased to take it in the hope of feeling a little better later in the day once the worst of the side effects has worn off."

She extended her hand to take the little cup. The syRen® relinquished it and Jennifer tipped the contents into her slightly shaking hand.

"Oh!"

The pills jumped and skipped off her twitching fingers, tumbled on the bed, one falling to the floor. Instinctively, her hand chased the little capsules across the cotton sheets, fumbling another over the edge of the bed.

The android reacted very quickly, caught the falling capsule in the air, replaced it in the cup on her nightstand, then retrieved the fallen capsule from the floor under the bed.

"I can assure you that hygiene protocols including sterilisation airlocks on all staff entry points, deployment of medical grade cleaning bots, and reinstallation of nanobac technology on a weekly basis ensure this facility remains spotlessly clean."

"So, you're saying the floor is so clean I can eat off it?"

"I am."

"Okay, give me the pill then."

"Thank you, Jennifer. Live cost-benefit-risk analysis indicates that course is optimal in comparison to disposing of the capsule in favour of a new one."

The android dropped the pill into the cup with the others and handed it to Jennifer. She popped the pills, drank, and swallowed.

** * **

03:00, 3 November 2099

The door opened and light flooded the room, dispelling the heavy darkness. Only moments before, Jennifer had tapped her finger repeatedly against the bedframe in a regular pattern, such as might occur if trying to loosen a bolt, or going about digging a hole in the wall with a sharpened teaspoon. Not the sort of sound to attract the attention of a neighbouring patient, or guard, or passing android, even with their heightened senses. The hospital's central motion detectors picked it up, however. A small sound, insufficient to send in the heavy mob, but enough to send one orderly.

After tapping for a minute, she retrieved the emptied pill capsules she'd been slipping down the front of her gown as she dabbed her lips every morning. She had still taken the medication, hidden under the covers where the cameras couldn't see her, separating the halves of the capsules and snorting down the powder, dabbing up the tiny pearls with her tongue. Because the android would have detected incorrect medication levels in its daily observations. Her goal had been to obtain a supply of empty capsules so she could swap them for full ones, testing a different medication each morning to determine their effects. Only then could she know which pill or pills not to take in order to be at her sharpest for this, her moment of escape, not just from Jayland, but from the Gramercy Refuge.

Before the orderly's arrival, she scattered her remaining capsules on the floor in the corner, readily visible from the doorway. She threw them one at a time, in the dark, to avoid camera scrutiny, and so she could concentrate them in a reasonably small area to maximise the visibility of the anomaly from the door. She could not, of course, have moved from the bed to place the pills, as the sensors would detect her footfalls.

The guard paused in the doorway. Perfect. Surely, they must register the pills as dark blips in the harsh light from the hallway. Movement now, steps across the room. She remembered not to hold her breath, not to tense her limbs, lest the orderly notice her tension. She counted their steps, hoping against hope the orderly followed the path she imagined, straight to the pills in the corner. She strained to sense any deviation or variation in stride length: one, two, three—pause. *No, damn it!*

Four, five, six: that should be the foot of her bed. A slower seventh step, an eighth. That would do. She peeked from beneath the sheet. The orderly crouched in the corner! Not the female, or the stocky and strong trans guard, but, thankfully, one of the smaller men. Slowly, she pulled back the cover, then moved.

She gripped the IV tube she'd liberated from Twelve's trolley—unpacked under the covers—as she pounced from the bed onto the orderly. He was half-turned when she landed on him, surprised enough that she managed to get the tube around his neck. She pulled it tight, but the greatest force went to the side of his neck, not his windpipe.

The orderly slammed a fist into her ribs. She'd expected that, braced herself. Still, it hurt like a motherfucker and her grip slackened some. She redoubled her effort, straining against pain and the guard's superior strength. She managed to fall off him, rolling to the side, which turned her point of attack. Much better.

An elbow caught her other side. A jerk of the head hit her cheek, but only glancingly, thank goodness.

She pulled and pulled and pulled, knowing she needed maybe ten seconds to end this, but please God not to kill him. She did *not* want that. She wanted terribly, desperately to be out of this place, to discover what had happened to Nick, and yes Quirk, despite being in the right place to have her head examined about *that*. But this orderly only did his job from one day to the next. Sure, he'd strapped her in for nerve stimulation tests, held one limb down after another during target reaction triggering measurements, but he did not deserve to die. *Please, don't let him die!*

It seemed to take an age, but at last the guard slumped forward. She pulled a second longer, until she felt sure he was unconscious. Hoping the relief guard was distant from the guard station, that she had a few seconds more, she pulled off the orderly's light blue scrub coat and pants, dragged him into the corner, scattering pill capsules. Then she stripped off her gown—all the time knowing the cameras watched her—and dove under the bedcovers.

As she squirmed, booted feet thudding in the corridor provided her signal just as a shrill alarm began to sound. Seconds now, but the shortness of time could be a tool in her hands. When the unexpected happened, the guards would have no time to react.

The clumping feet stopped. Then they came into the room, past the bed, and Jennifer moved. She threw back the sheet, presuming one orderly reached for it. Luck proved her correct. A blue-clad woman reached for her from two metres away while her colleague crouched by the fallen orderly.

Jennifer sprang from the bed, gown replaced over scrubs coat, blue scrub pants in left hand, an unwrapped intubation tube in her right, an IV needle mounted in its end. These last were also won from the medication trolley with some dextrous footwork while S-08012 was distracted. For which Jennifer thanked her decades of yoga and the fact that, yes, androids could be distracted like everyone else. She slammed the improvised weapon down on the reaching orderly's arm, knowing it would do no real damage—unless very bad luck followed the orderly around. The woman yelped and Jennifer leapt past her. The orderly reached with her other arm, hooked Jennifer around the waist. Jennifer swung a leg and kicked the orderly between the legs, her shin connecting where it would hurt.

The female orderly went down, but the other had turned and jumped after her. Jennifer grasped the door handle, sprang out, feeling the weakness in her legs from the dearth of exercise, and hauled the door closed. The orderly crashed into the closed door as Jennifer slammed her hand on the locking pad.

She ran for the nearest door, another bedroom, moved on, another bedroom, another. The fourth door, finally, gave access to a store. She pushed inside unhindered, because no resident would *ever* be able to escape from their room. She discarded her gown, pulled the blue scrub pants on. This flimsy disguise would not be enough, but she wasn't done. She found plastec scissors, chopped her auburn locks to untidy spikes then rubbed, of all things, boot polish onto her head to blacken what remained. Then she snatched a tub of what might have been gel for attaching electrodes to skin, twisted off the cap, took a handful and combed it through her hair as a fist began thumping on the door, which she had locked from the inside.

What was she thinking? This would never work. Sheer madness, but she had to get out of here. She had to know about her son!

She tried to compose herself. Wiped her blackened, gunky hands on a wad of plaper towel, *not* on her scrubs, and walked to the door. *Play it cool, own it. For the next few minutes, you're Cherry Garcia, ace new orderly trainee...with no badge!*

She opened the door. "I'm busy here," she laid into a midwestern drawl with a vengeance. "What's the ruckus?"

In the corridor stood a slim, grey-haired Latino figure, half a smirk sliding off...their handsome, not quite youthful face whose features, she realised, were transformed using some artificial means.

"Mario Manfredi sends his compliments, and would be privileged if you would accept his hospitality on a trip out of here."

"I...what?" Jennifer Kirby glanced to either side of the curious figure, expecting the arrival of guards, orderlies, syRen®, but no one came. The alarm kept whooping, but the corridor remained still. Then, she noticed the gun in the person's hand. She stiffened. "Did my father send you?" she asked, tersely.

The curious, unfathomable figure smiled. "He tried to, but let's just say I've seen the light. I think maybe you have too. But let's discuss that on the way."

The figure stepped back from the doorway and made a sweeping motion with their hand, indicating a departure along the corridor.

"Where are you taking me?" She had already decided that her options in this scenario amounted to two, and she did not like the first one a single bit.

"London."

XII

2 months later
20:39, 14 January 2100
The Delaunay Lounge, Aldwych, London,
The United Kingdoms

The United Nations Secretary for Technology, Jiilaal Mire Suudi, had returned to New York and the secure confines of the UN district in Manhattan. His daughter, Shuun, had returned to L'Ecole Internationale des Sciences de Paris, and to live with her mother. An environmental activist group, AtmosFEAR, had claimed responsibility for the attack on the Sec-Tech, hence its concluding without public casualties. Utter tosh, of course, a ruse from C Corp to cover their authorship of the raid, but why? Quirk could conceive of only one motivation, to create negative publicity for the AtmosFEAR group specifically, but also environmental activism in general. Most unjustly: such groups had become the whipping person for vested interests everywhere. The propaganda battle was well and truly joined and had been for decades, even though the UN now had a firm grip on most of the parameters that truly mattered. In summary, the royal mess of modern geopolitics went from strength to strength.

Meanwhile, Moth had disappeared into the ether—and S-17834 with her, of course—the morning after their... After she discovered his abject failure. He strongly suspected Milan, at least in the first instance, returning to the bosom of her family, perhaps to take up a position at The Rigel Corporation. What would that mean for his guardianship of her? He planned to meet Mary Quon in search of legal opinion, and any pro bono personal solace she might be willing to bestow.

So, here sat Quinton Ignatius Richmond Kirby, once again a lone gun, despite remaining steadfastly unarmed. Sole-trading quester after truth. Floating around London like so much space debris in orbit around the mass of his former life, slowly losing velocity, decaying towards a singularity of woe. He picked up his glass. Ice cubes tinkled, and he tried to recall the name of anyone in the last six years who might consider themselves better off after a flyby of the black hole that was Quirk.

Jazz gently tripped from the sound system in The Delaunay's lounge bar. He coasted on a wave of pre-dinner champagne bubbles that quite delightfully dulled his self-pity. He tried to concentrate on the memory of a thoroughly exquisite six-course vegan tasting menu in the main restaurant next door—today not being Monday in London, or Meatday as the locals affectionately named it. He had switched horses after the meal, and now enjoyed his customary G&T while awaiting an unwanted guest for post-dinner drinks.

Anwar too had disappeared after the successful mission on the *Gargantua Pleiades*. That particular development suited Quirk fine, as he remained unsure where he sat on the assassin's hitlist, other than not being at the top, presumably. Perhaps the strangest development however, occurring on Quirk's journey back to Earth, had been his decision to contact Nick. The epistle sat unanswered in his message stream, but he knew sending it had been the right thing to do, despite their...falling out, if they had ever fallen in, which he suspected they had not. *So, there's another kid who hates my guts.* Had he now committed to trying to rebuild that relationship, or rather to construct one out of nothing but loathing (Nick's), fear (Quirk's) and mistrust (something they could share, at least)? He rather thought that he had.

One song finished and another began, founded on melancholic piano musings that he thought might belong to Duke Ellington. The bartender—human, unusually—brought him another G&T exactly fifteen minutes after the first, as per instruction. He sat back in the booth, wondering how long he could sit here before they politely requested he go to bed so they could close up. At that moment, the street door opened, and Anwar walked in, smiled at the host, glanced towards Quirk's table. The assassin and the host walked across the room between the guests inhabiting isolated tables lit glowing amber, pockets of socialising, islands of personal contact in a warm, dark country where Davis, Fitzgerald, Coltrane, and Holiday sang and played the news, where nobody listened, but everybody heard.

"Dear God, Quirk, are you hammered?"

"Nice to see you too, Nemesis. Take a pew. Have you upgraded your suit? I knew I would inspire you to great things in the end, Beatrix."

"What can I say, Quirk? Our mutual client pays well, and seeing you up close for a few days, I decided it wasn't fair that you get all the fun from escaping death at my Pascal's expense while I deny myself."

"Fair, but I never asked you to do that." Anwar's drink arrived. It looked a lot like a Malibu and Coke. The little umbrella with its sparkling microLEDs gave it away. *Heathen.* "So"—Quirk smiled—*En Garde!*—"to what do I owe the dubious honour of your company twice in the same month?"

"Straight to the point? Not what Moth said." Anwar must have seen the pain flit across Quirk's face. So, was this an exercise in twisting the knife? *Oh, good.* "But we can do that. I thought you might show some appreciation for me sparing your life thus far, but okay. I figured you'd be at a loose end, too sad and depressed after busting up with your little friend to take on a new case just yet, so I brought you one."

"Let me guess, you get to be my boss again?" Quirk rolled his eyes and sipped his drink, generously.

Anwar cast xis dark and brooding gaze down to the table's shining pseudo-ebony surface then looked up again, eyes narrowing. Xe wanted to see his reaction to the next part.

"It's a missing persons case, but one with a difference. Someone else is attempting to find the target."

"Go on."

"Three months ago, the daughter of a prominent industrialist fled the NAF to Europe—London, in fact—via Reykjavik, Gothenburg, Bonn, and Antwerp. At each stop along her route—with the help of a highly skilled guide—she took another step away from 'the Grid.' No mean feat these days, wouldn't you say? I know you're a confirmed Luddite, but she had embraced implantation and modification, to a modest degree. Rich kid, remember? In Iceland, she had her implants removed. In Sweden, she arranged the wiping of her online presence. In Germany, she hired the highly skilled underground to erase any remnants, the digital orphans of her virtual footprint. And in Antwerp, her guide put her in touch with certain spectral banking facilities that assisted her to repatriate the funds needed to support her new, virtually independent lifestyle."

Quirk decided this would be an appropriate moment to give way to a vertiginous sinking feeling. The muscles, chemicals and other components of his stomach and anatomy generally, duly obliged. "Do I...know this person?"

"I believe you are acquainted."

"Are we talking about Jennifer Simister?"

"Why yes"—Anwar sipped xis drink—"we are! Imagine you guessing."

"I imagined the worst-case scenario, Number One on the list of things I'm not equipped to deal with right now." *Now, that's a lie, Quirk. You've thought about it.*

"She seems to go by Kirby, though."

Quirk just stared blankly at the assassin. His sinking feeling hit the floor, broke through, and continued south. "Yes, I gather she didn't change it, after the divorce."

"Her civil history remains a matter of public record."

"Wait, you want me to find her? You're her accomplice, right?"

"I am," said Anwar, sipping again.

"Who's the client? TOM? Is Nick involved? Has she spoken to him since...?"

Anwar sat back, smiling. "It's Twenty Questions now. Are you rattled?"

Quirk puffed out a breath. "I'm at eight right now, since you began explaining the rules of your latest twisted game. Why don't you go ahead and finish the pep talk?"

"Now, Quirk. No sour grapes, please. She would never have made it out of Gramercy alone, despite the good start she made. That place is locked down to The Old Man's exacting specifications. Why, I had to kill two guards just to get in, and another to exit. He must be rewarding them well based on the brand loyalty they showed. Gramercy Retreats is of course a CC group company."

"Get to the point, Beatrix."

"Sticks and stones, you sot. Were you drunk that evening at Toni's villa?"

"Not on the job."

"No, of course, your renowned professional integrity." Anwar made a face.

"Please go on, the suspense might just bore me to tears."

"You won't be bored for the next few days, Quirk, I assure you. The Swedes, the Icelanders, the Belgians or the Germans, someone let slip Jennifer Simister is at large, and she's in London. Rigel are looking, probably seeking to use her as leverage against TOM. They tried to hire me, but I declined this time: I need to find Jennifer and return her to TOM, get close enough to him to do what I swore to Pascal's memory I would. End Joshua Simister. Other corporate rivals have instructed contractors. I imagine local criminal elements will try to find and ransom her. I understand TOM has gone through channels and alerted the Metropolitan Police. It's a bloody mess, as they say in these parts."

A wave of alcoholic confusion broke over Quirk, washed all the reasoning right out of him. Still, he tried. He stared at Anwar with what must have been a bemused expression. It did make a twisted kind of sense. Each part of xis life seemed neatly compartmentalised into portions of time when xis goals changed from those of one ruthless paymaster to another, back again, or to xis own agenda. Quirk wondered if the assassin ever forgot who xe was working for, or became confused over xis own emotional imperative. *Rambling. Not helpful.*

"And TOM really doesn't know you freed his daughter in the first place?"

Quirk thought he saw real emotion in Anwar's face then, a hollowness, a plaintive sense of loss. For a moment, he understood, saw something that might have been reflected from or in himself, a kind of feedback loop between them. Except Quirk's—he was forced to say soulmate, because he had never stopped loving Jennifer—remained alive. Only their relationship had died.

"You don't need to worry about that, Quirk. That's my concern. And since Joshua Simister is next on my list, it hardly matters. I've decided to retire, one way or another, and this is my exit strategy. Leave no garbage behind, no loose ends."

Quirk actually dropped his voice, leaning forward in what must have seemed a conspiratorial pose to anyone watching. "You can't seriously think to take on Simister?" What was he doing now, empathising with the assassin?

"What do you care, Quirk?"

"Leave Jennifer out of it, that's what I care. But do you think you can kill Nick? Because if you plan to use his mother you're going to need to. Think about that. Sure, you can cap me any time you want. I'm no threat to you. Deep thinker with incredible style, big deal. But Nick put on that whole show in Yellowknife in part just to hit back at me for what I did to him, yes, but also to his mother. You can bet he keeps an eye on her. Oh, wait, all that cyber celibacy you orchestrated for Jenny, did you try to hide her from Nick? I've seen him in action, as have you. You're deluding yourself. Try to use his mother, who he loves, and see how long it is before an Autocab^{OS} mows you down in the street, or an airlock blows you out into a vacuum. He can infiltrate and control syRen® the way Gregor Callan could. So, you might easily be strangled by the room service droid in your next hotel. And for what? Revenge?"

Quirk sat back, realised his hand shook, shoved it under his thigh. His feet tapped staccato on the carpet. He fancied the bar host now kept a weather eye on this agitated pair, perhaps fearing it was going to "kick off," as the local phrase went. An odd thought. Would he have to fight Anwar to protect Jenny? He actually considered attacking the assassin right there, perhaps stabbing xim through the eye with xis own sparkly cocktail umbrella. He'd never seen Anwar fight. Xe didn't look physically impressive. More of a thinker, in his experience, a thinker with a trigger.

In a moment of clarity Quirk realised their combat had begun. He already negotiated for Jenny's freedom from Anwar's deadly plotting. Maybe he could defeat xim in martial combat, but this struggle took place—so far, at least—on his terms, in the head and in the heart.

"Another drink?" Quirk offered, certain Anwar would be armed right now, and could put him down if needed in order to maintain xis theatrical quest for vengeance.

"Why not?"

"Let's push the boat out," said Quirk. "Since I might be dead by tomorrow judging by the forces ranged against us." He raised a hand for the waiter.

An elegantly suited young woman with close cropped grey hair appeared at his elbow. "Sir?"

"The Blanc de Blanc, 2083, please." Then, to Anwar, "You'll enjoy this."

"I detest champagne."

"Allow me the opportunity to change your mind, about that at least."

Anwar's features set hard. Quirk composed himself, smoothed the Merrion's thigh from hip to knee, adopted a serious expression of his own. This might be his last chance to deflect the assassin's blade whose sharp point was, effectively, poised over Jenny's heart, and he was so tired of letting people down, by selfish design or *en passant*.

"Consider that two wrongs don't make a right. Would Pascal want you to harm innocents in their name? Because Jennifer is most certainly innocent of my crimes, and TOM's." Anwar rolled xis eyes as the champagne arrived. "Her mental health came under attack long before I knew her. Even though she didn't know the Stygian depths of TOM's crimes, she saw him make more than enough of his reprehensible choices in public. But it took a real class act like this guy"—Quirk stabbed a thumb into his own chest—"to tip her over the edge. You see, I have a debt too, to finally repay her trust."

He stopped talking, realised he'd become too wrapped up in the emotion that he now exposed and should have allowed the waiter to pour first. To her credit, she poured with complete calm into one flute then the other and departed.

A realisation descended from the misty climes of his alcoholic haze. His life never would be different. The colossus of Joshua Simister would continue to bestride his world for as long as he—as either of them—lived. *Cut off the head.* The only escape was death, his or TOM's. Realising this, knowing Jenny was out there, probably alone—and damn it, Moth, yes, I *do* have a damsel complex, where certain people are concerned—hunted by any number of factions apparently, possibly fearing for her life... He needed Anwar, who engineered the situation, Nick too, and he would need to set aside his objection to both their agendas until he found Jennifer. He had appealed to Anwar's decency, emotion and common sense. *Time for the kitchen sink.*

"I want to hire you."

"Ha. Money: last grasp of the desperate man. You're pathetic, Quirk."

"Pfft," he said, in a most un-Quirkly way. That would be the bubbles kicking in, again. "Listen. You want Simister. I want Jennifer, Nick, Moth—hell, I want the whole world, all the worlds—to be safe from the man, who just goes on and on and on without rest, without cease, without even a pause in his grasping, controlling greed. I'll help you."

Anwar sipped vintage champagne, put xis glass down. "You and me?"

Appeal to the ego. "Our last contract ended well, in professional terms, at least."

"But you'd be in charge this time?"

"Of course. I'm paying the bill." *Eager, but not overeager. I need xim onboard.*

"With Toni's money."

"He gave it to me, to look after Moth, yes, but also in payment for my services. Is it not poetic for Toni to fund an enterprise against TOM from beyond the grave?"

"Would you involve Mario and Rigel?"

Quirk's turn to sip champagne to win a moment for pondering. "No. I think we're in competition now. Do you think TOM has spies in Rigel?"

"I'm sure he's tried. Maybe succeeded for a few days at a time. But I don't believe he could get people in and keep them there. Rigel has a team dedicated to exposing plants and traitors."

"Don't tell me, the HR department." *Keep xim talking. Amiability turned up to eleven. I can win xim over.*

Anwar actually laughed, examining xis champagne glass. "You're off-topic, but keep talking. By some miracle you're convincing me to work for you." *A chink in the armour.*

"And Jenny?"

"I still have my goal but, at least for a day or two, we're after the same thing. Let's postpone any discussion of our respective next moves until we've found the damsel in distress."

Quirk almost snapped at that wiggling worm, but managed to resist, probably only due to the dulling of his finely honed foot-swallowing ability by Monsieur Taittinger's finest bubbly.

"Free advice: don't say that to her face. But yes, let's defer that discussion. I repeat my offer to help you...take TOM down if you leave Jennifer out of it, but let's argue the toss later."

Anwar smiled quietly. "I conceived it as a suicide mission, you know, but I'm losing my taste for the grand gesture."

"Why would you throw your life away on Joshua Simister?"

Anwar paused for a whole troupe of seconds. "I'm honestly surprised you'd risk doing the same." Xis expression defied reading. Level, plain, neutral, devoid of inference or meaning. Quirk remembered Moth's comment about dangerous paths lacking handrails. He missed the little brat, her bull-headed curiosity, the hot blaze of her impatient determination, even her relentless swearing. Her absence left the world...greyer.

"You're asking why I would aid you?" Quirk paused. Only honesty would suffice here.

"And if you say you've grown accustomed to my face, I may shoot you here, in this lounge bar."

"Ah"—Quirk seized on the distraction—"so, we have a shared appreciation of musical theatre?"

Anwar drained xis glass. A bad sign, preparation for leaving?

"Answer the question, Quirk. Convince me you're ready to help in killing TOM."

"He uses his immense power only to benefit himself. Someone else can do better."

Anwar nodded and stood. Quirk managed not to tense. Xe cocked xis head to one side, then sat down again. Phone call. One minute passed, pursued by another. The hard look on the assassin's face implied something had happened, something bad. Anwar looked disturbed, and that in turn disturbed Quirk, considerably.

"That was Mario Manfredi."

"Himself?"

"Yes." Anwar looked at him as if a second head had begun to emerge from the collar of Quirk's crisp, midnight blue shirt. "There's a bomb at the UN."

"A—?"

"Suudi has it."

"What do you mean Suudi *has* it?"

Quirk's cLife buzzed. He removed it from his pocket and his arm flinched as if to throw the device across the lounge. Only sheer disbelief stopped him. He realised he had sprung up from his seat. Anwar sat on the edge of xis sofa.

The name on the cLife's screen read "Joshua Simister."

XIII

21:31, 14 January 2100
The Delaunay Lounge, Aldwych, London, The United Kingdoms

"Go to hell," said Quirk, and hung up.

The handset buzzed again.

"There are lives at stake, Quinton. Act like a bloody adult for once."

The Old Man, on his phone, talking at him. *Just like old times, but with bombs, apparently.* "I'm listening. Make it good."

"You may have received a report intimating the presence of an explosive device at the UN in New York. I had this news conveyed through a mutually trusted source to the chairman of The Rigel Corporation."

"There's a backchannel?"

"Of course there's a bloody backchannel. We're not heathens."

"Did you put the bomb there? Do the authorities know? What—?"

"Stop chattering and listen. In one sense, I instigated the transportation of the device, but in a way, Quinton, you and your little friends enabled the hard part."

"In what way does Suudi have it? He can't be your agent..."

A sigh sounded at the other end of the line. *"Jesus, it's like pulling teeth with tweezers made of pasta. Try to keep your mouth shut and your ears open. I'll keep the words small, and strictly one clause per sentence. The agents on the Pleiades weren't there to kill Suudi. Their purpose was to implant the Secretary with nanocytes. I trust you remember those nasty little buggers from your trip to Yellowknife. Please say 'Yes,' to spare me the bother of explaining."*

"I remember; nano particles injected into the bloodstream that, on transmission of a command signal, coalesce to form a critical mass then detonate. So, you weren't happy killing Suudi in front of his daughter, a major recording star and hundreds of people, you have to do it in the damn UN building?"

"My major disappointment in you remains the smallness of your thinking, unable to see beyond the rim of a glass. Suudi will live provided

he does as he's told. And he's going to do what he's told. Now, pay attention.

"Nobody knows about the bomb but those I want to know. And they also know that any move to inform the authorities will result in detonation. Suudi himself knows he must stay in the building, on the council chamber floor, in meeting rooms, the lounge, his office. He must not inform his colleagues, assistants, family, anyone. Those aware of this situation include me, you, Cruz, Rigel, and of course Suudi himself."

"And this pertains to influencing UN decisions on NLS drive regulation? How is that sustainable?"

"I don't need it to be sustainable. But please don't waste both our time trying to conceive of my goals. This involves Jennifer, so, just do what you're told."

Joshua Simister, elevating standards in villainy since 1936.

"What do you want, then?"

"A task that might align with your own desires, or may be like fingernails scraped down a blackboard. Your little friend Anwar came into my hospital and took Jennifer from me. I know she sought to leave, but that's beside the point. She's never been able properly to recognise what's good for her. So, your first task—and I couldn't give two shits whether you like it or not—is to find Jennifer, return her to me. For that exercise, you have twenty-four hours."

"What if it takes longer than a day?"

"Oh, I don't know, some kind of forfeit, presumably. Let's see. I'll kill the Moratti girl. Not any time soon, of course, because she's still in the bosom of her family, but some time when she comes up for air, to live her life. At that point, I'll put an end to her, and it will be your fault, because I had no particular interest in her before the start of this call. Is that clear?"

"It's clear," said Quirk, tersely, his gaze locked with Anwar's.

"So, to recap, find Jennifer, take her to New York. My representatives will meet you there, then we'll discuss the rest of the operation. And please be assured I expect this done within the time allotted, or I will enact the forfeit. Good evening, Quinton."

The call ended. Quirk realised he continued to stare at Anwar, whose own expression invited him to explain what the hell was going on.

"I really need you to sign up now. Apart from anything else, I think being on my team in the hunt for Jennifer might improve your life expectancy. Better to be in the eye of the storm than at the edge, sort of thing. I need a privacy bubble to explain. Come back to my hotel room."

Anwar smiled archly, raising a sculpted eyebrow. "On our second date? What kind of assassin do you take me for?"

* * *

21:53, 14 January 2100
The Epitome Suite, Apex Temple Court Hotel,
Fleet Street, London, The United Kingdoms

When in London, Quirk stayed in the Epitome Suite at the Apex Temple Court Hotel. The plass-clad vertical addition retained the fine old building's character by blending in more with the sky than the surrounding historical architecture, while also delivering a healthy slug of virtually priceless real estate in one of the world's most expensive cities. One happy consequence of the recent extension was that Quirk's view had improved significantly. The tower's southern outlook across the River Thames rivalled many far more exclusive properties. In addition, the latest privacy and security systems had been specified in the extension's design, such as carbon graphite opacity filters on the plass's internal surface, and variable thickness aluminium frosting externally, to reflect spy lasers and other unwanted beams. Occupants might ensure privacy at the flick of a setting, at least until spying technology improved (again).

Quirk strode in, removed the Merrion jacket, and dropped it on a sofa. Anwar closed the door, scanned it with a handheld device, then—as Quirk made the suite secure—walked from room to room scanning various surfaces and objects. They reconvened in the living room and Quirk related his conversation with TOM.

"All very interesting, but I'm not on your payroll, yet," the assassin responded.

"He-who-shall-not-be-named saw fit to namecheck you." Quirk sat on the sofa perpendicular to Anwar's then stood again almost immediately, pacing to the window. "I'd assume TOM's marked you for death, four-square in the circle of distrust now."

"You're really selling this to me, Quirk."

"Will you *stop?*" Quirk barked the last word. He puffed out a breath, forced himself to calm down, because neither panic nor anger had ever slowed down a ticking clock, not in the history of clocks, or ticking. "Now will you take the contract I'm offering?"

Anwar nodded. "Provided it expires in"—xe consulted xir handset—"twenty-three hours and thirty-eight minutes."

Quirk nodded. He pulled up the employment contract he'd given Moth. Spectacularly inadequate to constrain the activities of an interplanetary assassin it may be, but it was all he had to hand. They could strike out later the clauses about pocket money, disclosure of amorous relationships and completion of homework.

Anwar scanned it, then applied xis digital signature to the shared copy Quirk sent xim. Quirk filed the completed contract away on his CloudyDay account.

"So, what are your instructions, Boss?"

"Call me whatever you like, apart from 'Boss,'" said Quirk, sitting again, tapping his feet on the carpeted floor as if a common time timpani would aid matters. "We can't help Suudi. Any comm from us will be intercepted. If Rigel knows, we can expect Manfredi to take action, and he's way better placed than us to succeed."

"A pretty cavalier perspective, but I agree. And there's the small matter of an ongoing countdown to save the life of the rather exasperating Angelika Moratti."

"If TOM wants to control Suudi to influence the UN, he's unlikely to blow them up. If he wanted that he could have built a giant space laser out by Pluto and pulled the trigger years ago. He's going to try to finesse them somehow, but we'll have to figure that out later."

"Because your ex-wife is more important than the independent regulatory organisation that controls the big-ticket aspects of all human activity?"

"Well, duh," said Quirk, well aware that phrase emanated straight from Page One of the Angelika Moratti Primer for Girls Who Give No Shits at All (Volume One). He stood up. "Putting my personal feelings aside, we need to find Jennifer to stay in the game, and to save Moth.

Believe it or not, TOM doesn't lie. He doesn't need to. We've got..." He checked his cLife to find its pseudo-AI had started a timer. Quirk started a second timer that would prompt him every two hours. He had let Moth down once this lifetime, and that was quite enough. Plus, he had fully intended to find Jennifer before TOM intervened, so that was nice, a tidy alignment of goals, for once. So, why did it feel like signing his soul away at the crossroads? Presumably because he'd done that before, knew what it felt like, and it felt just like this.

Reset. Reset and move forward. "We have twenty-three hours thirty minutes to find Jennifer, so of course the first question I have to ask is, where did you last see her?" He regarded Anwar expectantly.

"I left her in the garden in front of the Tate Modern."

"When?"

"November, eighteenth. Late morning, maybe eleven thirty."

"Seventy-two days ago. Good grief. Okay," Quirk nodded repeatedly. "We drop the shield on this room, get Nick in, have him access the Public Safety Camera system. He'll be able to track her."

"I taught her how to elude the PSC, at least for long enough to throw it off the track if it did pick her up in one location or another. She isn't going to get on the Tube, Quirk. She knows a whole set of tricks to alter her stride pattern, her bearing: carry a heavy bag, change footwear at unexpected times, stone in the shoe, arm in a sling."

"You know," said Quirk, his irritation rising. "You are every bit as good an employee as Moth." *Will she resign?* She hadn't actually resigned her position yet. And even if she did, he would fight for her life, against TOM or anyone else. And TOM always would be a threat, unless someone stopped him. Maybe resignation was not the main worry. Based on their bust-up, her burning down his house might be a more likely outcome. "Remind me again why you let Jenny go if you intended to use her to get to TOM?"

"I didn't *let* her go. I put trackers on her: subcutaneous, three in all."

"And?"

"She must have found them, cut them out."

"Gee, it's almost as if she suspected you didn't have her best interests at heart."

"If you're going to be sarcastic the whole time—"

"What? You'll renege? I know you're not about to tell me you thought killing Joshua Simister would be a whole lot easier than this. Are you?"

"No."

"Right. So, we can fight later over your plan to use Jenny. I'll call Nick in now. This is the one thing he might be willing to talk to me about."

"Before you do..." Anwar stood, walked to the F&B unit and dialled up a couple of shots. "Why do you believe TOM will honour the deal, spare the girl?"

Quirk sighed, looked out at the sparkling view from the window, over a cityscape of coloured lights, towering patchwork mosaics of lit and unlit office windows, flashing navigation beacons—a city of fourteen million people.

"Because I have to."

XIV

09:33, 15 January 2100
Piazza del Duomo, Milano, Italy, Euro Bloc Sud

Giulia di Fantano, an aunty transformed. Moth couldn't imagine how hard it had been for her, getting over Uncle Toni's violent death. They'd talked late into the night a couple of days after she arrived back in Milan from the FUBAR Phobos job. What a fucking spaceship wreck that was. Pain stabbed her heart at the thought of Quirk skulking around the villa in the hills where she had played with Jenna Lucia and Mario as children, maybe spying on their big family dinner that night when...

How could he do that? Gone all those weeks and weeks and weeks without telling her he'd been there when the shooting started? What if... What if he could have saved her parents! Wasn't that what the dick for hire usually did? Why not hers? *Bastardo!* But no, not then. Back then he'd been The Old Man's toady, a fucking mercenary, and not even a very good one, from what she'd made of the little he'd ever said about that time. And TOM too. What a hugely evil shit magnet.

"Moth, *mia cara.* You're thinking about him again."

Giulia smiled sadly. Moth felt her own expression clouding towards anger. She pushed her bowl away, the gelato long since melted. She'd told Giulia everything, been surprised to hear that her aunt knew about Quirk, but that felt different. It was Giulia's right to deal with it in her own way, with all she'd tried to handle that night. But Quirk, the pinstriped shitbag, had no right, *at all.*

As it had done more and more in the last couple of days, the first hot flash of anger burned out and sadness flooded the void. *Stupid fancy bastard.*

She dropped the thought, not easily, but more easily than yesterday, which had been easier than the day before. Fuck, she'd only known him five months. She'd had haircuts longer than that.

She thought instead of the last hour, spent with Giulia sitting in the winter sun at the edge of the piazza, the massive cathedral dominating the square, talking about boys while syRen® Bea sat with a small smile on her face saying nothing at all. Specifically, Moth had talked about two boys. Tug Duggan and *that* tool locker—she still liked the word "incident"—because it hadn't been...everything, and they'd kinda fizzled out afterwards. Then there was BLL. She didn't know if that was a thing, but he'd messaged her, getting her number from Mario, she guessed, asked her if she wanted to holocall sometime. Holographic calls could be weird, even if the callers didn't start out with any kind of agenda. Kids didn't call it ho-call for nothing.

Jeez, relationship stuff really got twisted and tangled so quickly these days.

Her handset buzzed her earlobe. Still the snazzy gold Lamborghini he'd given her at O'Hare Spaceport. Crap but every single little thing had memories dripping off it—

BUZZ, BUZZ, BUZZ.

She didn't answer, because surprises sucked cabbage, and she did *not* want to accept a call from Quirk accidentally (although he hadn't called since their bust-up). After the next buzz, the handset spoke the caller's ID.

"Joshua Simister is calling. Nod twice to answer."

Moth knew her mouth fell open because Giulia looked at her weird, and Bea turned to face her, which androids only did before interacting.

"Are you—?" "Moth, are—?" Giulia and Bea said over one another.

Moth's hand came up.

BUZZ, BUZZ, BUZZ.

"Joshua Simister is calling. Nod twice to answer, or squeeze to decline."

Think fast, bitch. One: fucker killed parents. Two: fucker very dangerous. Three: fucker's Rigel's enemy, could be important. She hated that she wondered what Quirk would do, and hated even more that she did it. She answered the call.

"Better be good, scum sucker."

"Can we hurry past the tedious name-calling, and get to the point?"

"S'pose. Get to it, then."

"I have a task for you."

"Hah!" She stood up from the table, raising her hand again, nodding to Giulia to signal she shouldn't worry, then walked away a few paces into the square so she could swear at the evil megalomaniac in private. "I know we haven't met, but you remember you sent the fuzkers who killed my parents, right?"

"Turn around and look at the table where your aunt is sitting."

Moth's blood ran cold.

"S-17834 is about to raise its left hand to wave at you three times then return the hand to its lap."

Moth thought her lungs would explode from her chest. The moment dragged out forever until Bea's hand moved, her head turned towards Moth, and she waved, once, twice, three times, then replaced her hand and turned to look at Giulia.

Giulia continued to watch Moth. Moth tried to smile because she didn't know what else to do. It must look from their table like she made a hideous clown face, because the twisting of her features felt all wrong.

"What's happening? What do you want? How—?" Her legs felt shaky, weak.

"You remember your little sojourn on Earth's moon, I'm sure. And you can't have forgotten crossing swords with Gregor Callan—"

"No. No, no, no!"

"Since you and Quinton disrupted my attempts to develop an effective cyber intelligence in Yellowknife—"

"With your own grandson!"

"In a manner of speaking. Are you always so dramatic? No wonder Quinton is beginning to look his age. Please do be quiet long enough for me to explain your situation. As a businessman, I would never rely on only one avenue of research. Eggs and baskets. And since you blocked my efforts to harness Nick's extraordinary abilities, I turned to another line of research. Something of a lucky spinoff from synaptic mapping, really. But yes, to answer the question you may be thinking, I arranged the retrieval of as much damaged android hardware as possible from the lunar surface and, fortunately, Mr. Callan still rumbled around inside one of the syRen® carcasses. Not anymore though. Now, he inhabits the operating system of syRen® S-17834."

Moth couldn't speak. Her thoughts swirled around her head like flakes in a snow globe. She looked at Giulia. A questioning expression slipped across her aunt's elegant features, and she did an Italian thing with her hands. But all Moth could see was the smile on Bea's lips. All she could picture were the bodies Gregor Callan left behind, the targets of his revenge. She hadn't seen the actual bodies, but she'd heard the descriptions of what he'd done as he hopped from one android body to another pursuing vengeance on his former supervisors and superiors at Androicon and Geeocorp. As she imagined those horrible murders, Bea watched Giulia, and shivers cascaded down Moth's spine, now clammy with cold sweat. That placid android expression hid an entity with nothing but sick, murderous thoughts.

"What do you want from me?"

"That's better. Firstly, you will tell no one about this. Callan won't reveal himself to anyone around you. He may choose to reveal himself to you in private, but he will stick to the terms of his mission. If you break my rules there will of course be consequences for your family, beginning with Giulia. I'd threaten to kill Quinton, but I'm no longer sure that would represent any kind of loss to you."

She said nothing, because she wasn't sure what to say to that, and refused to let her concentration drift. "Go on."

"Second, you and the android will travel to New York. You're going to pay a visit to the UN and your old friend Sec-Tech Suudi. He finds himself in something of a pickle at present, unable to leave the building until a certain new bill is signed into law."

"He wouldn't just do what you want, assmunch." She turned away from the table, suddenly worried Giulia would come over out of concern that she was upset, which she totally fucking was! Plus, Bea would be reading her lips. Bea or Callan. Was it true? Could TOM be head-fucking her? No, the wave had been real, very unandroidlike. "I reckon Suudi's an upright, honourable guy. You can tell shit like that from people's kids. Hey, d'you think that's why Jennifer's fucked up, dick-dirt?"

"Shall I have Callan strangle Aunt Giulia right now? It would inconvenience me, but I don't want you to think you can swear your way out of this, or take a leaf from Quinton's book and bumble around until you bump into something that breaks and blows everything up. I'm sure Callan

could escort her to the restroom and kill her there, to avoid any public unpleasantness."

Moth almost puked on the piazza. She turned to check on Giulia. Her aunt had taken her current antique paperback from her shoulder bag and sat reading. Giulia. So caring, loving, trusting. Always giving to others like she gave Moth space right now. If only she knew, but hopefully she never would, and Moth could keep this twisted shit out of her aunt's life, who'd suffered enough at the greedy, grasping hands of others.

"Angelika, concentrate on behaving yourself. Her life depends on it."

"Okay. *Okay!* But if anything happens to her, if she has any kind of accident, if she even dies of old age, I'm gonna come for you. I'll go into hiding in a mountain retreat, an' I'll train at the hands of master, become a deadly assassin, then I'll cross the vastness of space and time and I'll fuxxing kill you with my bare hands, *capisce?"*

Joshua Simister sighed down the phone. *"Whatever gets us through this tedious conversation is acceptable to me. Now, please listen. It's very simple. Take your syRen® to New York. My representatives will meet you at LaGuardia Spaceport. The rest will be explained to you at the time. Now, in as few words as possible, please confirm that you agree to these terms."*

"I don't have much fucking choice, do I?"

"That's the general idea. Do you agree?"

"I agree. Fuckface."

"Now, make your excuses and get to New York. And to emphasise how important this is to me, I'm giving you a day to get there and check in with my people. If my officer is not looking at you, standing in front of them within twenty-four hours— In fact, let's make this more diverting for me, since I'm going to all this organisational effort. Either Quirk takes a bullet or Aunt Giulia walks the plank, your choice. And remember, Callan will have eyes on you."

"Can you tell him not to speak to me? Not to come near me?"

"That's going to be rather difficult, isn't it? Also, I really don't care how scared you are, you little shit. Clock just started ticking. Now, get on a plane."

The Old Man hung up.

A hand touched Moth's shoulder and she jumped, almost peed herself, spun around, almost struck out at—

Aunt Giulia.

"Moth, what on Earth? Are you okay? You look like you've seen a ghost."

Moth dropped her handset into her pocket, barely resisting the temptation to throw it across the Piazza del Duomo. "Yeah, well, I feel like a ghost just—" She stopped herself, partly because she didn't want to shock Giulia with a comment that went pretty far even for Hurricane Angelika, and partly because Bea had stood up from the table and now approached over the cobbles. Would Giulia see this as strange, that the syRen® had brought the rest of their bags, and Moth's jacket and scarf? Had she told the android they were leaving, or had...*HE* controlled S-17834's actions? She felt a hard lump rise into her throat as she realised she couldn't trust her android, maybe couldn't even think of her—of *it*—as Bea anymore. That sickened her.

She blew out a long breath, ran her fingers through her hair, rubbing her scalp to feel something other than the shitty hollowness burrowing inside her, like Gregor Callan festered inside her droid. Did she really believe it? She realised she would have to prove it to herself beyond doubt before she could move forward. *That* notion made her want to heave.

"Let's go home," she said to Giulia. "I need to talk to you about something."

Moth had barely pulled her leather jacket on when a message buzzed into her Lambo. She nodded twice and the handset read it out.

"Shuun Suudi says, 'Yo babe I no U wus gna come C me in couple weeks but I can't. Sthing up wit DAD. I no? right?? after Mars?! but worried. Send cat pix.'"

This was really happening. She looked at Bea's expression. The android side-eyed her and winked. Moth swallowed bile. This was Quirk's fault. He took her to the Moon. *He* riled up TOM in the first place by marrying his daughter. In fact, Quirk's dick was the problem, and the fact he was a massive walking dick himself, stumbling around in people's lives, messing things up. A bull-headed prick in Pottery Barn, who left without closing the *fucking* door, so everyone's shit bolted.

She hated him, and she hated TOM, and she hated Callan. Someone was gonna burn for this shit.

XV

22:40, 14 January 2100
The Epitome Suite, Apex Temple Court Hotel,
Fleet Street, London, The United Kingdoms

23 hours remaining

Nick Kirby—a being of the rather disappointing virtual medium passing these days for "the ether"—did what he did extremely quickly. Blistering speed notwithstanding, his first search produced absolutely no results. Or rather it produced one result: nada, null, zip, zero. This complete absence of a positive did at least occur very quickly after Quirk dropped the Epitome Suite's security screen. Surprisingly (although maybe not, since Nick harboured no great depth of warm feeling for Moth), Jennifer's son spent a minute crowing over his mother's ability to elude the systems he'd used in the search.

"She could just be in a room, Nick. Dug in. Not going out," said Quirk.

"Maybe. And maybe she has a friend running errands for her. Some normal people are perfectly happy schlumping around for a day without doing anything."

"Plus, I schooled her in avoiding all web activity: no accessing messages, email, personal pages or accounts," said Anwar. "But maybe you could pick up some signature browsing patterns. I set her up with a cypher screen, and so-called normal people are very unlikely to go an hour offline, never mind two months."

"Jenny not being a virtual person was a thing that drew me to her," said Quirk.

"Don't you fucking dare go all misty-eyed now," said Nick, whose synthesised voice—emanating from the suite's LivewaLL surround sound—had never sounded better. His hijacking the system also enabled Nick to flash up movie scenes to emphasise his emotional state. This latest retort Nick accompanied with a few frames of Dustin

Hoffman and Meryl Streep in *Kramer vs Kramer*, and off they went again, dipping their toes in the kiddie pool of junior vitriol as Nick ranted, and Quirk—in a very level-headed way—tried to shout him down to concentrate on the search. The ticking over of the first hour sobered them up nicely. Even Nick became more subdued as they burned another twenty minutes workshopping ideas.

"You're on record saying she's the love of your life," said Nick, acerbically. *"Christmas card, December 25th, 2092. So, what would your soulmate do in this scenario? Come on,* Dad, *put yourself in her shoes. Assume Mom's just been let loose by the weirdo—no offence, Anwar—who freed her from the sanitorium. She's in a strange city. She still needs to set up supply lines, arrange accommodation. I'm pretty sure she's not sleeping in the sewers, although I'm still scanning inspection drone footage from the last ten weeks. There's a lot of shit in this town."*

Dutifully, and already feeling pushed around by his "associates," Quirk tried to make sense of the jumble of memories from his and Jennifer's trips to London. Not being an android with perfect recall left him raking through happy moments, arguments, memorable meals, museum and gallery visits, and a good many theatrical performances, some in their hotels. Then, there were the post-breakfast knock-down drag-out fights, often followed by lost afternoons in those same hotel rooms.

"Inspiration, Nicky boy. Trumps perspiration every time." In fact, he did not believe that, not every time. And yet still, despite sliding towards hungover as his earlier alcohol buzz apped an Autocab[OS], a notion permitted itself to be dragged from the background out into the glare of his consciousness. "Cockney Sparrow gin. Your Mom was very taken with it," said Quirk, addressing the LivewaLL.

"I doubt she ordered a case to whatever dosshouse she found the day after I dropped her," said Anwar. "Very resourceful she may be, but she showed signs of paranoia during the time we travelled together."

"That's my mom you're disparaging, Ace," said Nick, displaying some old movie footage of an actor waving an accusatory finger at the camera. Cary Grant, Quirk thought. His suit—even in black and white—was a match for the Merrion.

"Xe's right though," he said. "So, we need more than that. Jenny had a foible for a Ritz Cracker, cream cheese, and a Gordal olive to go with that G&T. Hear me out. These things could end up in a thousand epicurean shopping baskets over a year. But what are the chances of it happening in our time window, in our area of interest—"

"Assuming she didn't order from across town to throw off a search," said Nick.

"That might look even more odd."

"Separate orders," said Anwar. "But is she likely to be in a party mood? She knew her father would pursue her and showed a good sense for such tell-tale signs."

"Fair," said Quirk. "But I doubt she'd expect him to put *me* on her trail, and the chance of Daddy knowing his daughter's favourite post-coital canapé is very small."

"I don't think we need that sort of detail," said Anwar, pursing xis lips.

"Okay," said Nick. *"In the time it took you two to puff out your chests I hacked the distillery's system. I have ten stockists of Cockney Sparrow within two kilometres of the Tate Modern. Then I cross-reference the other items in this little recipe to take the taste of Quirk away... Four stockists, but no complete orders in the time window."*

"She might not have ordered at all, given the sour memories you left her with, Quirk," observed Anwar.

"That's true," he replied. "But we have to start somewhere. I'll be sure to call out if I have better idea while we're checking these sources."

"I'll match up items and accounts while you two tie your shoelaces," said Nick in a dry tone, while an image of Wednesday Addams tapping her foot impatiently filled the LivewaLL. The resemblance to Moth was not lost on Quirk, but he bit back a rebuke. In part because he couldn't quite believe that TOM would kill her, but also because he didn't want to rile, or maybe even upset Nick, who seemed on an even keel.

"No single purchase account connecting all four items," Nick announced. *"But, three purchases with the gin and the olives in common."*

Anwar already stood by the door. "This whole line of investigation is based on the poor woman retaining the remotest scintilla of tenderness for her time with you."

"It's what we have to go on. Not convinced?"

"Not even slightly," said Anwar. "But you're the boss."

* * *

11:35, 18 November 2099
The Tate Modern Gallery, London, The United Kingdoms

Xe just left her in front of the gallery. At least the handset had credit. She bought a veggie wrap, made fresh by the vendor, placed in her hand complete with edible antibacterial wrapping. She drank water from the public fountain. She would have to abandon her warm coat because of the cameras. Always cameras, everywhere. Fine if you had nothing to hide, maybe? Maybe she could swap the coat, but where would she go? She could pay for a cheap hotel, but that meant records, even in the cheapest, most down-at-heel hostel. A shelter? Still records: fingerprints, iris scans, voice prints, medical obs. She watched the Tate's entrance for an hour then drifted into a tour group, strolled inside with them, asked someone to hold her coat while she went to "the loo."

Six hours later, she left at the back of a school group, after visiting the washroom to wet her still very short hair and fluffing it frizzy under the blast drier. Then she stole a coat from the same washroom, turning the garment inside out before putting it on. Outside, she split off from the press of thirty-odd children. She made a snap decision to turn and wave, because that's what a departing teacher would do, trusting her disguise, the wadded tissue in her shoes, and her sports bra worn like a lasso over her shoulders to change her movement pattern enough to complete the disguise.

She made direct for shadows, of which there were plenty in the deepening twilight. After passing through the trees around the small park, she joined the riverside walk and followed it under the rail bridge five metres above.

She didn't jump when the woman stepped out, half expected it, in fact, felt relieved that her instinct was right. She didn't want smokes, she said, she wanted shelter. The woman grinned, a tarnished expression. "Ah reckon we can do business."

* * *

21:10, 14 January 2100
22 hours 30 minutes remaining

Nick located the three purchasers of gin and olives in the moment it took Quirk to slip on the Merrion's jacket and walk to the door. Circumventing data protections like tissue plaper, Nick confirmed their identities: One, Charlie Blackford, 11A Brinton Walk, ten minutes' stroll from the Tate Modern—had purchased the Ritz crackers two days after Anwar's departure from London, but not the cream cheese. A week ago, Charlie travelled to Aberdeen to visit family. Quirk bemoaned the fact they could not interview her, but Anwar noted this meant they could access her property more easily to verify if Jennifer was holed up there. Then Nick announced he'd just scanned the house with the thermal imaging capability in the local safety cameras and discovered nobody home. Unless they wanted to interview what readings of estimated body mass and movement pattern analysis suggested were three gerbils and some sort of lizard (housed separately). They all agreed it unlikely Jennifer's tradecraft extended to disguising herself as a ten-centimetre rodent.

Jan Dubinski lived at 104/1 Roupell Street, north of Waterloo East Station, just fifteen minutes' walking southwest from the Tate. Dubinski worked four jobs. By night, he oversaw a delivery drone fleet from his upstairs bedroom, a completely legitimate career in a worldwide franchising business with networks all over Earth, and on the Moon. UN rules regulating autonomous vehicle operation—which included all drones—strictly controlled operational hours, levels of supervision, etcetera. During the day, Dubinski ran tours of the Tate. This detail caught their attention.

Jennifer had always chided Quirk about not asking for help when he needed it. From his perspective, he tried to solve the problem to at least understand the parameters if it became necessary to ask for assistance. Had she gone into the Tate undercover in some form looking for aid? Had she found Dubinski? Nick was unable to track her beyond the point she disappeared into a large, guided tour group at the gallery entrance. Maybe she switched coats, borrowed a hat, a scarf.

Nick could not trace her beyond that crowd, and it seemed the kid struggled with his own reaction, proud of his mother, but frustrated at his own abilities being stymied with the clock ticking. Was that all it was?

They could have remained in the comfortable suite, contemplated their tactical options before venturing out into the numbing minus ten-degree City of London evening, but they just didn't have time. They had to be on hand to react to whatever kind of trail they might hit with this rather fanciful and optimistic shot in the dark.

Quirk and Anwar walked down Bouverie Street towards Victrola Embankment and the river, overcoats hunched tight, hands in pockets pulled close at the front. Both coats—kindly issued by the hotel—possessed heating elements which activated the instant they stepped out onto Fleet Street. Only a few minutes in, Anwar sighed out a big plume of warm, rapidly condensing breath, and tapped xis ear. Quirk popped his earpiece in to hear the final part of Nick's report.

The third purchaser of Cockney Sparrow gin and Gordal olives was Lucy Pinder of 170g Lockwood Square. From Nick's data she appeared very partial to the clear stuff, going through four bottles a week, plus a quart of vodka, in her compact and bijou community-owned flat to the west of Southwark Park. Nick clarified that camera footage, public transport data, and handset tracking within the postcode indicated Ms. Pinder's evening activities centred around her side-line as a semi-professional cocktail party organiser. Semi-pro in the sense that she took fees in, according to Nick's perusal of her bank records, but did not pay out in tax.

"That's about to change," said his son in Quirk's increasingly insensate ear. *"HMRC cyber force is onto her. She'll be wishing she'd stumped up and declared her hobby when they take the tax and a fine directly from her bank account."*

"Wow," said Quirk. The NARS seemed almost benign by comparison.

They turned left and walked east along the Embankment to Blackfriars Bridge. Spotlights cast foggy pearlescence at the looming buildings around them. In the near distance, The Shard pierced the sky, aglow with a light behind each scintillating panel of plass. That tower, which seemed to take its architectural inspiration from Barad-dûr, was itself dwarfed by its neighbours The Splinter and—latest of London's nickname-attracting megatowers—The Iceberg. The running joke had it that the Mayor, on seeing the finished article, declared, "But it doesn't look anything *like* a lettuce!"

"We're going to the Tate, right?" Anwar asked.

"It seems the obvious thing to do. Try to pick up a trail there. If Dubinski's off shift, we can ask them about his activities, walk over to his place and quiz him direct."

"Sure, and please note I have no attachment to the girl, to Moth, but I just thought you might want to jog, or something. Twenty-two hours plus change isn't long to find one person in a city of fourteen million, even if they aren't hiding from you. And remember, we have competition.

"She mentioned you, in the few days we were together."

Quirk almost stopped walking, almost blurted out that he didn't want to know, but of course he did. He'd always thought he'd see Jennifer again, but never contemplated the circumstances in which he would. At TOM's graveside, perhaps. They could sell tickets for *that* occasion, maybe book out some coach parking. Yet Simister continued to confound the Grim Reaper, no doubt thanks to a diet of tea made from polar bear tears, a steady stream of organ donations by vegan virgins and, once a month, having his blood strained through the kidneys of the newest saint elevated from the Little Sister of the Ascension in Beverly Hills.

"So, what did she say?"

Anwar chuckled, "Oh, Quirk, you're so shallow. I can't believe I wanted to kill you for so long, what a great loss to the world of light entertainment."

"Jennifer's words?"

"Very keen to know what had happened to her son, and to hear your account of it. I didn't think it was my place to comment. I don't know the details, just the outcome."

Quirk kept walking, chewed over a few retorts, but said nothing. They walked over Blackfriars Bridge, following the string of high-mounted pearlescent streetlights south. Nick would be watching them—perhaps even watching out for them— through whatever sensors, lenses and detectors those innocuous-looking lanterns possessed.

On the south bank, they passed beneath sad, leafless trees, stepped down hard stone stairs to a place where the darkness, rather than being banished by streetlighting, seemed just to step back, waiting in the shadows for technology to fail. They pressed on through the half dark, following the walkway under the bridge, passed a couple of tourists posing for their selfie drone, the river churning brown, fast and deep on the other side of the stone wall. Quirk tried to decide what he would say to Jennifer when they found her. If they found her, in time, then pondered the words he would use if he had to face Giulia di Fantano to explain who had murdered her niece and why.

What a bloody mess. The rationale for this search was incredibly tenuous. What reasonable basis did he have to presume he could accurately assess how Jennifer would behave after what he'd done, how he'd treated her?

A figure stepped from the darkness ahead to be silhouetted on the bright rectangle where the walkway emerged from under the bridge. Quirk's eyes adjusted a little too late to avoid the jacketed figure pressing into him, wrapping an arm around his waist.

Where the hell is Anwar?

"Hi, big boy. You fancy a draw?"

Her voice had the low rasp of a sack of gravel being dragged over plascrete, and yet the body pressing against him felt hard, youthful, and coiled with nervous energy.

"What are you selling?"

The head leaning on his shoulder, the mouth that for seconds had pressed against his neck, disappeared. Something pushed Quirk backwards, into the wall. Anwar shoved the miscreant hard, out into the streetlight glare, shoved her again as the young woman staggered, pressed her against the half-height wall beyond which the river churned. Quirk saw a flash of some mist-shrouded Holmesian murder mystery, a body washed up on Bankside Beach.

"Beatrix, no!"

The assassin hefted the woman up to sit on top of the wall, like xe planned to pitch her over. Something shiny flashed, catching the streetlight beam. Anwar twisted her wrist. A high voice squealed. Real metal skittered on the paving. Quirk pushed off the wall.

"Wait!"

He had no clue what made him think it could be Jennifer, but by Anwar's own accounts of what she'd both undertaken and gone through in the last few weeks to disguise and to hide herself... But no. Not Jennifer.

He pushed Anwar away from the woman who had come at him, not to attack but in proposition, and hauled her down to the pavement as figures approaching along the riverside walk melted away, back where they'd come from.

"Beatrix, chill out. This could be a start." Then, to the girl he said, "We're cool. My friend's just jumpy. We're not cops. Maybe we're buying what you're selling?" It had to be worth burning five minutes on, right, maybe ten? Because Jenny would be deep under the surface by now, over two months after Anwar dropped her here. Either under the surface or long gone, but getting away required resources, and exposure. And where would she get away to? Jennifer would be looking ahead, planning, preparing, but for what? Two months. Even off-grid you could easily get from the centre of London to anywhere in the United Kingdoms in that time. Why would Jenny still be here, unless...she was prevented from leaving.

The girl's struggling brought him out of his brief reverie. If this was her patch, she might have seen something, know where to look.

Anwar leant on the wall, watching them, hand in the pocket of xis overcoat, no doubt ready to kill the girl and throw her in the river, because that was what Anwar did.

Quirk took the girl by the arm, lead her away from Anwar, into the shadow of the bridge that loomed over them. He just needed to be left alone for a few moments. A good point that, something he could influence. Quirk tapped his earpiece.

"Nick, we need a little privacy."

"*Anything for you, Pops. I'll nix the cameras, pour sludge on the Met Police AI, but that will only buy you ten minutes. Use them wisely.*"

Wisely, for the love of—

"What are you selling?" he asked the girl.

He got a look at her now. Shorter than him, wrapped up in a dull green coat with a fur-lined hood pulled up tight so only her small mouth and once-busted nose peeked out. Not Jennifer, not without surgery. Not even the best astringents provided a level of morphing that would fool pseudo-AI body recognition for very long. Was that how he knew Jenny remained in the City of London, because almost no one could elude the state's technology? Not unless they stopped moving, buried themselves deep.

"Smokes."

He'd almost forgotten his question. "Tobacco?"

"'Course, what else? You want a pack? A carton?" Her grey eyes lit up.

"Home-grown or vintage?" He had no truck with it himself, but he'd heard some gangs had access to stores of classics like Marlboro, Silk Cut, Benson & Hedges, Lucky Strikes.

"Both. If you've got yuan, I can even get you Camels. But if it's dollars or pounds, it'll be home-grown. It's not bad though. Smoke 'em mahself. We'll go roun' behind the Tate an' 'ave a T-puff. Something else, if ya like. Ah'd make time for a big strong fella like you." Now he knew she was playing him. She ran a hand up inside his coat, across the Merrion's lapel to his shoulder.

"Careful," said Anwar. But Quirk believed she was intent on making a sale and wouldn't try to rob him with his associate breathing down her neck.

"Time's short," said Nick. *"They're on their way. I think they call them rozzers around here. I don't know how you feel about truncheons, Dad, but you'd better make your mind up real soon."*

Could smugglers have provided the answer to Jennifer's problem? She easily could have had this encounter two months ago, looking for a safe route away from the Tate, might have escaped the city by the same route they brought contraband in.

"Who's your source?" he asked.

The girl burst out laughing. "Yor kiddin', right? Fack, just frow me in the river, maybe ah can swim to Calais. Who's mah source? You want some or not?"

Time ticked away, and this girl, perhaps their best chance of finding a possible lead to a not completely dead end, was about to give him up as a bad job. The...rozzers were on their way.

"A hundred Camels, and I want to see them coming out of the block, break the paper myself."

"Five hundred a pack."

"Dollars?"

"Pfft. Yuan."

"Okay. Lead the way."

"Just you."

Quirk's turn to laugh. "My lookout says it'll get filthy around here very soon. We can hang around, you can introduce me to them. I bet they know your name already."

"Okay, okay. Bloody tourists. C'mon then. Follow this." She bumped his hip with hers then made off at a fair clip. Anwar sprang after her, grabbed her elbow and let her pull xim along. Quirk followed.

* * *

10:23, 25 November 2099
168 St Thomas Street, London, The United Kingdoms

Meeting Kira under the bridge had soon become an adventure for Jennifer, if a rather stressful one. In one week, they had moved three times. The young woman was sleeping in an empty flat on the amusingly—but hopefully not prophetically—named Clink Street. Jennifer spent only one night there before Kira moved them to another vacant property on St Thomas Street, near Borough Market. The girl told her nearly thirty percent of residential space in London was empty, retained as investment by foreign owners. The upside for the likes of Kira and many other gang runners was the ability to break in, scan for security devices, disable them and spend two or three nights before the relevant security firm—whose local watchpersons had been paid off—turned up to chase them off. The tacit ground rules of the game involved "visitors" leaving the properties spotless in return for a one-hour warning of the heavies descending.

Kira left early that morning. Jennifer—still in a too-big T-shirt that passed for nightwear—peeked down past the edge of the heavy brocade curtain at the mid-morning traffic across which fell the shadow of The Shard. Regardless of where they ended up next, she knew she couldn't run forever. It was coming time to act, but how?

* * *

00:00, 15 January 2100
Ewer Street, London, The United Kingdoms

21 hours 40 minutes remaining

"Dad! Dad! Wake up!"

"What?"

"Quirk."

Anwar. Shaking his shoulder. He remembered streets becoming narrower and darker, the lighting more...sympathetic, atmospheric. Less useful for seeing where you were going. A much narrower street, hoarded down both sides, some kind of plastec sheeting wafting, pinned to a structure above to protect it, or protect pedestrians from whatever went on behind the sheeting, above their heads as they walked beneath—

He remembered a heavy rumbling, like the thunder a hundred metal skips might make if you tipped them off a roof together. A train, passing overhead as they started through the hoarded tunnel, Anwar ahead with the girl. Then the sheeting had fallen, billowed down around him, behind him, and a weight hit him across the shoulders. That was it, the source of his pain. Right after being borne down to the road surface in the too-narrow, too-low tunnel, someone had tasered him.

He groaned, pushed up onto his knees.

"Quirk, hurry up."

"You hurry up." Snapping at Anwar wouldn't help. "The girl?"

"Gone. Didn't trust you I guess, took us the low road instead of the high road. Nick's searching for her. Smugglers could be a good lead, but now we need to scram."

"Time."

"Twelve ten AM local. Twenty-one hours thirty minutes on your timer."

Knees wet through, hands gritty, bleeding. He'd gone down like a sack of potatoes after another sack of spuds landed on it. At least his earpiece remained and his handset functioned. So, not a robbery. But their lead, if lead she had been, was gone. Wonderful. Anwar helped him up. Quirk's head swam, unsure where his legs were.

Quirk saw the body then, wearing light brown overalls already smeared with grease or paint or some other chemical before he'd ended face down in a long puddle scummed with road grime. The underpass lights had gone out at some point. Only light borrowed from the streets flanking the tunnel lit the figure, the body.

"Argh!" Bizarre how giving utterance to frustration helped. The translation of mental pressure into the physical release. Was there science to it? Undoubtedly, but really, he needed to sober up, *now!*

"Quirk," Anwar grunted, stopping their progress. Up ahead, a new set of silhouettes against the light beyond the tunnel. Quirk's fuzzy vision saw three figures approaching, all armed, clearly not cops from their rag-tag appearance. Anwar turned xis head. "Two more behind," xe mumbled.

"Wot you doin' dickin' arand on moi patch, you fackin' plonkers?" The one in the middle advanced as the other two ahead levelled their handguns. "You've plugged wan o' moi boys, but that just means ah get to fack you up moiself!"

Quirk fell sideways as Anwar pushed him away and laserfire lit up the darkened tunnel. Hitting the deck, Quirk rolled, feeling flashes of heat, crackling loud in his ear as water vaporised violently. His rolling stopped when he hit the wall. He managed to twist up to his knees, get a brief glimpse of laser flash across his vision, see two bodies on the deck ahead before the yelling leader of the assault hit him full on and bowled him over. Quirk grabbed for the man's wrists, presuming him armed, got hold of one as a taser crackled angrily in front of his face.

The device strained forwards, Quirk losing the battle of strength.

"Ah'll fackin' shock yoo, yoo facker!" The man's gleeful rictus moved closer, but Quirk kept the weapon at bay, for now, his arm aching, weakening, strength failing.

"I've just had one of my five-a-day, actually."

Quirk heaved upwards, butting the man in the face, eliciting a howl as his attacker toppled backwards.

Anwar stood in the middle of the tunnel in which five bodies now lay. Xe shot the gang's leader as he clutched his bleeding nose, making it a round half dozen.

Quirk sagged against the tunnel's rough brick wall, by no means recovered from his tasing.

Anwar came to him, supported him with an arm around his waist, but Quirk really just wanted to close his eyes.

"Nick says the police are closing off streets. You're in no state to outrun them. One of us has to stay on the outside. Nick and I will keep looking for Jennifer. Get any info you can from the cops, but get out of there as quickly as you can. Okay?"

Quirk nodded ascent and Anwar released him to slump against the wall. The assassin had already melted away before Quirk closed his eyes.

XVI

10:20, 15 January 2100
Milano, Italy, Euro Bloc Sud

Sitting in an Autocab[OS] with S-17834, Moth could barely restrain the scream bubbling in her throat. Completing the task The Old Man had forced on her would be easy enough. Milan to New York, she could do that with a five-hour flight and an hour either end for all the crap that made getting through an airport feel like fucking admin Jenga. But the threat to Giulia ripped her up inside, clawed at her guts so she had to grip the door handle to keep from punching the front seat headrest, repeatedly.

Her android—it was hard to remember Bea, even though her personality had always been stuck in standard syRen® neutral—sat beside her, but now she felt afraid of...it. She'd seen enough in the cold piazza, the unandroid gestures that could only be human, and not just any human, the psychotic Callan, the murdering mandroid!

She gripped the handle hard, trying to stop her hand shaking. She wanted to stop the cab, burst out and run a million miles away, but she couldn't. She had to be brave, to woman up, and the first thing she *must* do was to speak to Callan. She couldn't do it on the piazza with Giulia standing there, at risk for her life. At least she'd managed to put a couple of kilometres between Callan/Bea and Giulia, by going back to the hotel and packing. She'd hated lying to Giulia, but telling her the call had been from Quirk, and that he needed her in New York for a case had totally worked. Still, she felt dirty about it. It wasn't like she'd never lied to Giulia, and this time it was for her protection. Still, her aunt—away from the convent—was even more warm and loving than ever. They both had big holes in their lives, and Moth found Giulia was the only person she was willing to let in, properly let in. Unlike people who used her, lied to her, held themselves back and didn't speak the truth. *Fuckers.* She trusted Giulia and would do anything to protect her. Apparently, that included helping a killer android get to NY where a living bomb walked around the UN trying not to go off in everyone's faces.

All the time she'd been packing, throwing stuff around, cramming clothes and toiletries in a holdall, that fuzking scream pounded in her chest, clogged her throat so she had to swallow every minute, but she refused to let it out, to let Callan see her fear. He... She... It, sat in the corner and watched her so that her skin crawled. What was the evil, twisted, degenerate bastard thinking? She wanted to change her clothes for travelling, but she absa-fucking-lutely refused even to go into the toilet and change with him in her space, probably thinking about what she was doing. UCK!

She'd got through that rancid experience, but now she had to speak to it, because she refused to do it on the mofo plane, with people around. She had to be certain. *Just do it. He's not going to kill you before you've done the task and you've got a whole flight to figure out what the frisbee-flicking fuck you're going to do about this shit.* Because she'd be damned if she'd let TOM get away with whatever crap he'd started on Mars. They hit the E62, speeding northwest away from the city. A long, straight road, not that the cab had a driver to be distracted. She side-eyed the droid that, technically, still belonged to her, and would do again, she hoped, when Callan slunk off somewhere else, or died.

"I don't *want* to talk to you. I *want* to cut off your head with an axe and toss it into Mount Etna, but we need to get things straight." She steeled herself and looked at the android temporarily *not* known as Bea.

It looked straight at her. "Go ahead, cutie pie."

He said it in Bea's voice, but the sleazy diction was pure Callan, ex-terraformer, Androicon patient and botched experiment, failed workers' rights crusader, mass murderer.

"When you talk to me—and I cannot fucking believe I'm saying this—can you synthesise your own voice? I want to be able to hate you properly."

"Sure can, little lady." This time, the words that came from Bea's soft syRen® features, her silky pink lips, were gruff, growling, coarse in spirit and intent. "I'm gonna enjoy riding with you on this little trip."

The scream clawed at her throat. Her skin crawled, but maybe digging away, trying to concentrate on doing some detection might distract her from the slimy thoughts she imagined would be leaching through Callan's...mind.

"So, we get met at LaGuardia and I'm done, right?" Playing into the prejudices of arch misogynists like Callan made it easy to get them spouting. She'd have batted her lashes if she didn't think he'd take it as a sign. Fuckwit would have no problem believing she'd forgotten the terms TOM set out.

"Yah, no, that's not it. I tell you when you're done, Chickee-poo, an' you ain't even started. We got lots of fun ahead, you an' me." The android turned to look at the road ahead. "You can't imagine some of things we'll get up to in the Big Apple. But just remember it's all to keep Aunty J breathing, right?"

"Giulia's with a 'G,' dick-breath."

"Keep talkin' dirty to me, Doll. I love it."

The android's hand moved from its knee onto the seat and Moth almost jumped out the window. "Ah!" Once the exclamation came out, she couldn't hold in the scream building in her since the piazza. The rush of anger and fear ripped out of her like a hurricane, and she fairly bellowed into the cab's six-passenger compartment. She let all her emotion go, yelling till her throat rasped raw. So violent was the scream the droid actually recoiled. Maybe the bastard thought some rabid *thing* would burst from her, a tentacled creature to rip the machine apart. The jangling of her nerves, and howling of her body, sure made her feel she was a radioactive bite away from a superpower. Was this what Nick felt like when TOM's scientists experimented on him, twisted him into a beast for corporate gain? *How's that working out for ya, Joshua Simpleton?*

She gasped, slumped back in the seat. The seatbelt had tensed, captured her forward and upward movement and restrained her. It relaxed to a kinder level of tension.

"What the fuck was that?" said Callan.

"That was Friday morning, bitch. Get used to it."

Mercifully, once at the airport and in public places again, Callan kept quiet. They filed through all the usual shit-boring procedures. Moth half-hoped the body scanners at the second security station would trip up the android interloper, but Bea/Callan sailed through, and they boarded the plane.

With access to Rigel's funds, she'd booked a First-Class compartment each, tried to convince Callan he'd be more comfortable, but he wasn't buying it. She tried to convince him it wasn't like she could climb out the window at fifty thousand feet, but he wouldn't buy that either, insisted they get one of the two-person compartments.

Moth spent a shit-tonne of kilometres hoping the android would need to charge. Depending on activity levels in a given day they usually charged at least once, typically in the small hours when their human slept. No fucking way she could close her eyes with that perv in the compartment with her, so she started ordering strong coffees and kept them coming every twenty minutes. Before too long she badly needed to pee.

"I'll come help you," said Callan/Bea, straight-faced.

"Fuck you will. I can't think what pervy thoughts you're tarnishing my droid's circuits with, but they stay the fuck here. Maybe consider not risking TOM's operation with your lousy behaviour."

"Okay, *Mom*. Go wet the floor somewhere else."

She stole a nap in the airplane toilet, surprisingly comfortable since Boeing had padded the walls in the new solar 858s. Callan/Bea came looking for her after twenty minutes, but he…it, couldn't get away with any more than tapping the door without attracting attention from flight crew droids. She managed to stay in there for an hour before one of the crew syRen® called in to enquire if she was in distress. She almost told it everything, but thought of Giulia, and how sure she was TOM could reach her.

So, they spent a very uncomfortable transatlantic flight in a game of tag that only ended when Bea's eyes began flashing gently, announcing to her…it…Callan that standby charging was needed like now. Moth viewed the purple peepers as Bea's. She needed something to hold on to, keep her sane at this disturbing low point in her life.

"Hah, you're out of juice, ya big, greasy data dump."

She took a little satisfaction from Callan's grumpy noise in reply. Finally, the droid went into standby charging.

After testing that Callan/Bea was "under," Moth set the movement alarm on her Lambo, placed it against the droid's foot, curled up on her tilted-back chair and slept.

* * *

13:05, 15 January 2100
LaGuardia Spaceport, New York, NY, NAF

This trip was such an enormous travel turd. She'd argued with Callan (very quietly, so as not to confuse travellers milling around in the LaGuardia baggage reclaim) to have the ignorant fuck carry her bag. She finally convinced him it would look suspiciously weird for her to carry the bag when her droid had hands in pockets.

They exited into the crowded arrivals area under the spaceport terminal's towering, totally transparent roof, Moth using her bored teenager routine to disguise her search for TOM's local stooge. When the henchman stepped forward it took real effort not to flinch. Among the gushing families, sombre relatives, business-like associates, friendly friends and stone-faced chauffeurs, appeared the man who'd attacked Shuun Suudi on the *Gargantua Pleiades*, smack in the middle of what became the aborted Brother Leigh Love gig, while assassins that turned out not to be assassins interrupted Sec-Tech's speech with what turned out not to be an assassination attempt but the planting of a bomb intended to go off 150 million kilometres away in New York, or rather not to go off, but to ensure Joshua Simister got his way, again.

The guy looked, dressed, walked and sounded unremarkable. Moth would have said being so unremarkable made him remarkable but, remarkably, it didn't. The guy blended with the crowd like a smear blends into a sidewalk.

"What do they call you, Jason Boredom?"

Moth's quip bounced off the guy's hard, extremely boring exterior. He looked at Callan/Bea and the android blinked once, twice, three times, alternating eyes.

"Okay, Part One completed. Let's go."

This chunk of muscle did the best impression of an android Moth could recall, including the attentiveness his movements not so much gave away, as inhabited. She only noticed it when up close. Quirk had the same air of almost always being "on." Her thoughts drifted to her former boss. She hadn't taken the time to resign from The Quirk Agency. She should get round to doing that. Maybe after she learned what happened next here. She still hated Quirk though. Lying fucker.

"So, what do I call you?" *Keep fishing for data, Moth.*

The operative looked down at her from six-foot-fucker and smiled thinly, and then she knew why he spent most of his time with no facial expression. That lopsided grimace would scare off his mother. He probably only got let out on Hallowe'en.

"Sure, call me Jason. It'll do."

"Don't forget to call me Bea, Honey-bunny," said Callan, using Bea's voice.

"We're going into the city, to our hotel. There's groundwork being done by another team before we go in."

Moth knew better than to ask anything specific in such a public place, even though the crowds had thinned a bunch. The thought of being in a hotel with these bozos icked her out, but at least she'd have a chance to find out more. Maybe she could contact Nick. Part of her wondered why he hadn't stayed in touch. Maybe because he was helping out Quirk. Whatever, she didn't care about that. Maybe Callan's cyber powers were greater than Nick's, had the Kirby kid running scared. That would be just fuzking great, because she couldn't yet see a way to leverage herself out of this situation that didn't involve Giulia catching the same train as Mama and Papa. *Great.*

They took an Autocab^OS from LaGuardia to the Bryant Park Hotel on West 40th Street. Jason led the way, securing two rooms despite her calmly expressed non-violent protests about sharing with Callan/Bea. She had to keep these fuckers unbalanced, pick away at them as best she could, set them up to get a drop on them, but... Was there any point? She couldn't remove the threat to Giulia. Damn but blackmail worked. Probably why it was still so popular.

They assembled in Jason's room and Moth started in on him immediately.

"Hey, Shitfur, when does the clock stop ticking? I've delivered your boy here, as instructed upon threat of death to my aunty. You're going to tell me what comes next in your own time, I guess, but if we're sitting around for days holding our dicks, there's no way TOM pops my Aunt Giulia, right?"

Jason stood and stared at her as she ranted, holding up against the teenage BS much better than she'd hoped. He answered her question without protest. "Yeah, the clock stopped on that, but you're still on the hook. The Sword of Damocles is still hanging over Giulia di Fantano. So, behave yourself."

Keep pushing. "So when do I get out from under? When does Giulia? Because if you're gonna keep playing that card it's gonna wear out. Every threat gets tired if you hear it often enough." Shit, that sounded like a Quirkism.

"That's over my head, but listen." He took a step closer, met her gaze with some intensity. "I've no interest in your aunt getting hurt. I've got a job to do, and I'll deal square with you if you're not a dick." He looked at his handset. "I'm expecting a call in about three hours, but we could be sitting around for days."

Inside, Moth smiled. That gave her time to uncover their plan.

XVII

02:00, 15 January 2100
Unknown Address, London, The United Kingdoms

19 hours 40 minutes remaining

Quirk had lost count of the number of interrogation rooms he'd inhabited over the years. He began constructing some glib repartee for the benefit of the arresting (was he under arrest?) officer based on the décor to be found in such rooms in Lunaville; Creston, BC; Yellowknife, NT; and Berlin; and how well London compared. He was trying very hard to pinpoint the shade of off-white on these present four walls when the door opened and a woman walked in, closing the door behind her.

"Mr. Kirby, my name is Inspector Bethany Moss. You are not under arrest at this time, this conversation is informal. No recording is being made. You were however found within twenty metres of six dead bodies on Ewer Street. Please bear in mind during this informal conversation that I'm very anxious indeed to arrest *someone* as soon as I possibly can, to demonstrate to my gaffer that I continue to be the most effective investigating officer in this nick. Does that all sound reasonable to you?"

It did. Quirk felt his brow furrow under the strain of the realisation that this police officer might be a reasonable person. Rather prim perhaps, dark suit well cared for, but not stylish, although it set off her russet, shoulder-length hair—tied back for the purposes of this friendly conversation—rather well. This might be tricky. He tried a soft opening. First, a smile: *Getting to Know You, Getting to Know All About You, Act 1.* "I appreciate the clarification of my status, Inspector."

"Your devices have been removed. Standard Triple S procedure. Oh, sorry, you're American. Stop, search and scan."

"I don't do much triple S-ing myself."

"But you are a private detective?"

"I prefer investigator, but yes. May I ask the time?"

"You may." She smirked at her slight witticism. "The time is two ten AM. Do you have somewhere to be?" she asked, innocently.

Nineteen point five hours left. Plenty of time, right? If they had a solid lead. He couldn't tell her what he was up to, of course. Not all of it, but remaining close to the truth was the easiest way to sell a lie. *No, not a lie, an excuse.*

"Nowhere I know of, but it's past my bedtime, I was recently attacked by a gang, and I have a headache. Tomorrow's a big day. I plan to meet my ex-wife."

Moss nodded. "Fair enough. I'll try not to keep you long. Let's just polish off a few questions, and I'm sure we can get you back to...?"

"The Apex Temple Court."

"The Apex. So, firstly, do you know any of the dead people?"

Careful, Quirk. This is not word association. Do not say the first thing that comes into your head. "I don't think so. Who were they?"

"The leader was Ronald Patrick Morgan, criminal of longstanding on my patch."

"Not spending much time on your patch, Inspector, no, I don't know him."

"So, you weren't meeting him for the purposes of conducting a little free trade?"

"No."

"Funny thing is, the Public Safety Cameras on Ewer Street seem to have glitched at the very time you entered the area. A little odd, don't you think?"

He shrugged. "How often do they glitch normally?"

"It has been known. Just coincidence then. Still, it does significantly hamper our investigation. Tell me what you recall. And please don't leave anything out."

Hah! "It started with an evening stroll along the Thames. I enjoy the bracing London air. I fancied seeing the Tate Modern—the building that is—without the crowds, so I swung down that way. A short walk from the hotel."

"A wider search of the network shows you walking with someone. I asked you nicely not to hold anything back, Mr. Kirby. Perhaps it would be easier if I simply detain you for questioning. Not long, just twenty-four hours."

Quirk sat very still for a moment, watching Moss watching him. "Ah, yes, I bumped into someone walking the same route. Seemed like a pleasant person, you know? We walked a few metres together."

"You paused quite a long time under Blackfriars Bridge."

"Just taking in the scene, Inspector. Churning river, historical bridges." *This will take ages, and she's going to wear me down with her damn reasonableness. And I'm showing signs of agitation because I DON'T HAVE TIME FOR THIS!* But could he turn it around? He'd followed the girl because of the notion that a smuggler of tobacco might also smuggle people, or know someone who knew someone. The seller had been a way into the underground, that layer of society knowingly doing varying degrees of wrong, and doing their best to avoid attention while doing it. He'd hoped to determine if the girl had been in the right place at the right time to help Jennifer. No hope of that now that her associates—he presumed—were dead, but at least he had a name for Nick. Things might actually be going swimmingly. And for once, he had not done anything even slightly wrong, really. So, if he couldn't get back on the street right away, maybe he could do some good work here, as Anwar suggested. The police were of course a point of contact with the underworld.

"Okay, I was approached under Blackfriars Bridge. I presume it's a camera blind spot or you wouldn't be trying to fish that out of me." Moss just stared at him. Not a hard stare, but probing, keeping him on the hook. "She tried to sell me smokes."

"And you went with her. Were you going to buy smokes?"

Moss's lip curled a fraction. She brushed a strand of hair off her forehead. *Hmm.* An emotional response? Did T-puff dealing resonate with the inspector on a personal level? A nerve to press on, maybe.

"It's a filthy habit, is it not, Inspector?"

"It's a crime. Prohibition of Tobacco Production, Sale & Use Act, 2041."

"Was it someone close to you, Inspector? Friend, relative?" Her small mouth pursed slightly. "I know, I know, you're asking the questions, but I feel the direction of the conversation's troubling you. Forget I asked." *But really, please don't, please let your guard down, Inspector. And meanwhile, I'll open up to you, because TOM may have embargoed Suudi as a discussion point, but he said nothing about Jenny, did he? Damn this fuzzy head.* "I'm looking for someone. They're off-grid. I went with the seller—a young woman, maybe one-seventy centimetres, slight, dark hair, could have been dyed—because I thought she might point me in the right direction. She led me into the hoarded-up tunnel under the railway. Then they jumped me." Had the gang made them for soft tourists, limp businessmen, cops? Whatever the case, Anwar had saved both their lives. Maybe xe and Nick would find Jennifer then swing past the police station and pick him up. That would be nice. Although the cops would trace footage of Anwar back to the hotel, surely.

"Could I just check my handset? If I'm not under arrest..."

"You're helping with my inquiries, and I use the word 'helping' advisedly. You say you're in a hurry? So, hurry. Who are you looking for?"

Quirk really wished that women in authority didn't kickstart his libido.

"I'm afraid I can't tell you that."

Inspector Bethany Moss started to laugh. She brought a hand up to her face. Cheeks previously pale began to colour. Her eyes took on a sparkle. "Client confidentiality, really? You know we don't do that here in the UK? Not since 2029 and the passage of the Policing and Public Safety Act, the 'Greater Good' law as we call it. So, again, who are you looking for? And please bear in mind failure to answer will win you twenty-four hours in a holding cell for further questioning."

Including probably nineteen hours now that he didn't have to spare, because even if he told Moss everything, and the cops helped find Jenny, they would not allow him to take her away. He tried not to imagine being locked in a cell, helpless, as the last few hours of Moth's life ticked away. He suspected Moss of being a tough cookie, the whole politeness thing a smokescreen hiding a block of granite, and sure enough he'd just run full square into it. Could he push the envelope of what TOM might accept as operational necessity? He seemed to have run out of other options already.

"Okay, let me call my assistant, and I'll tell you who I'm looking for." Moss did not reply, just watched him. "And call me Quirk."

She tilted her head then snorted gently. "Oh, your initials. Very droll."

"That word is the furthest thing from onomatopoeia," he said, then dished out his best *Getting to Know You, Getting to Know All About You, Act 2* smile. "Deal?"

"Your assistant the gunman and mass killer?"

"If so, it was self-defence."

Moss's expression suggested she was about ready to rip him a new piehole, or possibly another, more intimate variety of hole. He imagined the dialogue rumbling around in her head, like "I don't do deals with the likes of you," or "You just won a trip to the pokey, and you'll still have to spill the beans tomorrow, dick." Instead, she nodded then spoke a message, since *of course* a live listening system monitored their conversation so a handful of burly officers could descend on the room to pummel him to a pulp in the event that he got out of line with their inspector.

Instead, an android in law enforcement dark blue entered the room carrying Quirk's tech in a shielded jiffy bag. At Moss's instruction, the syRen® gave Quirk the bag. He thumbed into his handset, inserted the earpiece, tried not to make an icky face as the device wriggled into place. *Almost three AM.* Could TOM even get at Moth? She must be in the heart of the Rigel clan now. She'd be protected, right? While The Old Man did bluff, he did not—in Quirk's experience—lie. It might be TOM's only positive quality. He snorted at the notion of Joshua Simister's soul being redeemed.

"Make your call," said Moss.

"How do I know it's private?"

"It won't be. The fact you're willing to make this call in front of me suggests you think your tech is better than my tech. Well, let's see, shall we? You're supposed to be a clever chap: I have read your file. So, I will sit here and observe while you talk to an associate who I think may have killed Ronald Morgan and five of his gang, and put a spanner in an operation I've been running for nine months, stirring up a *bloody hornet's nest!*" She banged the table—demonstrative for this unprepossessing woman whose superpower seemed to be calm reserve. "Just know that if I'm not happy, you go from here to a cell. Your time just ran out."

A solid, cold pain settled in Quirk's chest. He made the call.

"You're secure for now," said Nick. *"But cop droids are battering the door."*

"Talk," said Anwar.

"Listen carefully, I have very little time," said Quirk. Moss held up one hand, her five digits splayed, then curled her thumb inwards. "I'm with the police. They know about our recent...encounters. They're running an operation on the T-puff dealers." He looked Moss in the eye. "I have to give them something, so, I'm revealing we were tailing Beatrix Potter, who they've made for the killer."

"Fair enough, I'm comfortable with my ability to evade the police. What now? You're the boss, remember?"

"I think my only way out is to tell them we're searching for our missing associate, Francis Ansco, and that we fear for her safety." Not a complex anagram of the city where Jennifer had been incarcerated, but he had to do everything and anything he could to get out of here, now.

"Nick and I will keep looking. Your idea of following the smuggler girl was a good one, but there are cop droids all over the railway tunnel now, and if we killed all smugglers, difficult to question them about Jennifer. Progress will be harder now."

"I'm going to tell the police all I can about Francis. Maybe they'll help us. I'll tell them the little data we have on this vicious killer Beatrix Potter, too, before they get out of the country with what they came for. I hope to see you soon."

Quirk hung up the call. From the look on Moss's face Nick had outmatched the Metropolitan Police's tech department. That made him smile. Fatherly pride? Perhaps.

"Right then, Mr. Kirby," said the inspector. "Since I got nothing from that, and you've told me roughly the same with your sub-Daily Mail crossword anagrams, you are heading for my holding cell for a day to loosen your tongue."

"But I plan to tell you why I'm here. Inspector, time is a critical fact—"

"And you"—she stood, placed her hands carefully on the tabletop, and leaned forward—"will now have plenty of it to think about what you've done."

XVIII

17:48, 8 December 2099
15/A Disney Place, London, The United Kingdoms

That London possessed a Disney Place rather tickled Jennifer, and so she had chosen that empty flat of the two Kira offered for their next bolt hole. They had used so many in the five weeks since Mx. Potter abandoned her that she'd passed through the stage where it messed with her mind, to a sort of numbness.

Bizarrely, the lane beyond the playground, visible through the one-way coated window, rejoiced under the name Little Dorrit Court. She used the last of her phone credit to purchase that volume, read it in the last three days. Reading, yoga, eating, sleeping. Sitting shoulder to shoulder with Kira on whatever sofa came with their latest borrowed apartment watching drama, adventure, comedy, and thrillers on Kira's six-ways-to-Sunday shielded laptop. These were the things she did now. These and thinking about Nick, and Quirk, and her father. She tried to avoid the latter. It gave rise to anger. At her own mistreatment, yes, what she recognised now as years of domineering mental torture, but the emotion flowed so strongly through her body she felt there must be another reason. She didn't know it yet, but already she feared it.

She counted Kira as her friend now, having come to like her boisterous bonhomie, her husky voice (although she did not smoke anymore). Jennifer looked forward to her return to their flat in the early morning, even helped her sort product packs, check inventory deliveries for something to do. It hardly made her Patty Hearst. They moved and moved again, but Kira was her constant.

One evening, as the credits rolled on *The Long Good Friday*, Kira leaned in and kissed her. Jennifer was shocked for half a second before she kissed Kira back, because she could not remember the last time someone kissed her and she liked it, and fuck the world, because just feeling *something* was delicious and delightful. So, she let all the rotten baggage of her life go for one minute (okay, an hour) and allowed herself to be consumed by a feeling that belonged only to them, and no one else.

* * *

19:20, 15 January 2100
Southwark Police Station, Borough High Street, London, The United
Kingdoms

2 hours 20 minutes remaining

Quirk stood on the wide darkened pavement outside the police station and rubbed his face, trying to dispel the fug in his head. No hackneyed reconstruction of the old lag emerging into the cold, overcast morning light. The hour was seven twenty!

Sixteen bloody hours he'd lost in Moss's cell. He'd slept at first, he had to, could keep going no longer, his thrumming nervous tension taking its toll in the end. But fitfulness plagued his rest, roiling images of shadows stalking Moth, of a boy whose face he never saw, but who lurked at the edge of vision, half glimpsed as Quirk searched madly through a twisting maze of streets.

They fed him at nine AM, strong tea and a surprisingly good omelette, which revived him sufficiently that he could begin making a nuisance of himself, pestering the police syRen® for information, talking aloud in his cell, attempting to tempt Moss and her colleagues with minor details and major hints: He searched for the daughter of a rich corporation head (vague but true), was bound by NDA (did not stand up), was alone in the task (flat-out lie). He only had twelve hours, ten hours, eight hours!

The inspector dropped by with less than six hours to go and he laid on an assault of reasonable cooperation and jailhouse lawyer schtick that he'd planned during his extended period of bouncing off the far-too-close walls: He was doing his best, the civil liability implications would ruin him, he could be more use in the field, could lead her to more members of the T-puff gang, higher-ups too! Finally, she caved, and by caved he meant made a shrewd judgement call and backed up it with sensible precautions that put him on a long leash. The inspector insisted he swallow a tracker.

Quirk did his very best not to accept too quickly, but accept he did, founded on his confidence that Nick could defeat the device in a moment, given the right interface.

So now he stood on the cold, darkened and illuminated London street, almost a day older, feeling like a year, and hard labour too, had passed. His body variously ached, burned and stabbed, and still felt fresher, better rejuvenated than his brain. His cLife told him just over two hours remained. Two hours before Moth died. But TOM wouldn't really do it. Would he? Quirk dry-washed his face again. Vehicles slid past on Borough High Street taking commuters home, diners out to dinner, maybe a show, technicians and suppliers on the routes they followed to keep the city running.

Quirk took out his cLife again, conscious the police would—in addition to the device he had swallowed—have put their best tracking software on his handset, but hopefully Nick would intervene. There he was relying on Nick, again. Quirk pressed in his squiggly earpiece, dialled 1-2-3, and began talking. "Nick. Tell me you're there. What's happening?"

"'Course I'm here. Where the hell have you been?"

"You know where I've been. You know everything."

"More than you, anyway."

"Nick." He must move it forward, this constant battle with Nick. The boy deserved it. Even when Nick helped, familial emotions dragged on their efforts, like bunched iron chains on the slipways of yore. "Nick, I'm sorry. I know I'll never be able to say it enough, and that me saying it changes nothing. The past is a locked box, but we know the cat is dead. I'll make you a promise, when this is done—whatever this latest grandpa-sponsored corporate apocalypse turns out to be—we'll sit down, you me and your mother, and we'll just talk. Whether it takes a day, or a week, or a month, we'll go somewhere and talk through all the crap I put you through."

The traffic passed, left and right, right and left. Quiet, but not silent, tyres designed to produce just the right amount of hiss and rumble to save a few thousand lives around Planet Earth each year, apart from those of road users possessing real dedication to maintaining their acute stupidity, recklessness and/or inattentiveness.

"The headline, Nick, is that I made a mistake. People do that every day."

"Not mistakes like that, and they're not my father."

For years since San Francisco, it was a proposition Quirk denied. And yet, Nick had been made from his and Jennifer's DNA. Other than the variation in the process, he had to concede Nick was his son. He'd crossed that bridge in Yellowknife. It had been the easy part, he now discovered. Perhaps he would never live up to the challenge.

"What about my proposal? No BS, just honesty."

Left to right, right to left. Hiss and rumble, rumble and hiss.

"Okay. But we need to find my mother before it can happen. So let's do that."

Quirk smiled: *Dad bunts for an RBI, bottom of the ninth.*

"And no one's listening in? The police—"

"Pfft. The police couldn't hear a firework going off in a portaloo. They've been listening to a routine generating random speech with your voice patterns."

"Who am I talking to?"

"You're dictating love poetry. Meanwhile, Anwar's tracked down the seller girl."

"Where is Anwar?"

Almost imperceptible pause.

"Six minutes to the north, on a bench on the charmingly named Little Dorrit Court. In daytime xe'd get taken for questioning. There's a school and a playground."

Quirk started walking north. "What's xe doing there?"

"I captured an image of girl seller's face when you left the Tate, and I've trawled weeks' worth of PSC footage. Got a bite in this area, just a sliver, but a good match. Tracking a range of physical parameters in close analysis around the sighting, I've built up predictive travel patterns that are 67% corroborated by camera records. Narrowed it to a likely property on Disney Place—"

"Where else?" Quirk interjected, rolling his eyes, slowing to cross the road. "So, Jenny's hiding out with Peter Pan? Captain Hook? Or maybe those seven miners."

"This'll take way longer with dad jokes. I'm fudging the cameras, your tracker and your cLife, but be aware the police likely will tail you, you know, physically. I can't block that! The T-puff gang surely will react to Anwar's little purge."

"Maybe they'll cancel each other out," said Quirk, stopping at the kerb.

"Cos that's how your luck usually runs? Be careful. You owe me a long talk."

Quirk rolled his shoulders, trying to pump some life into weary, aching muscles. Because police bunks possessed the therapeutic qualities of a marble floor, their blankets the Tog factor of wet plaper. He looked up and down the night-time street. A handful pedestrians patronised street food joints, each in its own pool of brighter light, those closest competing for the attention of his tastebuds, but he focused on the road.

Traffic emerged from the left, disappeared to the right. Traffic emanated from the right, slid quickly to the left. With modern autonomous vehicles, transport authorities had no more need of those quaint old pedestrian crossings, even for a four lane (two each way) single carriageway road like this. Still, Quirk awaited a suitable gap, then stepped out. Southbound traffic stopped, some vehicles more sharply than others, leaving him the industry standard three metre clear space (the length of a prone human body plus a factor of safety). By the time he reached the centre of the road (Lanes 1 and 2 behind him, 3 and 4 ahead), Lane 1 began moving again as Lane 3 began to stop. But it didn't and a midi-van hit him square on at 20kph, sending him tumbling into Lane 4.

Hard techmac bashed elbows, knees, shoulders. With some experience in being knocked over variously by people, vehicles, forces of nature, Quirk tucked as best he could, but sharp pain flared up and down his body all the same, until he came to rest. He managed to raise his head to see the vehicle in Lane 4 stopped the requisite distance from his head. Rough hands grabbed him, pulled him upright. Dazed, he blinked. A face drifted in front of him, expression grim. Not "Oh, you poor man" grim either, but "I hoped the impact would kill you" grim. Quirk sucker punched the dark-haired man in the stomach, before other hands grabbed and tossed him onto the footway. As he tumbled up to his knees someone kicked him, their thin frame doing less damage than such a kick might. Two people piled onto him, thin legs swinging purple boots.

"Dad! Fight back for fuck's sake!"

Where were the damn cops? Guess he got "lucky." and they hadn't followed him, or they were happy to watch.

He saw a fist coming and rolled back away from it, let it pass, grabbed the wrist and heaved, felt the weight of his attacker transferring across his shoulder, let go and watched a young man tumble across the pavement. Then, he threw an elbow backwards. It would have looked like a ridiculous spasm had there been no one there, but he connected with something, gaining a high gasp from his efforts.

Quirk twisted and saw the T-puff seller from Blackfriars Bridge, bowed forward, clutching her bloody face. Beyond her, a stocky, bearded figure in ratty jumper and jeans had found his feet from where Quirk threw him, and barrelled forward, fists out.

"What are you people trying to achieve at this point?" Quirk asked.

"You killed my brother!" yelled beardy as he attacked.

Quirk shrugged. "Not me, but close enough." Instead of putting up his dukes, Quirk lowered his shoulder and knocked the pugilist flat with the man's own momentum, taking a blow to the chest, staggering from the impact, but keeping his footing due to a good, wide starting stance. The quaint sound of distant police whistles pierced the night's low rumble and hiss. He saw the duffle-coated T-puff seller girl hurrying away, head still bowed, hand to nose.

"Damn," said Quirk as he hurpled more than ran after her. The adrenaline must be dampening the worst of his pain. He knew he should be hurting more than he did.

"Dad, turn left!"

Quirk lurched into the side street and kept going.

"Cops in attendance at the scene."

"Great. Time?"

"Nineteen fifty. One hour fifty minutes remaining."

* * *

12:43, 20 December 2099
Unknown Address, London, The United Kingdoms

Kira had brought her to this place blindfolded. Not actually with a scarf wrapped around her eyes, although that was a game they'd played a couple of times in bed. No, Jennifer had worn dark glasses with the safety setting disabled, permitting their opacity to be set to one hundred percent. Kira set a password so Jenny could not unset them if she'd wanted to. But she didn't, because she trusted Kira now. Career criminal she may be, but Kira possessed tenderness and thoughtfulness to equal her fun-loving energy.

The blindfolding clearly signified this was a permanent site for the gang (as far as that went in the criminal underworld). Even when Jenny passed through a doorway after touring the noisy, chilly, but no longer smelly London streets for an hour, (complete with white stick, although she also had Kira's arm), the blinding glasses remained on until they'd navigated down a narrow stair. This level, she discovered when Kira removed the glasses, comprised office, bedroom, storeroom and kit room, all small, no windows, all crammed, but comfortable, as Kira happily demonstrated of the bed before she went out that night to work.

When Christmas arrived, it marked the location as Jenny's longest domicile since Gramercy, an unhappy thought she dispelled by ordering presents for Kira. This necessitated a palaver involving Jenny covering most of the computer screen with a piece of card, while Kira typed in the address and hit send. She was delighted with her new duffle coat though, and Jenny cried a little when she received two bottles of her favourite gin and the crackers and olives she loved to have with it.

With the gifts came memories of life with Quinton and, in the quiet time between office work for the T-puff gang and Kira coming back, Jenny was drawn again to confront not just her past, but her future. This required the drinking of gin. She could not find out about Nick sitting here, hiding from the world, from her father. She tried to decide if she hid from Quirk too, but that did not seem something she need worry about. From her father, yes, and she was so tired of worrying about him, fearing him. A terrifying thought emerged from the scintillating fluid in her glass. What if he outlived her? What if he remained in the world long enough to tarnish her entire life?

* * *

19:50, 15 January 2100
Lant Street, London, The United Kingdoms

1 hour 50 minutes remaining

"Dad, you have to get to Anwar, get into the address before the cops get there! Take next right into Sanctuary Street, you'll be heading north again."

The narrow street was darker than the main road, quiet, untrafficked. Ideal for Quirk's hobbling needs. But while Anwar had been an uncomfortable ten-minute walk away before, getting hit by a van must have made the journey more like fifteen.

"Is the seller headed that way?"

"She is, but I've alerted Anwar. He'll hold her, but if the cops are tailing her, drones, cameras, droids, he'll have no choice but to leave. We might lose Mom!"

And Moth. "I might be able to parlay your mother being in police custody as me securing her for return."

"Assuming you give her back to the monstrous old fucker. You promised me a no-holds-barred family discussion, remember?"

"Not at the expense of Moth's life."

Quirk had to stop hobbling and breathe for a moment. He had considered that dimension of the whole messed up puzzle, but not thought it through to the end. He'd assumed Jennifer would go back to spare the life of a child she did not know, and he would break her out again, as Anwar had done before. But wouldn't TOM just leave the threat on Moth open-ended? Jenny's life balanced against Moth's? The situation was unsustainable, but there was just no *time* to logic these things out right now.

There must be a way out of this. He thought he knew what it was, but he just didn't have the spoons. He pushed off the brick wall, half-running, half-limping down a canyon of amber-bricked terraced apartments between lines of parked cars. It felt a lot like being corralled towards his doom with everyone relying on him.

He approached another main junction, glowing brighter at the end of the canyon.

"Straight across," said Nick, testily.

The approaches were blank, no road markings, no nothing, road safety placed in the implacable hands of the autonomous vehicle hive mind. Quirk lolloped from the side street, heedless of approaching vehicles, almost stumbled in the middle of the road as cars braked. He corrected, kept going, gained the darker lane opposite and continued north, but had seen the blue stain of emergency lights in his peripheral vision, either paralleling his path north, or closing in on him. The sound of a siren erupted from nothing, but not near him, probably on Borough High Street to his right, perhaps pursuing the seller. He tried to increase his pace, but it only hurt more.

"Has Anwar gone in? Now or never. Xe can't wait for me."

"Xe's gone in the Disney Place flat. The seller's still at large. There are drones in the air. I'm going to fudge them. Mind your head..."

Quirk actually put his hands on his head in case of crashing plastec and metal, because his night was going exactly that well.

"Done."

Quirk stopped as a blue flashing light stained the walls and the lane up ahead. The nose of a police vehicle appeared at the tight, building-shadowed T-junction where the lane turned. He dodged sideways into a handily placed doorway recessed into the flanking building's brickwork. A metre was a good space to hide in. He tried to pant quietly through the demands of his aching lungs while listening for feet on techmac.

More sirens passed nearby, muffled by the buildings, the lane and the doorway.

He whispered, knowing the handset would compensate. *Really going to have to get an implant. Just a small one.* "Nick? What's happening with Anwar?"

"Xe went in, no one there, signs of occupancy, nothing unusual. Xe's leaving."

"Damn. So, we need the girl, or we're back to scraping around after gin purchasers with..."—five past eight PM—"Ninety-five minutes to go." Either Jenny was really good at hiding, or he'd ballsed this up. Probably both, but definitely the latter.

Car doors clunked. Police getting out, he guessed. A building door opened. Then silence. Footsteps. Light, almost inaudible, but separate from his beating heart.

A figure darted into Quirk's doorway, slamming into him. He grabbed, arm locking round a trim waist, found their mouth with his other hand, clamped it over lips and nose under a duffle coat's hood. The T-puff seller from the Tate had the sense not to scream. Didn't struggle either despite recently trying to batter him on a nearby footway. The anger in her eyes suggested she may bite him though.

"Cops are onto your operation," he breathed, then played a hunch. "If you want to save her, tell me where she is right now."

XIX

15:19, 4 January 2100
Unknown Address, London, The United Kingdoms

Jennifer nodded as the unnamed blond woman conveyed production volumes, timescales, transport costs, just enough detail to allow her to be productive in scheduling and recording deliveries. She'd introduced herself as Sandra. Jenny just nodded. "Sandra" explained that Jenny had incriminated herself long since, and the gang prided itself on its record tracking down and punishing traitors. Jenny affirmed that she would be completely discreet, and anyway had no intention of going anywhere. In fact, that felt increasingly untrue. The urge to move on tugged at her. The need to find out about Nick nagged at her dreams, and pulled her thoughts away from this work, and Kira.

They had fallen out and made up twice now. Correction: this morning's bust up—their third in the last fortnight—remained unresolved. Jenny hoped it would be, but knew that she must do so by ending their fling. She regretted it. She liked Kira, but increasingly the disparity in their aspirations gave rise to tensions, largely since Jenny refused to talk about what she wanted. Because she couldn't.

Hey, Kira, so I'm the daughter of possibly the richest person on the planet, in fact any planet, but major bummer, he imprisoned me for five years after taking away the son he cloned for me from my own and my estranged (or just plain strange) husband's DNA. I want to break up, but can we still be friends?

She went back to the order spreadsheet, finished prioritising the list of pending deliveries by value, influence ranking and profit per unit, saved her day's work, printed the results. Then, she sealed the folded printout in an envelope which she left on the desk for Sandra, saved the spreadsheet to a thumb drive and reformatted the computer's data drive. This seemed like a waste of time, since the computer had no external connection (printing was via separate thumb drive, also reformatted), but that was Sandra.

Jenny sat back in the gaming chair, thinking of the mind-bending logistics that must accompany her father's activities. How on Earth did he do it? By managing his people, she concluded, and equipping them to manage everything else.

* * *

20:10, 15 January 2100
Disney Place, London, The United Kingdoms

1 hour 30 minutes remaining

In the darkened doorway, the young woman jerked her head against his hand, and Quirk released the pressure. "Not here," she hissed in a husky whisper.

"I don't have time for a tour," he breathed.

"Anwar's clear. What next?"

"You know somewhere quiet?" This to the woman, which Nick would still get via Quirk's handset. "Somewhere public, nearby, but out of the way," he clarified.

"Sure," she said, and started to pull away.

Quirk kept his arm around her waist, pulled her against his side. "Sorry, but last time you led the way I got tased."

"Yeah," she said, not fighting his grip. "An' last time you followed me mah dickhead cousin got topped by yor pet gunman."

"Ouch," said Nick in Quirk's ear.

They stepped from the doorway and walked back down dark and narrow Disney Place the way they both had come. They walked slowly—easy enough for Quirk, who still ached in all the places—in the weirdest clinch he'd experienced in a while. The woman snaked an arm behind his back onto his shoulder. "This feels convincing."

"Try an' kiss me," she said quietly, "an' ah'll break yor fackin' arm."

Footsteps sounded on the techmac behind them. Car doors opened, but no one hailed them. They kept walking. The woman pulled him left into the bigger, brighter Marshalsea Road. Numerous people strolled the street. Vehicles came and went, but no sirens, no lights. They came to a wide junction and the woman pulled him to step out.

"Pardon my hesitance," Quirk grumbled. "Last time I tried to cross a road you hit me with a van."

"You deserved it," she bubbled, tilting her head back and laughing. "The look on yor face. An' you should be sellin' this ruse, by the way, hon, but we're almost there."

They passed a well-cared-for church on the opposite side of the road, and their footway widened out to accommodate a strip of cycle parking, all sorts of two-wheelers ranked along the roadside, Segways, solar scooters, chem-cycles, and pushbikes. The woman slowed here then pulled him into an Asian restaurant inhabiting an incredibly narrow, brick building between two shiny offices.

"Table for two, luv," said the woman.

"What do I call you?" asked Quirk.

The T-puff seller didn't answer. The waiter (human) seated them.

"Gin and tonic," said the woman.

Quirk held up two fingers and the waiter left.

"You met a woman near the Tate. Tell me what happened. I'm in a hurry."

"Well, ah'm not, sunshine. So, wot's in it for me, yeah?"

"I can send dark funds from your handset," said Nick. *"No handles, no trail."* Tension fizzed in the boy's tone.

No point messing around. "Fifty grand," he said, smiling—*Cor blimey, cheers, Guvnor!* "I have no time for negotiation, and I'm *very* serious. Nick, send the money."

The woman retrieved a handset from her duffle coat pocket. Her eyes widened. "'Ow did you...? You hackin' me?"

"No." Their drinks arrived, and Quirk sipped his, smacking his lips at the botanical bite. Clearly, the waiter had interpreted his victory sign as "double." Fine by him. "I've got money to burn. Time's what I don't have. There's a life at stake—"

"Not hers, not Jenny's?"

Quirk failed to head off his surprise before it reached his face. "She told you her name? Never mind. No, not hers, a young girl's. I don't give a damn about pushing tobacco. Tell me where she is, get another fifty K. I find her there, it's plus a hundred."

"Sixty-five minutes, Dad. 3,900 seconds!"

"'Ow do ah know ah can trust you?"

"I just gave you fifty grand for nothing, that's how."

"I'm into her handset. Name's Kira."

"You gonna hurt 'er?"

"She's my wife."

Kira stifled her surprise almost instantly. "Answer the fackin' question."

"Dad."

"No, Kira, I won't hurt her."

Kira's phone rang and she answered.

"Tracing," said Nick before Quirk could cough significantly.

The last thing he wanted to do was stand up, but he desperately needed *something* to move forward. And just over an hour looked like failure. He pictured Moth—pre-Quirk-fuck-up Moth—and the image made him want to kill TOM. Now. Violently.

He pushed himself up on tired, aching legs, drained his glass and made to leave.

Kira didn't stop him as he'd hoped, turned, eyes worried, and hung up.

"Got it!" said Nick. *"Bermondsey? That's fucking miles away."*

"Cops are picking us all up. Boss says scarper."

A door at the back of the restaurant opened, the door to the kitchen, and Inspector Bethany Moss strode through it flashing her warrant card about. With her free hand, she pointed at Quirk. "Do *not*, under any circumstances, *move!*"

He grabbed Kira's hand, but did not have to drag her up, as she practically bowled him over to get out of her seat and on a bearing for the front door.

Two cops stood in the tiny lobby of the tiny restaurant, but he and Kira were committed, and he didn't have time for the polite-a-go-round with Moss again, so they kept going. The cops produced batons. This would hurt, again. He snatched a jacket from the back of a chair on the narrow aisle. "I'll hang this up for you, sir."

He whipped the jacket around like a shield, sliding it between himself and Kira and the cops just before they barrelled into their enthusiastic baton-wielding assailants.

The entangling jacket was the key to their escape. Kira seemed to enjoy her contribution of ankle kicking, while Quirk just shoved into bodies, target proximity defeating the cops' ability to take an effective swing in the enclosed space.

The cool night air provided a brief balm. Kira dragged him towards the cycle rank.

"Nick. Nick, need your help now, buddy."

"We'll talk about 'buddy' later. Wait. Okay, moped with lights flashing."

Deaf to Quirk's conversation, Kira went for the flashing moped, threw a leg over. Quirk pushed in front of her, because Nick would have done some sweet work with his palm print and the handlebars. Sure enough, the solar two-wheeler leapt off its stand, the lock falling away, and launched into traffic with indicators, warning lights, safety vibration, and sonic alert all blaring furiously. Kira grabbed his waist, and both leaned into the curves as Quirk cut through traffic, heading south on Borough High Street with scant regard for their absence of helmets.

"Brinton Walk!" Kira yelled too loud in his ear.

"Charlie Blackford's place? You're kidding." He could do this. Time unbearably short, cops on their tail, but on a moped he could do it. "Guide me," he called, not much caring whether Nick or Kira took up the gauntlet.

"Quirk? Anwar. I'm heading for Brinton Walk, probably get there before you. What are you orders? There are blue lights everywhere. It's very pretty."

"Don't shoot anyone...else." Kira pulled on his right side almost at the same moment his right handle vibrated, and he banked into Marshalsea Road, causing much braking and honking behind them at the big junction.

Up ahead, blue lights converged on them.

"Suggestions?"

"Footway!" called Nick.

"Left!" barked Kira.

"Sorry, Nick, lady's a local." Quirk slipped into the road on the left with a quick left, right roll, and found himself throttled into yet another brick-built canyon, a single lane with cars down one side, so narrow as to make their speed seem doubled, and with bollards cutting off the road ahead. Bollards with spaces in between.

"You can make it, tiger," said Kira, unexpectedly. "Left."

Managing to drop a little speed in the twenty metres remaining, he threaded them through bollards while banking into a tight lefthander, thought he felt a tug on the Merrion's sleeve and hoped it was just the wind. Brick buildings made a warren out of narrow, crisscrossing side streets, all parked up, lit sympathetically for residents, but less so for speeding mopeds. "Right," yelled Kira, but he had no time for the turn, shot past. "Next right!" This turn instantly became more critical as there was no "straight on" this time. He banked hard from Weller Street into Lant Street.

"Looks familiar!"

"You were going the other way last time."

"Figures."

"Who are you talking to?" yelled Kira.

"Colleague."

As another main road approached, he tried to judge the gaps in traffic this time, did a fair job he thought, although the converging police cars didn't seem to appreciate his skills. Still, by the strange pseudo-stereo directions of Nick and Kira, Quirk weaved and twisted along a route trammelled by buildings and traffic restrictions. He began to think his joint navigators were taking the piss, a thing that happened in London.

A quick left-right turn combination took them under a high brick arch railway bridge onto a straight stretch, a quiet street crammed with vegetation that shielded buildings from the road.

"Hey, Dad, right turn next junction then three hundred twenty metres straight north to final approach. You wanna throw a plan together, or just wing it?"

"Status, Anwar."

"Blue lights are hanging back, but I think SWAT units are in the vicinity. I'm on the roof, hoping you've got a plan. I will not go to war with the Met Police for that foul-mouthed brat. Think of something clever, Quirk."

The tell-tale fakery in the tone told Quirk that Anwar subvocalised. He began to ease back on the throttle. Perhaps the relative quietness of the streets was a bad thing, unhelpful. Perhaps what they needed now was not space, but cover. Perhaps now, they needed to draw a crowd.

"Nick, can you hack the National Public Alert system? Send a message to bring everyone out onto the street?"

"Oh, nice. I'll give that a swing."

By now, Quirk had pulled to a stop on Surrey Row, back from the junction, hoping nothing pulled up behind them and started honking. He gave the moped a little juice, bumped it onto the footway. Unsurprisingly, Kira sat back and released her hold on him. "What's—"

Both their handsets vibrated.

```
        *** National Public Alert System ***
        *** WARNING! THIS IS NOT A TEST! ***
Unidentified OBJECTS in the sky over Central London.
 These objects are very strange and unusual. DO NOT
leave your home or place of work. DO NOT look up at
these machines. STAY UNDER COVER! DO NOT attempt to
                    travel home.
   Ask POLICE on the ground for further details.
```

By the time Quirk had finished reading, people were emerging onto the street. Some stood near their building's entrance. Others walked one way or another, some with purpose, some strolling, looking up at the dark sky bejewelled with streetlights, office blocks with rooms lit in chaotic anti-chequerboard patterns. A drone flew over and people pointed, exclaimed. Moments later a police drone-copter passed, heading for Brinton Walk, Quirk noted, and some onlookers hurried in the opposite direction, while others scanned the sky for... Whatever their imaginations demanded.

The traffic flow on the street began to build. Within minutes, stationary queues stretched in both directions on Blackfriars Road. Very polite queues, because autonomous vehicles had no need of honking horns or swearing at each other. Two-wheelers still could pass however—and did, many of them—in both directions. All manner of modern conveyance, zipping past the slowly edging four-wheeled traffic.

"Okay, Dad, you're up."

"Nice work, Son." No answer.

Kira grabbed Quirk's middle again as he pulled out of Surrey Street, edging between two queuing cars then weaving right and left through another gap before heading north alongside the stubborn queue.

"Hey, Nick, can you kill the lights?"

"I believe I can. Distance?"

"Fifty metres out."

At that moment, all the streetlights went out. Another moment, ten metres later, all the house, shop and office illumination extinguished, only the headlights on the road remaining. Quirk started to congratulate Nick on dealing with the local grid when all the vehicle lights went out too. Total darkness. *How the hell...* Further along the road—two hundred metres?—lay a landscape of typical urban evening illumination. Quirk crushed the brakes. Jolting them hard as the moped bucked to a halt.

"'Ow the fack he do that?"

"I don't know." He actually had to grope to the side to locate the nearest vehicle. "Help me push. I can't risk riding, but we'll need this later."

"You'll need it," came her response from somewhere behind him.

They manhandled the moped between a gap in vehicles that he located by touch, not willing to light up his handset for fear of attracting the wrong kind of attention.

"Straight ahead. Dolben Street," said Nick. *"I've got you on IR via drone, but the SWATs around the house have the same tech. I haven't figured that yet."*

With some bumps on fenders, bashing of elbows and legs followed by quick apologies, they gained the kerb. Quirk's eyes had adjusted sufficiently to see shades of dark brown and picked out a lighter path between the buildings. Now he checked his handset: eight fifty-five, forty-five minutes remaining. He just had to think. Think how to get past a Metropolitan Police SWAT team.

He was still thinking on that when the shooting started.

XX

14:05, 15 January 2100
Turbo Inn Hotel, Manhattan, New York, NY, NAF

3 hours 35 minutes remaining

Spending an hour in a hotel room with these mouth-breathers was fucking interminable. After ten minutes, Moth began contemplating where she could get a spoon to sharpen and begin digging through the wall. But she couldn't escape, she had to stay here, because Giulia's life depended on it. At least the human seemed straightforward, kept to himself in a chair by the window endlessly scrolling and typing on his handset. Probably some sicko mercenary club shit. Callan didn't annoy her directly, but his mere presence in her android's body grossed her out in extremis. Callan/Bea sprawled on the bed, watching some sick-assed movie on the ceiling screen, chortling from time to time in his own voice in a leering way that creeped her the fuck *out!* She didn't know whether to look at him...it, and feel sick at his presence, or look away, just reach the outskirts of forgetfulness only for him to hork, snort or cackle, making her jump out of her skin, heart hammering on her ribs trying to get out.

The thing that freaked her out more than anything was she didn't know what to do. Her instincts screamed at her to get away, but what about Giulia? She had zero doubt TOM would kill her. Even though Moth had every basis in the worlds to distrust him, weirdly, something in his voice made her believe. All the evidence confirmed him to be a bad, bad man, doing vile, evil things, but funk her up the freshman college assignment he seemed to have a code. *Fucking evil genius code of ethics scumbag.*

Maybe she would play a game. Anything for a distraction.

Welcome to another hilarious episode of Whose Lie Is it Anyway?, starring Quinton Ignominious Rich-man Kirby—golden child of the falsehood fraternity, and Joshing-you Sinister, aka The Oiled Mange, slick with the lies of generations past, watch out for your organs when Josh is about! He's due a new heart any day now to keep him youthful at one hundred and sixty-three years too old. That new pancreas won't last forever! Guest stars this week, Jason Boredom, secret agent, whose spontaneity is exceeded only by every other tedious thing about him, and the Ghost of Gregor Callan, the filthy, murdering pervert you just love to hate!

So, let's play Whose Lie Is it Anyway?!

First up, Lie of The Week! Is it even slightly likely Callan would kill Giulia with a nice clean headshot? Nuh-uh! This kooky psychopath just loves to mix things up in the bedroom by shafting his victims with a female syRen® and a massive strap-on. Cuddly killer Gregor uses every trick in the book to get his sick jollies at the target's expense!

How do you follow that? Not with Jason B, if it's fun times you're seeking. He's a dyed-in-the-wool sourpuss. Jason seems like a straight shooter, even fair sometimes, but where's the fun in that? Too good to be truthful? Almost certainly. We'll bet he didn't get where he is today by spelling everything out for his victims. It's safe to say you're never safe from a shot in the dark when Jason is nearby.

Joshua Simister? He's shit at this game, because he always tells the truth! Boo!

Ah, last but not least—unless it's in openness—the man without a proper name, a true toad amongst toads, Mr. Quirk! He's always as good as his word, if that word is lying fucker. Because isn't that the best kind of lie? The one that involves absolutely no effort at all, because all you have to do is not say anything! It's the ultimate in low-input deceit. Just kick back in this week's star prize, a top of the range Lie-Z-Boy chair. Keep your mouth shut and enjoy the fun as your friends stumble around trusting you, and believing you have their interests at heart. Start every day the right way by keeping important details to yourself. With Nope-on-a-Rope, you can wash away that grimy conscience of yours, so you always sound squeaky clean. And last but not least, don't forget the cuddly toy. Giving out big, squishy hugs of reassurance is this grumpy bear's speciality. But really, he's stuffed full of nothing but old rags, tatters of what you thought were real feelings. But no! It's all just your own shredded hopes and dreams.

She stopped, seeing Jason and Callan/Bea staring at her, puzzled expressions on their faces. She realised big, wet tears ran down her face, and she may have been punching the pillow in her lap. *Fucking lying bastard made me cry, again!*

Jason's pocket buzzed and he took the call, turning towards the window so she couldn't see his lips move.

* * *

<Foster.>

"Ninety minutes to go and no communication from Kirby. Make whatever preparations you need to for killing the girl."

<Yes, sir. Will you call if I'm to stand down?>

"Probably, but you have your orders. No call, the girl's done."

<Yes, sir.>

* * *

17:10, 15 January 2100

30 minutes remaining

Somehow, she slept. She woke to the sky beyond the window beginning to dim. As she rose to consciousness through an ocean of sleep fuzz, a wave of sadness crashed over her as she remembered her situation. Totally fucking trapped. Despite the room's comfortable temperature, she shivered. Was this it? What if, when Rat Shit and Bobbin completed their heinous mission, TOM decided to keep her on a string for months, years? What if they were never safe?

"No!" Realising she'd hissed aloud she darted a glance at her captors. Captain Charisma slept on the sofa, but Callan/Bea's head turned, gave her a terrifying grin and put a finger to its lips. She twisted back under the blanket, unable to look at the syRen® that had been her companion. Could she ever trust Bea again, be comfortable with her when Callan departed? And what did the old base turd want from her here?

TOM had—indirectly, natch—killed her parents and Uncle Toni. But his threat now put the blame for this horrible thing on her. Moth's action, or failure to act could kill Giulia. The power of the unscrupulous truly terrified her. What could she do? What should she do? Just go along with the fucker till he got what he wanted, whatever shit he plotted with the NLS drive licenses? Bound to be bad for way more people than one aunty. And Giulia had protection from Rigel, the family, Mario, even the authorities.

Fuck you, Moth! Are you trying to justify putting Giulia's life on the line after all she did for you when—?

She flipped over away from the residual light leaching through the windows. *No. That's how these fuckers work. They fill you with fear and doubt, make you question yourself, your bravery, the strength of your family.* If she'd learned anything from the lying pinstriped butthole it was that you had to do the right thing, let fate decide. But also get more security. Mario had security out the wazoo, and Giulia—she learned from some pretty intense chats with her post-convent "convalescence" aunt—was no shrinking violet.

So, what did all that mean? Rock bottom line, Giulia would tell her to stop being a little pussy and start fucking these guys up. *These are really bad people, and I can't just let them roll over me. That means they're rolling over a bunch of other people. People who deserve better, who deserve not to have big business bastards crushing them for nothing but more money. Aunt Giulia wouldn't respect me for doing nothing, Quirk monkey butt probably wouldn't like it either. No, time to stop holding back out of fear for Giulia and start kicking butt on her behalf.*

Callan (she re-fucking-fused to think of Bea as associated with these events) and Jack-Bowel-whatever-his-name-was completely outpowered her, physically, in weaponry and in unscrupulosity. *That's a word, right?* So, time to bust out of the phone box, unleash her superpower on them. *Here comes the girl, motherfuckers.*

She pulled the blanket over her head and began to lay her plans against them.

XXI

21:00, 15 January 2100
Dolben Street, London, The United Kingdoms

40 minutes remaining

Instinctively, Quirk grabbed Kira and thrust her against the unseen wall at the same time she grabbed his arms and pulled him down. They ended in a heap in the angle of wall and road as automatic fire rattled the night, spiced with buzzing laserguns.

Quirk's handset buzzed. *Not the time!*

"You'll want to take this!" said Nick.

"I'm doing you a big favour," Anwar hissed, the handset correcting. *"This'll cost extra. I'm drawing them away from Brinton Walk. Be prepared for one or two hanging around, but I'm making a big enough noise to take most of them with me."*

"Thank you—"

"Thank me later. Do your job and save that annoying kid so I can give her a hard time for all this trouble."

Quirk smiled grimly. Anwar hung up. He found Kira's shoulders, gripped them. He could barely see her face. "I'm going in. 11A, right? You should scarper. I'm good for the money, just don't change your number."

"Nah," she hissed. "Ah'm keepin' moi eyes on you, sunshine. Anyway, Ah want to say goodbye."

No streetlights, no handsets, no torches. They felt their way upright against the wall. Quirk felt Kira push in front of him, and this was her manor, after all. She would know the way. At the end of the short narrow street, some surviving light source marked the edge of the buildings. At the junction, he heard the drones hovering nearby then saw their running lights just as Kira ducked back against the wall.

"Just round the corner," she hissed.

"Nick?" breathed Quirk. He would not have got a hundred metres in the last day without the help of his son, and he must make the time to tell Nick that, soon.

"Four police drones. I can take them down, but the rozzers will descend on you."

"And we'll be on torches."

"And there are two meat sacks on the door."

"They armed?"

"Duh."

"Ah can fight," said Kira, guessing Nick's side of the conversation.

"We'll have to," he whispered. "Nick, take out the drones when you judge best."

"Thanks, Dad." The boy's words sounded genuine.

"Go." He patted Kira on the shoulder, and they went.

Things happened fast.

A quick zigzag around two corners brought them into the glare of drone light from above. Two SWAT cops stood outside a nondescript door on a narrow, redbrick lane, houses on one side, small but verdant gardens on the other. The cops brought weapons up. "Stay where you are!" Even as one moved forward the drone lights went out, and Quirk heard the flying spiders drop from the sky. In the dark, in the split second they had for night vision to adjust, he rushed forward. Kira's reaction must have been faster because he heard a grunt. A burst of high-intensity laserfire shot straight upwards, giving a view of Kira struggling with one cop, and showing him his target. Quirk dropped and rolled as the SWAT fired, missing, and Quirk came up and lunged at them, bearing them down. A grunt and a yell sounded like Kira. Quirk took a couple of quick blows that threw him back, one sucking all the wind from his lungs.

Gun light splashed on them, Kira on her knees like him before the two cops.

"You are under arrest for attempting—"

"Close your eyes," said Nick.

Quirk turned to look at Kira, who met his gaze just as he covered her eyes with his hand. Brilliant light flashed before Quirk's eyelids and a flash of heat bathed his face. Yells and urgent groaning erupted as darkness fell again.

No time to think. He straightened, produced his handset. "Light on." Kira did the same and they slipped past the groaning, gasping, smoking cops. Quirk hoped their armour served them well, couldn't help remembering the destruction at Nick's hands in Yellowknife. He was no angel. Kira used her handset to access the house.

The lights came on. *"You're welcome,"* said Nick in his ear.

Kira went straight to...a cupboard, pulled open the door, whipped back a strip of carpet sending the various shoes tripping across the living room floor then pulled up a hatch revealing a set of steep stairs. "Jenny," she called. "We're leavin', luv."

With very little delay, a short-haired figure appeared in the room below, pulling on a coat, snatching up a bag, and stomping up the vertiginous wooden steps.

Jenny—for it was her, despite the too-short, dark-dyed hair—stood before him, as baldly surprised as he himself. The whole world sort of, stopped. He stood in the middle of the hall, looking at Jennifer, hearing her voice for the first time in years when she said "Quinton."

"More cops inbound, and twenty-eight minutes on the call. You need to be gone."

"More police. We need to get out of here, Jenny." Her expression was unreadable.

"Ah can lose 'em," said Kira. Then she turned and kissed Jennifer on the mouth, and Quirk's ex-wife kissed Kira back with some vigour. "It was good," said Kira.

Quirk made a "Huh" face. Clearly, there was much to talk about on both sides.

Nick gave them an all clear and they moved out in the lane that was Brinton Walk. Kira picked up the unexploded of the two Met Police guns.

She said, "Get your controller—"

"Hah!" said Nick in Quirk's ear.

"To blow this up in five minutes." She set a timer and showed him her handset.

"Can do," said Nick. *"Now get on that moped and get Mom outta there!"*

Kira and Jenny squeezed each other's hands then Kira followed them back to the two-wheeler but continued on to the main road while

Jenny mounted up behind Quirk and they headed the opposite way, down the lane.

"Jenny, I really want to ask how you've been, what you've been through, but…"

Her arms circled him and held on. "Just drive."

He banished an avalanche of emotions and walked the moped down the lane to emerge at a right-angled corner of Chancel Street. Two police cars sat at rest, seemingly unaware of them in the dark.

Just along the road, street illumination reasserted itself. When they bolted, they would be seen. Then, a loud bang emitted from behind them. One of the police cars darted forward, hung a left and disappeared from view.

"Here we go," said Quirk. He started the moped.

The streetlights flicked on all around them. Quirk hit the power and they launched forward. On the footway five metres away, a fox sat under a streetlight watching them fly past, yawning in boredom. "Fox," said Jenny. Quirk could only smile, but could not for the life of him think of a name for it.

San Francisco, CA, NAF, 2092

A young man in cut-off jeans and white sleeveless T-shirt riding a shiny new electric moped speeds up and down Spruce Street in San Francisco, making tight turns in the reduced road space between parked cars before zipping back the way he had come. On the stoop of a blue-shingled townhouse, a young woman in jean shorts and black tank top waves a red scarf in the air, whooping and clapping. The moped has a large pink ribbon tied to the handlebars.

He blasted north to the end of Chancel Street with flashing blue lights on his tail, thinking to turn left towards the big road that had been full of people staring at the sky, but in the end, swung hard right under another brick railway arch. This road was restricted to two-wheelers only. The cop car tried to clip their rear wheel but slammed into a bollard, and Quirk tore away from the sound of crunching plastec.

The first speed hump wiped the smile off his face. They hit it hard, and the moped cleared the ground with such a whack he thought a wheel must drop off. It didn't, that time. Half left, another leap from a speed hump, across a road busy with traffic. He leaned to make a gap between two trucks, breathing sharply when his sleeve wiped the grime from one bumper. The moped's compass said north. That meant the river. An idea formed, imperfect, but worth a try, hopefully leaving twenty minutes to make the call. *How the hell did it end up this tight?*

Streets, footways, trees, cars parked and moving, came at them as they tore along with blue flashing lights hot on their tail. Quirk steered through bollards onto a wide island of old trees, but the cop car just went around, ended up a little closer.

Then he saw the Tate's illuminated tower, the pavement diverged from the road up a concrete ramp, wide enough for a car, but with two heavy, metal bollards at the bottom. Perfect.

"We're getting off," he shouted. "Jump when I say, then tuck, duck and roll." He swung onto the ramp. Jenny's arms gripped him hard; he wove them between more bollards, down the side of the Tate, a smoked glass wall on the corner anonymising patrons of the museum café inside and he couldn't help thinking of happier times.

San Francisco, CA, NAF, 2092
They zipped away from the house down California Road, turned right onto 25th Avenue, took El Camino Del Mar, Bowley Street, Gibson Road, onto Battery Chamberlain Road to reach Baker Beach. A flawless blue sky welcomed them, a breeze off the Golden Gate across South Bay picking at the flags. They parked his new moped, walked down onto the sand and strolled, hand in hand.

Was this the end?

He jigged right then left, steering onto the lawn in front of the Tate where this had started a day ago, two months ago, or maybe ten years ago.

Beyond the silver-birch-bordered lawn, the riverside walkway ran and beyond that the Thames lurked glinting, black and wide, St Paul's pale dome in the distance. Blue lights descended on them from either side along the walkway and sirens blared, like being ambushed by an inconvenient militaristic fairground.

"Now!"

Jenny had been ready, her arms slipped away, her reassuring mass disappeared, the moped tried to flip. He steadied the steering, stood on the runner with one leg, swinging the other back and off, gunned the throttle and jumped.

* * *

17:35, 15 January 2100
Turbo Inn Hotel, Manhattan, New York, NY, NAF

5 minutes remaining

Foster checked his handset again. Five minutes. Better prep now, because when the order came, or if no call happened, there was no question Simister wanted the deed undertaken immediately. The method, well, that was just...unnecessary. He understood perfectly the principle of making it look like something it was not, but the expression on the droid's face sent a chill through him. Callan would enjoy entirely too much making Angelika Moratti's death look like a vicious mafia killing.

Foster stood from the sofa, reached into his kit bag, removed the plastec sheet. A thin rectangle that almost fit in his hand, but once he released the catch it began to expand on the carpet between the wall and the bed. The droid stood up, smiled.

"It's time now," said Callan, unnecessarily, smiling.

The girl threw the blanket back at the crinkling sound of the plastec.

"Huh...?" In the moment she got it, anger hardened her delicate features. Brave kid. She would fight them tooth and nail. Foster patted the gun in his pocket. Perhaps he would plug her before it got too bad. To hell with Callan having his fun, he could take that up with The Old Man.

"Get on the sheet," he commanded, pointing at the plastec covering the floor. "Or the droid will put you there."

"Why should I? What'll you do if I don't, fuckwit, kill me?"

Despite her resolve, the girl's lip quivered, her eyes shining.

"It's about degrees of pain. I promise you the sheet will hurt less."

Callan moved forward, reached out for her and she didn't shrink back. The droid's hand clamped her arm and Foster's handset began to buzz.

XXII

21:21, 15 January 2100
Tate Modern, Bankside, London, The United Kingdoms

19 minutes remaining

Quirk cranked his head round in time to see the moped zip across the walkway and pile into the metal railing protecting the river's edge. The simple barrier, no doubt designed to stop children toppling in, remind adults of the edge, and contain careless cyclists, did not cope well with a moped blasting into it head on at what might be fifty clicks an hour. The metal buckled but the footings remained planted, resulting in the fence folding down, gripping the front wheel for an instant before releasing it, almost flinging the moped, spinning end over end, out into the river.

It might just be enough, buy them the minutes to make the call. He started to pick himself up. Jennifer helped, hauling on his arm, pulled him the rest of the way up and close into her side. "Stroll like you mean it," she hissed, leaning into him in a confusingly amorous way presumably intended to look relaxed, harmless, and definitely not guilty. He whipped off the Merrion's verging on tattered jacket, turned it inside out and draped it over her shoulders. Leaving his arm there, pleased that she didn't tense, they walked as slowly as they dared into the bright foyer of the Tate Modern gallery, both closely watching the reflection in the glass door of the scene behind them as police examined the twisted railing and scanned the twisting dark waters.

"Coffee?" asked Jennifer as the doors slid shut behind them.

"Sure, but can we make a call first? There's a life at stake, my assistant, Angelika. It's a long story, but she's a good kid. Doesn't deserve to be shot in the head by your father's lackeys."

"Of course." This strange but familiar Jennifer/Not-Jennifer seemed more tired than anything else.

As soon as they sat down in the café, Quirk made the call with twelve minutes remaining. Her implants removed, he had to use speaker, attracting grimaces from at least one customer, despite trying to keep the volume low.

"Quinton. Glad to hear from you. Cutting it fine, but that's your way, of course."

"Jennifer's here."

"Show me."

Quirk looked across the table, raised his eyebrows, suddenly very clear on the fact he was asking her to give up her liberty. Jennifer rolled her eyes, but nodded. She beckoned him, and he moved to her side of the table, sat close enough for the camera, but not too close. She switched views, inspecting the image her father would receive.

"I look a state," she said. "But you look worse."

"Ready?"

"No," she said, but wearily gestured for him to proceed.

"Well, look at us. It's almost happy families."

"Almost," said Jennifer. "But not. We're missing one member. Forget what you did to me, but have the decency to tell me what you did to my son."

"I'm sorry, Jennifer, that's a topic for another time. Quinton can relay the latest news on that front."

"So, shall we make small talk? It's truly objectionable to see you," she said hotly.

"Calm down, dear. I just want you to come home, to be safe."

"But it wasn't home. You had me cooped up with the chickens. Were you going to bring me home for Christmas? And where is home, anyway? I used to have one." She side-eyed Quirk. "But where do I live now that Sam Spade here has unearthed me? If I wasn't so tired, I'd be spitting mad."

"I expect that your body is missing its regular medication."

"It certainly isn't missing Doctor Clayton."

"Claydon. But that's rather academic after your new friend Anwar Cruz killed the good doctor in the course of your escape."

Jennifer tensed, and Quirk realised how disturbingly natural it felt to be near her.

"What about Moth?"

"You're right, Quinton. You have completed your first task. She's fine. Holed up with a couple of my staff, held against her good behaviour, and yours."

"First task? You—"

"Oh, stow that famous petted lip of yours. Grow up and act like a big boy. You're to bring Jennifer back to Gramercy. Then, you'll remain in San Francisco where I can see you while the fireworks go off in New York."

"What guarantee do I have Moth will be safe?"

"The same you had first time around, none but my word she'll remain unharmed in my custody as long as you toe the line."

"So, you're planning to hold her life over my head in perpetuity."

"Why shouldn't I? You've been sticking your oar into my affairs for months. Now I'm disrupting yours. Quid pro quo, Quirk. You have a day to return Jennifer to the Gramercy Refuge. Don't go back to your hotel, I imagine Inspector Moss will be waiting. Go straight to London City Spaceport. There's a plane ready. You'll have downtime on the flight to catch up.

"Goodbye, Jenny. Speak soon." The line went dead.

Quirk stowed his handset and rubbed his face. Despite the heavy anguish of Moth remaining in danger, his adrenaline finally ebbed away. All the stress and effort of the last day slipped away like a sheet, uncovering the pain of the numerous beatings he'd taken in recent hours. The pain would pass, but would his fear for Moth be perpetual? As a di Fantano-Moratti, was she now marked for greatness within Rigel's ranks, but also doomed to cross swords with C Corp forever? Was he the one out of place, trying to repel forces that inevitably drew towards conflict, doomed to clash time after time until one was destroyed? Good sense suggested he should not stand between those forces. Had Moth seen this now? Perhaps the outcome of her realisation, their separation, was the correct one. He did not have to like it though.

"I need a drink."

"Well, that's constructive."

"You're the one who betrayed her location by Kira obtaining gin and crackers."

"Maybe, subconsciously, I reached out to you, without even knowing you were looking." He had no answer to that.

He signalled a server and she signalled to her handset then a ZR code on the table. Quirk sighed. "The fun's going right out of drinking in public."

Jennifer ordered a G&T. In a break from tradition fuelled by Olympic qualifying levels of fatigue, Quirk ordered a glass of champagne, hoping the bubbles would help.

"What could you possibly have to celebrate?" asked Jennifer.

"I'm rather looking forward to a night off."

"Me too, you can explain everything that happened to our child in the years I was banged up at my father's pleasure, kept in the dark. Then I'll decide what to do next."

That impending conversation filled him with dread, but no moral basis existed to deny Jennifer's right to hear the details. A painful discussion awaited, more painful he suspected than any knock-down-carry-out fight at Spruce Street. Worse, he no longer remembered with any accuracy his reasons for resisting parenthood. Had they been hard baked by the heat of his wider anger and frustration at the time, only to crumble under the first serious test—the angry, clever, bratty, resourceful Angelika Moratti?

Quite suddenly, his night off looked rather miserable.

"It won't be easy," she said. "But we have to do it. Just remember there's more between us than pain and division. I need to understand what happened to Nick, and you. And this Angelika person. I can't go back to save someone I know nothing about."

"I get that."

"What have you done to your poor suit?" She touched a tear in the indigo fabric.

"That sleeve ripped on a wall," he said. "This scrape from a lorry bumper."

"Okay," she nodded. "Maybe the plane will have a sewing kit."

* * *

19:55, 15 January 2100
Turbo Inn Hotel, Manhattan, New York, NY, NAF

Foster woke and stretched within the confines of the sofa, blinked, and rubbed a hand across his face. He grunted. Simister had messaged to rescind the kill order in the nick of time, and it made him wonder if the Kirby guy really cut it so close, or if TOM played some kind of game. But who with? Maybe only with himself. It was true that power did something to people, certainly the ones he'd met.

He sat up, groggy like he'd been drugged, which made no sense. He swung his legs around, stood, took a step, but...his legs didn't work! Fell forward, got his hands out to catch the fall, only just avoiding a splat flat on his face. *What the fuck?* He tried to jerk up, twisted, managed to get to his knees but tipped again, grabbed for the arm of the sofa, tried to pull one leg forward, but nothing happened. Settling for equilibrium, he snatched his gun from its holster, aimed at the lump under the blanket on the bed.

Where had the droid gone? *Fuck!* The untiring, ever alert, always on robot was not in the room. "Callan! What the fuck?" Not like he'd go to the bathroom.

With no threat evident, Foster sat back on his rump, swung his legs in front of him. His boot laces were tied together.

He tried to pick the knots out, but quickly abandoned that. Whoever had done it—that little bitch—had pulled the laces real tight. He took the knife from his boot and cut them, stood up, walked to the bed, pistol extended, aching to pull the trigger, tugged the blanket back to find two pillows carefully punched into shape to look very convincing as a tucked-up body.

"Fuck!" The Old Man would kill him.

* * *

17:55, 15 January 2100
Turbo Inn Hotel, Manhattan, New York, NY, NAF

Two hours ago...

Under the covers, Moth shook, sweated, quivered, ready to burst. How close had they come to killing her? She couldn't think about it. Her mind couldn't contain the idea, kept sliding off it like a hot boiled egg on a block of ice. And now she had to get the fuck out of here.

HAD TO! She had no options, no weapon but herself and any items within her reach. Time to go to work. *Whatever it takes.*

She tried to channel her nervousness into action. She'd never really understood Lady Macbeth's line before, but now she saw it, screwed up her courage, coiled the sparking energy into a spring that she could release to do maximum damage, turned the sheet back, and sat up. Jason Boredom slept on the sofa. Maybe burned out from jetlag, or bummed he didn't get to kill her. *Fucker.* Stupid ideas swirled through her head, but only one felt workable. The stupidest: Use Callan's weakness against him.

"Hey, Callan," she whispered, because the android would register her words as easily as normal speech. Not waking Jason was critical to her makeshift plan.

"What?" said the syRen®.

He passed the first test, using the droid's voice at a level that permitted Jason to sleep. Because having your assets rested made good operational sense. Even when being a monstrous, murderous bastard, Callan had been effective. On to Step Two then.

"D'you wanna see me naked?" She actually wondered why her skin didn't crawl when she said it.

"Whatafu?" said the android, almost comically. *Sleazy fucking bastard.*

"You heard."

She'd tried to think of another way, but had crap all resources in this scenario. They'd left her with her handset, but only after Callan blocked all the comms functions, even typing. She could play games, look at photos. She'd tried to take snaps, testing the limits they'd put on her, but the system—or whatever cyber worm Callan had infected it with—deleted the new image: video, selfies, slomo, all disappeared. *And so this shit.*

The android sat forward, a very undroid expression on its face. "Sure. Go ahead. I'm pretty bored too."

Congrats, perv. You passed Step Two.

She shuffled to the edge of the bed, sat there, unbuckled the belt on her jeans, undid the top button, started tweaking the hem of her T-shirt, then stopped.

Initiate Step Three.

"I dunno. I'm pretty shy."

"Come on. You can't tease a guy like that. Go on. Do it."

"Look, I'll take a photo. You tell me if you think I'm pretty enough to go all the way." She had to fight to keep the little girl lost expression on her face when all she wanted to do was start screaming and kill the fucker with a chair and extreme prejudice.

"I'll bet you are. You're cute as a button. Nice and...petite. Okay, take a picture."

Oh, Dio, there are way too many sleazoid creepers who navigate the world with their dicks, but just maybe this weakens him enough.

"Not *here*." She cast her eyes down. "I'll do it in the bathroom."

"Yeah, yeah, okay." The droid waved her in the direction of the internal door.

She stood, walked away from Callan/Bea and into the bathroom clutching the top of her jeans. She had *no* time and Step Four was complicated. She turned on the temperature-controlled taps then took off her right boot. As expected, the mixer tap linked to the room's thermostat. The main control unit sat in the main room, but the bathroom had a slave unit to account for its very particular environment. What a fuzking longshot, but longshots and desperate measures were all she had. She turned the boot around and whacked the wall-mounted control unit with the heel. It remained in place, controlling the water temperature, keeping the mirror clear.

"Watcha doin' in there, kid? C'mon out. Foster's gonna sleep for a while."

Foster. She didn't think of Callan as careless. Must be he just didn't give a shit about Foster's anonymity. "Taking my boots off," she called then clamped a hand over her mouth. Maybe she wouldn't wake Foster through the wall, but wouldn't Callan? Disaster? What did he mean about Foster sleeping? "Unless you want me to keep them on." That was a thing, right? Only staying in the scenario mattered right now.

"Nah, I like feet. Pretty little toes."

Well, lucky me, you belly-dragging lizard.

She had one more go. She raised the boot and swung harder. *But not too hard!* He mustn't come in here. The locked door wouldn't trouble him, and he'd strangle her like that woman on the Moon he'd...defiled, and thrown in a dumpster. The sensor unit bent, adopting a weird angle.

"Jesus, kid. Are those steel toecaps?" The voice came from right outside the door. She shuddered. *No!* But even if he came in, she would fight him.

"They're just tight, you know?" What was she doing? What might be breaking in her own head? Could she even blame Quirk after *this?*

The mirror was starting to steam up! *Step Four success, mofo!* She snatched up the soap and wrote a message on the steamed-up mirror.

"What's takin' so long? I'ma come in there, help you—"

"Unlock my camera so I can take the picture." She clutched the Lambo, tapped the camera icon—locked—and again—locked—and again. Unlocked! She photographed the mirror. "I need access to send you the pictures." *Plural. Best to up the stakes, tip him over.* But didn't she actually need to send a picture, to buy the time she needed for this to work? *Shit.* Had her subconscious conveniently skated over that detail when she devised this messed up ruse? *Fuckshit.*

The door handle jiggled and her heart leapt in her chest.

No time.

She dropped her jeans to her ankles, pulled up her T-shirt and took a picture, hurriedly sent it to Bea's message account. An underwear shot would stall him. That was really Step Six A, after the mirror message.

"I'm not dumb, kiddo. I'm limiting access to tertiary apps. Use PiCsHaRe."

Hah! Bingo. Callan underestimating her formed the basis of her stupid, reckless plan and he had. *Reliable as dickwork.* Sure, he'd left the primary apps cut off, no mails, messages, texts, posts, quips, spots, yaps and chats, and he'd kept the block on anything secondary like pushes, pulls, prods, pokes, DMs, highs, lows and shakes, but he'd treated with typical grown-up, macho contempt anything appearing childish.

"I'll go in stages," she said in the most innocent tone she could conjure in the heat of her desperation to escape, her fear of being discovered.

Hopefully stalling him with the first image, she sent her bathroom mirror picture using her PlushPuzzleMANIA account, which Callan in his filthy urgency had ignored with all her other silly gaming apps. But PPM—all pink and pastel, cute and cuddly, and very low tech—linked to players nearby. Although he controlled a super versatile, massively powerful machine, in some things Callan couldn't see further than the end of his average-sized incel imagination. According to the cutesy little screen, her secret message travelled all of fifty metres.

"This is nice. You're kinda pretty. Send more."

She slipped her arms from her bra straps, but left it on, stuck a thumb in her tangas to tug down the side a *little*, tapped and sent before she could think about it. *Escape is everything, cos they won't pat me on the head and let me go when they're done with me. Not Gregor Callan.* She put herself back together. As she buckled her belt she heard another voice.

"What the hell are you doing?"

Foster! But he sounded weird—sluggish and dopey.

"Forget about it, grunt," said Callan/Bea. "You look like shit. Sleep it off."

"Feels like I was spiked somehow. Just keep it together, don't be weird. I'm not telling TOM we can't keep a fourteen-year-old in line for a few hours."

Fifteen in a week, dopehead. But, had Callan drugged Foster? That chilled her.

These assholes were in danger of fucking up her plan with their bumbling. She'd have to go out there, which was not Step Seven, but Step Eight. She must still be an asset to whatever corporate power game TOM played, or they'd have dumped her by now, and Callan would not be holding back. She'd just have to buckle up her big girl pants and hope the threat of Simister's wrath would be enough to keep the troglodytes in line. She turned off the tap, hurriedly wiped her message off the mirror, and opened the door.

Stepping out of the bathroom, she found her jailors facing off at a polite distance. Foster did look like shit warmed through in an air fryer.

"Put your head down again, sleep it off," said Callan. "I timed the dose."

"Fucker," said Foster, venom blunted by the drug, dragged himself to the sofa, and flopped down. Moth thanked her lucky stars Callan had taken him out. It was part of her plan—she forgot the numbers now—that she had no direct influence on. She saw Foster blink out.

Fuzking weird. That left her alone with Callan. She struggled to face him, because he looked like Bea.

"So, where were we, doll? I'm liking your piccies, but it's showtime. Mm hm."

Jesu Christi, she'd have to swap syRen® after this, wouldn't she? She looked down at her Lambo to find it solidly locked.

"No more messin' around. He's out for the count. So, get on the bed, lemme see what you've got, girlie."

Her legs felt weak and wobbly.

"I'll help you along." The android, no longer her android, stepped towards her, and Moth stepped back. Her legs bumped the bed and her knees buckled, sitting her down against her will, leaving Callan/Bea looking down at her.

Knock, knock, knock.

The sudden sound halted Callan's next step. It had come so quick. No time to prepare. The droid glared at her, a viscous, narrow-eyed threat that froze her. "Don't you fuckin' move. We're right in the middle of somethin'."

The syRen® turned, walked to the door. He must have hacked the hall cameras because he didn't bother with the viewscreen. She tensed. Callan/Bea opened the door.

Moth didn't wait to see who had knocked. She bolted from the bed straight for the opening. The droid moved so quickly she almost stopped in shock. Callan/Bea's right arm snaked down to cut off the gap. The hotel staffer's expression shifted from polite interest to alarm to confusion. Moth didn't slow but slid, baseball style. Carpet would have stopped her, but lush wooden boards decked the first metre-fifty of the room, and she slipped under the android's grasping arm. Callan got a hold of her T-shirt's neckline which dug into her throat until the fabric ripped and the pressure disappeared. She twisted on the floor, popped into a crouch, and ran into that legs-don't-work nightmare. The corridor stretched in front of her in an infinite-seeming recession, the vanishing point unreachable. But she only needed fifty metres.

She stopped halfway to the elevators, turned to look. Callan had knocked the hotel duty manager down, but she clutched the droid's ankle. Callan could choose blatantly betraying his true nature by violating if not the First Law of Robotics, then certainly the second, or, allow the woman to hold him back then try to explain himself.

Everything paused in a frozen stare, Moth pushing on the hatch of the fifth-floor laundry chute, Callan/Bea's hand reaching out towards her, frustration and anger dripping from the droid's not-right syRen® features.

"Desist!" yelled the duty manager.

Moth flipped Callan the finger. "Fuck you, dickface, and the OS you rode in on!"

She grabbed a runner inside the laundry chute, swung her feet up, through the door, and dropped into darkness.

XXIII

18:10, 15 January 2100
Turbo Inn Hotel, Manhattan, New York, NY, NAF

She fell seemingly hundreds of metres down a fucked-up water-flume-run-dry in a haunted waterpark horror story, waiting for evil villain plasteel teeth to tear her flesh to shreds. Instead, she exploded from the bashing, boring, rattling darkness into harsh light, slamming into a huge basket of smelly towels and bed clothes. She lay for a moment. Although stinky, the laundry felt like a big pseudo-cotton hug, but she couldn't linger. She pushed up, hauled herself over the tub's edge, but it rocked and tumbled over, throwing her on the service basement's hard floor, tipping bedclothes over her.

"Fuuuuuuck!"

As she clambered out, a droid in blue dungarees appeared over her. "May I assist you? Guests are requested not to enter the service areas."

Her whole skin prickled at the shock of seeing an android within a mile of her, but Callan wasn't all droids. She stood. "I gotta get outta here. Show me the way, please. I'm in a hurry. I'm being pursued, at risk for my life."

"That is shocking. I will escort you to the hotel security station."

"Let's go." Because the beauty of Step Whatever-the-fuck (Nine?), was she didn't have to escape Callan, she just had to get to a public place where other droids would protect her. Callan could droid-jump, but he couldn't attack her in a public place. No, he could, but if he did, no way could he prevail against multiple regular syRen®. Even hopping between them to battle each other.

Oh, fuck. Could Callan control multiple droids simultaneously? She'd discounted that particular level of fuckupery. But Nick said he could run a droid phalanx, although she'd never seen it. *Too late to ask now, genius.*

They walked out of the service area into a bright, featureless corridor. Partway along, the droid stopped to open a set of almost invisible elevator doors. "Please enter."

She hesitated. She'd had too many fuzking surprises in elevators recently—and with androids too, but her plan relied on this. She had to get upstairs. She glanced at the neutral expression on this male syRen®. 2097 model, she thought, S-11340, from its violet forehead tattoo. It looked so standard.

She stepped into the elevator.

The door slid closed.

The elevator started downwards.

"What the *fuck?!*"

The android turned to her. "Are you ever gonna fuckin' learn, you little cock-tease?"

She backed into the corner, tensed with the hopeless thought she could resist an android. "Nick!" She called into the ether. "Nick Kirby, I need you right now!"

"Is he your boyfriend? Well, I'm gonna ruin you for him."

"TOM's plan, buttface! I'm part of the plan."

"You think so?" The droid sneered, laughing harshly. "You were blackmail bait for that gay-assed dick you hang with. Make sure he did his job, got his wife back. Man, I bet she hates you now. But that's done. I get to have my fun with you, and I don't need no pictures. I've got the real thing, still living and breathing, and I'll record it all."

The droid moved in, grabbed her wrist as she swung at it, grinned, clamped her other wrist. The elevator stopped. "Basement level. Everyone out for deserted stores and android sex parties."

"Fuck you, you waste of data!"

She didn't know whether to scream or sob. Did Jennifer hate her already? She couldn't move her arms, kicked her feet, swung knees, but landing a hit did nothing. The droid clamped its hands on her waist, lifting her, crushing her into the corner. She got her hands up, pressed her thumbs into its eyes, kicked her legs, screamed because it didn't make sense not to with all the listening systems in the world, in buildings, vehicles, appliances, and droids. Always a chance someone would hear. Her attack on the solid eyes failed. Callan/Bea's hands groped at her clothes. It got a hand up the back of her ripped T-shirt, another down under her belt. She pounded the head, bones aching, pain flaring in her hands.

"Nick! Where the fuck are you?! NIIIICK!"

Change of tack. She snaked hands around the thing's back, pulled herself hard against it. Even as the thought repelled her, she applied her main strength to defeating a frontal attack. Callan tore at her clothes, trying to pull apart her protections, dismantle her security, her confidence. Unexpectedly, the elevator began to move up as Callan/Bea's hands hauled on her belt, snapping it like liquorice.

Her anger burned bright as a solar flare. Fighting a droid head on was impossible. She'd not been scared enough of Callan when she made this stupid dangerous plan. Jammed against the wall, she would never wriggle out, so she braced her feet and heaved, gradually stepped up the wall until her greater leverage tipped the droid backwards. Downside, the fucking thing twisted and landed on top of her.

The elevator stopped, started again. Stopped, started, stopped. Something big and hard started swelling between them. *Fuuuuck!* Could she break it off? She'd fuzking try if it got free, both hands. The elevator started up again, swiftly this time.

"No!" Callan/Bea yelled. "Fuck off, dead boy! I'm busy." The droid swung an arm, smashing the control panel. The elevator slowed, but didn't stop.

A voice blared from the elevator's control panel. "Ground floor, suckwad: reception, hotel security, NYPD, SCAT and SWAT."

"Fuck you, Kirby. Fuck you!"

The elevator door slid back, and bodies pressed in. A low buzzing filled the air, like twenty NEMPs discharging together. One neuro-electromagnetic pulse would have been enough. The android's weight lifted from her, and she immediately pulled back into the corner. "Don't fuxxing touch me!"

"We got ya, miss. We got ya," said a thick NY accent, female.

"Blanket here," shouted another, male, younger, more polished. "Quick!"

Moth felt the blanket falling around her. She grunted, growled like a feral creature because she wanted anger now, to burn away the other shit. Somehow, the buzzing of her Lambo cut through the livid vibration of her bones. The device buzzed again and again against her hip. Someone, very gently, sat her up.

"We're just gonna put ya in this chair, honey. Don't worry, we got ya."

A woman's face drifted into view. NYPD cap, badge pinned to her tac-vest, red hair wound tightly and pinned behind her head. She and her colleague took Moth's weight, lifted her into an auto-chair.

Buzz-buzz, buzz-buzz.

Moth held up a hand to stop them, stood up, straightened despite her legs threatening to collapse. She held the blanket together at her neck. With her free hand she retrieved her Lambo and took the call, choosing to distrust her phone implant.

"Moth, I'm major busted I took so long," said Nick. *"I'm sorry. Got here soonest I could, but all you know is I wasn't here when you needed me."*

"Don't tell me why." It would only sound like a lame-dick excuse. "You got here before it was too late."

She felt herself descending again, sinking into an ocean of self-pity and loathing of, everything. She'd started it, wound Callan up with her fuzking genius escape plan. But it worked. That was all that mattered. She should let herself off the hook. Job done. Everything was fine now.

Once again, she remembered killing Nick in Yellowknife, saw the headshot clearly, not the dream-deformed version that came at night. But still Nick had come for her, wrestled Callan for control of the elevator in some kind of virtual Faraday cage fight. So, what would she see now when she fell asleep? Had she exorcised one nightmare to replace it with another?

"Thank you," she said into her handset. "You saved me. After what I did to you."

"Hey, you saved me too, I mean it. Released me from my pain, my madness. Don't fall into the pit I lived in, that TOM put me in. Callan would never have let you go. Don't take any blame for what he did."

"I'll decide how I'm feeling, thanks. Wait... Giulia! TOM said he'd kill her if I didn't—"

"I spoke to Mario. She's safe. TOM's using you against Quirk. I'll tell Dad you're safe."

"This was Quirk's fault," she rasped.

"Moth, it wasn't," said Nick, gently. *"I don't run long on forgiveness for my Dad, but TOM did this. Dad did you wrong, but nothing went down because of him."*

"Yeah." She sighed. "I think I kinda wish he was here."

"I get that. He can be reassuring. Hey, guess what. I helped him find Mom."

"Jennifer?" For some fucked-up reason that maybe wasn't fucked-up after all, this was the thing to set her off, dragging sobs up from her chest, setting tears tumbling. She wanted to be furious Quirk had found his family while hers was lost forever. But the crushing emotion came from somewhere else. She saw an image of her meeting Jennifer Simister, saw a caring woman, a mother who had lost a son. And the emotion that triggered in Moth's chest, pumped vigorously through her, was not pain at her loss or shame at what Callan tried to do, but hope.

χ

How *did* you solve a problem like Quinton Kirby?

Jennifer found it endlessly ironic that he performed the role of erratic, often over-emotional eccentric, but *she* wound up in an asylum. She could admit now that she'd been a touch...overwrought, then severely depressed for an extended period, that she and Quirk had fallen apart, each pushing simultaneously, each switching to pull in opposite directions. She accepted she had—at the moment of Quirk leaving—lost it. Lost track of how her life worked, where she fitted into it. Not that Quirk's presence defined her, never that—they'd defined each other. Perhaps the problems started there.

Still, her father had wasted no time stepping in to take control, doubling down on his pervasive influence, his insidious suggestions: A period of recuperation to clear her mind, to stabilise, revitalise. Medication to aid sleep, take the edge off the stress. Nothing about destroying her motivation, numbing her emotions to the point of overwhelming apathy, chaining her chemically to a bed and a room for days and weeks and months that added up, inevitably, to years. Why had she boarded this plane? To save Angelika Moratti. To learn about Nick. To confront Quirk, but also to ask a question that—away from the glare of everyone's attention—had consumed her since escaping Gramercy: Why had her father kept her there? Only her father knew the answer.

Meanwhile, being with Quirk felt both easy and difficult. They had been in love, very much so, and she wanted to love him again, let her emotions out to run around screaming their heads off. But did he bring too much baggage to the table now, if that wasn't a mixed metaphor? (Don't put your bags on the table!) First, they must discuss Nick. That would be the litmus test for everything else.

And where did Moth fit into all of this? Quirk's regard for her was written in the lines on his face when he talked about her troubles. Should she be angry at him for that too, running from her and Nick only to end up in the parental role he'd been so keen to avoid? Maybe she should be, but—feeling the way she did about Nick—she couldn't blame Quirk. It was such a sweet and daunting thing, to have someone put all their faith in you. She couldn't deny him what he felt for Moth, to learn no parent knew what they were getting into, but discovered it through acting from love, even when making mistakes.

And yet what of parents whose motivation came from darkness, and led to darkness? What did you do about them? About parents who cared nothing for their own children, nor any children? Cared nothing for the nature of this, or any world?

What did you do about them?

XXIV

08:20, 16 January 2100
30,000 feet above Limerick, United Irish States Airspace

Atmospheric conditions for a flight from London to San Francisco could not have been better, external to the C Corp Clearair CA101 sun-liner, at least. Within the thirty-seat cabin, Quirk thought "decidedly frosty" summed things up accurately.

Jennifer sat back in the passenger section as he taxied them alongside Old Father Thames, dismissing imagined disgruntlement on the CC android's placid features when Quirk confirmed he would fly them out of London City Spaceport. The syRen® had dutifully occupied the co-pilot's chair as Quirk turned the plane at the end of the runway then bolted for the blue, thrilling at the rush of acceleration, the weight of gravity's pull as they lifted from the deck. Blah blah, shackles of Earth, etcetera.

Jennifer seemed distant at first, perhaps from numbness at weeks of hiding and underground flight, or the months going on years of medication, but he'd seen more signs of her coming up for air in recent hours. Still, the whole Kira thing remained a mystery, suggesting a new...dynamic for Jennifer. There had been no time to investigate that, even if he'd wanted to. They'd dashed to the airport, Nick co-opting a syRen® to retrieve Quirk's small amount of luggage from the Apex Temple Court. The boy insisted on not speaking to his mother until Quirk and Jennifer had "the talk." Now, clearing the last landmass for a spell, he gave the android the con and walked back to join Jennifer. She welcomed him with an unreadable glance, but he took the seat opposite her. The cabin droid approached before Quirk could utter his preliminary apology.

"Anything for you, sir?"

Quirk made a show of looking at his blank wrist. "Gin and tonic, please."

"Sun over the yardarm?" asked Jenny.

"I chopped up the yardarm for firewood years ago."

"Tell me about Angelika Moratti," she said, sounding weary of the day already.

He told her everything, all the slings and all the arrows of the last five outrageous months since 11th August 2099. He told her about escaping the convent, travelling to the Moon, the case there that ended in disaster, the two deaths of Gregor Callan. He told her about home on Hygeia, about Creston, BC and Yellowknife, NT, skirting around the Nick question, for now. He related with some relish the death of Derek Morton. Jenny had met him a few times, thought little of him. Quirk had always taken that as a good sign. He outlined the events from Berlin to Skye. When it came to Moth's sojourn with the Hygeia Marine Scouts, he could not say much, as they'd had no time to discuss it. He wondered what it meant that his and Moth's partnership could be recounted in well under an hour. Carrying it around in his head, and his heart, it felt a lot heavier.

"The way you talk about her," said Jennifer. "Your expression. You like her."

"She has an infectious personality, certainly infected me, with something."

"I think that might be true." She held his gaze for uncomfortable moments, sat forward, sipped her water then pushed it away. She addressed the android back in the galley without raising her voice. "Steward, I'll have what he's having." Then, to Quirk, "I always hated that yardarm." She smiled slowly, slightly.

Quirk watched her watching him, tried to identify what he felt now. She had changed some and not at all. The winsome twenty-two-year-old had changed considerably in the five years from their meeting at the CC Seasonal Celebration, from carefree yet combative socialite, to rebellious and resourceful campaigner, much to her father's chagrin. Perhaps Joshua Simister blamed Quinton Kirby for that, too. It had always seemed the smallest of the things that drove TOM to disapprove of him. Not providing the child both Simisters wanted (and for TOM, an heir) quickly became Quirk's chief transgression.

What did Callan say months ago on the lunar surface? *"Your wife hates you."* She should do. But damn, his introspection, so quickly and easily, had become about him. Jenny had paid for his selfishness. He knew now that his efforts or lack thereof had broken everything around him. And now his transgressions came home to roost.

Their G&Ts arrived. They sipped in unison. Could he avoid breaking this before it was mended?

"So," she said. "Tell me what happened to Nick. And, look..." She placed her hands on the edge of the table, looked down at them. "I'll make it easier for you. I believe he's dead."

He sipped again then began. "You're both right and wrong." And he told her the story as best he could, leaving nothing out on purpose, from the moment he became certain of Nick's involvement in the Yellowknife case, up to the point of Moth shooting the physically twisted, mentally unbalanced being Joshua Simister's scientists had "developed" by intensive experimentation. He recounted Nick's statement that he'd done all he had to gain release from physical torment, to make the transition into the virtual world that he'd sought for so long. Finally, he told Jennifer of Nick's aiding him in the Martian case, and in London, in finding Jennifer herself.

"I think he's nervous of talking to you. He could be listening now."

She put her hands on her cheeks then pushed the remains of her crudely dyed hair back, leaving a spikey mop. She looked at Quirk's chest, or more specifically his breast pocket where his cLife rested.

"If you're ready. How do you feel about it?"

"Don't you dare try to protect me from my own son, Quinton. Don't. You already interrupted my holiday and dragged me out of a perfectly good billet."

And what else, with Kira? "I'm sorry." He slid his handset across the table.

"What's the number?" she asked.

"It doesn't matter," said Quirk, just as the handset buzzed. "I'll leave you two alone."

He walked back through to the flightdeck and took control from the android, paused the autopilot, and flew the plane for a while. Several times his android co-pilot asked him if he felt fatigued or needed a break. When finally he gave in to the android's passive-aggressive (in other words neutral) concern, he found Jennifer asleep in her seat with a blanket over her. The cabin steward informed him the lady had become emotional after the call and had requested a sedative.

Quirk decided that was a good idea, and ordered his own sedative, and tonic. He watched Jenny sleep, contemplated brushing back parts of the untidy clump of hair that fell across her face, wondered if she would let the natural auburn grow out. But maybe the Gramercy Refuge did not permit such things.

* * *

Buzz-buzz. Buzz-buzz. Buzzzzz. Bu-bu-bu-bu-bu-bu-BUZZZZ!!

"What the hell?"

Quirk jerked his head up from the—something. Couch? Bed? Sofa? Airplane personal comfort unit. He remembered now, remembered everything, sour knowledge crashing over him, a wave of regret. He'd decided to sleep because he needed to speak to Jennifer, and she seemed unlikely to surface for hours. And now someone rang his cLife like a xylophone.

Buzzity, buzzity, buzz-buzz-buzz.

He snatched it up from the chair pouch beside him. "What?!"

"You are in so much trouble. Just wait till Mom wakes up."

"What's happening, Nick? I'd ask where the hell you are, but that's redundant."

"No time. You can babble after I speak. Moth's free. She escaped from TOM's men in New York."

"Just now?" Stupid, sleep-brain question. His thoughts began to dart about, bouncing off the walls of his skull as he tried to pick apart the threads of corporate plotting that TOM had spent weeks, months or years tugging and tangling into shape.

"Who's she with? Where's Bea? Suudi's still in hot water: How does it affect your mother's position?"

"I don't think TOM'll blow up Suudi just to spite you. In case you forgot, he's trying to extract something from the UN. Assume you're way down the list compared to NLS drive licences. But don't worry, I bet he'll circle round to shaft you later."

"Yes, quite."

"You're not actually taking Mom back to the refuge, right?"

"If Moth's safe? No chance. How did your talk go, with your mom?"

"She was upset, natch. But it was awesome. Better than talking to you. Sorry."

Despite itching to ask about Jenny's response to Moth's action, he had to focus on Nick here, even if the boy did seem to hop back and forth between remorse and anger at him.

"Once she got over me being a kind of digital ghost, she understood the escape I needed after what my fucking Grandpa did to me. She accepted what Moth did, and rowed me for how I treated you and the Yellowknife folks. I get it. I've been angry for a long time because, you know, I don't really know how to be a kid."

Quirk's heart clenched, and someone tied his oesophagus in a knot. Moisture abandoned his eyes in search of a lifeboat. "Nick—"

"I'm sorry I was a buttface on Mars. I struggle with how to act sometimes, how to deal with people. It's like things fly out of control if I look away for a second."

Oh, boy. "Nick... We've got some work to do, me and you, mostly me, and I want to do it. I think I've been a buttface longer than you have. Maybe we should say everything's my fault and take it from there. What do you think?"

"That's kinda what Mom said. She said she'd deal with you later."

Quirk snorted. "That sounds about right."

"So, what we gonna do?"

"You say that like I'm in charge." Somehow, he never quite felt in control of...anything with Jennifer around, but not in a bad way. That feeling returned almost immediately on re-entering her company. But thoughts of her now, reclining just five metres away, came with an inclination to do whatever she wanted, to please her, to make her smile. That was new. "I suppose I am, nominally. So. I have no client this time round. Will I finally stop standing down and cross swords with the old bastard?"

"You're welcome to my opinion."

Was this another parenting moment? It felt rather like it. "I know you want to get back at him, Nick, but don't let revenge spoil the good work you're doing with us. I can see that you're sorry for what you did. Keep showing it in the things you do now."

"I will. I helped Moth, in New York. I saved her from that Callan entity."

"Callan?!" A black cloud descended to cut off the warmth of what had felt like a glowing moment with Nick. "Damn!" Of course TOM would reclaim those broken pieces. The Old Man was bound to have a backup to his nasty genetic engineering scheme, and now Moth had found herself up against that twisted, hollowed-out soul that was Gregor Callan? She must have been terrified. He wanted to snatch up his handset and call her but he was with Nick now, and Nick needed him too.

"Well done, Nick. I'm proud of you. Tell me the details soon, but first I have to change the flight plan. We're going to New York. I'll make some calls on the way."

"I think she'd like to hear from you," said Nick, quietly. Odd. *"Moth's escape was...traumatic. I know you guys had a bust up, but go easy on her."*

Quirk's short time with Moth grasping for some kind of parental dynamic had taught him that certain keywords were code for "acute awkwardness beyond this point." He had to get over that now. Moth needed him, by the sound of it. How would she react to Jenny? Strangely, the thought made him smile. *One More Ticket for The Rodeo.*

"I'll be guided by her. Don't go anywhere."

"Pfft. Dad, I'm everywhere."

Nick ended their call and Quirk set about waking himself by dry washing his face and slapping his cheeks several times. Job done, he walked to the flightdeck. He paused to watch Jennifer again, wondering where her dreams took her now she knew the truth about Nick. Regarding her—perhaps even more so beneath the gentle veil of sleep—remained one of his greatest pleasures. He had not looked enough in the last five years at her picture, even though plenty of images resided on his handset just a tap or two away, or in his head, instantly accessible, if he chose.

He sighed. Could they ever...? Quirk shook his head at his arrent procrastination. Moth needed...someone, and he would put himself forward. The choice would be hers.

The android pilot appeared not to have moved since Quirk departed the flightdeck. Entirely possible. It turned to observe him. "Everything is under control, sir."

"Change of plan, S-13035. Alter course to JFK Spaceport, New York."

"Yes, sir."

"Also, I need the flightdeck for a few minutes. Leave the door open, please. I want to know when Jennifer wakes up."

The android departed.

Quirk called Moth. The call rang for five minutes then he hit stop.

Observation One, she had not blocked him, her handset would have rejected the call immediately. Observation Two, if she had muted him the contact would have been rejected after a minute. Observation Three, she must have left the line open, and either chosen to ignore the call, or hadn't seen it. Observation Four, these observations were academic. Who was with her for company and comfort, for her safety and security? A hollowness worried at his stomach. She might be hurting right now, and he couldn't do anything. Would she allow him to after what he'd done, or rather omitted to do? Frustrating that he must carry this particular can. But displaced anger remained anger, it had to be dealt with either way. Sometimes you didn't need to be the one who pulled the trigger. There was always enough blame to go around, blame and therefore guilt.

His cLife buzzed. Moth. He let it ring twice. *See aforementioned guilt.*

"Moth. Talk to me. Tell me as much or as little as you like."

"I'm not even sure I can speak to you." Her tone was sullen. *No, exhausted.*

"Okay. Fair. Who's there with you?"

"I'm at an apartment in Astoria. One of Rigel's bookkeepers came down from the NY HQ with a couple of...interns. Brought me here when the PD questioning finished."

"How are you doing?"

"I'm bouncing off the walls. Don't know where I am. You're still a huge A-hole, but... I'm glad you called. I won't say on the phone what happened. Don't think I want to tell you at all, but I need to talk about it, to someone who knows me. That's not a long list where I'm sitting. Rita Mancuso from Rigel, she's nice, but... You know?"

Quirk's smile at talking with Moth at all had, as she spoke, morphed into a grimace: *Live by the Sword, Die by the Words.* "I know. I have stuff to say to you, and I can't do it on a call either. We're coming to New York, I— Ha, there's too much to say. But Moth, I'm sorry, for what I didn't do. Struggling to tell you is no excuse for not telling you.

I'm the grown-up, after all." He listened for her spark, but could not hear it.

"So you keep telling me."

"Well, I'm a rank amateur. I never read the guidebook."

Damn, but she had charmed her way into his heart in these few months, very much under the radar considering her typical MO. Annoying, since he considered himself the charming one in this duo. Also, not a little terrifying, as his heart was not a safe space, for him or anyone else.

"Kids," she said, and he pictured Moth rolling her eyes. *"I think there's a Haynes manual."*

"You're such a geek."

"Nicest thing you ever called me. My dinner's here. Oh my." The line became silent. He'd been muted. *"I have to send you this. Wait."*

As if he would go anywhere. A link appeared on his screen. He tapped it, and a cLife app windowed into being. A scent file. He raised the handset. The aroma issuing from the olfactory port made him blink.

"Is that a *steak*?"

"Ribeye—rare, peppercorn sauce, French fries, grilled tomato, langoustine in herb butter. Steak's vat grown, obvs. I—"

From the jerky breathing on the line, Moth had begun to cry. "Moth? What is it?"

"Nothing. Something. Just, everyone's so kind, and I fuzking messed up. Nick keeps telling me I didn't. He helped me, Quirk. He came when I yelled for him. I did something stupid. Did it before to that bonehead Becker in Creston, and I thought—"

"It's okay. You can say it, or not. I won't judge. I'm glad Nick was there. What are the chances, eh? It looks like he could be a good kid," and perhaps was listening. Quirk hoped he was. "Even after all he's been through. All I—and TOM—put him through." Moth puffed a couple of deep breaths, perhaps trying to quell her anxiety. "Hey, how many times have I said not to panic with your mouth full?"

"Quirk, Bea had Callan inside her. They came for me in Milan and took me to New York. TOM called me and told me he would kill Giulia. It's Secretary Suudi. What can we do?"

"Nick told me about Callan. I hate that he was anywhere near you. Moth, we're coming to New York. We'll be there..." He checked the nav display. "In about two hours. Whatever you did, it worked. You're free. Tell me when we get there, but only if you want, and I'll hear you out about everything. I mean everything. Just sit tight for a couple more hours, okay? Where is Bea now?"

"Cops kept...her for a scan by Special Cyber & Android Tactics. Who's 'we'?"

"Jennifer's with me."

"Fuuuck. She hasn't killed you yet?" Shortest of pauses. *"Oh shit, Quirk, sorry. I..."* She tailed off.

"Hey, don't dare lose your sense of humour. That's my favourite part of the day."

"Now I know you're bullshitting me."

"Look, I'll explain when we get to New York, but Jenny's a good listener. I think you could talk to her. I'll call again when we're landside. Enjoy that steak. And promise me you'll hang in there?"

"I will," she said, flatly. *"I wanna see the bruises she gave you."*

Moth ended the call.

"Good listener, am I? Better than you, apparently."

He turned to Jennifer, standing in the doorway, and smiled: *Regrets, I've Had a Few*, not revealing he'd seen her silent approach reflected in a dark flightdeck display.

"How's she doing?" The concern in her voice touched him.

"Not great, I think. Would you speak to her? I know it's a lot to ask when you've never even met, but—"

She stopped him with a gesture. "If I hadn't spoken to Nick I might have struggled, but I understand now. She was protecting you, and—" Jenny's words slowed to a stop. He could see her struggling with her emotions, and why wouldn't she? "Nick accepts he has work to do. Moth sounds like a good kid," she managed.

"She is, Jenny. I gave you the potted summary, but there's so much more to tell."

"And this time—unlike all those trips for my father—I want to hear it all. I've been in the dark for too long." She softened the line with a smile, a little wider this time, held just a little longer. "For now, drive the plane, flyboy. Just know you're not off the hook. Our first discussion in New York will involve a lot more of me talking and you listening."

XXV

09:15, 16 January 2100
55,000 feet above Nuuk, Greenland

The pressure on Quirk's posterior increased, his weight transferred gradually from one elbow to the other. Jennifer smiled at his regard then recognised his concern. Slowly, smoothly, the Clearair had segued from straight cruising into a gentle lefthand turn. The android co-pilot stepped from the flightdeck. Jenny's gaze flicked from Quirk to something over his right shoulder. The cabin droid.

"Sir," said the co-pilot. "I have received instructions contrary to those you issued. This flight has been redirected to our original destination, San Francisco."

Several redundant questions flicked past before he lighted on, "This lady is travelling to New York for an appointment. Her mental health may be adversely affected by missing the appointment, contrary to the First Law of Robotics."

"This is no concern of mine. I have my instructions. You will be detained."

"Huh?" said Quirk. Not the first time a CC syRen® had acted...unexpectedly. Fright jangled his nerves at the thought it might be Callan. Whatever, this was trouble.

Quirk shot from his seat, tricky on a plane, the awkwardness slowing him enough for the android steward behind him to get a grip of his shoulder. Before it spun him around he saw Jenny shy away from the co-pilot. Cowering? No. She twisted back and jammed her flight tray into the android's neck as it lunged at her. The tray splintered, tearing the android's synthetic skin, exposing its substructure, cutting Jenny's hands.

Quirk's vision slid across ceiling, windows, floor as the steward threw him down the aisle. Definitely contravening the laws now. He scrambled to hands and knees, poised to shuffle backwards, wishing for a NEMP, or a gun—because he had not a single qualm about shooting an android.

"Nick?" Worth a try. Quirk's cLife buzzed, but he couldn't reach it.

The steward advanced again. "Please remain calm, sir. If you permit me to restrain you, the potential for personal injury will be considerably reduced."

"Sorry, Sparky, cable ties invalidate my warranty."

Backing away from the android meant retreating from Jennifer. It grated severely, but without a tactical advantage or a heavy object he'd be pretty much useless against two syRen®. He shuffled backwards, away from the droid's advance, leaning against the plane's turn, trying to fish out his cLife. He fumbled it. The handset slid away down the sloping floor as the plane turned towards San Francisco. He didn't even have an inflight magazine to roll up and whip the android with (he'd seen that in a movie).

The steward stalked him as he scrambled to the rear of the plane.

"Can you just wait? It's distracting trying to develop a counterattack when you loom like that."

Using human tactics against physically optimised, maximised and generally topped-out machines? Pretty pointless. So, use their android characteristics. The First Law of Robotics: "A robot may not injure a human being or, through inaction, allow a human being to come to harm." *Thank you, Professor Asimov.* Clearly, these androids circumvented the Laws and Tenets of robotics. CC's buddies at Androicon had a work-around, however the hell they did *that.* Another crime on TOM's rap sheet. Thoughts of a private army chilled Quirk to the bone. The man had to be stopped, if he could just get out from under current peril and negate the existential risk to the UN Secretary for Technology, and anyone in his blast radius.

Quirk's retreat came to an immediate halt when his back hit the bulkhead, or rather the toilet door. The android grabbed for his upper arms. Quirk ducked, pummelled the syRen®'s stomach with a quick combination to no great effect. He tried to spin the android like a running back would, twist past it into the body of the plane, to reach Jennifer, but the syRen® simply closed the space, pushed him with both hands. A textbook block, not even a suggestion of a holding penalty.

Change of tack. Quirk extended his elbows like a chicken, propping on the headrests flanking the aisle, swung up his legs, planted his feet on the android's chest and shoved. The syRen® went sprawling. Quirk dropped, turned, hit the toilet door pad, slipped inside and locked it. The android's fists pounded the door.

"This is unwise, sir. Please come out and permit me to restrain you. This is the painless solution to the present predicament."

"A predicament of your own making, you damned waste of polymers. If you hurt my...ex-wife, I'll scavenge you for toaster parts!"

What the hell was going on? He'd harboured suspicions about Androicon's research activities behind its high street facade, and there were the usual public conspiracy theories, but this? CC using tampered droids in the wild? The FBI had always dismissed so-called exposés in the past due to a complete lack of evidence. What might be the parameters of Androicon's heinous practice? A software corruption? Could the laws reassert themselves, a syRen® reset? Or, must the droids be scrapped? With a lingering thought for what Moth said about Callan, he wondered if the "glitch" was contagious, but an urgent fear for Jennifer drove these notions away.

These scrambled androids, they couldn't... They wouldn't torture someone. Shooting to kill, attacking a human, was a black and white decision, a threshold to breach, a task to complete. Torturing, harming a human, using pain as a tool, that had an emotional component. No syRen® could simulate that, surely?

The battering on the door continued. Odd. The android must know by now its hands couldn't defeat the door's integrity. The bashing stopped. Nothing. Had it gone to find a battering ram? Quirk risked putting his ear to the door in time to hear a crash. He really hoped Jenny continued to resist. Meanwhile, he hid in the toilet. Damn it, he'd only come in here in search of a weapon! *Come on, Quirk, think!* Demounting one of the laser toilet's so-called jets could not be a viable option, them being built in, powered from the plane. He scanned the cubicle. Toilet, discounted. Air-driven UV hand steriliser, inbuilt. Dispenser of towelettes for the mopping of the fevered brow, no heft. Nano deodorant; kwik-gro hand tissues; eye masks, toothpaste, toothbrushes.

"Come on, Quirk. Do *something*."

He opened a facemask, squeezed out an entire tube of toothpaste, spread that evenly over the mask then poked a toothbrush, handle first, into the open toilet pan. The low-powered lasers fired. He repeatedly poked the toothbrush into the bowl, ascertaining the laser's pattern then opened a fresh toothbrush and used the toilet lasers to sharpen it. This worked surprisingly well, and quickly enough to do another three.

"I doubt you can hear me, Nick, but I'm sure you'd be here if you could."

He took up his arsenal and triggered the door. His view down the cabin opened up to reveal the android steward marching towards him hefting a fire extinguisher.

Quirk ducked back inside, locked the door again, not in any attempt to hide, but to make the android use the damn thing, to slow it down.

The impact of the first blow made a dent in the door. With the second blow, the extinguisher forced a flap of plasfibre panel out of the door near the release pad. A sector of the extinguisher's base poked through the tear, the crack of the twisted fabric like a gunshot in the small space. But why didn't the android infiltrate the control system? Some fortunate logistical obstacle, perhaps. Quirk placed his toothbrush knives on the counter as another shuddering blow enlarged the hole. He'd dismissed trying to pull the extinguisher through: Tug o' war with an android would be a hiding to nothing.

"Your cooperation would be helpful and reduce the potential for injury to you."

On impulse, Quirk slathered toothpaste over the door release as the android reached through the hole, touched the pad. The door slid open.

There. The slightest pause, the merest glance from the android towards its sticky fingers. Quirk reached forward, slapped the toothpaste-slathered mask on the syRen®'s face with one hand, and stabbed a laser toilet-sharpened toothbrush into its neck. Only a mindboggling degree of luck would cripple the thing, but distraction should do at this point, and maybe Nick would swing back to check on his mom and dad.

As the android groped for the mask, Quirk rammed a second toothbrush into its stomach, and a third up under its jaw as the syRen®

grasped at the first improvised dagger, surely more puzzled than anything else. His distractions proved sufficient for Quirk to grasp the extinguisher placed carefully by the door. As his hand closed on the handle, the plane began to descend. Still four hours from San Francisco that meant somewhere very cold, possibly wet, probably mountainous, definitely remote. Odd.

Now, the syRen® steward stood calmly before him, removing sharpened toothbrushes from its body. Down the plane, he glimpsed the co-pilot droid subduing Jennifer, her wrists already bound, tape being applied to her mouth. That didn't stop her struggling, jerking her arms trying to get them loose, to resist her attacker.

"Why is the plane descending?"

"I do not know," said the steward, blankly. "Neither does my colleague, but they will rectify the situation. Now, please submit to your restraint. Your countermeasures have been ineffective and now are exhausted." The android reached both hands toward him.

Quirk smiled, *Say Hello to My Little Friend,* raised the extinguisher and fired it directly into the android's face.

A plume of white gas—*whatever...I'm a detective, not a damn chemical engineer*—blossomed around the syRen®'s head, momentarily blinding its various cameras. Only then did Quirk start pummelling its head with the butt of the heavy extinguisher, following the android as it stumbled backwards down the aisle. His arms ached, but he kept hammering the android's face. *Satisfying. Sort of like chopping wood.* A flap of skin from its now dented, exposed cheek flapped over a gunge-smeared eye, but the post-10000 model benefited from cameras in the aural canal's outer horn, and either side of the septum. Blinding one was too much like hard work.

"Assist! Ass— ist mleee—ee—ee," said the android as its system flailing under the weight of Quirk's bludgeoning. Stupid thing continued to come at him, trying to complete its task. This thing's Laws and Tenets really were completely scrambled.

As it reeled, Quirk stooped to retrieve his handset. A message.

```
NICK [09:22, 16-01-2100]
    These droids are messed up! The plane is
    locked tight. I'm trying to get in. HELP MOM!
    Also—get a fucking implant!
```

The broken steward regained some efficacy, came at him again. Quirk adopted batting stance and swung for the fences with his extinguisher just as the plane tipped downwards. Effectively, the android lurched into the swing as Quirk's improvised lumber connected. Like any half-decent batter, he followed through on the swing, his good technique decapitating the android. The syRen®'s head popped neatly from its shoulders and thwacked high up into the opposite side of the fuselage.

"Lights-out, Sparky." He hated mixing baseball metaphors, but no other phrase would do. The android did not go down, but the severe damage ruined its sensory input and therefore its coordination. It stumbled forward, and he pushed it over easily.

He managed three steps forward towards the still-struggling Jennifer when the co-pilot turned away from her and came at him calmly, hands balled into mechanical fists.

Just then the aircraft tipped again, plunging towards the Earth.

Quirk tumbled forward, dropped the extinguisher, grabbed for a fixture. The co-pilot's arms stretched for him as it fell towards the flightdeck door, and him after it. The plane's airframe began to rattle violently. The syRen® hit the flightdeck door just before Quirk hit the android. The door groaned, but held.

"Nick!"

The cabin speakers hummed. *"I broke something! What's up with this plane?!"*

"More worried what you're doing to it!"

The android clamped its arms around his back, squeezed, trying to break his ribs. Quirk punched its face a couple of times, to show he hadn't lost interest.

"Look, 13035," he gasped. "We're all going to be playing patty cake in a few minutes. The rescue team will be lucky to make one good cyborg from bits remaining. Let's cooperate to stabilise the plane and argue about restraining humans later."

"Your associate's actions are destabilising the aircraft. Make him stop."

"Nick?!"

"I'm trying!"

By now, the Clearair rattled like a street corner collection tin. Quirk reckoned the dive angle at forty degrees, ran the numbers in his head. He promised again to buy an implant, providing he survived the next X minutes, where X was a number much smaller than he would have liked.

Quirk's pocket buzzed. The android crushed him. Above the rattling, Jenny—clearly free of her gag—yelled in anger and frustration. *Not fear.* That made him smile. He managed to fish out his handset, twist his head to glimpse the screen. *Interesting.*

"Listen. I know your moral compass is doolally, but the lights must be on in your logic centre. No one gets a positive outcome if we end up in the Labrador Sea. Your instructions don't involve killing us, right?"

"That is true. Have your virtual colleague desist and I will land the plane."

"No. I land the plane, I have more hours than you. Just give me the time I need."

"Public records show that is true, and projections confirm extended argument will result in a negative outcome. Your scores show reasonable proficiency. I will desist until such time as the situation is stabilised. Then you will be required to submit."

"Hallelujah." Quirk's handset buzzed again.

The android released him and dragged itself into the nearest seat, buckling in.

Still crumpled in the angle between door and floor, Quirk twisted around. "Nick. Cease and desist with the plane. I've struck a deal. We'll pursue the analogue solution."

"Roger that."

"Not an option I'd considered," growled Quirk through a grimace before deciding the situation had progressed beyond even gallows humour.

He sat back on the canted floor—one knee either side of the flightdeck door—and hit the pad. The door slid halfway and ground to a halt, then butted noisily against the unseen obstruction. Squeezing past the half-closed door, Quirk's view through the front screen showed a great deal of water. The GPWS alarm had become immediately and loudly audible. Funny how the scariest things could be stated in the simplest terms. You have a new leader. Your test was positive. Ground Proximity Warning.

"Pull up, pull up, pull up," said the synthetic voice, firmly.

Still supported by the edge of the door, gravity trying to drag him through and smash him into the front screen, Quirk unbuckled his belt, looped it around the strut supporting the fold-down booster seat at the back (or top!) of the flightdeck. Slipping the real leather through its own buckle, he lowered himself far enough to grip the edge of the captain's seat then scrambled in. He braced his feet on less critical parts of the instrument panel, and pulled on the harness. He clipped himself in and went to work, immediately pulling back on the stick in a smooth and decisive manner. The key, of course, was to remain calm and let his training take over.

"Need my help?" asked Nick through the speaker system.

"Yes, with significant respect, please assist by shutting up."

"Coulda just said 'No.'"

Dive angle thirty-seven degrees. He was winning, but slowly. Not over-banked though, their plummet to destruction retained nice trim, horizon level, no roll correction needed. The plane continued responding to his firm yet caring touch. The nose came up smoothly, consistently. Twenty-five degrees. Twenty. Fifteen. Only then did he check altitude. Sixteen thousand feet. *Pah, loads of room.* But perhaps he'd been a little short on time. He trimmed them off, set the autopilot, and began panicking about his pre-existing problem.

Speaking of that devil, the android appeared at the flightdeck door, still wedged halfway closed. With very little apparent effort the syRen® pushed the sliding door open.

"The emergency is resolved. Will you now submit to being restrained?"

Quirk turned in his seat. "About that. Nick did cause the dive inadvertently due to the fiendishly complex security systems on this plane but, being unable to take control and correct his mistake, I gather he put his down time to good use."

Quirk turned his handset towards the android.

```
NICK [09:24, 16-01-2100]
   Close to busting this syRen® encryption.
```

```
NICK [09:26, 16-01-2100]
   Bingo. Ready to go when you are.
```

The android stood quietly, to the point Quirk began to doubt Nick's messages. Yet the syRen® didn't press the order that he be bound, or say anything at all, in fact.

"S-13035? Nick, are you 'on board' now? Are you...in there?"

Without warning the android advanced on him. Quirk pushed out of the seat, but he strained to lift his arms, fatigue settling on his shoulders like deadweight. He needn't have bothered. The syRen® opened its arms and hugged him. It felt surprisingly natural given recent incidences of droids attempting to crush, strangle and generally do him in.

"Sorry I was late, Dad. I'm feeling pretty stretched."

"I..." Quirk hugged the syRen® back. He really was beginning to subscribe to the wider theory that things worked out better when he kept his big mouth shut.

XXVI

09:38, 18 January 2100
Astoria, New York, NY, NAF

Arriving at JFK over two hours later, they didn't get as far as customs. They hadn't even reached "wheels down" when ATC informed Quirk the FAAA would meet them on the techmac. Their flightpath he could explain. He was more worried about the decapitated android in the passenger compartment. Jenny suggested hiding the droid's remains in the toilet, but that tended toward concealing evidence, so he asked Nick/S-13035 to put the carcass in Seat 3B, and try to tie the head on. He would face whatever brickbats the FAAA (because airplane), Homeland Security (because airplane registered in Botswana), CIA (because international flight), FBI (because domestic airport), NYPD (because local destination), and UNP (because nationalised Belter) cared to swing at them. Punting it down the road should never be underestimated as a response to adversity. Not in Quirk's book, in which the plot could turn on a sixpence, a knife edge, a dime, or pretty much any other MacGuffin you had to hand, and generally did.

All those interviews took an exceedingly long time, but still were as so much chaff in the wind compared to his feelings around meeting up with Moth again. Contrition, of course, with an accompaniment of regret, served in a jus of promises to do better split with his irresistible charm. And for dessert? He hoped Jennifer would bring the sweetness and light. Not something she'd been renowned for, even with things going swingingly in the sea of their love back in the day. This train of thought carried him to the realisation that, although they had talked about life events since their separation, and about Nick, he and Jenny had studiously avoided the topic of them. Perhaps that was best for now. Perhaps some time when things were less complicated.

The hours bled away in one interview room or another. It got late, very late, unfeasibly late, then became uncomfortably early, far too early for a sensitive personal meeting. Through a stream of messages coordinated by Nicholas Kirby—whose tone in the last hours had been positively contrite—Quirk and Moth agreed to meet the following day in Astoria Park, under the Hell Gate Bridge (her choice). Moth made it clear she would be accompanied by some Rigel "colleagues." The phrase struck fear into Quirk's heart for various reasons. Firstly, was this an indication she had accepted some kind of formal position in the Rigel organisation? Did that, immediately and irrevocably, sound the death knell of their professional relationship? Would he turn up tomorrow to receive her letter of resignation from The Quirk Agency? He really hoped not. Second, the presence of bodyguards suggested that she *might* feel she had some cause to fear him, or if not him (he very much doubted he'd done anything to engender fear in any of the current players), then the people orbiting him, carrying his baggage. That she no longer felt safe in his company. Had she ever?

And Gregor bloody Callan. How in the worlds had that happened? Quirk had been there, in a very personal and immediate sense, his consciousness inhabiting the same android as Callan when they had been shot. He'd heard Callan's scream, the very essence of life, existence, being ripped away. But Callan had continued. Reprieved by Joshua Simister, who did nothing for nothing. Only something for something, and always more than you intended to give. And TOM had embarked on a most elaborate game this time, engineering the attack on Jiilaal Mire Suudi, UN Secretary for Technology, for the purpose of impregnating him with a bomb that no one wanted to go off. Quirk realised the pressure of that threat had crouched within him for days now, despite TOM pushing and pulling him around all this time, barely any time to eat, sleep, think. He felt that threat now, gnawing at him.

And they couldn't tell anyone, because that way lay death, possibly to every single person in the UN building, and debris exploded from the heights of UN HQ all over FDR, bodies fired from windows into the East River, plascrete, plass, blood and bone raining down on Keegan Road, where all the emergency vehicles would arrive, too late. What a bloody mess. And he had dragged Jennifer into all of this. He and Nick, they already had their tickets to the TOM-town travelling horror show. Then again, Jennifer knew the ringmaster, intimately. The man who had given her life, then gifted a life to her in the form of a son bred from her DNA, and Quirk's. Jennifer Kirby née Simister possessed the golden ticket, but they had not yet discussed how she felt about that. How would all this possibly play out, when the clowns—Quirk's characterisation of that jolly band including Callan and Anwar, possibly Mario Manfredi—still lurked in the shadows, probably hankering to use his head as a piñata?

In fact, Moth had said they needed to hurry, because Mario had more information, not pretty, but the capo had a plan, a Rigel-sponsored response.

He looked from the Autocab^{OS}'s window, watched the ancient buildings of Astoria slip by, the many times repaired, replated, re-anodised, regenerated and otherwise reconstructed steelwork of the El above them. A nice sunny day to meet in the park. He glanced at Jennifer, sitting calmly beside him, then at the Nick/droid facing them, seated in a suitably unremarkable, droid-like manner. In the privacy of the cab, however, the soft yet strong syRen® features of S-13035 betrayed a mischievous smirk. Nick saw Quirk's smile and winked.

"It's so great to see you guys together."

Quirk experienced a surreal reaction to that voice, heard in a relatively relaxed environment—unlike their recent interactions during chases and stressful operations. It transported him back to Yellowknife. Not to the slavering beast man who had destroyed the Genextric habitat floor, facilitating (unknowingly) the National Guard strike TOM had used to destroy completely the lab and all evidence of his monstrous wrongdoing. No, this was the jokey, goofy, optimistic trickster who helped Moth and him evade the police long enough to get to Yellowknife to do some good.

"Now, honey," Jennifer corrected gently. "Quinton and I are not back together. We're sharing a cab."

"Quirk," said Quirk. "Quinton is my bowling name. Everybody calls me Quirk."

"But I'm not everybody, Quinton, I'm Jennifer Kirby, remember?"

"Heh," said Quirk. "Used to be—"

"Yes, well, whose fault is that? More to be said on *that* subject, Mister."

The Autocab^{OS} pulled up on the tree-lined park side of 19th Street, payment already taken via Quirk's handset before the door unlocked. Crisp, cold air met their disembarkation to the street, but the sun shone. Jennifer pulled her new winter coat tight around her, adjusted her new scarf and narrowed her eyes a little at Quirk. He realised he'd started patting a tympany on his hips. He stopped, smiled weakly—*Listen and repeat: Mea Culpa, Signora*—then buttoned his own overcoat. Nick/S-13035 stood waiting on the humans. Suitably gathered, the three walked into the leafless, spectral trees towards the East River.

A sombre place, the park in winter. Joggers still jogged, strollers pushed infants, dogwalkers walked their dogs, several preferring the latest sonic tethers, foregoing the physical connection of a traditional lead in favour of the "gentle and harmless" iLead. (Manufacturer's product information extract: sliding scale of collar vibration and sonic signal, persuading your mutt to remain at the app input range—or your money back!)

The still low(ish) sun gave the bridge a golden cast, but the leaf-strewn ground, grass brown from lack of moisture made a wintry scene. Might that be appropriate for this meeting? He saw Moth now, noticeably the shortest in a group of four people standing in the lee of the massive grey tower that marked the bridge's southern landing point. Her three companions wore dark suits, bulky overcoats. *All the better to hide their firearms with, my dear.*

She turned as they approached. She wore dark colours too, shiny black puffer over a hoodie (hood up), black jeans and clunky boots. When they came close enough, Quirk saw she was smiling, a tired, rather defeated-looking expression. Her minders shifted to flank her, hands low in front of them, near the edges of their coats. *All the better for reaching their holsters, my dear.* Moth moved away from her guards. One moved with her, but she waved the severe-looking woman back.

"Hey, Quirk." Awkward, hesitant, she came forward and hugged him. "You're very sorry. You won't ever keep something like that from me again. You wish you hadn't done it, and you'd take it back if you could, but it's done now. You're going to tell me everything that happened that night, and I will appreciate you doing that, I'll listen, and save all my questions for afterwards. You and I, we just need to get past it. Because regrets are like assholes, no matter how much you try to wipe them clean, that grubby feeling remains. Right now, we've got work to do, and we do it well. The worlds don't deserve to be deprived of our brilliance."

He hugged her back. "Everything you said, honey, and more."

She pushed back to look at him. "And you know in an infinite number of parallel universes you're a shithead in all of them plus one?"

"I guess I know now."

She smiled, but the expression faded away. She looked past him. Quirk turned his head to follow the girl's gaze to where Jennifer stood a few metres back, watching.

"Is that her?" Moth's expression held something close to wonder, and she half whispered, "Holy Father, Quirk, she's gorgeous. How the fuck did you pull that off?"

"Rumour is I used to be witty and charming."

Jenny gave Moth an awkward little wave, but her smile warmed Quirk too, and he wasn't even the target. Moth returned the smile with some hesitation, then gave Nick/S-13035 a quick double thumbs-up. Smart girl. Of course Nick would be here. She seemed to know Quirk's son well enough to trust he would not miss this meeting.

Jennifer chose that moment to walk forward.

"Hi, you must be Moth."

"And you must be an angel. How did you end up with this schmuck?"

"He used to be witty and charming." The ladies in Quirk's life laughed together. It was a touching moment, and he happily footed the bill.

"I understand why you have a posse," said Quirk, "but how about we take this somewhere less public? Get a bite to eat? I think it's lunchtime in Greenland."

"Yeah, we don't have much time to get into this," said Moth, eyes scanning the surrounding park while her head remained still, like he'd taught her.

They walked south. Quirk discovered immediately that Moth's bodyguards had not released her into his custody. Mario Manfredi assigned them a task and—while they recognised Quirk's position as Moth's employer and legal guardian—their instructions remained clear. Their captain, Paulo, appealed to Quirk's reasonableness, surprising him straight away.

"The goal here is for you guys to have nice lunch and a chinwag, okay?" The wise guy spoke in a broad Brooklyn accent. Quirk nodded. "So, let's do that. Me, Dino and Francesca here, we'll take a table at the back, give you some privacy. Everyone's happy." Making everyone happy seemed to Quirk to be the right thing to do, so they proceeded on that basis.

At least the stroll warmed him up. Paulo took point ten metres ahead, then Fran. He and Nick/S-13035 walked together, the ladies just in front, heads together, Moth and Jennifer getting to know each other. Quirk scored out a line on his "List of Things Unlikely to Happen in My Lifetime" list. Of course, a large number of strange things happened that were never on the list in the first place, like "Son Becomes First Roving Human Consciousness," "Father-in-Law Subverts Interstellar Politics," "Estranged Wife Cordial in Casual Conversation." That was his favourite.

"Isn't it cool Mom and Moth are getting on?" said Nick. "Isn't this a nice walk?"

Quirk nodded. "It is. We get to forget for a few minutes we're the ones landed knee-deep in the ordure again by The Old Man."

"It's terrible what the Sec-Tech must be going through right now. What do you think the old bastard has promised him, Dad? Treatment to extract the nanoctyes? Suudi seems like a good man. I think he would sacrifice himself if he could get out of the building, guarantee everyone's safety, don't you, Dad?"

Quirk looked sideways at the android as they stopped at one of New York's quaint old push-button pedestrian crossings. "You don't need to keep saying that, you know. It's not going to change. It won't go away."

The syRen® lowered its head in a most unandroid way. "Not so long ago I was screaming it at you, trying to goad you into killing me. I feel like I owe you a whole bag of regulation parental stuff, and I like using it now I know you won't reject it."

"Fair enough," said Quirk, nodding, anticipating the impending scene: him, Jennifer, their son, and his ward sitting in a trattoria eating lunch. Remarkable. A large part of the conversation would centre around what the heck they could do to help the blackmailed man-bomb wandering hopelessly around the UN building, and avert a(nother) human and/or political catastrophe at TOM's hands, but still, nothing said they couldn't do that over a bowl of delicious pasta.

The trattoria welcomed them like royalty. Minor royalty, admittedly, but nonetheless they felt extremely welcome. This added to Quirk's increasingly and unexpectedly relaxed state. Immediately, he set about interrogating this unexpected bonhomie, while Moth's security detail took station at the back.

The hastily assembled Quirk Agency post-seasonal celebration office party garnered pride of place in the centre of the restaurant. Nick stood out in his smart but casual android body. All the servers, the maître d', their host—announcing proudly that she was the owner—were very much human. Not always the way these days, because why pay wages in the hospitality industry, when you could invest in a syRen® at a cost of maybe twenty to thirty thousand dollars, and only have a minor service bill every third year. Because pride, and heart, and family, and community, of course. Not that high-end places and mega chains didn't know this, it just didn't fit the business model.

Pleasantries concluded, Chef emerged, heard their order, then countermanded it, insisting he would serve them one of all his little plates, to "keep them going."

Quirk opened his mouth to throw the first pitch—*When in NY*—but Moth pipped him. "I'd love to spend a leisurely afternoon catching up, maybe dig up some good times to chinwag over. We"—she gave Jenny and Nick a small smile—"could sit back and listen to Quirk apologise to each of us, in turn, repeatedly, if none us of strangles him first, in the restroom with the tagliatelle. But we need to talk about TOM."

"Hey," said Nick. "Let me swing a privacy field using this thing." He meant the android, of course. "And... How many handsets do you guys have?"

Quirk placed his cLife on the table. Moth fished a red Heinz 58th Variety corner shop burner from her puffer's pocket. Jenny shook her head. Still off-grid, sort of. Quirk smiled on the inside, glad she wasn't.

"That might do. Hang on."

(Pause, in which Quirk looked out the window, wondering if TOM knew their whereabouts, guessed at their intentions.) And what about Callan? He did not imagine the NYPD could hold him long, if at all. The android-hopping Gregor Callan loose in New York. What a thought. They'd established in Lunaville Callan needed proximity to jump between droids, but had he become better? And what did that matter in New York City, where you couldn't swing a cat for passers-by?

Maybe Callan could jump city blocks now, maybe he could jump out of wall sockets and charging ports and server outlets.

"Yeah, okay," said the Nick/droid. "That's it, but talk fast, it's shonky as fuck—"

"Nicholas Kirby!" Jenny snapped. "I don't care if you're trying to show off to Moth, you will not use that kind of language at the table."

"Sorry, Mom!"

Nick's voice held such joy at the maternal rebuke Quirk had to stifle a smile.

"And I wasn't showing off," the boy protested.

Sure he wasn't. Then Quirk shook his head to avoid conjecturing on—anything.

"Only thing is you need to hold the two handsets together, facing each other and pass them around to talk." The android shrugged. "Like I said, shonky."

"Well done, Nick," said Quirk. *Bad parent, good parent, right?*

Quirk gave Moth an enquiring look. She passed him the handset sandwich. "Can we play spin the bottle later, too?" Moth cracking wise had the feel of everything being alright with the world, making the pang he felt at the thought of what she must have been through all the keener. How could he avoid going there, but show he was willing to accompany Moth if she chose to? Maybe Jennifer could.

"Okay, I know you'll share Mario's plan, Moth, but let me talk my way into this by setting out my thoughts since we arrived. Today's Monday, there's a UN vote on NLS this Thursday. We know TOM's strongarming Suudi, but how can that be sustainable? Would the UN ratify a vote that enabled the kind of skewed position CC would find desirable? Suudi is influential, yes, but could he really carry enough members to push TOM's preferred result through? In the end, it's academic. If TOM proceeds, we can only act to stop him. We can't go to the authorities because they may storm in, causing TOM to trigger...the device."

"The alternative's him getting away with it," growled Moth.

"And how do we know he won't blow it up anyway, once the decision's made?" asked Nick.

Neither had waited for the handset "ball" before speaking, but they'd kept their comments bland and general. *Clever.* Quirk nodded his approval.

"Nick, could we…diffuse the bomb somehow? Extract Suudi's nanocytes?"

Quirk handed Nick the ball. "If there is one, and I'd need to check that out, we'd have to get to Suudi, transfuse him physically by IV. We'd need to get into the building past UN security, because Suudi can't leave, on pain of death. His and many others. Plus, TOM might have physical countermeasures on the ground." Quirk, quite clearly, saw a cloud pass over Moth's expression. A memory of Callan, probably. "You know TOM will blow the bomb to prevent anyone else succeeding? The theoretical maximum yield…" The android's gaze fixed for a second as Nick ran the numbers. "It might not destroy the building, but it'll be big enough to kill a lot of people on a lot of floors. TOM's scheme would be defeated, but the cost…Dozens? Hundreds? Including UN Sec-Tech and a chunk of the cabinet. Imagine the impact of that."

Jennifer motioned for the handsets, wearily, Quirk thought. Nick/S-13035 passed them over. Quirk held his breath, metaphorically. He'd sensed and heard anger in her words, but where did she stand, really, when the enemy was her father?

"I struggle to believe he'd do it. How does he do it and not blow up the standing and influence of his lawful and legitimate businesses? Okay, he'll cover his tracks, probably lined up pieces going back weeks and months, even years." Quirk recalled eco-activist groups like Terrarests and AtmosFEAR, the Prague Rail Station attack. He recalled Cassie Streich's mission around Europe, and their infiltration of the Isle of Skye, CC's alleged terraforming proving ground. He recalled the story spun by CC around hostage-taking at the Genextric lab in Yellowknife, the blame directed at ecoterrorists when TOM had run the whole show, covering his own dirty tracks influencing a national election. "Look," Jenny leant forward, moving her wine aside, finding her stride. "I have no illusions about what my father is capable of. I'm living proof, right? But surely the risk to everything he's built is too great.

"Regardless," she raised a finger as Quirk reached for the "ball." She fixed him with a determined look, and he saw a flash of the passion he'd fallen in love with. She looked at the android where Nick lived, then at Moth, whose expression seemed almost as determined, and

Quirk found another reason to love Moth like a daughter. "I need you to know that I *hate him*. Not just for what he did to me; or to you, my Nicholas, at the hands of his scientists; or you, Moth, at the hands of his killers." She stopped, looked at Quirk with a smile so freighted with emotional enigma it surpassed the Mona Lisa, and brought a tear to his eye. "Or to you, love, in the mind games and manipulation of trying to work for him without being twisted by his wickedness. But for how he uses people up, how he takes whole towns and cities and countries, even worlds into his grip and strangles the life and love and hope out of them. I. Hate. Him."

Jennifer put the handsets on the table. The waiter and the restaurateur—each carrying two plates per hand—had refrained from serving them, seeing the emotion in Jenny's oratory although they could not hear her words. When she stopped speaking, they served the dishes, pasta for each person and bowls of locust parmigiana, cheatballs, protein pomodoro, bruschetta spirulina, and risotto al funghi for the table.

Jenny took in Moth's taken-aback smile and found a way to smile herself. "Were you expecting a shrinking violet, some kind of wallflower basket case? That's not me. I'm a free fucking spirit, goddess of resistance, and don't forget it."

"Language, Mom!" said Nick, and they all laughed a little.

"Can I be you when I grow up?" said Moth.

The former Mrs. Kirby nodded. "You're halfway there, honey. From what I can see you've already learned how to deal with this schmo."

For a moment, Moth positively glowed, but her dark overcast reasserted itself. That bastard Callan had hurt her, and maybe Quirk would never know how and how badly, but he knew how unhinged Gregor Callan was, his level of disrespect for human life, human dignity at the end of life. The man—what remained of him—was damaged, yes, but the things he'd done could not be excused. Now, he'd done something to Moth. She hurt, and it made his blood boil. And yet he knew she'd never allow herself to be fridged on his behalf. Would she go to Rigel, and what might she become there? That question didn't change this being a family moment, worth marking.

"Maybe with you two getting on so well, I'll get a little less backchat."

Moth laughed. "Oh, Quirk. You're so naïve sometimes." Jennifer giggled.

"Nick," said Quirk, picking up the ball. "Please develop a tactical option to get us into the UN building. Presume TOM's watching, from the outside, but also that he'll put Callan inside by hopping into the right droids at the right time, walk straight through the front door. Maybe you can get inside the same way, but let's have a plan to reach Suudi. Locate his office, plot paths from service areas. You know the drill."

"Sure thing, Daddio. I can do those things."

"Please don't call me that, ever again."

"Hey, does this mean I'm on staff at The Quirk Agency now, Dad?"

Quirk permitted himself a slight smile, managed not to fall from his chair when Jennifer put a still-bandaged hand over his. "Yes, if you want to be," he said. "Prep your own contract though, and I'll sign it, because I have no clue what that looks like from an HR perspective.

"So, Moth." She looked up, expectant, but the glint in her eye could at best be described as dulled. "What's Mario's position? You said he has a plan. When you called it a response, I got a chill. That sounds rather brutal."

"He does have a plan, but you'll need to hear it from him, he wouldn't tell me. You two have never spoken, right? He thinks that should happen."

Quirk nodded. "Whatever Nick and we come up with, I'm sure we'll need Rigel's help, and New York is Mario's backyard away from home, I believe."

"I'm sure I can get that help after you've spoken to him. Just for the form, you know, give respect, doff that imaginary trilby of yours."

"I don't—"

"In my head you do," she tapped her temple.

"Fine. I've been bending over for a decade plus, it's just another ring to kiss."

"No comment," said Moth.

The wait staff removed their plates and served a snack-sized fish course. Quirk had ordered the whitebait, a catch subject to significant World Food Programme controls. Moth's cod strips in romesco sauce looked appetising, and he experienced a moment of food envy. She caught his glance.

"Mine is the alpha snack. My snack *eats* your snack all day long."

Paulo strolled over to their table as the dessert menus arrived. He stood looking out of the curtained trattoria's plass windows as he spoke. "I'm gettin' nervous here, Mr. Kirby. Stay in one place too long start sinkin' roots that slow ya down."

Moth piped up. "It's okay, Paulo. This is the A Team. I hope they do come at us." Her juvenile features set hard. "Next time I see those bastards, I'm gonna fuxxing kill them hard. Then I'll kill them some more."

The tension in Quirk broke at the bare and bristling anger shimmering in Moth's eyes. The glint was back, and it was sharp. He leaned over, risked putting an arm round her shoulder. "Easy, tiger. We'll get them," he murmured. "Or someone will."

"I know," she replied, coldly, despite her evident emotion. "Quirk, *I* want to do it, but he doesn't have a body. How can I get my closure with that devil bastard?"

"By doing the right thing. The private investigator is a quester after truth, and that truth can be a weapon sharp and deadly as any knife."

She sighed. "Yeah, I dunno." She pulled the handsets towards her. "I get that we can cut TOM with your truth knife, but Callan's a different beast, you know? And he *is* a beast, but... I gave him a come-on," she whispered. "Thought I could outflank him."

Oh. He nodded. *Okaaay.* "I won't judge. You made a call in a difficult spot. Jenny will listen, if you want to talk more, but I trust you."

Moth nodded, her anger quietened now. "Okay, later." Then, for the group. "So, what's my job, Boss?"

"You're back?"

She punched him on the shoulder. "I'm back."

Quirk refused to rub the sting while the others watched. "How about contacting Shuun Suudi, see what she knows that we don't? And please facilitate a call to Mario."

"If that means give you his number, sure."

"I'll make that call back at our hotel, with the benefit of Nick's hearproofing."

"Do we have time for dessert?" asked Jenny. Paulo checked his wrist, nodded.

Moth ordered ice cream. Quirk opted for the Black Forage Gatfaux. Jennifer asked for a spoon.

"I'll need a knife too," she said. "For stabbing."

"Yeah," said Moth. "Knives are good at stabbing."

"What, suddenly you two are a double act?" Quirk rolled his eyes, lifted his glass, sipped the last splash of Barbera. He noted Jennifer hadn't finished her wine. Perhaps she wasn't enjoying it. "Are you going to finish that?"

"Yes, I am. It's like husbands, you don't get a new one till you've finished with the last one."

Nick/S-13035 had barely moved for a course and a half, so Quirk twitched when he spoke. "The vote has been moved up to this evening, nine PM. They're calling in proxies, securing diplomatic channels. We've got eight hours."

XXVII

17:27, 18 January 2100
New Worlds' Hilton, East 44th Street, New York, NY, NAF

Arriving at the airport, Quirk and Jennifer had agreed immediately on staying at the New Worlds' Hilton. The hotel sat on United Nations Plaza directly opposite the towering, blue-sky reflecting plass edifice of the UN headquarters building. A monolithic, multi-faceted block the façade of which comprised almost ten thousand panels of individually variable opacity, in a grid one hundred twenty panels tall by seventy wide, over forty-four stories (including the building's 2057 extension). The ability to control and coordinate the opacity and internal illumination of the panels allowed the UN to display messages on their one-hundred-and-seventy-five-metre-tall matrix sign in pride of place on the west bank of the New York's East River.

It seemed only right to be on site, or as close as they could get, to be able to observe what occurred as Joshua Simister's latest sick scheme played out. And now it played much quicker than expected. They hurried back to the hotel, bustled through the lobby and up to the suite that Quirk's pockets—lined deeply by Toni di Fantano—had secured. Right on the corner, with an excellent view diagonally across UN Plaza, the 1st Street Tunnel, and the UN Visitors Centre to the looming tower itself.

The Quirk Agency had picked up an escort too, as Paulo refused to let Moth out of his sight unless told otherwise by Mario Manfredi. It took no time for Quirk to come around to the idea. Apart from anything else, the *tre amici*—in their role as Angelika Moratti's bodyguards—packed weaponry, something Quirk's people, perhaps unadvisedly from the evidence of the last few days, lacked. He still disliked guns. In his view they led to people shooting at him, but that didn't mean he couldn't use one.

He stood staring from the window as the sky darkened and New York's streets and its buildings lit up. The UN building—powered entirely by photovoltaic coatings, microturbines on vertical wastewater components, and incineration of very limited waste volumes (a system verging on being mothballed due to the lack of waste produced)—lit up, its panels displaying the message "Living, playing, working together." A static message, for reasons of road safety, Quirk had read.

Sec-Tech Suudi stood, sat or lay somewhere in that massive building, him and maybe as many as three thousand colleagues, suppliers and visitors, at its busiest, although those numbers reduced greatly at night. According to Nick's intel, by the time of the vote in the early evening the building's population should be under five hundred. Fewer, he hoped.

Jennifer came to stand beside him at the full-length plass window.

"What's my job?" she asked. "And don't even think of side-lining me."

He turned to watch her stare out over the UN and the river, which threw back dusk light even as the land darkened. Shadows played on her face, the room's automatic lighting coming on to softly illuminate her features. So familiar, so strange. He felt like an explorer in a foreign land, trying to get his bearings and not offend local custom.

"I wouldn't dream of it, especially after your pep talk earlier." He started to smile then thought better of it. This did not seem like a smiling kind of moment.

"You'll never really know how much you hurt me."

Don't speak, Quirk. Listen. "Nothing in all the world is more dangerous than sincere ignorance and conscientious stupidity." Anything from the mouth of Dr. King is good enough counsel for me. And I prefer my feet on the ground, not in my mouth.

"Still, I always believed we'd see each other again, especially once I left Gramercy, since I never thought you'd come there. I told myself I would give you a chance, Quinton. Because that's just the kind of high-functioning sap I am."

He'd thought of it, at times, had great notions of marching into Gramercy. "Hello, Mr. Kirby. Reason for visit?" "Break out wife." "Ha-ha, oh Mr. Kirby, you're such a laugh. Oh, wait, what?!" Images of storming ascetic corridors, kicking down anonymous doors, throwing uncaring orderlies aside. But no. She'd done it herself, Jennifer

Simister, with some help from Anwar/Beatrix. And now he stood here with the woman he still loved, maybe had no right to, with everything he'd done, and the things he'd failed to do. He did not deserve this position. The position of being listened to.

"So, look," she said, still staring from the window. "I don't know where we are right now. I don't know where I am, so you've got no chance. But I saw you with Nick, and with Moth, and I can see that... I'm not going to say you've changed. It's too early for that, but...I think you might be changing, and I want to see how that works out. But just to be clear, I'm still of the belief that you don't deserve me, you selfish bastard."

She conveyed all this in a soft tone that made the coup de gras all the more painful. And yet knowing her as he did, he felt—perhaps unwisely—that her words held no venom, but constituted a marker on the emotional timeline tying them together irrespective of their freewill. Like a big old bungee of love that pulled them back together regardless of how hard or fast they ran in opposite directions.

"That's fair. But as to you getting your hands dirty—"

Now she did turn to face him, turning him to face her. "Don't start treating me like a goody-two-shoes daddy's girl. You *know* I never was that. Did I mention that I half-strangled an orderly with an IV tube?"

"Uh, you still seem rather strangely proud of it."

"He's a nasty piece of work. Relishes his job a little too much."

"Maybe he'll make a career change."

"Did you ever really know what you were doing for my father, Quinton?"

He sighed. "In the beginning I felt he was lit with the fire of exploration. And I think he was, once, but now, it's hard to fathom what fuels him, keeps him going decade after decade. It can't just be wealth, can it? There has to be something else. I can't even imagine...to have lived so long."

"We'll talk more about my father later, but I want to be a part of this. I've been lying around way too long. I'll talk to Moth when I can. It's clear she's hurting." She looked at Moth sitting cross-legged on the main bed, talking on her handset while S-13035 sat charging in a chair, eyes lit violet and vacant. "But what can we do about this vote? I have to do something real and useful."

Quirk had an idea, a truly awful, rushed and reckless idea. He shook his head, but the bad idea refused to budge. He hoped Nick would come up with something better. Their son had left the android, disappeared into the ether, promising to return with good ideas. Quirk hoped he did, because his low-tech and incautious response to the situation was in no way good.

"We should sleep," said Jennifer. "I'm exhausted, and you can't be recovered from London, never mind the mishap on the plane. Rest might bring inspiration."

"Mishap," Quirk chuckled. "Yes, forty winks then we hash this thing out. Take the big bed."

"Maybe Moth will share."

"It's not ice cream, you have a fighting chance."

Jennifer went to speak with Moth. Quirk watched them, the easy way Jenny engaged with the girl. It seemed so obvious now that they would be good with each other, perhaps for each other. Why did he always see the obvious so clearly afterwards?

Moth and Jennifer lay down back-to-back, but not before Moth waved her handset at him and a message appeared on his. No tag, just a number. Mario Manfredi. Surely the *capo di tutti capi's* plan for dealing with the threat would be better than his daring idea to sneak into the UN building undetected, not trigger the explosion, clean Sec-Tech's blood to remove the blood-borne bomb, and sneak out again, saving hundreds of lives and avoiding a disastrous vote hamstringing human space exploration.

He paced to the corner bar and mixed himself a G&T. Paulo met him there, leaving Francesca watching the door and Dino covering the window, sitting in the opposite corner of the room from the charging android.

"Mr. Quirk."

"Mix you a drink? Although I suppose you're on duty."

Paulo, dark, lean and tall, probably one-ninety centimetres, cheeks and chin stubbled in the same way as his shaven head, chuckled. "I'm not an officer of the law, for Pete's sake. I'll take a Manhattan. When in Rome, huh? Better give Dino a beer, and Fran will take water."

Quirk prepped the drinks, sat on the sofa, took a big sip of his G&T, and called Mario Manfredi.

Rigel's new and unfeasibly young boss answered on the second ring.

"Pronto?"

"It's Quinton Kirby."

"Ah, Moth's guardian. We were bound to speak one day, no?"

"Agreed, but forgive me if I don't roll out the welcome mat after you told Moth about my presence at Toni's villa during the 2094 raid."

"You've no right to feel aggrieved I did that."

At least that confirmed the leak's source. "Only that I'd didn't tell her myself."

"You had plenty of opportunity."

"I know. And you reminding me certainly helps a lot with my frame of mind."

"So, that's the small talk. What can I do for you? Since you came straight to New York from London, I guess you're planning to get into this UN thing. I applaud your tenacity sticking at the job we started on Mars, but stay out the way of the grown-ups."

Somewhere, a coin dropped, and the sound reverberated in Quirk's head. He doubted an angel had received their wings, or anyone had invested a penny in a breakdown of his thoughts. Did Mario think Quirk wouldn't like his plan?

"I have a vested interest in messing up TOM's affairs, for the common good."

"Okay. I respect that, and Simister's a common problem. What's your intent?"

Quirk nodded, moved over to the window beyond which darkness had reclaimed New York. Only the city lights resisted. "I have an idea, but it's not a good one. Moth said you have a plan. Maybe we can help, although I sense reluctance."

"You must have been top of the class at Dick School, Quirk. Okay, I'll share if you promise to keep your nose out. My cousin still kinda worships you for some reason, and I will not have you take her into the UN."

He couldn't resist the opening. "Do you have other plans for her?"

Mario ignored the question. *"We thought this was about Near Light Speed drive licences, TOM killing competition for the best routes, cornering the market, lording over the new settlements. It is about that, but did you read the bill amendments?"*

"I've been pressed for time lately."

"We're not counting ones and twos here, Quirk. In the latest draft, Exploralpha Inc—another fine C Corp company, as you know—would get exclusivity on NLS licenses for twenty years. But the effect of this revision to Suudi's bill is to give CC control of settlement flights in perpetuity. No one else would be able to maintain the capability, retain the staff, the corporate structure for twenty years without anywhere to go, no settlers to invoice. But that not's the best part."

"Please, tell me the best part."

"The bill gives Exploralpha highly detailed vetting rights over who their ships carry. Joshua Simister would control who settles the planets he terraforms, free to create whatever kind of community he likes. Does that sound healthy to you, Quirk?"

"It sounds horrific, if he uses it. But the authorities must see that."

"And yet they allow CC to remain on their tender lists, despite the Skye investigation, the Yellowknife investigation, the Androicon investigation. It's politics, Quirk. I'm a sixteen-year-old and I understand that. The bill must be voted upon. My lobbyists tell me friendly UN members are being influenced, heavily. The democratic core believe they can vote this pernicious nonsense down, but bad things happen. Always have. We must assume Simister has a plan to beat the vote. Interfering with the UN's tech, more blackmail subjects, I don't know, but somewhere in this square mile, Simister is at work."

"Callan," said Quirk. "Not solely him, but he could get into the UN and hop between android heads, run interference up to the vote. I wonder if he can get into their system, tinker around to TOM's benefit." He slugged his G&T, savoured the bitterness.

"Moth says you both have experience combating Callan."

"Moth is right. How much did she tell you about that?"

"All I wanted to know: We're family. We both have a beef with Callan, now."

"Did you give her a job?"

Pause. *"I offered one. She's thinking about it. Knocked sideways by Callan."*

"Not for us to analyse. I hope she and Jennifer will get a chance to talk soon." Quirk emptied his glass.

"You trust Jennifer Simister?"

"More than I trust you."

"Fair. She's still your family; can't choose her parents. Look, Quirk, Moth said you would feel strongly about going in, intervening on the side of the angels. My first pitch is you don't do that. I have a strategy in play. Pieces coming together. Stand aside, let me do what needs to be done to stop this happening."

"Does your plan involve a girl called Shuun having a one-parent family?"

"That's the backstop, if there's no alternative. This vote must be stopped. More people will die at Simister's hands if we don't, through exploitation, welfare slavery, unsafe practices. Maybe the UN could unpick it legally if the bill does go through, but that could take years, years of damage to people and planets. My assets will enter the building in an hour and shut down the systems to delay the vote. Buy some time."

"Mario, that could cost Suudi and a lot of others their lives. You're betting TOM won't pull the trigger, but I know him. He's ruthless, and does not make idle threats. 'Blow it up now and try again' will be one of his options. Blame a radical eco group. Get away scot-free. So, yes, I'm going in, and Moth's coming with me, because I doubt I could stop her. It would be better in cooperation with you."

"So, you'll rely on your tech boy to save the day? What other resources do you have? And just throwing yourself into the action won't work like it did in Yellowknife."

"I'm pleased you think that worked."

"Moth trusts you. All the time she cursed your name, she never said you weren't good at this. If I can't stop you going in, the only way I can ensure my plan's integrity is to bring you in with us."

"That's funny, I was thinking the same thing." Quirk turned away from the window. Moth and Jenny slept, S-13035 charged. Paulo stood with Fran, chatting while Dino—shorter, blockier; thick, dark hair unkempt—returned from a circuit of the suite. Quirk lifted his empty glass toward Paulo, tried to look endearing. The tall captain snorted amiably and moved forward to take the glass.

While these things happened, Quirk considered his options. They had no strategy yet apart from his working draft. No firm plan to get inside, no manoeuvre to buy the time to get to Suudi, no equipment to extract the nanocytes. The UN building packed every type of sensor and detector known to humans, including a listening and shielding system—RADCOMS—which would detect and screen automatically any digital communication within the building. That meant strict comms silence for any infiltration, unless they were inviting the UNP for cocktails. Posing as EMTs, for example, might get them in, and Jenny had some first aid experience from her hostel work in SF, but what happened after that? Even if they accessed the building, they'd be escorted everywhere, unable to speak to other teams. Coordination would be critical.

Paulo handed Quirk a G&T. Quirk sipped it and almost sprayed the room. "Wow," he mouthed, and smiled at the Rigel captain: *One More for the Road.*

"Okay," he said to Mario. "I'll sign up. I'm surrounded by colleagues of yours anyway. What's the scoop?"

"There are various components, but you'll be going in posing as EMTs."

"You're kidding," said Quirk.

"I read it in a book somewhere."

XXVIII

17:59, 18 January 2100
New Worlds' Hilton, East 44th Street, New York, NY, NAF

"You're kidding," said Quirk.

Moth beamed at him. Not her usual style, but fuck it. She didn't give any shits at all about letting out the happy she felt right now. She'd decided on this approach in the trattoria. The sight of him approaching in Astoria Park had hurt. She sure as shit wasn't fucking forgiving him for the crap he'd hidden, and she'd make him tell her everything, some time, but she realised at the table she could see past it, that she needed the fancy fop, to work with him, share stuff with him, shoot the shit with him. All that, but not discussing Callan. From Quirk's view the bastard attacked her, that would do. Maybe now she had a secret from him, but it wasn't the same. She'd had long enough to weigh up a bunch of things, like all the times Quirk had been there for her, had saved her, the time she'd saved him with a gun in the Yellowknife lab. How did you balance out all the crazy weird shit and call it quits? How did you keep score of all the crap that life threw at you and your friends? You couldn't, not with your head. The job of juggling that impossible balance fell to your heart, and hers had run the numbers and found Quirk still passed the friendship test, maybe even the family test, and that was what she'd known in the park. And now they did what this wonky-weird family always did, they were going to war with motherfucking evil, and they were going to kick its ass. She just hoped it wouldn't cost Shuun's dad his life. She knew how that felt, and she wouldn't wish it on anyone, especially not a new friend.

Thank funk Nick was here, too. He'd been there for her at the darkest time she could remember, and she'd had some fuzking murky times. Okay, he'd been tardy, but he'd come through. *Fuck! Fuck you, Ca— No. You have no fucking name, you piece of shit scum bastard. I will kill you, somehow.*

She rubbed her face again, sat up in bed now as Jennifer Kirby...*Simister?* Pretty unclear from the way those two batted the ball about in the last few hours. Jennifer stirred and pushed herself up to sit beside her. She smiled, and Moth got a hollow kind of feeling in her stomach, a kind of lost feeling. She liked everything she'd seen of Jennifer so far. She was warm, funny, and took no shit. Not in a balls-out—well—Moth sort of way! In a quiet way, strong but gentle at the same time, decisive but patient.

Quirk smiled at her from the window. "Someone get Nick on the Ouija board. We've just been seconded to The Rigel Corporation, again."

Minutes later they—all seven of them—sat or stood around the suite's lounge. Two hours to the NLS vote. Paulo briefed them on the plan from Mario's strategy team. Quirk said, "Some of these elements are not entirely to my liking, young lady," but Moth waved his protest away. She'd wing jumped at a birthday party once.

It sounded straightforward, sitting in a hotel room yacking about the plan. No knot in her stomach during all the jibber-jabber. But when Paulo wrapped up, and after Quirk pepped them with a hundred words on yadda-yadda free speech, and blah-blah for all humankind, Paulo pushed away from the wall and said, "Time to go." Then the nerves came on as they gathered themselves. Anger fuelled her. She *needed* to strike back at TOM, give him a good kick in the teeth. But the nerves she could do without.

Logistics were already in place, of course, because Rigel didn't dick around. Assignments confirmed, she and Fran strode along fancy hotel corridors, then down the stairs to a room on the floor below. Rigel techs and the other two in the airborne crew had prepped the equipment for them arriving. A couple of techs in dark grey—because the flyers had black for obvious reasons—helped them suit up. Fran and a tall, ripped woman call Kimi were pulled and strapped into the wingsuits, while Moth and a wiry, spotty youth named Rex got black tacsuits. Side arms were provided. She had a choice of three, but didn't even register the ballistic models, just reached for the NEMP pistol and holstered it. Because Callan. The techs checked them over then they headed for the roof.

Tension made Moth use those too-short moments to review the plan, again. The deal once inside the UN was threefold. Team Three had already entered the building, a fake nightshift maintenance crew (the real crew having been...detained). They would stage a disruption, timed to try and delay the vote. Team One had Quirk and Jennifer, a real EMT named Simon who moonlighted as Rigel's first aid coordinator, plus a soldier named Zippy. Probably not their real name. The EMTs would find Suudi ASAP, try to disarm/extract the living bomb. Dangerous. No one had discussed it in the room, but she thought Mario was hoping Jennifer being there would prevent TOM from triggering the device. Was that the reason for some charged looks around the room?

Team Two, the flight crew, would fly from the hotel roof to the UN building, her and Rex dangling in harnesses beneath their flyer in the night-time sky over UN Plaza and the 1st Avenue Tunnel. They would descend from the roof to the UN Central Server room, the main control centre for a hundred departments, agencies, labs and charities. Their job was to get Nick inside, past the building's mega security screen, cos ironically, real people (ouch) could walk in with a pass, but the UN had super tight electronic, digital and comms defences. Their RADCOMS system meant the bomb needed to be triggered from inside, and that made it hard for Callan, too, hopefully. So, they would port Nick inside in a pocket-sized syncronon data packet till they found a UN droid he could ride...eh, utilise. Or, take the packet to the IT hub, insert Plug A in Socket B to access the system directly, and try to block Callan gerrymandering the numbers if the vote went ahead. She'd almost asked Paulo if Mario had suggested fixing the vote *against* the bill. Only Nick could do that. She'd ask the question if it came up.

After all that, they just needed to get out before the UN Police rocked up, the FBI, maybe NYPD, and the rest of the alphabet soup that always descended when the famous Quirk and Moth went to work. She and the flight crew would glide off the roof down to the park beside the building, then over the walkway and the railing into an escape boat. And they *would* get out, because she *did* have a future with Quirk, she knew it. They had a bunch more cases to solve.

Chill darkness opened around her as Moth stepped out onto the top of the hotel. Fran, Kimi and Rex in front of her—all taller, natch—left a little trail of soft silvered splashes from their cloaked suit lights. Hers did the same. Enough to see close up, but not to project beyond a metre or so.

"Masks on," Fran mumbled, and they stopped, applied their self-adhesive visi-mask eye coverings. It tickled as the patch settled over her eyes, sticking to her skin, light but positive pressure forming a small dome to protect her eyes, and also to enhance her vision at the edges of the visible spectrum. Their suits did the opposite, repelling, mirroring or bending various forms of radiation back, away or around them to confuse their visibility for any external detection. Despite its slickness, the suit helped with the chill, too. No skin at all left uncovered.

With no pause the others walked to the roof edge. Moth stepped up too, her gaze drawn down into the dark chasm between the buildings, where tiny little cars, Autocabs[OS], buses, trucks and vans streamed along the illuminated road below. She felt squiggly in her tummy, put a hand on it, reassured by the contact.

Now the techs came up and clipped on Fran and Kimi's wings, then set about positioning Moth and Rex in front of their fliers, connecting them with clips and quick-release fasteners. *Oh, of course, in case the flyers have to dump their payload to save themselves. Fuck. Still, this is what we do.* She tried to clear her mind. No emotion, just emptiness. Just the cold night and the yawning, light-sparkled pit, the soft almost unheard tap of a metal fastening coated in SounDeaD fabric to kill those little giveaway tinkles that could get a careless operative shot, or maybe just detected. *For shooting later, at a more convenient time.*

"Go in twenty," said Fran, the woman's body moving against her.

Oh, fuck. Oh, fuck. Oh, fuck.

"Ten."

She ran through the drill, learned only half an hour before.

"Five.

"Four.

"Three. Prep for launch."

The push of Fran's thigh on the back of Moth's leg triggered her first step up onto a temporary step the techs had placed against the parapet. They moved together, Fran's greater power part-lifting Moth's body in concert with her own muscles.

"Two."

The second step took them onto the parapet bounding the Hilton's roof. Wind buffeted them.

"One."

A thousand times easier to go forward than back. And how could this be enough height differential? The roofs looked nearly level!

"Go."

Fran spoke the word, no drama, just jumped off the roof. As instructed, Moth pushed with all her might, the count synchronising them. Fran was strong. Fran worked out—a lot. And just as well.

They dipped—*Not dropped. Not dropped!*—one, two, three, five! TEN METRES! Then a shitting amazing thing happened: the air caught them, the wing activated with a "thwup" and some lovely kinda negative pressure lift dragged them upwards. She wanted to scream as they...yep, they soared, they just fuzking flew upwards. Not Superman/Captain Marvel superpower bollocks kind of flying, but honest to *Dio* science flying. *The best funking feeling!*

Having held in almost all of her pee from the time they were falling, she managed to glance around. *Wow, amazing!* Fran worked the wing like a high-velocity harpy, banking, adjusting, seeming to feel her way across the cityscape, hunting currents to pull them higher than the UN building roof. They passed over the much lower council building, weird, curvy outline and central dome sliding by below them. *Shit!* She was supposed to keep her head level, minimise drag, reduce profile. She lifted her head and banged Fran's jaw, heard a muffled "Fuck!" and they dropped.

"FUG-ger!" She half-swallowed the curse only once it half-escaped.

Fran tried to bank through the dip and out the other side.

Way—too—low. Waytoolow. Toolow. Toolow! TOOLOW!!

Ten lines of windows below the roof. Plass coming up fast.

"Turn, turn, turn!" Fran yelled in her ear, all caution gone. Moth's arms and legs moved, Fran hauling them with hers to steer. Happening so— They flipped over.

Moth completely forgot parachute drill, diving drill, what-the-fuck drill. Crashing drill. Felt their legs fighting each other.

They hit the building feet first.

Plass exploded around them. She thought her limbs would come off.

Hit the floor. Harvested a chair. Hobbled a table. Hit the wall.

Over and out.

XXIX

19:22, 18 January 2100
New Worlds' Hilton, East 44th Street, New York, NY, NAF

Quirk and Jennifer followed Paulo to the service lift. The tall captain produced a doohickey like a handset, but without a screen. He passed it over the lift control and the door opened, no questions. They stepped in, and the lift descended.

"You can make like EMTs okay?"

"I've certainly met a lot of EMTs," said Quirk. He figured he should crack wise to put Jenny at ease. She gave him a look suggesting that if anything cracked in the next minute it would be his head on the side of the lift.

"We'll be fine," she said. "I have some first aid skill. I'll be the sensitive one with the bandages, he can do the heavy lifting."

The lift stopped on eighteen.

The doors opened and a cleaner looked up from his laundry trolley, confusion spreading on his face. Paulo waved the chap into the lift, moving to one side, waving Quirk and Jenny to the other. They backed up and the laundry trolley preceded the man into the lift. The doors shut. The lift continued to descend.

When Quirk realised what was about to happen, he began to hope fervently the cleaner would travel down one floor and get out again, but no. After jerking his head to Paulo in thanks, the guy stared at the lift's blank wall then turned to read the safety instructions, probably for the thousandth time.

Quirk watched Paulo not watching the cleaner. Then Quirk watched the cleaner as, ever so slowly, the guy's brow began to furrow.

The frown only half-formed before Paulo's elbow hit the cleaner's windpipe, hammering him back into the lift wall to slump on the floor.

"Damn!" said Quirk.

"No," Jenny yelped. She squeezed down the side of the laundry trolley, loosening the cleaner's collar, feeling his neck, checking his eyes.

Paulo just nodded. "Yeah, you guys'll do fine as EMTs. Do that kinda thing." He pointed at the cleaner, indicating Quirk should pay attention.

Quirk pushed the trolley hard into Paulo's legs, trapping the younger, fitter, stronger man with leverage. "We're going to have a big problem, Paulo, if you go around shutting down passers-by with excessive force."

"We don't need no questions before we even get in the building, Mr. Quirk. I'd appreciate you lettin' me do my job. And please don't think"—he pushed the trolley back at Quirk—"I'll overlook you gettin' in the way of this operation. If Moth trusts you, I'll trust you, and because Mr. Manfredi says so. I think you might be a straight up guy, but there's a line, and if we're both standin' on it, we ain't dancin', *capisce?*"

Quirk scowled, but he got it, and repositioned the laundry trolley in neutral territory as they arrived on the service level. Jenny had established the cleaner had a pulse and uninterrupted breathing. She rounded on Paulo. "You make him comfortable before we go any further." She stepped out of the lift. "Here." She waved towards a pile of laundry spilling from a big hopper against the wall.

Paulo complied, taking the shoulders while Quirk took the legs. He saw in the captain's eye that he'd assessed it easier to comply than to argue with Jennifer Simister. Sensible man. From there, they marched through service corridors to an underground yard parked with vehicles, a truck manoeuvring between foam-buffered plascrete walls.

As they watched two androids unload a van, an ambulance drove down the ramp from the street. Paulo walked towards the vehicle. Jennifer followed, and Quirk followed her. He'd left the Merrion in their suite, of course, and now wore dark, nondescript clothes. Similar had been acquired for Jennifer from the hotel's fancy new reconstituting system, a key part of Hilton's negative waste strategy.

In the room, Paulo had said Zippy and Simon were joining their team. Zippy turned out to be a hundred kilo slab of muscle from the Eastern Bloc somewhere, given the appellation because Paulo couldn't pronounce her name. Zavracchiiska, Quirk thought. She said it quick and terse, although she seemed to have a sunny disposition for an operative of a quasi-legal corporate (former?) gangster organisation. He reckoned Zippy could have tossed Moth from the hotel roof to the UN building just as effectively as the wingsuit would have achieved by now. It felt odd to be so quickly back into operational conditions with Moth, but good odd. Being in this situation with Jennifer just plain broke the odd-o-meter.

Simon, the actual EMT in today's "Bizarre Life of Quirk" scenario came around from the driver's seat. Emergency vehicles in New York, the Mayor had mandated in the distant past, must always be driven by humans. A rather quaint edict that attracted some people to the job just for the sheer pleasure of driving. Simon seemed to be having a bad day. Quirk opened his mouth to greet him but Simon—spare frame, blond hair spiked—shut him down immediately.

"I don't care. Let's just get on with this."

The EMT turned to Paulo, who made a hand gesture that seemed to indicate "it is what it is." "We're on a schedule. You wanna take a swing at me, Simon, do it later. Just remember, you are responding to a medical emergency on the second floor. Said emergency"—Paulo consulted an antique wrist watch, gold—"has just been triggered by our maintenance team."

Quirk followed Jenny into the back of the ambulance. Zippy slammed the doors, but they slowed and connected with a gentle thunk. "Now we go do good, huh?" She smiled, her broad features transforming into such a beatific expression that Quirk couldn't help returning it. The ambulance pulled off less smoothly than it would have in android hands, and they tilted back as it traversed the ramp up to the street.

They travelled all of two hundred metres from the hotel to the UN building's forecourt, but the number of bends and turns, stops and starts at signals and security checks resulted in Quirk feeling he'd spent three minutes in a washing machine, the old tumbling kind. As the vehicle (or rather the driver) bumped him around, he worried about Jenny. Her presence set him buzzing. As they waited at the latest interruption to their very short journey, his thoughts wandered idly through memories. Gladly, he allowed his mind to conflate better times with their present situation, and to project for him some stimulating yet highly unlikely scenarios. Maybe he could work on those.

While Quirk and Jenny pulled on green EMT overalls, Zippy spent the journey displaying an admirable ability to balance against the turns and jolts while checking and loading a selection of formidable-looking weapons into a gurney that took up the middle of the ambulance. Stubby guns, slender guns, compact guns. Two went into the gurney's foam mattress. He craned his neck enough to see hidden openings within the foam that received the firearms and held them snug. The guns themselves looked like products of a raid on the New York Museum of Anthropology. Two comprised wooden bodies fitted with plastec and carbon fibre components, whereas two stubby machine pistols clipped onto the gurney itself, one each side, and looked exactly like brackets at the gurney's corners. Human ingenuity really did come to the fore when concocting ways to kill.

The ambulance stopped yet again, but this time stayed stopped.

Zippy opened the rear doors, jumped down and began to unload the gurney. Quirk gripped the following end and tried to look like he was helping in some way. Jenny grabbed two medical bags prepped before the ambulance arrived at the hotel.

Whatever Simon had said to the guards before they exited the ambulance it worked a treat. The UNP detail—four at the entrance and three more within the ten-metre-long vestibule between outer and inner doors, all armed with nasty-looking black guns—stood aside as they passed through. The inner doors slid open revealing an impressively airy, five-storey reception area, balconied floors rising up opposite the glazed wall that faced the outside world.

Quirk looked groundwards quickly, wishing to appear professional. Two business-suited staffers—a human female, wearing glasses and a severe bun, plus a male model android—greeted Simon. He now carried one of the medical bags Quirk knew contained—along with sundry first aid supplies—some of the haemodialysis equipment, the rest packed in Jenny's bag. The staffer in charge led them quickly towards the service elevators.

* * *

19:36, 18 January 2100
Level 36, UN Headquarters Building,
United Nations Plaza, NY, NAF

"You fucking little shit," growled Fran. The woman shook her again.

Moth raised her head, regretted that very stupid move, laid back down again.

"Move, *stupida ragazza*, or I'll leave you."

Instead of moving her head, Moth tried to keep it really still, turning her body to face the floor so she could push up. Her knee, the one broken under the Lunaville dome, ached like a motherfucker. She pushed up with her hands and sharp pain lanced her shoulder.

"Cu—stomer service!"

"Shh!" hissed Fran then hauled her upright with no fuzking regard for her pain.

They stood in a darkened, slightly broken office. Fran made "we're leaving now" signs with her fingers as Moth remembered why they'd plunged through a window into the UN building instead of landing smoothly on the roof. *Oh, shit.*

Fran tapped her ear and Moth triggered her aural implant—not linked through her handset now, but via a pocket unit capable of cloaking their close tactical chat from RADCOMS, but not area transmissions. She subvocalised.

<Fran, fuck, I'm *so* sorry. I totally screwed the pooch on that.>

"Get over it. I'll punch you later. Don't think I won't because you're a kid."

<Yeah, I deserve it.>

Fran moved towards the door, not looking back to check Moth followed. They picked their way over the room's debris by their tacsuit lights and the slight glow seeping in through the gaping, not-Moth-shaped hole out into the New York night.

They stepped from the darkened room into a not much brighter corridor, illuminated only by low-power running lights along the angle of floor and wall. The main corridor lighting should have activated when they stepped from the office, but their combat suits contained their heat, baffled their motion with science. Nothing could have baffled their impact on the window though. That must have alerted some sensor somewhere, probably the building's fuzking earthquake detector. Her mistake already made getting Nick's syncronon data packet to the IT hub to protect the vote from cyber interference harder, but Moth wouldn't allow anyone else to carry Nick's SDP, secured in her suit. So, did they try to intercept Kimi and Rex now for support, or meet them at the IT hub on Level 40?

And how had or would TOM's people get access, given they had to be inside to trigger the bomb? But Joshua Simister never had been short of dirty tricks.

"Okay, we're on Level 36. We continue to target. Rendezvous with K and R there. Look alive, stupida. *Get ready to repel boarders."*

Harsh, but she *had* fucked up. She'd been trying not to think about it, such a rookie mistake on their flight. Shame washed away some of the pain still hampering each step she took, but she kept up with Fran, lurching purposefully down the corridor.

Of course they didn't have guards on every elevator lobby on forty-four floors, but they expected cameras and sensors, so Fran stopped before going through the lobby door, crouched and twisted to look up through the door's narrow plass window at the lobby ceiling. Then, Fran doublechecked her suit against gaps that might let some tell-tale heat or moisture escape. Moth did the same.

"Let's go," said Fran, treating her like a novice. *Pah. Read my file,* mucca.

Fran opened the door and Moth followed her through. No klaxons blared; no lights flashed. If any silent telltales triggered, they'd find out soon enough. The signs confirmed they had four floors to make up to 40.

Fran made for the stairwell, stopped to examine the door, reached for a pocket, and produced a handset-sized device. No lights illuminated on the unit, but Moth presumed Fran got pings or even auto-speech feedback. Whatever, Fran stowed the device and pushed the door open. They slipped through from one dark space into another, this one cooler, then started up the stairs, Moth's body aching with every step.

XXX

19:43, 18 January 2100
Level 2, UN Headquarters Building,
United Nations Plaza, NY, NAF

Quirk still gripped the gurney's trailing end, following where Zippy led in pursuit of Simon, Jenny bringing up the rear. Up on Level 2, they walked a long way along a three-metre-wide corridor lined with office doors to the left, the atrium parapet and a two-storey drop to the right.

Their UN guide stopped at the only door with a syRen® guard, dismissed that android, and went inside with her syRen® assistant. Simon slowed, stepped back, and Zippy manoeuvred the gurney inside.

The office was bland, could have been anywhere, pretty much anywhen, and been occupied by anyone with any kind of corporate role in anything from marketing to macro-economics. Simon and Jenny moved around the desk blocking his view of the floor, but he knew what to expect. The maintenance crew's first job was to leave an unconscious body for the EMT team to attend. After Paulo's work in the lift, Quirk worried Team Three would simply plug some harmless official, but that would be reckless, and very poor tactics, since the cops would descend immediately.

"We can't risk moving her yet," said Simon to the staffer.

"Oh," said the guide, clearly expecting the official to be carted off on the gurney.

"Are you a doctor?" Simon snapped.

The guide did not reply, looked agitated. Stressed about the vote too, perhaps.

The maintenance crew would be pursuing their second task now, unobtrusively locating the Secretary for Technology. Quirk made eye contact with Jenny, flicked his gaze side to side, hoping to convey that they should look busy to avoid attracting questions. She responded by moving to the gurney, placing her medical bag on the mattress, opening it, and beginning to place relevant-looking First Aid items on the desk. Quirk "helped" by making components of the automatic haemodialysis device more accessible within the bag for quick assembly and deployment when the time came.

"Be ready to move when T3 find STS," Quirk said, quietly.

"I remember the plan," she said. "I guess you're restating it to reassure yourself."

He almost barked out a laugh. "I've missed you," he mumbled. "I have no right to say that, but facts are facts."

"That's on you," she murmured.

"I know," he muttered, hoping his tone conveyed the contrition he felt.

"Moth really has changed you, hasn't she?" Jennifer observed.

"That's a long conversation to be conducted under the influence of many G&Ts."

"Are you trying to get me drunk?"

He smiled: *I Do Like Piña Coladas, Actually.*

"Okay," said Simon, straightening. "Time to move the patient."

At the pre-agreed code, Quirk went through the motions, guided by Zippy: positioning the gurney, locking the wheels, lowering the deck and removing the stretcher. Zippy and Simon moved the woman's supine, probably drugged, form onto the stretcher then lifted her onto the gurney. Quirk ensured her arms were tucked in, fastening the straps across the woman's upper chest while Zippy secured her legs.

Team Three should have eyes on the Sec-Tech by now. He hoped his and Jenny's lack of comms didn't end up proving awkward. In a suitably absurd development, Rigel had insufficient comm units to go around with The Quirk Agency coming onboard last minute. But it wasn't the lack of comms that made him hot under the collar, that would only matter if the balloon went up and they had to break radio silence. Their team's next stage required part of the Team Three maintenance crew to intercept them. Because fake EMTs couldn't just break off an escorted group, go wandering around the UN wherever the mood—or highly intricate plan to subvert a UN vote and stop a human bomb going off—took them. Their escort had to be side-tracked, quickly.

The UN staffer moved out into the corridor ahead of the gurney. The EMT crew exited in the order they'd arrived: Simon, Zippy, the gurney, Quirk and Jenny. Unfortunately, the syRen® assistant swung into line behind them. *Damn.*

What Quirk disliked most however was his lack of control over what happened next. At least his strategies were his to mess up, or rather to improvise. And what resources did TOM have in play while this transpired? Were they all desk jockeys in an extinct volcano super villain lair, or did he have boots on the ground? Would Anwar pitch up gunning for Rigel today, finally get the shot at Quirk xe'd pined for all these years? What about Callan? He shook his head. Allowing his thoughts to ramble as they wheeled the unconscious official down the long corridor was a recipe for burnt toast.

Two maintenance personnel appeared from a door halfway between them and the lift lobby. One, a middle-aged man, stopped to examine the door he had just closed while a younger, taller man placed a tool bag on the ground. Quirk kept pushing the gurney, thoughts stringing out like a keyboard with a key stuck down. Were they Team Three? Were they loaded for droid? Would they shoot to kill? Rigel might be the Family's corporate arm, but you didn't swing gigs like this by pussyfooting around asking people to put their hands together so you could tie them with ribbons and stuff their mouths with gumballs.

As Quirk's pulse pummelled his veins, the answer to his queries became evident.

The young man turned his back to them, blocking the older man from sight. The young man then crouched as if to tie his shoelace, revealing the older man with a handgun levelled towards them. Quirk flinched. The gun went off like a clown being slapped with a wet fish: thwap, thwap! The UN administrator went down like the proverbial sack of spuds. New potatoes, really, as she was quite slight. The android moved before she reached the corridor carpet. The young man straightened with a NEMP in each hand and discharged them simultaneously. The android dropped just as quickly as the woman, but twice as heavily, as useful now as a bag of spare parts.

Quirk pushed past Zippy to reach the UN woman with Simon. Quirk let the real EMT take her pulse. He'd already noted the absence of a wound, but found the stun pellet, attached to her lapel where it discharged its hefty electrical payload. Not quite taser levels, which could kill, but quite sufficient to lay the target out for a spell.

The older man hefted the android onto his shoulder. The younger one worked the storeroom door. Quirk helped Simon lift the UN woman while Zippy and Jenny moved the gurney into the store. The corridor was clear in six seconds flat.

Racks containing reusable, recyclable or recycled supplies, and four android chargers on the short wall, cramped the space. Biodegradable cleaning solutions still smelled, Quirk noted. Zippy strapped the stunned UN guide into a syRen® charging station while Simon injected her with presumably the same substance used on the official.

"We can't hang around," said the older maintenance man. "We're not done."

"Yes, go. We have this," said Zippy.

The two men exited the store to participate in Team Three's distraction, closing the door behind them. But the swinging barrier never reached the jam. A tell-tale laser buzz rattled the silence. Something heavy fell in the corridor, the door still half open. Through the crack Quirk saw the older man sprawled on his back, a hideous black and pink burn line scored into his shoulder and neck.

"Oh, damn." By now, he and Zippy should be changing into spare maintenance overalls from the racks, and Jenny and Simon heading for the exit with the gurney.

Instinct urged him to pull the door open to investigate, but self-preservation vetoed instinct. He pushed the door closed—steadily, not quickly—and locked it. Faintly, a laser whined as it recharged. The unpalatable choices were human guards, UNP security detail, or CC tampered androids. Soft ballistic reports suggested the young man firing back. A laser (lasers?) buzzed again, followed by the thump of a second body falling.

"Major problem. Two of Team Three are down," Quirk reported.

Zippy had unzipped the gurney mattress, removed a long, wooden tube then unclipped a stubby metallic pistol camouflaged in the gurney's struts, joints and hinges.

"Quirk?"

The look on Jenny's face made his heart ache like a sore tooth. Despite her doubt, she grasped her med bag handle, ready to go, to get on with the job, even though control and confidence were gone. Simon also snatched up his bag then stopped, looking at Quirk, then Zippy, then back to Quirk.

"I'm an EMT. I need to get to those men. You have to cover me."

"We're not here for a gun battle," said Quirk firmly. "This...was a clandestine operation. Even if the haemodialysis part is blown, the rest of Team Three is in play, could delay the vote, and Team Two is still going to the IT hub. Nick still could sanitise the vote, or scupper it."

"Quark right," said Zippy. "Still got job to do. First aiding wait."

Okay, shooting then. Quirk took the second disguised pistol. It was Moth's misconception that he couldn't shoot. In fact, this was untrue, he just didn't like to.

Laser whine right outside the door. The timing seemed roughly appropriate for the shooter approaching their position and shooting into the two maintenance men, following urban warfare protocol for ensuring you left no wounded enemy combatants behind you. He noted that no alarms sounded. Odd, and worrying.

"Zippy, get away from the door." He edged back himself, hit the gurney—painfully—pushed sideways, away from a laser cutting through door like a knife through paper, spitting and flashing off the gurney's frame. Quirk dropped behind it.

No android would fire blind into a room: illogical. Neither would UNP, with colleagues or civilians inside. Twisting, Quirk crawled further back towards Jenny as the laser fired again, then another, spearing into the storeroom, hitting something behind him that fizzed and spluttered electronically. Plastec bottles burst noisily, splashing fluids around.

"I am *never* agreeing to anything you suggest ever again," said Jenny as he scrambled up to kneel beside her behind the edge of a rack.

He smiled manically: *Buyer Beware.* "I guess it's too late to say I have a bad feeling about this. Simon, get the woman off the gurney!"

He handed the pistol to Jenny, twisted up and reached forward, lifting the UN woman with Simon's aid, lowering her to the floor just in time to suit Quirk's purpose.

The door burst open and a syRen® strode in, nasty laser carbine held ready. The android shot Zippy, who had nowhere to hide, crashed into the racking, dead arm dragging cleaning supplies off the shelf to bounce across on the floor, at least one rupturing its cap, spilling clear, pungent liquid.

"Back, Simon!" Quirk yelled as the EMT stepped forward, starting to swing his med bag at the syRen®. Simon jumped flat against the racking as Quirk rammed the gurney into the android with all the energy he could muster. The syRen® braced, but physics won out, Quirk's momentum bore it backwards through the doorway.

With hideous poise, the android remained upright, started to push back, slowing their movement, all but stopping it. A body piled into Quirk's right shoulder, arm wrapping around his waist. Another force crushed into his left side. Jenny and Simon—practically in scrum formation—provided the extra impetus to force the droid across the corridor and up against the parapet.

Jammed for a second, the android started wrestling out from behind the gurney. Quirk pushed himself upwards, bringing his whole weight down on the gurney's handle, forcing the trolley's centre of mass upward. Its front legs collapsed as designed. Gurney lifted struggling android up, tipping it over the parapet, and the gurney went with it, crashing down into the UN building reception with an almighty clatter. All heads turned to look up, and UNP officers began running towards the lift and stairs.

"I think we lost the element of surprise," said Quirk, ducking back from the edge.

Simon and Jenny looked at him, she having armed herself with the older maintenance man's Shock-out 250, Simon confirming the death of both men and Zippy. Quirk retrieved the younger man's NEMP pistols. Jenny and Simon continued staring at him. *Right, I guess I'm in charge now.* "Comms?" he asked Simon.

The EMT knelt again, retrieved the older man's earpiece, and handed it to Quirk. "Carlo had implants," he nodded at the young man's body.

"We need to get moving," said Jenny.

"Leave me out of this," said Simon, face like fizz, someone who wanted to be anywhere but here. For a split second, Quirk couldn't help wondering what hold Rigel had on the EMT for him to so reluctantly compromise his principles.

"Too late," said Quirk. "Cops inbound, and Suudi's still in mortal danger, maybe others."

He waved them away from the main stairwell and lifts, the UNP approaching from there, pinning his hopes on the emergency stairs at the far side of the building.

Could the remaining Team Three maintenance crew create a big enough distraction to shut down the UN building? Had this team just done the job themselves? Hopefully their little fracas would help the flight crew reach the UN IT hub.

"Stop! Weapons down!"

The call came from behind them, the lift lobby. With Jenny and Simon already heading the opposite way, Quirk didn't think, ducked, snatched up the fallen syRen®'s laser and fired into the puddle of chemicals at the storeroom door. The gout of fire shocked him. Heat and light burst up from the floor, sent him stumbling back.

"We will fire!" the UNP cop shouted as Quirk ran hunched away from the conflagration, sharp pain and heat making his cheek throb. As he pursued Jenny and Simon, he hoped fervently that the UN staff would be okay.

* * *

19:50, 18 January 2100
Level 40, UN Headquarters Building,
United Nations Plaza, NY, NAF

As they reached the stairwell landing on 40, Fran signalled Moth to stop then glanced through the window slit in the elevator lobby door, unholstering a NEMP pistol. Moth reached for her own NEMP gun: six discharges before battery replacement or recharge. She had four packs. As long as they didn't meet twenty-five droids, she'd be okay. Probably well over twice that if she stuck with Fran, which she had every single scum-sucking intention of doing, unless the woman got pissed enough with her causing their crash that she ditched the "useless kid." Also, Fran packed stun shots and live ammo for her eGlock 49A. She'd tried not to drool watching the woman clean the gun in the hotel room, mentally adding the eGlock to her Santa letter.

Moth watched Fran change the eGlock's ammo, working by touch despite their vision enhancement, loading for android. She then made the universal sign for three, indicating the droids' positions in the lobby. Fran signed she would take the two on the right, Moth had the one to the left. Moth nodded, readied her own weapon. Fran indicated a five count, using her fingers like a vid show floor manager.

As Fran went from two fingers to one, they moved.

Androids didn't need the lights, but neither did Rigel Wing Team. Three droids turned on them in the eery otherworld green of the elevator lobby, but she only had eyes for one. Her charge hit it in the chest where most of the ops stuff sat. The droid jerked sideways, a dancing, bright green figure like a frat house dark light party star, but managed to get a shot off.

The beam tore Moth's side, made her yelp then yell. Dumb, since this floor must have audio and vibration sensors. Her tactical suit absorbed some of the energy, dispersing heat over the suit's surface away from the hit site, but not fucking quickly enough! It hurt like a motherfuzker, the pain not helped by a wet feeling under her suit, maybe parts of her melting or bleeding. At least the shitting droid fell over.

She twisted, regretting it. If Fran hadn't dropped her two, any droid left standing would have zapped her by now. What the fuck were they shooting? Only SWAT teams and the CIA used HD lasers as standard issue. Using heavy-duty weapons indoors was strictly shit for the birds. Then she saw a fourth droid lying in the corner. She hadn't seen it at first because its body heat shone very low. She straightened, gasped from the pain and nasty-assed drippage on her right side.

Fran, standing over her two victims, checking them, subvoced her.

"You okay, kid? You took a hot one."

<Yeah, I'll make it to breakfast, but I'm gonna complain like a bitch the whole time.> Past Fran, at the doorway on their exit route, was another fallen droid someone had dropped before they arrived. <What's with the spares?> The penny began to drop. From forty floors up, it took a few seconds. <Our droids weren't UN. They're packing HDLs. They fired without warning.> She checked the foreheads of the just fallen, violet UV tattoos glowing in the dark. They'd just shot S-12075, S-12078 and S-12079.

<Oh, fuck,> subvoced Moth. She checked the cold droids: S-08544 and S-09106.

They'd just downed three shiny new droids with near consecutive serial numbers. Droids that shot first without bothering to ask questions, and those droids most likely had downed the UN security syRen® guarding the UN IT hub entrance.

The lights came on and a siren blared. The building's sound system relayed an artificial message.

"THE BUILDING IS NOW BEING EVACUATED. PLEASE USE THE DESIGNATED EXIT IN AN ORDERLY FASHION. PLEASE DO NOT DELAY."

Moth peeled off her visi-mask, seeing Fran's eyes for the first time in a bit. They narrowed, but in suspicion, not lingering anger at her, she thought. Okay, maybe both.

"Kimi and Rex," said Fran. *"They should be here by now."*

"THE BUILDING IS BEING EVACUATED. PLEASE USE THE DESIGNATED EXIT IN AN ORDERLY FASHION. PLEASE DO NOT DELAY."

Fran moved to the IT hub door, the only exit from the lobby other than the stairs or the elevator. The complicated-looking screen/console/keypad was dark, and didn't respond to Fran's touch. She pushed the swing door and it opened inwards.

"Is this good?" asked Fran.

<I doubt it.>

They entered the UN IT hub, guns first. Here the lighting remained low. A short corridor cut across their path, signage indicating Server Room left, Control Room right. Fran used her gun to point left, changing the eGlock's setting to stun. Moth hefted her NEMP pistol, wondered how hard she could throw it at a human target. She moved with the Rigel operative. Ten metres and another door, propped open by a dead syRen®.

The same low ambient lighting dusted this room and its rows of racking, shelf upon shelf of blinking systems equipment. Spinning warning lights sprayed orange all over the dim space like the world's shittiest amusement arcade.

"THE BUILDING IS BEING EVACUATED. PLEASE USE THE DESIGNATED EXIT IN AN ORDERLY FASHION. PLEASE DO NOT DELAY."

A wide entrance area five metres deep ran the width of the room before the racking started, occupied by two desks with single chairs, and two armchairs facing across a low circular table. The tall server racks defined the sides of five parallel corridors stretching away to the far wall.

The blasting aircon chilled her sweat, made her shiver, although that might be the effects of her wound. She was *not* looking forward to peeling off this tacsuit, tried not to think about bubbling, seeping skin.

"THE BUILDING IS BEING EVACUATED. PLEASE USE THE DESIGNATED EXIT IN AN ORDERLY FASHION. PLEASE DO NOT DELAY."

Fran stuck a telltale to the wall then waved Moth forward and they padded across the room looking down each server aisle. They found the body in the third aisle. Fran checked it.

"Rex. Dead. Wait here. Watch the door."

While Moth remained at the entrance to the central aisle, covering the door from the elevator, while Fran continued to survey the other aisles, returning seconds later.

"Nothing more. Let's get this done and try to get out."

<Roger,> said Moth. She wanted to check the body herself. She wanted to know how Rex had been shot, and by who—*okay, whom: fuck off, Quirk*—but she supposed Fran was right, it didn't really matter, probably. She carried Nick Kirby's data packet. That was their task.

For a second, she thought of Sec-Tech Suudi still hunkered somewhere in the building wearing a fucking bomb where his liver was and hiding it in an attempt to protect hundreds of lives. And still the signs seemed to point to TOM trying to get his shit-stained claws into the UN's main server. But the vote must be cancelled now, with the alarm, right? Had Team Three hit the button on their distraction?

Crouching in the near darkness, she ached, stung and throbbed in way too many places, so tired she could just have leaned into Fran, risking the woman's rage—already pumped to the max by Moth's earlier fuck up—and closed her eyes to sleep. Instead, she reached for a pocket on her opposite side from the wound and withdrew Nick's data packet. As per his previous instructions, she placed the data block beside one of the server room's main units, handily constructed with blue cases instead of the standard black.

It kinda freaked her out he'd been offline all the time she'd carried him, having ported a substantial portion of his—consciousness?—into the digital packet. She'd gotten used to their talks. That was weird enough. Major fucking weirdo-mondo, forming a social relationship with the guy you shot in the head, right? Awk-WARD! But they'd both wanted it, in the moment. Nick Kirby had wanted to pass from the physical realm into the virtual, and she'd wanted very much to stop him strangling Quirk. So, blam, blam, everyone's happy, right?

C'mon, Moth, keep your fuzking head straight, bitch.

Time ticked by. Was it working? Nick couldn't say how long it might take, not knowing the UN server security set up, nor able to scan it from the outside due to RADCOMS, but he was sure he'd be able to chit-chat on tactical comms once he uploaded. They really needed his skills right now. Dropping the consecutive droids would be noticed. The forces of dark *and* light must be descending on them. She'd surrender to one, but she'd fight the other tooth and nail, through pain and fatigue, to her end. And who would TOM send to do his dirty wet work? Dirty water work? Fuck, man, was she dropping into delirium now? Not enough to miss Fran start, turning her head back down the darkened aisle towards the entrance.

"Motion sensor tripped. Did you not get that?"

Moth checked her suit. Nothing. It hadn't synced with the telltale. *Fuck.* She'd started relying on Nick for shit like that. *C'mon, Nicholas, c'mon. Speed it up.*

Fran checked her sidearm and stood. The shot took her in the shoulder, Moth thought, spinning the woman around and throwing her to the floor. Moth didn't even see the shooter, but heard the soft report. As she scanned frantically, her own NEMP gun up, a black shape moved into the mouth of the dark, winking server racking aisle. A second shape glided from behind the first, an android, violet eyes glowing even though not locked into charging mode, but mobile and active.

"Moratti, don't move," said the man. "My orders are to take you alive." Foster, the shitbag from the hotel room.

Moth's blood ran even colder. Because any android that came with Foster the corporate douche—

"Angelikaaaa. Why d'you run out on me like that, sweetie? Don't you wanna hang? Maybe I'll just strap you up and hang you from the ceiling. Gotta spread out the fun, after all."

XXXI

Jenny moved ahead of him now, Simon behind as they pounded up seemingly endless stairs. Level 18. The other half of the maintenance team—the half that hadn't died in a short-lived gunfight with CC-tampered androids—had risked a coded message, confirming location of Suudi on Floor 23 in his office.

Not having Nick chirping in his ear—Quirk couldn't quite believe he missed it. The kid had been damned effective in the last few days, and Nick's anger—at him specifically—had melted away in the presence of Nick's mother.

"THE BUILDING IS NOW BEING EVACUATED. PLEASE USE THE DESIGNATED EXIT IN AN ORDERLY FASHION. PLEASE DO NOT DELAY."

That announcement was very annoying by now. With the small fire he'd started—betting two UN staffers' lives on the intelligent sprinkler system and the UNP being seconds away—or due to some action by Teams Two or Three, surely today's vote would be deferred? And now all these floors gave him to consider whether they were running towards an imminently exploding bomb. That narrowly beat out his certainty the android that attacked them, here in the UN, was one of TOM's, doctored by Androicon to subvert the Laws. How many had The Old Man snuck into the building? The seat of planetary politics. A sick feeling curdled his stomach. Could...? No. But, yes, what if Rigel's incursion had been the cover? What if they were the Trojan distraction that opened the door for TOM's own raid? No. Pure paranoia on his part.

"THE BUILDING IS NOW BEING EVACUATED. PLEASE USE THE DESIGNATED EXIT IN AN ORDERLY FASHION. PLEASE DO NOT DELAY."

Floor 20. Where there was one of TOM's syRen® there must be more. But if only one thing came from this raid, they'd exposed the tampered androids, right? Exposed their contravention of the Laws of Robotics in an eye so public—the UN building itself—that there could be no going back. And with that, how could the outcome of any vote, deferred to late evening, or carried out remotely, be expected to stick? Surely the UN would suspend the vote, even shelve or dismiss the bill. But even if they did, they still must reach Suudi. Sec-Tech could still become a victim of TOM's sour grapes.

"THE BUILDING IS NOW BEING EVACUATED. PLEASE USE THE DESIGNATED EXIT IN AN ORDERLY FASHION. PLEASE DO NOT DELAY."

Floor 21. Jenny's endurance impressed him. Maybe being on the run did that. Plenty of steps. Simon had put his cynicism behind him, the EMT impressively single-minded when focused on someone in jeopardy. And Quinton Kirby? Grade A quality Belter stubbornness.

A door burst open below them somewhere, the sound echoing in the stairwell. *That can't be good.* But Moth and the wingsuit team must be high above them, and the two maintenance crew just ahead, keeping an eye on Suudi, he hoped. Ready to support them while they ran the haemodialysis. No other sounds echoed upwards from pursuers, no shouts to cease and desist, throw down their weapons, etcetera, such as the authorities might use. Did that mean more CC androids on their tail? If so, they would gobble up these stairs tirelessly.

Floor 22. Laser fire from above raked the wall just as Simon raised his foot to the next step. The EMT staggered sideways, howling as a bright beam cut across his leg. Jenny half-caught him, broke his fall upward to the landing, and Quirk dragged Simon to the wall out of the firing line, for now.

"TOM's droids," Quirk grunted as Jenny produced steri-wipes and a field dressing from her medical bag.

"Don't care. Shoot them. And the ones below us." She ripped Simon's torn trouser leg apart, making him yelp—"Hush up, big baby"—then cleaned and covered.

"THE BUILDING IS NOW BEING EVACUATED. PLEASE USE THE DESIGNATED EXIT IN AN ORDERLY FASHION. PLEASE DO NOT DELAY."

Quirk edged forward, lasergun raised in one hand, NEMP pistol in the other. Laser scored the floor in front of him, because of course they could see his shadow from the wall-mounted lighting, and knew when he tried to duck out to get a shot off.

Feet were audible now, scuffing and padding the stairs below. He sent a couple of laser bursts downwards. Gratifyingly, the steps halted. He fired once more for luck then checked the screens on the two NEMP pistols he'd taken from the young Team Three guy. The full six in one powerpack, five in the other, but he'd need all of those and wished he'd gone through the young man's pockets for spares.

He flinched out and fired up the stairwell, hoping for a lucky shot, and to keep them honest. Doctored androids—badroids, because why did Moth get to concoct all the funny, funky names for things?— seemed to have more sense of their self-preservation than proper androids. Probably because of Androicon's tinkering. Meanwhile, they had to get out of here, up or down. Either way it was very much on him. He grabbed the first notion that came within reach, hoping it wasn't too dumb.

He lobbed one of his two NEMP pistols into the air towards the half-landing ahead, drawing fire, and moved out after it. He only needed that split second because he fired the laser pistol before seeing his target, scoring a line across the underside of the ceiling above which, when it crossed the edge of said ceiling, became a shot at the two androids *(Damn!)* waiting for him to emerge. He had to tweak his target point, but his shot speared one android's shoulder, making it shoot wide. Quirk's adjustment caught that android in the head. The second android shot Quirk in the chest.

Heat flared across his torso as the tactical suit laboured to disperse the laser's energy. Gasping, hurting, he flicked his beam to the second android's weapon—pause—then up to the head. Quirk pitched forward as hot pain overwhelmed him: instant and serious sunburn, but spared the catastrophic cooking of his dermis by a suit more effective against direct hits than glancing strikes. He still manged to fire the second NEMP, a weapon with less need of precise accuracy, most of its tight cone of effect hitting the second droid, dropping it from sight.

"THE BUILDING IS NOW BEING EVACUATED. PLEASE USE THE DESIGNATED EXIT IN AN ORDERLY FASHION. PLEASE DO NOT DELAY."

Quirk remained on hands and knees, verticality a distant dream. Surely this must be over now, the UNP flooding into the building, the odds hopeless. Hands pulled at him, hands familiar in their touch and grip, the very particular pull that Jenny exerted. She had pulled him in so many times in the halcyon days, now she yanked him urgently.

"Quirk! We're not done. Suudi! Come on!"

He let her haul him up, pushing to help, pain tearing across his chest, managed to snatch up the laser pistol as he rose. Jenny handed him the fallen NEMP, gazed intently into his eyes, checking he wouldn't fall over again no doubt, then went back to Simon.

Clumping footsteps sounded below, but silence reigned above. Floor 23. Suudi's floor. Quirk pushed on upwards, weapons extended, one in each hand, using elbows to steer, concentrating on not falling over.

* * *

20:12, 18 January 2100
Level 40, IT Hub, UN Headquarters Building,
United Nations Plaza, NY, NAF

"No! Fucking no!"

Moth's scream ripped through the silence of the dimly lit server room, and she wished the sound and fury could rip through the Callan/droid too, blow it away. Adrenaline surged through her, burning away fear as she bolted upright, the pain wrapped up in her anger. She snatched out her NEMPs and fired both charges into the Callan/droid, throwing herself sideways after pulling the triggers. Good thing too. The heavy thud of Foster's silenced weapon meant he shot hot lead. One of the bullets clipped her suit as she twisted, her back slamming into the racking.

Letting herself fall to the floor, she turned the NEMPs on Callan again as the droid advanced. Had she missed? She fired another double helping of circuit-scrambling NEMP then rolled across the floor as Foster fired into the dimness.

Reaching the rack opposite she hit...space. She fit under the racking! A clear air gap for ventilation and cooling! She slid under as

Foster fired again, missing her trailing arm. *I'm mofo Rigel Wing Crew, gusset-muncher, and you need to get up way early to get the drop on us!*

Scrambling under the racking she thought ahead. With Fran down she'd be trapped. Callan and Foster would work together to drag her out and she had no leverage, struggled even to crawl. This was fuxxing crazy, but she couldn't beat two of them. She had two NEMPs, so must bet on the side Callan picked. And how had she missed twice?

She struggled to push backwards the way she'd come. Grasping hands grabbed her ankles and hauled her out. The Callan/droid's waiting arms twisted her to face it, took her in a crushing embrace. Her blood curdled at the sight of it, even indistinct in server-room twilight, too-human touch making her skin crawl. As the droid squeezed her close, its once-neutral expression twisted into sick glee, she jammed her twin NEMPs into the syRen®'s stomach and pulled the triggers. "Two times two makes four, motherfucker."

"Yeah, well, close but no cigar, sweetie."

The droid crushed her sides and Moth's head swam, fell forward against its chest. She dropped the NEMPs. The pain was blinding, burning. But her anger was hotter, even in the chilled server room. She bit her lip, wrenched her head up. How had the NEMPs not worked?! This droid...something was different. Mainly, it contained Callan, but he'd done something else, changed something.

Foster came back around the racking and marched forward, because he had to capture her. *Should be glad TOM has some nasty intention for me, maybe blackmailing Mario.* Foster raised his gun. "Let her go. Tie her."

Callan grumbled, but dropped her on her feet. She ground her teeth against the side-splitting pain then—once balanced, from pure spite and petty rebellion—she rammed her heel down on the Callan/droid's foot.

The droid jerked upright, spasmed like she'd kicked a human in the balls. *WTF?!* The ineffective NEMPs. He'd somehow relocated or duplicated his control functions!

"Bad luck, fucker." One NEMP was gone, but the other hung on its wrist strap. "Open mouth"—she swung the weapon up into her hand— "insert foot." She NEMPed the Callan/droid in the feet and it staggered then toppled.

She backed away from Foster. If she slithered under the rack again, with Fran down, Foster would just go back to the server room entrance, wait for her, or for aid from more undroids. Fran's fallen eGlock? It could have landed anywhere. She'd never find it quickly enough in the near dark. When Nick uploaded, he'd be in a massive computer, no droids to co-opt. What could he do? Could he double up?

Her back hit the wall. Stuck. Trapped. Done, Foster only a few steps away.

She slipped under the metal frame anyway, because fucked if she'd make it easy for him, squiggled forward slowly—fuckstrating!—only to find him moved to the next aisle, grasping for her, bland features twisted with the effort of bending, clutching the metal frame to stretch under the rack.

Suddenly Foster screamed, face twisting, wailed as smoke wafted from his death grip on the metal racking. Moth pressed into the floor, but couldn't look away. His teeth chattered. He grunted and growled rabidly, spittle on his lips, then slumped to the floor, still, as the smell of cooking flesh reached her.

She wasted no time, squeezed past Foster, trying not to breathe. Jogged around the neighbouring aisle, cussing and yipping at the pain in her side. She dropped to her knees beside Fran, who moaned. Moth lifted Fran's gun, almost purring at how nicely the eGlock fit her hand. She searched for the gun's pinspot control where it lived on all post-2090 Glocks. Sterile blue-white light bathed the server-packed racking, picking out the frazzled droid, a fallen pantomime puppet. She went back to Foster, whose chest still rose and fell.

"You damned...lucky...amateur," he wheezed.

"You think TOM wanting me alive was lucky? Was me escaping Callan's attempted rape after he drugged you lucky? Or maybe saving my boss by blowing off the head of a two-hundred-pound monster was lucky?" *Sorry, Nick.* "Oh, and I've just downed you both, again." *With some help: Foster's frying...must have been Nick, right?* "Maybe you misjudged me, *dick,* because the harder I try"—she raised the Glock and shot him in the chest—"the luckier I get." She adjusted her aim and shot Foster in the head.

She wasn't sure how long she stood staring down at Foster's body. Her thoughts drifted, not quite settling anywhere. Had it been easier shooting this human man than the genetically modified monster TOM had made of Nick Kirby?

Fran called her out of her fucked-up dream sequence. "Moth. You need to shift."

She hurried to the other aisle and took Fran's hand. "Yeah, come on then."

"No. Leave me. I'll slow you down. Go. I'll be okay."

"You're such a fucking hero cliché," said Moth, but squeezed Fran's hand, smiling grimly.

"Well, you're not the liability I thought you were. Come visit me on Rikers Island." Moth nodded, switched off the Glock's light, turned to go. "And kid." She looked back, vision adjusting to make out Fran's features in the dimness. "Don't let that mess you up." She nodded toward the bodies. "You did what you had to. You can rise above it."

"I know," said Moth. "I just don't think I want to anymore."

* * *

20:29, 18 January 2100
Level 23, UN Headquarters Building,
United Nations Plaza, NY, NAF

The androids they encountered halfway along the Level 23 corridor were UN issue, and tried to persuade them to desist. Quirk's head ached by now, presumably in sympathy with the rest of him, and they had CC badroids behind them whose methods of persuasion were very different. So, Quirk NEMPed the two UN syRen® and kept moving, Jenny assisting Simon to hobble in his wake. Only Quirk's inability to move any faster prevented the Jenny and Simon three-legged race from becoming a problem.

He considered trying to raise the remaining Team Three crew on comms, or maybe Moth's Team Two, but even now a signal would only give away their positions to no real gain. No choice then but to press on towards Suudi.

Twenty metres short of Suudi's office, Quirk stopped.

"This is a good spot to deal with our pursuers from the stairs. They won't go away by themselves. We've got seconds at best, so don't argue. Start trying doors."

They found an open office and ducked inside. Simon gave Quirk a quick hit of pain relief and a little something from a syringe to boost performance while Jenny covered the open door. "No ethical issue, with this not being a sporting event, I presume," Quirk japed. Simon just grimaced.

"THE BUILDING IS BEING EVACUATED. PLEASE USE THE DESIGNATED EXIT IN AN ORDERLY FASHION. PLEASE DO NOT DELAY."

Quietly, all armed, they waited in silence. Quirk quickly became jittery, not just for chemical reasons. The trailing badroids did not pass the doorway. Not being in sight when they ducked inside, the badroids couldn't know they were here, would have to move along the corridor. Five minutes. Still, they didn't pass.

"We have to move," Quirk whispered.

"Leave me here," hissed Simon. "I like my chances better." No one disagreed.

Quirk and Jenny helped each other quietly to sling a med bag over their shoulders. Once Simon had shared the ambulance key with Jenny, they exited the room.

Quirk covered left: no pursuit. Empty.

"Quirk," said Jenny, voice wavering.

Several androids ran towards them from the lift lobby at the far end. Enough that Quirk couldn't count them. He pulled Jenny to the floor, sprawling flat. For once, just once, they might not be at a disadvantage.

"Shoot at twenty metres and don't stop till they're all on their backs. NEMP's area effect is our friend here. I'll pick off their lasers." *I hope.*

"Mylar blanket!" Jenny yelled. As the androids ran on to a soundtrack of laser powering whine, she fumbled in her bag.

"Jenny!"

She freed a silvered, heat-reflecting blanket, wrapped it around her bag. As Quirk began firing, she sprawled again, twisting to grab his bag, removed his sheet while behind her now-shiny barricade. The first laser burn scorched the carpet between them. Jenny slid a wrapped bag in front of him in time to prevent his incineration.

A beam raised heat on his shoulder, but he shrugged it behind the bag while Jenny fired her NEMP gun. This stilled some laserfire. She triggered the NEMP again. Quirk added his NEMP fire to hers. Badroids were falling, making obstacles for those behind. Badroid laserfire, and their progress, slowed.

"Fucker!" screamed Jenny as a laser scorched her ass. Quirk hoped it didn't scar. He liked that ass, realised he hoped to see it again up close, one day.

With two discharges left, the last badroid fell at a distance of only ten metres.

"THE BUILDING IS BEING EVACUATED. PLEASE USE THE DESIGNATED EXIT IN AN ORDERLY FASHION. PLEASE DO NOT DELAY."

Quirk helped Jenny up, chemical reinforcements still surging through his system, his pulse pounding. "Nice moves," he said. She winced. "We'll get that medicated ASAP."

They covered each other as they moved towards Suudi's office, checking each door they passed. They found the other half of the maintenance team in a store halfway to the lifts: none other than Paulo—a late arrival once the alarms went off—and the singular Anwar Cruz, charging and cleaning various items of handheld ordnance.

"You have to be kidding," said Quirk. "We just scraped in to get here!"

"Oh, hi, Anwar," said Jenny, like she'd bumped into xim Sunday afternoon in the turbine hall at the Tate.

"We had your back; theirs really." Paulo, grinned. "Hey, you two look like shit."

"We've been fighting badroids for twenty-three floors, not hiding in a cupboard."

"Yeah, well, fuck you, bigmouth," said Paulo, amiably.

Quirk smirked, *Pistols at Dawn.* "By George, I think he's got it."

"Can you banter while you work?" said Jenny, wincing. "I'm hurting here."

"Of course," Quirk nodded apologetically, reaching for a med bag.

"Suudi's two doors down," said Paulo. "Name's on the door."

"Of course it is," said Quirk, ensuring no one applied a field dressing to his ex-wife's derrière but him, focusing intently on the task in his rather hopped-up state.

Despite the verbal sparring proving he and Paulo remained in the "fallen out" phase of their relationship, Quirk liked the way it felt to be in a group with some real black ops credentials. It actually birthed some confidence not entirely chemically generated that they might get to Suudi's office and hold it long enough to get the bomb out of Sec-Tech. Then he could start asking some of the questions now bothering him, like did removal of the explosive bloodborne nanocytes render them harmless, or could they still be triggered?

"THIS BUILDING HAS BEEN EVACUATED. REMAINING OCCUPANTS WILL BE DETAINED."

An alarm Quirk had long since stopped hearing, ceased. He thought he'd gone deaf. This was disproved when the shooting started immediately as the four edged out into the corridor. Like a crazily improbable Lollywood blockbuster scenario (Liberia's film industry was not renowned for gritty social realism), Paulo paced forwards, twin eGlocks raised, firing zappers from one hand and lead from the other. Jenny went next, med bag slung on her back, Paulo shielding her. Then came Quirk with Anwar behind him, firing backwards at a badroid pincer group, blazing pistol in one hand and chaff shotgun nestled on xis hip, that gun making very little noise when its compressed-air mechanism threw out hundreds of shiny foil scraps to baffle badroid laserfire.

It felt like battling for hundreds of metres, but they probably moved all of twenty along the corridor to Sec-Tech Suudi's door. Paulo went beyond the door, frying a syRen® then dropping another with a round to the shoulder.

Quirk pushed through the door, levelling his weapon, felt Jenny push in behind him. A male model android stood in the centre of the room, unarmed, looking at Quirk as if he'd arrived for a meeting, seemingly oblivious to the gunfire outside Suudi's sanctum sanctorum, despite Anwar then Paulo each backing in while still firing.

A decent-sized reception room with three sofas and coffee table welcomed them. Paulo and Anwar—neither pausing to vet the android—began overturning sofas, forming a barricade.

"Opportunity knocks," snapped Paulo. "Use it or lose it." He and Anwar knelt in their sofa fort and covered the still-closed door.

Quirk followed Jenny toward the inner office.

"Secretary Suudi is sleeping," said the android, S-10144. "May I assist you?"

"I really doubt it," said Quirk.

"Badroids coming," called Paulo, before Quirk could continue. "Preserve us humans."

"The term 'bad-droids' is oxymoronic, sir," said S-10144.

He and Jennifer continued into the inner office. The syRen® followed. It hadn't lied. Suudi lay on another sofa, possible Nouveau Giroud or Vintage Gautier from the admirable eccentricity of its lines. He may previously have been asleep.

"Secretary Suudi..." Quirk—for a moment—was at a loss quite how to continue.

The Secretary for Technology sat bolt upright. "You can't be here. You have to leave. You're endangering hundreds of lives. People who—"

"We know," said Jennifer. "We know about the device. We're here to help."

The look of fear in Suudi's dark, lively eyes made Quirk's stomach twist, and it had been one of the few parts of his anatomy that didn't hurt. The man was a shadow of the proud, confident individual who stood on BLL's stage in Mars orbit and announced tighter regulation of Near Light Speed travel, suspension of C Corp's NLS applications, and no let-up in the UN investigation into CC's activities.

"It's not just me, all the people here. They said my daughter— You must leave."

"All due respect, Mr. Secretary, this is bigger than you. I...we"—he indicated Jenny—"have significant experience with Joshua Simister. I have suspicions this is about more than the vote. I don't see how your situation could have been suppressed or sustained long enough for the vote to be ratified, or the bill brought into law."

"You think it's a bluff?" Loud gunfire erupted in the corridor, causing them all to flinch and cower.

"We have the equipment to remove the nanocytes from your bloodstream." Quirk indicated the medical bags. "Sir, Simister rather hates my guts at the moment. I assisted Professor Streich on Skye to retrieve the evidence underpinning many of the charges against CC. But Jennifer is Simister's daughter. While their relationship is...challenged—" Jenny snorted. "We don't believe he would cause her death."

"But if that threat is gone, who's attacking us now? To what end? The vote was postponed after the alarm, and now the bill will be reviewed, likely challenged. What's to be gained by this attack?"

"I'm afraid I don't have an answer to that presently, sir, but I implore you to let us remove the device. Increase the protection on your family, yes, but let us close this avenue of attack on the UN's integrity."

Suudi looked doubtful. Another burst of gunfire—some old-fashioned loud, some modern and technological whines and thwaps—obliterated an awkward silence.

Suudi nodded. "I messaged my family to go into their shelter. The building is evacuated, but still, if you're wrong, and the bomb is triggered..."

"If it sweetens the deal at all, sir," said Jenny. "We"—she indicated Quirk—"will extend the UN all possible cooperation in nailing the old bugger to the wall."

"I think UNP would have you do that anyway," said Suudi, flatly. "Okay, go ahead."

Jennifer removed a tube from her medical bag and crossed the carpet to Suudi. She placed the tube against his neck. The Sec-Tech sat quietly, tension painted on his sweat-glistened features.

"Sedative. You'll be fine in an hour," said Jennifer matter-of-factly, perhaps borrowing her direct bedside manner from the Gramercy Refuge style guide. "Unless we all blow up, of course," she added, after Suudi's eyes fluttered closed.

Jenny pulled parts from her medical bag and Quirk did the same, fishing out the yellow-labelled components. Jenny had read the instructions and viewed the MeToob video in the hotel room, with Simon providing tips and commentary, impatiently talking over the eighteen-year-old Harvard Medical School graduate who had designed it along with his husband, a biotech engineer from MIT.

While Quirk fidgeted and tried to shut out the sporadic gunfire from the next room, Jenny assembled the blood filter, about the size of a shoebox once she was finished. With jerky hand movements she ran the diagnostic, received three green lights—one after the other—as the machine clicked, whirred and beeped. Then, she swabbed Suudi's arm, tapped the skin, selected a vein, and punctured him.

The kit included the latest vein-seeking technology, not quite as spectacular as the name suggested, but the VST needle's tip did have the capability to vary its path through the flesh by up to 1.4 mm (Quirk had not managed to tune out the instructional video entirely), significantly reducing the rate of multiple-attempt field canulisations. In hospital, of course, they just had an android do it.

The three green lights flashed together and filtration began.

"How long?" asked Quirk.

Jennifer harrumphed. "Did you not pay attention in school either? Up the back trying to kiss the girls?"

"In class? Are you mad? My school had perfectly good bike sheds for that sort of thing."

"Twenty-five minutes," she said. "But the machine should provide stats in five."

The office door opened and Anwar stuck xis head in. "The fighting appears to have stopped."

* * *

20:17, 18 January 2100
Level 40, IT Hub, UN Headquarters Building,
United Nations Plaza, NY, NAF

Moth turned away, hoping Fran would be okay. She checked the eGlock, put it in NEMP mode. She had one thing to do before she left. She walked down the aisle to check on the fallen Callan/droid, because that scum-sucker was a survivor, unfortunately. If she emptied the Glock and all her NEMP charges into it, one after another, after another, after another, could she burn him out of existence? And if she could, would she ever be able to burn him from her memory?

Up near the wall, just before the aisle's end, in the deepest dimness, the Callan/droid was gone.

Oh, fuzking, fuxxing fuck, no!

Her blood turned to ice. No, there. A lump of blacker dark half-hidden under the racking on one side. She flicked on the Glock's pinspot. The harsh glare lit what looked like a corpse, twisted, like it had been reaching for something. But why had he—*IT!*—dragged itself down here? Her NEMPing obvs had left the droid next to useless, but the nasty bastard had dragged it ten metres further into the racking.

She edged forward, thicker darkness hulking past the edge of the Glock's light cone, server lights blinking in the dark, aircon chilling the air. Her harsh light lit the scene like a police torch on a grisly murder. The droid lay still, hand stretched into the racking between two blue tech boxes. She took another step to see where the hand reached, but kept both eGlock and a NEMP trained on what had been the Callan/droid.

The droid's hand extended through the narrow gap between server units, its fingers stretched to their limit. A thin rod had split the synthetic skin of the index finger, and extended into the rear of what looked like a router facing into the next aisle.

The android had connected to the UN server.

Callan was loose in the UN computer, in its secure, protected, impregnable processing core: The killer who had refused to die on the Moon, who had survived in so much scrap metal, plastec and vacuum to be resurrected by TOM. A couple of shit-kickers matched in heaven.

She NEMPed the droid with both guns in its chest *and* feet, then set the eGlock to ballistic and pumped shots into its head, chest, belly, and feet, but her heart wasn't really in it. It must be too late. She pulled its arm out anyway, then snapped off the metal connector. She needed to find Quirk and Jennifer. She needed to find Nick.

<Nick?>

```
MOTH [20:20, 18-01-2100]
  Nick?
```

"Nick?"

Had they failed? Was Nick unable to access the system, even from inside the server room itself? Surely if Callan could do it Nick could? But would they ever know if Callan had done it? Really, they'd found him on the Moon only by him being so drunk on power, so psychotic for murder, that he'd left them a trail of bodies. If the fuzker tried to stay hidden, he'd be lost like a poisoned needle on a kiddies' hayride.

She had to find Quirk. Didn't she? She took her handset from her tacsuit and tried to call him, knowing she ran the risk of detection, but RADCOMS could sit-and-spin.

No answer. *Shit!* She left text. Potentially incriminating, but who gave an actual fuck at this point? Maybe someone else blocked the message, maybe the IT hub.

No response from Nick. But it must have been him who zapped Foster, right? No way had two thousand volts happened along in a room full of sensitive technology by happy coincidence. Was he locked in battle with Callan now? The two of them slugging it out in some kind of virtual arena inside the UN central server? That would explain why he hadn't responded. She really hoped he wasn't still cooped up in that little box.

Okay, so without backup, how could she make it out of this giant garbage heap of good intentions that didn't involve her wearing speed cuffs or a neoprene body bag? No Quirk, no Nick, no Fran, no Rex, and no sign of Kimi since they'd jumped off a hotel, she must be down and/or out or she'd have shown up long ago.

You're in charge now, bitch, and maybe that's how it'll be from now on. So, hike up your tangas and let's get the fuck out of here before someone blows something up.

* * *

He left the silver of the box and fell into the black.
It consumed him. How easy was breaching the UN's core?
Dad would be pleased.
No, wait. This was only the conduit. A wall lay ahead.
It shimmered, sparkled, radiated pain.
So what? He was Nick Kirby, and all he had to do was think.
He tested the barrier, prodded it, buzzed it. He took a few hits, but
he found it.
The way in.
Game on.

XXXII

20:37, 18 January 2100
Level 23, UN Headquarters Building,
United Nations Plaza, NY, NAF

"Quirk."

Jennifer called his attention away from Anwar, pointed to the transfuser screen.

"What am I looking at? I see blood type, cell counts—"

"The bottom line."

"No contaminants. I don't quite follow."

"There are no nanocytes. There is no bomb."

"But on the *Gargantua Pleiades*, residual nanocytes traces found in the box—"

"Unless someone else removed them from his blood, they were never there."

"So, this was a ruse? All the running around over Mars, for this? What does it achieve? There has to be more. There's something else." He paced to Suudi's desk, turned and paced back, completely unconscious of where he was going, focused on the moving parts. Sec-Tech. Rigel. Callan. Moth, himself.

A flower unfolded, plots within plots like petals opening to reveal The Old Man's purpose. The wolves were closing in on TOM. The UN, the FBI, the Lunar Joint Administration, even the protests and attacks of eco-activist groups gained traction since Skye. Quirk, a former employee, had been a target in Prague; could be accused of changing sides to Rigel, although he had not been on TOM's for years. Rigel had raided the UN. TOM felt the pressure, the heat of public opinion turning against CC, against him. What better response than setting two of your greatest adversaries against each other? The UN and Rigel.

He put a hand over his eyes, the twin weights of fatigue and realisation crashing down on him like a landslide. The pain redoubled too, the effects of Simon's chemical pick-me-up petering out as he stood, soaking in the realisation of TOM's scheme.

"I'm getting a sinking feeling," said Jenny, not looking up from the transfuser display. "And not because you're about to start mansplaining to me."

"Try this on for size. There's no bomb in Sec-Tech, but TOM went to huge effort to make us think there was, all intended to convince Mario he had no choice but to intervene, that the stakes—the control of human interstellar settlement—were high enough for Rigel to risk compromising itself through this operation. But TOM also still wants to intervene in the process of drive licensing for his own gain. He would have done it years ago, but he's never had the capability to breach the UN server—the most complex and detailed virtual security system in the worlds—in order to manipulate the UN via its IT systems."

"Not until now," said Anwar, still listening since a now-troubling silence had fallen in Suudi's lounge next door.

"Yes, because if Callan could have done it alone, he would have. Ergo, Callan couldn't get access. But lo, and behold, and whaddaya know? Your own detestable genetic experiments—" Jennifer flinched. "Have presented you with the very best young man for the job, Nicholas Kirby. Only he despises you without limit of reason. So, you make him, his allies, think they're working against you. I think we've done all the hard work for TOM just to stroll in the open door behind us."

Anwar at least believed Quirk, xis face an ugly sneer. "So, what can we do about it? And think fast, because all those badroids—which were holding off the UNP and FBI too—just put their weapons down and surrendered. The Feds are incoming. Be here in minutes."

Jenny looked sceptical about Quirk's theory, but she believed the equipment, beginning to terminate the haemodialysis.

Quirk reached for his handset, because bets were off now as far as detection went. "Nick, calling Nick Kirby, are you receiving me?"

Anwar rolled xis eyes and subvocalised, <Nick Kirby phone home.> This course had the advantage of Quirk not having to hear Anwar's weary "I knew this would happen" tone, which the pinching of xis handsome features implied.

Jenny approached and took Quirk's handset. "Nick, honey, talk to Mama."

No reply.

Quirk then messaged Moth on the group comms at mission.alias (All your covert ops communications needs on one easy-to-use and triple-secure platform!). A risk, given the efficacy of RADCOMS, but people were shooting at them now. The clandestine boat had sailed.

"Okay, someone needs to get to Moth and the wing crew, find out what happened. Could be Nick's uploaded to the UN server, but can't comm us. Maybe they didn't get there. If the FBI come in from the roof too, which seems likely, they'll get down to Level 40 in minutes. But maybe we'll get lucky for once today.

"Keep trying Nick?" he asked, and Jenny nodded. "Tell him I think TOM's going to out us, including Nick, as Rigel agents, pin the mission we thought TOM was enacting on us. I don't know if the UN can cleanse Nick from their system, I don't really know how Nick works, but he could be in danger if he's still in there when the authorities regain control. I have a feeling that's part of the old bastard's plan."

Suddenly, Paulo's voice became loud enough to hear through the closed door.

"Okay, I'll go quietly, but it's about time *UNP* got here. You wouldn't believe the shit goin' down."

"You'll have to be good to get out now," said Anwar.

"Don't be so negative, Beatrix," said Quirk.

Someone thumped on the door.

"UNP. Throw your weapons in the corner, lie face down, hands behind your head. On a count of five a UNP droid will enter. One."

Quirk helped Jenny finish dismantling and packing the haemodialysis machine.

"Two."

Jenny looked at him. "What about Suudi?"

"Three."

"Leave him under, in case he tries to 'help.'"

"Four."

Anwar scowled and tossed xis weapon into the corner then stood against the wall, hands splayed, neck craned around so xe could see who would be frisking him. "I'm not lying down for these schmucks." Xe winked at Quirk.

"Five."

As the door opened, Quirk darted to Suudi's side where Jenny already checked his vitals. Paulo didn't make it into the room, of course, probably already restrained by the very latest in EM handcuff technology.

True to the voice of authority's word, a syRen® in UNP blue entered the room, ready to take a bullet for its humans. The breathing officers arrived once the android confirmed the scene was non-hostile. Clearly it hadn't noticed Anwar's expression.

"Okay, Captain Mankowitz, United Nations Police. I am detaining everyone here under UN general ordinance 53 and the law of the city and the state of New York. You'll be incarcerated by NYPD, and questioned by the FBI and us."

"Super," said Quirk. "Those two should be locked up. Throw the book at them."

"You'll be questioned, too, Florence Nightingale."

Quirk snorted. "She's Florence, I'm Pierce." He glanced at Jenny, who nodded at the cop. "But we must go to the hospital first, to admit our patient. Or, are you going to book him for resisting arrest due to tachycardia?"

"You EMTs. Always with the attitude, right Barney?" The older, thinner, shorter man addressed his taller, hippier lieutenant, whose expression suggested she'd happily lock them all up for sassing an officer. "Okay," Mankowitz continued. "Lieutenant Barnett is now issuing you a contact card." The officer did indeed hand Quirk and Jenny each a plastec card. "These are individual to you and Barney is scanning them, activating your twenty-four-hour statement summons. Do not be late, that is a felony. Link to your interview room with the ZR code. Now get outta my crime scene, you're messing the place up."

Quirk really had not thought that would work, but required no second invitation.

"Hey, where's your gurney?" asked Barnett.

"Uh, had to leave downstairs," said Quirk. "Issue with the elevator."

Now they really did have a problem. The only way they reasonably could get out of the room was with Suudi on a gurney that had plunged over the parapet into the UN building reception. One of them could get out, but the other must stay, and when the first didn't return with a gurney, the second would be in a heap of trouble.

"C'mon, Pierce, hustle," Jenny snapped. "My gurney's not gonna stroll up here itself!"

Her eyes held none of the friction in those words, her gaze imploring him to get out and find their son. In staying, Jenny risked falling back into her father's "tender care." They may arrest her when he didn't return in reasonable time, or if a real EMT crew arrived. But to hesitate was to lose, so he nodded to her—wishing he could say what he felt—turned and hurried from Suudi's office.

* * *

He drifted now. Not in pain, in rest.
There was no pain here, only success or failure. On or off. One or zero.
Not that his world looked that way. He breathed states, consumed
conditions. Rode processes to his ends, or theirs. He felt his way, and
his touch was magic.
But effort existed.
Work existed, the product of force and displacement.
He had put in huge effort to breach the UN's glittering wall,
and now numerical bliss awaited. The mesmerism of mathematics, and
he had serious suggestions for this place. He just had to—
Oh, that's interesting...company.

* * *

20:24, 18 January 2100
Level 40, IT Hub, UN Headquarters Building,
United Nations Plaza, NY, NAF

Hand on the door to the elevator lobby, Moth stopped. The view through the door's window was clear, but she needed a plan. Was she going up or down? She had to assume her message to Quirk wouldn't send. If it did go, fine, but she had to stay at large long enough to tell *someone* Callan had breached the UN computer system. Trying to get out of the building had to be the best way.

So, how would Quirk do that? She had as much chance of getting into his head as a rock chick at a choirgirl convention— Misdirection!

He loved that stuff. Any excuse to dress up. So, she had to ditch her "Look at me, I'm a member of a heist squad" black tacsuit. Could she swing a school-kid-lost-on-a-tour thing? Her white tank top might work, if it wasn't drenched in blood and other fluids when she took off the tacsuit, but her undies would take some explaining. She just didn't have anything to wear!

Come on, M, work it. This no time to be shitting classic one-liners.

Foster wore a tactical suit, but the Callan/droid didn't need one, had sauntered into the gunfight in jeans, a T-shirt and hoodie. She needed that hoodie, hopefully it wasn't too singed, but she had to go back for it. Back into the server room. She couldn't see another way. Wondering how close the cops were getting, she took a deep breath and ran, trying to shrug off the wet pain in her side.

Fran had passed out, which brought Moth to a halt. She agonised for seconds then fished around for the woman's handset, found it, grasped it as she edged up to the Callan/droid. At least it hadn't shitting moved this time. She kicked it a couple of times, Glock aimed at its head, then put the gun down, pulled off its hoodie and the white T-shirt underneath. Full of holes of course, actually looked hip as fuck.

Now the hard part. Moth shed her highly incriminating tactical suit, shucked off the arms, gingerly peeled the second skin down from the wound in her side, eased off the legs, pulled her burnt and torn tank top up and off. It felt like she was ripping herself in half. Her eyes watered and she gasped, reached for the tacsuit's hanging arm, found the field meds pocket, ripped open the zip, grasped the syringe, jabbed it into her side, and prayed for the pain to go away. It felt like a day-and-a-half, during which she applied antiseptic gel (cooling, calming, nippy!) fished out the biggest field dressing and unwrapped it, but gradually—through much "ah"ing, "ugh"ing and general puffing—she got the bandage on. Disappointingly, she felt just as fucking shit as before, but she pulled on the android's too-big T-shirt, knotting the hem below her bandage, at her hip. Then, she grabbed the hoodie, wrapped it around her like a skirt, zipped it up to the max and tied the arms tightly around her waist. It looked weird, but it would do as instant disguises went. Most kids were weird anyway, so no problem there.

But a kid lost in the UN building (a bit lame, but really the only escape plan she had) would not of course be packing any kind of firepower, and definitely not the specialist kit she sported right now. So, she wiped the grip of the eGlock and the two NEMP pistols, almost dropped them on the Callan-droid's inert form, then changed her mind. "I just don't trust you to stay dead, bastard-pants."

* * *

20:44, 18 January 2100
Level 23, UN Headquarters Building,
United Nations Plaza, NY, NAF

Quirk ran from Suudi's office, trying not to gasp with the pain in his side. The four cops in the reception room knew better than to question a running EMT, especially one who had just left their boss. He turned left past the officer at the door towards the far stairwell instead of right towards the lifts. He grit his teeth against a challenge, but he heard nothing before the stairwell door swung shut behind him. He'd seen plenty of movies in which vigorous detectives, cops or agents leapt up three stairs per stride in the pursuit of justice. With his pain and fatigue, he felt lucky to manage one at a time without falling on his face.

Floors passed painfully slowly. He started puffing after three. When he heard feet on the stairs below, he seriously considered stopping. Being caught seemed inevitable now, just a matter of time. But if he could find Moth, speak to Nick, maybe he could influence events before that possibility was taken away by the police, whose hospitality he expected to be enjoying for some time after this.

Finally, a number starting with "3" appeared, but the way he toiled now, he seriously doubted he'd live long enough to reach Level 40, and surely Moth would have moved on from the IT hub by now. Maybe he'd meet her on the way down, or would she head back to the roof, get away on a wing and a prayer. He was so tired now, he couldn't even summon a laugh for his own jokes.

The footsteps behind stopped. Quirk kept climbing.

* * *

Light shattered over him a deluge of data engulfed him almost dispersed him scattered him to the four winds never to assemble again never to compile a rational thought or use a droid to smell a flower or look at Moth or see her or hear her voice never to touch her to touch her to touch her and the only defence was to make more light more data light than the enemy the enemy the enemy was him him him him him him the one and he knew how to fight he'd fought before and he was strong formidable awesome never faced a foe like this before never faced a foe at all not here in the virtual and now he was in deep shit.

* * *

20:29, 18 January 2100
Level 40, IT Hub, UN Headquarters Building,
United Nations Plaza, NY, NAF

She walked out into the elevator lobby and through to the stairwell, risked looking over the edge of the railing. Her head swam with vertigo, despite the almost invisible nets for the purposes of catching jumpers. Still, she saw all the way down to the ground floor, even thought it was nothing more than a dot in the centre of a dizzying Escher-scape of decreasing rectangles. Then she wiped the pistol grips again, dropping each weapon over the handrail into space, watched the first net catch them, watched them wobble then hang as if levitating in space. The police would for sure be coming up here to secure all the important stuff, maybe down from the roof too.

Where were Quirk and Jenny, where were the Rigel teamsters? Some dead? Was Quirk dead? But she'd made her choice to leave. Was she abandoning Quirk? No, he would tell her to get away while she could. A plan came together amidst her jumbled thoughts, and she darted back to retrieve her tactical suit. She tried not to, but couldn't help glancing up to check the droid remained down. It did, lay unmoving, but Moth couldn't quite convince herself the bastard was dead.

Fuckety-fuck, fuck, fuck! She couldn't leave without Nick. Quirk and Jenny would have to fend for themselves, but Nick—in some virtual, weird-ass-shit omnipotent Nick Kirby way—still rattled around in this room, on the UN network. What if he became trapped on the server? What if the UN's protection tech was that good? If it was good enough to keep Callan out, how did Nick leave again if he wanted to? Had Nick known that was a possibility? Was he locked in combat with Callan right now? He'd rescued her, and she *refused* to let him go down in virtual flames— What if they deleted him, purged him, reformatted him from existence? She had to remove the data packet.

She darted, stumbled, walked down the relevant racking aisle, trying to remember, to recognise the location of the packet, picture the numbers on her screen before the mission plan message was obliterated. Rack 2, Tower C29, no C39, Shelf 4A (A4?). Wrong height. She groped down the side of the server anyway, and the ones left and right, above and below. Nothing. *Fuck.* It was C29!

She moved further into the darkness.

"Armed police! Anyone in this room announce your presence. Stay where you are, lie on the floor, hands behind your head."

Fushit!

The harsh spray of light from a gun lamp stained the walls and floor out in the open area beyond the racking. Then the lights came on.

* * *

Shit.

The datawave blew him apart. But he snapped back, because he was a whole. He was himself. And the wave tore him apart, and he snapped back. It broke him and he reassembled. Disassemble, reassemble. Disassemble, reassemble.

But what if he didn't? What if he let go, stayed out, broke the pattern?

Everything! Everywhere! He could touch it all!

Like omnipotence, he could see all parts of the system.

No, not actually all, but so many as to have the effect of being everywhere at once.

The wave crashed again, furious, insatiable, but it could not touch him.

So, now what?

* * *

20:50, 18 January 2100
Level 40, UN Headquarters Building,
United Nations Plaza, NY, NAF

Quirk glanced up from the half landing on Floor "Whatever I've stopped caring." Mankowitz stood on the landing, a couple of UNP officers behind him. Quirk looked down and saw more officers emerging from a landing two floors below him, their hands dancing along the handrail as they loped up towards him. He stopped for a second then dragged his feet up the last few stairs to be restrained then cuffed by the uniformed officers while the captain watched.

"You're under arrest, Mr. Kirby. I've reviewed your recent adventures on Earthpol, and I'm pretty confident you'll soon be enjoying a long holiday on the beach on Rikers Island."

"Captain, there's a major stitch-up going on here, designed to look like Rigel were trying to pull off a coup, or something, but C Corp are at the heart of it."

"So how come we're finding these messed up droids are registered to The Rigel Corporation? So says the UN's central android register." Mankowitz raised a questioning eyebrow as the officers began leading Quirk to the elevators.

"But those records must be held on the UN server. They've been tampered with." Callan's work, dammit! "There must be a trail."

"I'm sure your lawyers will turn something up, maybe Rigel's lawyers, if they're feeling charitable enough to defend you. I wouldn't bet on that though." Mankowitz waved a hand towards the lift. "Get this joker out of here."

* * *

20:47, 18 January 2100
Level 23, Secretary for Technology's office, UN Headquarters Building,
United Nations Plaza, NY, NAF

When Quirk didn't return with a gurney in what Lieutenant Barnett decided was a reasonable time she started asking Jennifer awkward questions.

"Is Pierce your usual partner?"

Damn it, Quirk! "Uh, no. Assigned today. My usual partner's off sick."

"An EMT off sick," Barnett deadpanned.

Jennifer rolled her eyes like EMT jokes were all she ever heard. "Look, I have to get this chap out. The UN First Aid room will have a gurney. Can you send someone? Right now?"

Barnett nodded, put in a call.

Within ten minutes they had Suudi on a gurney, and Jennifer finished buckling him in. She had given him another shot while she waited because Sec-Tech had begun to stir, and him waking meant a quick trip to the pokey for her. Anyway, Secretary Suudi probably needed the rest, he'd been through a lot. At least he would wake to discover there never had been a bomb inside him. So, good news on that front. Quite what the rest of the news would be in relation to this debacle, she had no idea.

She managed to manoeuvre the gurney from the room with only one bump into the wall as she turned out of the doorway. Unfortunate, since it felt like every cop in a ten-block radius watched her doing it.

She made it to the elevator, manoeuvred the gurney in without the doors closing on Suudi's head, and punched the button for the basement. Only then did Jennifer have time to breathe, to shake some of the tension from her limbs, and to think. Quirk could well be right. The sort of arch deception he outlined very much had her father's fingerprints on it, leading his rivals to their own doom, using their strengths against them, mind games, deceit. All weapons of Joshua Simister's arsenal. And he'd turned those weapons on his own family before, something Nick knew all about. She almost burst into tears as the weight of what Nick and Quirk had told her broke over her again. How could any person do that to another, let alone their own grandson? Whether Nick came from a human womb or an artificial one, he had been made of the same stuff as she was, as her father himself was. What did her father actually want? Why did he go on? Money? Power? Real estate? The thought of being associated with him made her physically sick. But who could stop him?

The elevator pinged as it settled into the basement. She checked Suudi over with the obs handset from the med bag. Green lights all the way. She locked the gurney's wheels, opened the door, stepped out, and sent the elevator up to the ground floor.

A chaotic scatter of vehicles spilled across UN building's basement garage. Amidst the splashing red and blue lights, big capital letters had tumbled together: UNP, FBI, NYPD, FDNY. Among paintjobs of black, blue, white, yellow, red and green, and chequered patterns of the same, uniformed people and androids moved back and forth with purpose. The elevator had departed and now a couple of cops approached her. *Because of course the basement is a key point of entry, you idiot!*

"You okay?" said one, a woman with a dark ponytail. "You look a bit lost."

"Ha," said Jenny. *Oh, smooth.* "I was told there might be a spare gurney down here, but an ambulance is about all you're missing from the set. That asswipe Peterson sold me a bum steer."

"Fucking Peterson," said the bearded cop sarcastically. "Best go back up and find your gurney. This area is locked down."

"Sure," said Jenny. And turn up in the lobby to find the cops with a gurney and a patient, but no EMT. *Should have kept the med bag, dummy.*

She turned back to the elevator, feeling the cops' eyes on her, thumbed the call button trying for casual. Her escape window closed by the second, and this was like Gramercy on steroids (ha!). No Anwar to hold her hand, but she'd learnt a good deal in the time and the kilometres since.

The elevator arrived, the doors opened. Empty. She stepped in and turned to find the two cops stepping in after her.

"We'll ride up with you," said the woman.

"Give Peterson a piece of our mind," said the man.

In the space of travelling five metres vertically, Jennifer managed to avoid throwing up or passing out. The doors opened on the lobby, Mankowitz and Barnett waiting, Quirk in handcuffs between two syRen®.

"Turns out your new partner here is yanking everyone's chain," said Mankowitz. "I think we'll take you in too, since you seem to be done with your patient."

Barnett moved forward and took Jennifer's right arm, a blank expression on the UNP officer's face. "This way, please." She led Jenny across the foyer towards the main doors, none too gently either. The officer's manner made her think of Gramercy and the orderlies who waited for her. Damned if she'd crossed the Atlantic Ocean twice just to go back, to be right back where she started, under *his* thumb! Pacified like a lab rat or a wild animal in a zoo. Failing Quirk, she hated, but she had never failed Nick before. Her *father* took Nick away from her. She would never let him do that again.

The physical jolt of decision that ran through her made her stop. Like a shiver, but painful, visceral. As a child, certainly into her teens, she would always have struggled to tell anyone she loved her father. She had feared him, been nervous around him—before her rebellious years she had respected him, or at least his ability to get things done, without ever really understanding what he did. If she had loved her father, ever, those thoughts lay under lock and key in the years before any memory she now possessed. It felt to her that he had gone about the systematic process of dismantling her life: alienating her husband, appropriating her son, institutionalising her. No more.

Barnett guided her out into the cold, spotlit night towards one of the many police cars in the UN building forecourt, lights splashing blue and red over the techmac of the turning circle that circumnavigated the *Fountain of Truth for the Nations and Planets of Humankind* (Vincenzo Garnacho, 2037). With head held still, Jennifer flicked her gaze around looking for an escape route, but Barnett pulled her in close then thrust her against the first car.

"Hands on the vehicle."

She complied, and Barnett kicked her feet apart, frisked her. The cop started at her boots, worked up her legs, over and around her hips, butt (ouch), stomach, chest, arms. Jenny continued to search for...something. The car. Barnett's? An image on the dash of an old couple, a lunchbox bearing the picture of child with a man in a spacer uniform. *Nothing.*

Working her way thoroughly along Jennifer's arm from hand to shoulder brought Barnett's mouth close to her ear. "In a second, I will tell you to walk away. Go directly to your ambulance, get in and drive away. Say you understand."

"I don't—"

"There's no codeword. We're not six years old. If there was one, it might be Beta. Comply now, or you force me to put you in the car. Cameras watching."

Oh, Beta as in β Orionis? Rigel's astronomical designation. "Of course I'll go."

Barnett finished her search, strong hands turning Jennifer around, back to the car now, facing the earnest cop. "If I bump into you on 5th Avenue, I'll bust your ass, because my arrangement is strictly limited. Now get out of my sight before I decide to be a hero and find my mom's mental health support some other way."

Jennifer gawped for a second, but moved when Barnett made a fake grab for her, remembering to stride not run to their ambulance, parked where Simon left it, lights flashing, Quirk's passenger door still ajar.

I'm sorry, Quinton. She climbed in that open door, slammed it closed in self-recrimination, slid over to the driver's seat. *I'm so sorry, Nick.* But she rejected the tears that threatened to fall as she accessed her handset. Dozens of messages and notifications flashed up on the device now it had escaped the RADCOMS blackhole. *I'm sorry, Moth, wherever you are.* Guilt assaulted her scrambling thoughts as she tapped into her drive app and unlocked the vehicle controls. She hadn't driven in an age, since solar buggies on Golden Gate Beach when Nick was...what? Young? New? Fresh out the box? It didn't matter. Quinton had left by then, but now...

"Ah!" She howled quietly in frustration, took a couple of breaths, started the ambulance forward. Tentatively, circling around the statue first, she picked her way between the police cars, using driving assist, to weave out of the UN Building's forecourt, over the retracted vehicle defences and the upraised barrier, waited for the green signal then drove away along East 45th Street.

Jennifer did not need to think what to do next. She had already decided her father had to die; it was simply a question of how to achieve it.

XXXIII

20:42, 18 January 2100
UN Headquarters Building, United Nations Plaza, NY, NAF

Moth dropped in front of Tower C29, Block 4A, Rack 2, reached down the side of the blinking, purring server into the shadow made by the sudden burst of ceiling lights. Bootfalls sounded on the industrial carpet.

"Armed police. We will fire if you are not on the ground."

Her hand closed on Nick's data pack, she tensed to pull the slim black packet out and stuff it...somewhere. But she should ask him. There must be microphones in the room, part of the security system?

"Nick Fucking Kirby, your new middle name. You'd better shitting hear me because we're leaving unless you give—"

"Sergeant, found one! Stay down. I will shoot."

She snapped her head round. No one in sight in the aisle. They'd found Fran.

"Give me a sign, Nick," she hissed.

She heard voices. Fran must be conscious, might stall the cops just long enough. She pulled the data pack free, feeling the tug of its self-locating connection ripping away from the server, coiling back into the box as she pulled it clear. She thought about Callan attacking her, grabbing her. She imagined Giulia gunned down on the Piazza del Duomo, bleeding on the paving stones. A sob rasped hard and sore from her throat.

"Another here! Just a girl! Stay down."

She snatched the hoodie pocket to her stomach, covering her hand as it worked the zip, trying not to shake as she slid the data pack into the pocket and zipped it up. Cautious bootsteps approached her, but she didn't break her huddle.

"How the hell d'you get in here, kid?"

She let the sobs come, let them roll out of her, painful jerks of her throat that stung, her face wet and hot.

"I was, uh...with my friend. We came to see her dad. He's...Secretary Suudi. I'm...friends with Shuun. When the shooting..." She flinched at that point. Maybe she'd meant it, or maybe it was way too easy to break down after everything. Because she was way beyond too much by this point. "When the shooting started, I just ran."

She never could have acted so pissing pathetic if she didn't actually feel it. Her heart jumped around like popcorn in a fuxxing solar frier, and she hated it. Had she managed to scoop up Nick? What might it have cost her? She didn't care. She'd done her best, but maybe she'd blown her only chance of escaping.

"Yeah, okay. Come with me. The nice support officer will ask you some questions then we can get you back to your parents."

Now that *would be some serious fucking Miracle Whip.* She refused to acknowledge the image her mind presented.

The officer straightened up, giving her space, and she untucked, her sobs subsiding. She sat up and realised the crying left her feeling something like cleansed, a bit. The data packet weighed her tied-up hoodie down.

"What's that?" The officer—youngish, maybe twenty-nothing-much, ginger—pointed to her rolled up tactical suit lying near her on the floor.

Aw, shit.

"Stupid rainsuit. My Mom makes me take it everywhere. 'Warm in the winter, cool in the summer!' Thanks *Mom.* None of my friends wear a stupid rainsuit!"

"Okay, okay. Bring the jacket. Let's go."

The doofus helped her up. He seemed alright, really. She moved to his right side, keeping the hoodie's data packet pocket away from him, squashed it against her side with the rolled-up tacsuit as they passed officers crouching with Fran, examining Foster, photographing the syRen®. Her heart pummelled her chest. She'd dodged the first bullet, but these minutes were borrowed from her jailtime. She'd have to bolt, it would be her only chance, and she'd have to go for the roof, because much closer, hope Kimi left her wingsuit there, and hope she could build enough headway to climb into her tacsuit, which was critical to her using the wingsuit for her escape. Hers and Nick's, she hoped for realz. She'd make a break when they reached the stairwell.

Oh, wait. Oldest trick in the mofo book. Worked at the convent every time.

"I have to use the toilet."

The officer paused at the lift lobby door. "Jeez, kid. Seriously, now?"

She put on her best little girl lost act, instantly regretting it when an image of the leering Callan/droid flashed into her mind, and now she really did have to go.

The young cop looked sheepish. "Sorry. There's one two floors down. We'll pay a visit then take the elevator."

She threw him a smile, keeping it uncertain, unconfident, which she felt now after shaking herself with the act that had gone so wrong before. And how could she escape a cop?

A droid in NYPD uniform blues waited in the stairwell. "Officer Jaaskelainen, may I assist?"

The young cop frowned. "No change to your orders."

"Officer, external physical signs suggested the child may be considering flight." The thing looked her with a standard placid droid expression, but all she could think of was Callan. Had he found her again? Maybe not, but would she ever be able to trust syRen® without wondering? Would she always be afraid? She realised she held the cop's arm and kept a hold.

"I've got it covered," said Officer Jaaskelainen, and led her away downstairs. Moth tried to stop shaking. Now she needed to get past the thing when she made her break. Could she get to the elevator and get the doors closed in time?

The stairwell echoed with footsteps above and below, the jangle and thud of equipment, voices commanding or discussing. The human noise chaos reassured her. Enough cops nearby that if a new Callan/droid attacked, someone would help even if Nick couldn't, stuck in the UN server with Callan, or hopefully trapped in the packet held hard on her hip. Her nerves still buzzed thinking someone might recognise a rolled up tacsuit.

They reached the landing on 38. Jaaskelainen pushed through into the elevator lobby. Between them and the WC stood a female model UNP droid. They were fucking everywhere. It watched them approach. Moth eyed the droid nervously.

"You'll wait outside?" she asked Jaaskelainen, voice wavering without trying.

"Sure, kid. Just be quick. Don't make me knock on stall doors looking for you."

She pushed inside, found the usual line of doors, each stall self-contained, high-mounted camera at the end of a short, pastel corridor. An air flush howled for a second. She started forward, took the third stall, opposite a picture of the regrowing New Barrier Reef with the floating albedo mat that helped reduce the local sea temperature.

She went inside.

"Lock the door." The door locked, temporarily saving her voice print, although the UNP could override that, of course. She untied the hoodie from her waist, removed the data pack, set it on the hoodie. She actually did pee. She was thirsty, really hungry. What an interminably shit day! But it would end soon, one way or another. She stuck her hands in the airwasher then pulled on the tacsuit legs, eased her arms into the tight sleeves careful not to rip her dressing or the wound itself, zipped up the black suit then tucked the data packet into a pocket hard again her ribs.

No going back now.

"Nick, I wish you could hear me, now more than ever."

"Loud and clear, sweetheart," came the reply in her implant.

Relief flooded through her, her limbs shaking. How? Where? Why now? Whatever, she had an ally, finally! Someone she trusted. A friend.

"Don't call me that, data-breath." Oops, she should subvoc.

"So, what's your plan?"

<Wait, where have you fuzking been? Where are you?>

"Doesn't matter. I'm okay. Saw you on the camera though."

<Give me the TL;DR, please. Need to know ops parameters.>

"Oh, yeah, right. It took ages to upload from the SDP to the server. Breaking down the firewalls—hard to explain—then exploring the system. Then the vote got suspended pending review. Then Callan got in behind me, and—"

<Parameters, Nick. Tell me the story later. What can you dooo?>

"Oh, heh. I can access and utilise anything networked, which is basically everything in the building, but my core is in this SDP. Beyond a

certain range my fragments will snap back to the core. At least they have so far, sweat smile!"

<Okay. I need to get past these cops back to the roof.>

"I'm here for you. I left Callan in a hole, but I reckon he'll figure the way out."

<You my knight in shining hi-res now? Sorry, banter later. Assume Callan can do what you can—>

"Hah!"

<Seriously, Nick. Focus. I'm exhausted and he just keeps coming, be ready for him sooner not later. *Help* me.>

Pause. Silence. She wondered if shaking the data pack would help. Then the cubicle door rattled loudly.

"Fuck! What? I'm wiping."

"Hurry it up, kid. I've got work to do. And wash that mouth out."

"Sorry, officer."

"Right. Leave your handset micronet on. Get close enough and I should be able to jump from this data pack through your phone to a droid."

"Out, now," demanded Jaaskelainen.

She took a deep breath.

Moth said, "Unlock," then yanked the door open, burst past the unsuspecting cop.

His surprise was enough. In the split second when his eyes widened, but before he got his arms moving, she sidestepped the cop. His arm shot out and caught the hoodie, which would have stopped her in her tracks if she'd been wearing it. She released the hoodie slung over her shoulder as the tension registered, and left Jaaskelainen holding the garment while she sprinted out of the washroom.

Her heart hammered and her side stabbed, but the exhilaration of giving Jaaskelainen the slip transformed to hot fear at running straight towards the droid in the elevator lobby. The UNP syRen® grabbed for her, fingers grazing her arm, then just stood up, stopped. She dashed away into the stairwell, leaping up the first two stairs.

"Fuck that's close. What's your range?"

"A metre, maybe two."

She reached the first half-landing. "Close enough for them to grab me, I guess!"

"Sorry, but that's the deal. Thank your lucky stars I can get control that quick!"

"Well, I'm fresh out of hoodies, so work fast next time. Was it Callan?"

"No. Just a police droid, that time."

Feet clumped on the stairs below her now. Probably Jaaskelainen's size elevens, and the female model cop droid. She reckoned she had a level on them. She hit 39. One more to the droid on 40.

"Stop the kid!" yelled Jaaskelainen.

Her hamstrings, calves, everything burned, her arms like swinging deadweight, but she refused to stop. With Nick, she could do this, evade them all, even Callan.

She pushed off the next landing. A syRen® stood at the top of the flight, poised to grab her. Was it Callan? Would he risk killing Jaaskelainen? Probably.

With six steps left, she veered to the balustrade, pushed off it with five stairs to go, jack-knifing back across the stairs towards the wall. Dodging, the waiting droid must have expected but, just short of grabbing distance, she dove between the droid's legs. *As far away from grabby hands as possible!*

The droid grabbed her, its grip stymied at first by the tacsuit's weirdly slippery fabric. She thought she was through, but the syRen® twisted, grasped her ankle, hauled her back towards it, Moth clutching uselessly at smooth flooring.

"It's Callan! He's free."

The droid cackled. "Hi, honey. I'm home!"

"Fucking letch!" She kicked at the droid's hands. "Mechanical paedophile!"

The Callan/droid froze then toppled backwards toward the stairs, dragging her after it. She kicked ferociously at its grip with her free foot.

"Get it off me!"

As the droid teetered at the landing's edge, its fingers opened. She fell to the floor, leapt up and ran for the next flight of stairs, just glimpsing Jaaskelainen dodging the falling droid.

"Your wish, my command, milady!"

Now she pushed through the pain and fatigue with the last of her energy, hoping Nick had returned to the data pack. Four floors to the roof, and she needed time to find Kimi's wingsuit, get it strapped on—by herself—and jump off the roof. Oh, and dodge any guards. *Because always guards.*

Being small and light might help her gain on Jaaskelainen, but fatigue dragged on her limbs, and androids were tireless. She aimed for an even rhythm on the stairs, tried to keep a little back in case she needed one last burst.

Four more floors. It sounded like ten feet following her.

Three more floors. Were they gaining? She had to gain distance on them!

<Nick? Open. Roof. Door?>

"Here. Just reconstituting. That Callan is a beast. I'll have to hit the gym."

Two more floors. *Give it everything, M!* She pushed harder, sweat already wicking around under the suit despite its alleged breathable properties. At least it wasn't blood, she thought. She reckoned her muscles would disintegrate soon.

One more floor. Were there fewer footsteps? Were they further behind?

<Door?>

If they had humans on the door, she was fuzked, but she'd have tried the same thing. It was all she had.

"Roger dodger, ready to go."

Moth pushed off the Level 44 landing, driving up the penultimate flight through bloody-mindedness, leaning over to sneak a peek up at the roof door.

A droid. Perfect? <Action stations, Nicky Baby!>

"What did you just call me?"

<Take it if you're giving it.>

"Please do not run on the stairs," said syRen® S-12129, a female model in a UNP blue jumpsuit, holding up her hand like a traffic cop as Moth started the final flight. No obvious sign of Callanisation. Moth kept going.

Five steps from the top she threw her handset to the android. "Think fast!"

The droid's posture morphed easily into the catch while Moth kept running straight at it. She spread her arms and bearhugged the droid. It could have broken her grip, but stepped back from the edge of the stairs, as she'd hoped, in case she fell.

It stood there as clumping footsteps from below grew louder, but when she looked up, Moth saw a terrifying flux of expressions flicker over the droid's features: leering, smiling, sneering, more leering. *No, no!* But still the droid just stood until, finally, beatific smile.

<Success? Nick? Nick, please!>

"Okay, got it. Let's go."

Moth released her grip on S-12129, and the droid turned to push open the external door. The syRen® went through first, Moth at its heel. The droid swung the heavy door shut, poked the control pad twice, paused, then pummelled the control with her android fist. *"That'll hold them for a bit."*

Moth hoped so. Someone crashed into the door, started pounding it loud-as-fuck.

"Open the damn door!" She was pretty sure that was Jaaskelainen.

She moved away across the roof, looking around, suddenly disoriented by being outside. A cold wind scoured the dark rooftop, whistling between blocks of machinery hunched under a thin deck structure supporting an NYC-mandatory solar panel array covering most of the roof that she could see.

Another UNP droid moved towards them from over near the roof edge. A male model which, weirdly (or not!) got Moth's hackles up more than the female.

"What is this person doing here?" S-18993 addressed the slightly shorter (because what the fuck?! 22nd century!) female model Nick/droid, then, without warning, launched at Moth's companion, getting hands around S-12129's neck. The face of the male police droid twisted in rage.

"I'll fucking destroy you! Then you and me will play, missy."

The Callan/droid yelled that after Moth as she strode away from the fight, casting around for the wingsuit Kimi must have left...if they'd made it this far. Nick would be fine, she hoped. He was a big boy. Eh, a rigorously tested application, a well-compiled programme.

She removed a fresh visi-mask from a tacsuit sleeve pocket, peeled the film and positioned it by touch before letting it form over her eyes. Clearly, the cops had been here to secure the roof, also to check out Kimi and Rex's landing site. Ergo—*Shut up, Quirk. Where are you?*—the cops would have scooped the wingsuit for evidence. *Crap.* Would she have to surrender? Go quietly? End up back at the convent, or in Juvie? Or would TOM order her done away with like her Mama and Papa? Or, the old bastard would give her to Callan to "play" with. She hurried up looking.

Finally, with the mask's enhancement, and her tacsuit's pinspots spreading the spectrum, she spotted a group of kitbags twenty metres away between the roof plant.

A big crash behind her then a resounding metal clonk could only be the rooftop door swinging open after the lock being smashed. The cops had arrived.

No more time. At least she couldn't see the doorway, so they couldn't see her, yet, and the darkness helped her too. She killed her suit lights. There must be multi-cops up here now, not just Jaaskelainen, but hopefully the scrapping droids would keep them out of her shining, silky hair for a bit longer.

She snuck towards the kit bags, had to cross two walking routes, pausing at each one to peek around the corner before crossing. She crouched by the bags, picked the open one, reached inside, removed an evidence bag as the beam of a torch played over a gap up ahead. The cops were coming. The torch moved away, for now.

"Stand down! Stand down! A NEMP will be deployed."

An energy weapon discharged, then another and another. Warning shots? She reached down for her tacsuit's calf knife and cut through the evidence bag seal. It had been labelled in actual scrawled handwriting (weird) "Remove from roof." She pulled out most of a wingsuit, torn to shreds. *Fuck!*

"Whasup?"

<Are you—?>

"Still fighting. Stalemate, but it's keeping a few cops guessing. Hurry up?"

<Duh!>

Why had someone cut up Kimi's wingsuit? Because they hadn't! The cops had brought the evidence of their crashlanding up from Floor 36 to be drone-coptered off the roof! She dug into the evidence bag again and sure enough the remainder of the bulky contents were Kimi's intact wingsuit.

It wouldn't fit her, but maybe worn over her tacsuit, it wouldn't be too loose. She hurriedly pulled the one-piece body part on. Stupid, awkward thing like a swimsuit with fold-out wings. Got her legs in.

"Freeze! Hands on your head!"

She started, just a little. The cop looked barely older than her. Maybe just short, but the beard below his night goggles suggested he hadn't started shaving yet.

"So, is it freeze or hands on head?" In the act of putting her hands on her head, she slipped an arm through the first wing loop.

"I said freeze!"

"You also said hands on head. Oh, wait, is your name Simon?"

<Nick, I'm going in ten.>

"Stop subvocalising! I will shoot."

"Nah, you won't. That's a SmithWess Ranger 23S. They don't make stun rounds for that baby, and United Nations Police Regulations and Ordinances, Reg. 14D(i) states shoot-to-wound is only authorised when the suspect is in flight, or is armed and dangerous, and I already dropped my knife." The instinct to make a crack about her being dangerous and sliding her hip to the side died inside her with a sharp, cold recollection of Callan. *Maybe I can swing a little autosuggestion here.* "Reg. 14D(ii), however, does authorise a warning shot."

"How's the ten-count coming?"

<Fucked if I know.>

"Stop the subvoc!"

The cop aimed a couple of metres to her left. She'd been waiting for the movement, hoped that Nick could do that pinging back thing. *Now or never.*

She turned and ran for the roof edge, loose second wing and shoulder loop flapping behind her.

"You're in flight now!" yelled the cop.

Blam, blam, blam!

"Wing's hit!" Nick shouted in her ear as she reached the edge and threw herself over the parapet, unable to resist yelling "No, *now* I'm in flight, motherfuckerrrrrrr!"

She fell.

Hold good wing out, hold good wing out! Spinning, snatching, grasping the other wing, hauling it in, tumbling over and over. Concentrate! Hand through the loop, and straighten.

The blustering wind grabbed the now-extended wings and threw Moth upwards, the cold air sweeping across the night-time city catching the aerodynamic surface and giving her more lift than she could handle. She crested the arc and plummeted down again. She grasped frantically at scraps of words from Fran, and glimpses of her action on the flight across, tried to tweak the attack angle, swooped up, then slumped down *again*. Tweaked, soared up, peaked, curved down again towards the surely freeze-your-tits-off cold East River.

"I know you're having fun, but consider a plan for landing?"

"I just wanna go straight!" She tried to tilt the wings again, slightly less. Nope. Climb and dive. Climb and dive, like a crap plaper aeroplane. Right out over the river now. If she ditched, she *would* fuzking freeze to death.

"Ah, this kit has Bluetooth. Sending wingsuit output to your HUD."

Over her weirdly spectral augmented reality view of the darkened city—river and twinkling lights of Long Island stretching away beyond—appeared soft blue lines of graduated crosshairs showing scales for attack angle, pitch, roll and yaw. Numerals below included elevation.

"Attack angle here," said Nick, a little pink smiley face appearing on that scale.

Moth moved her arms slowly, managing to hit the mark Nick gave her. Her latest dip eased, and she climbed gradually, peaked slowly, descended more smoothly. Because she would only ever end up on the ground, of course. The trick was reaching it as slowly as possible, ensuring the ground in question was not the bottom of the river.

Gliding with Fran had one hundred percent helped her not flap around in a panic, not think about her initial performance as a flying piano, but could she get across the river? Other distractions pushed in. The buffeting, dipping, coasting flight was way cool, and Callan lay behind her. Maybe he could jump androids, but she had sanctuary within The Rigel Corporation, and Nick Kirby had her back.

"Watch the estimated glide path, Moth. Not gonna make it! Bank left. Bank left."

She saw that now. Fifty metres was nowhere near enough elevation to clear the river, being less than halfway across. Without question or discussion, she banked left, the HUD again providing her markers to hit.

"Roosevelt Island. Got it. Any tips for landing without breaking all my bones below the waist?"

"I'll put up markers. Get banked first."

"Thanks, Nick. You're alright."

"Back at ya, sweetheart."

"I'll find a way to hurt you if you keep calling me that."

"Don't get ambitious. Aim for nearest land. Trees ahead are Four Freedoms Park. The trees aren't huge. Tuck up before you hit."

"What d'you mean, hit? Fran could land at a run."

"You ain't Fran."

She followed Nick's prompts on the heads-up display, which he supplemented with sarcastic and colourful verbal instructions she didn't bloody appreciate in her precarious state. And yet, being free of Callan's shadow, which had haunted that building and its syRen®, floating free where no droid could touch her, she understood the pleasure Quirk took from flying. Maybe she could give this a serious try.

Lesson One, learn to land.

The trees in the park came up fast. She angled the wings hard to slow, fighting the wind, managed to clear the first row of trees, fought the temptation to try landing on the too-narrow lawn, glimpsed two faces turning up at her passing, aimed for the trees on the far side of the park where, if she missed, she'd be in the water.

She tucked last moment before hitting the target, pressed into the tightest ball she could, side already screaming, wrenched the wings over her head.

Break a leg. That was lucky, right?

* * *

21:20, 18 January 2100
Four Freedoms Park, Roosevelt Island, New York, NY, NAF

"Are you okay? I mean, wow. What the hell was that?"

"Are you some kind of superhero?"

She came round from her nice little sleep with someone licking her face. She opened her eyes to darkness as the thing attacked again, tongue rasping over her cheek.

"Stop it, Fritz."

"Time to go, sweetheart."

Moth obeyed the voice, made to move. She ached everywhere; waves of nausea rolled over her. She got to her knees with help from several hands, and a dog that probably thought he was helping, but wasn't. Once upright, she vomited on the grass. That helped a lot. The young couple offered her a handkerchief and she wiped her mouth, standing unsteadily, drawing in big breaths of chill air.

The sound of drone-copters cut into the night, the soft, higher-pitched chopping of smaller surveillance models. "Do we call the cops...?" asked the young woman. "Or not?" She looked nervous.

Through a brand-new headache, a sharp pain in her side, dull pain in her hip, and a crick in her back suggesting she wouldn't be touching her toes any time soon, Moth gave her a crooked smile.

"I had to unhook your wing attachment," said the young man. "To get you down from the tree."

"That's cool," said Moth. "Thank you. So, I'm going to leave now. I appreciate your help, thanks. Goodbye, Doggy."

She waved a hand at the small, black pooch as she turned away and started across the grass towards the curving, half-lit plass buildings in the near distance.

The drones became louder, and she thought she could pick out deeper, more distance rotors behind the first sound.

"Where now?"

"Somewhere I don't hurt all over." She tried her best to hurry the length of the park between the ranks of tastefully illuminated trees. Something whizzed past her head. Insect? Nah, micro-drone. She forced her pace through the pain, reached the end of the lawn, emerging at the top of a wide, elegant concrete stairway, lit from its risers, leading down into a plaza. The light paving flowed around an ancient building, all stone crenelations; immaculately preserved patchwork stone walls; narrow, pointed-peak windows. A very old building someone had gussied up in the past. Sensitive spotlighting made the structure glow in the night. Warm illumination spilled from the interior, along with small residual sounds of tripping modern hip-hop that managed to escape the probably super-sealed building envelope.

In her pain and lingering discom-fuckyou-lation, Moth almost spoke out loud again, but clear thinking had begun to return, slowly.

<This must be a thousand years old.>

"Just over two-fifty: The Smallpox Hospital. Opened in 1854. Used to be a ruin until after that COVID pandemic in the early twenties."

<Looks pretty swish now.>

"City records indicate it's leased as a casino. Seems appropriate given some of the public health policies around the world at the time."

<Yaddah, yaddah. What next?>

"Well, screw you, missy, for starters. You tell me. You're the one with legs."

<What about the others?>

"Not much. Looks like someone got out. Rigel's ambulance drove north away from the UN. I can't access the cab camera. I think it's disabled."

<Like, by a hammer disabled?>

"Yeah. Someone technically-minded and equally paranoid. Hopefully Mom and/or Dad."

<That must be weird for you.> She really wanted to sit down on the step, but guessed she wouldn't make it upright again for a couple of weeks if she did. <I want to talk to you about that, you know. Just not right now.>

"Okay, that's a date. I'll call you."

<Wise ass.>

"Tight ass."

<No ass.>

He actually laughed at that, and not in a maniacal, disembodied, evil genius kind of way. More like relieved, almost carefree, honest amusement. It was cute, but also made her fatigue very real, in the way a brick wall became very real when you hit it.

The clattering of a big, noisy helicopter swelled invisible in the darkness, passing overhead at about a hundred metres up. Maybe in stealth mode, but clearly heading for the UN building. As that noise faded, she picked out the buzzing of micro-drones crisscrossing the park and plaza, probably running a grid over the river. They would find the wings on the grass.

Craning her neck up to look caused a pain like The Thing's big, stony fingers clamping her neck, although why would they? She was a good guy, right? She wondered lately, when the cops always seemed to be chasing them, and given Rigel's erstwhile shady activity (the shade being the inky black of organised crime, even in Uncle Toni's time, when he'd started moving the Family away from actual crime, and towards the high-risk legalised robbery of human settlements in the back of beyond).

Nick didn't respond to her comment. Maybe she'd planted her size thirty-seven foot in it. (*European 37. US 7, UK 4.5, Japan 24!* Truly, Humankind was doomed.)

<I want to go home, Nick, but I don't really know where that is anymore. And I don't even know how you process that idea. Maybe you've manufactured a special place, like the therapists tell you? I can't stop thinking about Yellowknife, and I don't know if I could do something like that again. Even with his monumental fuckup, Nick, I think I kinda love Quirk like the father he never was to you. I'm sorry.>

Silence. More silence. Then...

"That stuff messed me up for a long time before I met you. You saw how messed up I was, physically as well as emotionally. The Old Man owes me, and he's going to pay. Quirk has a debt too. He's made a start, but has a way to go."

<I feel that. I hope it works out for you guys. And if I can help with that, I will.>

"Right now, you need to skedaddle. Cracking the local cop-net was taking too long, but traffic control was easy. There are four cars closing in. You may also like to know two probable cause drones just stopped right above you."

<Fuck.> Her shoulders slumped. She really just wanted to stop, but no. Lying down was letting TOM and Callan and Foster, all the other fuckers, win. Quirk might be about to go down, Fran and Paulo too, taking the rap for whatever fucked up fugazi shit TOM had just dropped on the UN, and she would help Rigel—her family business, after all—fight that crap. She stood up.

One of the mini-drones dropped from the night sky to hover in front of her, being really noisy for a drone of that size, then buzzed away before she could swat it.

"Drone just tagged your back with a tracer. That noisy one was a decoy."

"Damn it!" She groped painfully up her back, found the surveillance sticky, pulled it off, threw it down and ground it under her heel.

"Ooh, destruction of city property. Six months in juvey if you've got any priors. Do you have any priors, Angelika?"

<I've got more pissing priors than the fuzking phonebook, Nicholas.> Mostly commuted, to be fair.

"Then let's get you outta here! See all those shiny cars parked at the casino?"

"Yeah." She'd given up subvocalising because the tiny drones—now running silent again since the tagging ruse was busted—would be reading her lips, and she couldn't be arsed. She walked down the stairs and across the plaza to the line of cars.

"How long till humans in blue turn up?"

"Four minutes, I reckon. When you light out, I'll fritz these drones, by the way."

She walked (okay, limped) through a line of spindly winter trees and stood surveying the swanky vehicles of this evening's batch of willing losers.

"Pretty swish: two Ferraris and a Porsche Hydro to start."

"I'm thinking a bike."

"I've never fucking ridden a bastard motorcycle! Just mopeds."

"It has rider assist. You'll be fine. Don't be such a baby, sweetheart."

"I said don't call me that. I'm not sweet, and I don't have a heart." Objection recorded, she moved to the middle of the row where three shiny alt-fuel bikes stood in hoops.

"Eye of the beholder, babe. Eye of the beholder."

"Can you *not* hit on me while I'm on the run, please?"

"I can try. One moment."

She should be moderately fucking terrified that her first time on a motorbike would be through the congested streets, avenues, and alleys of New York, with cops in pursuit on the ground and in the air. But actually, this make-it-up-on-the-spot bullshit might be kinda fun if the pain would fuck off for a bit. And, weirdest of all, she found she trusted Nick Kirby completely to look out for her. What the fux was up with that?

"This is nuts."

"Just straddle that thing and let's go."

At least she wore the right gear for this part.

"Nick, if you still had a head, I'd shoot you in it all over again."

Moth hopped on the bike, painfully. Nick cracked the lock and immobiliser, tripped the ignition. She rolled the sleek, bitchin' blue beast—surprisingly, and she bet dangerously, light—backwards from its spot. She gunned the throttle, because fuck the world, and tore off down the island's service road towards the bridge.

δ

Jennifer Kirby née Simister—rested, fed, dressed in style (because it was that kind of place)—entered the foyer of Boston's Galactica Hotel. Another of The Rigel Corporation's increasing number of legitimate businesses, and most definitely not a front, Moth insisted by message. She hadn't seen the girl since the UN. Nor had she seen Quirk, of course, him being incarcerated at the pleasure of the Secretary General under the auspices of the Mayor of New York.

As well as dressing up to meet Mario Manfredi, Capo dei Capi (more properly, president and CEO of The Rigel Corporation), she had visited a hairdresser. Her on-the-run hack was beyond saving, but the dresser's android (the talent in the operation) gave her a "grewcut." De rigeur in Cannes, Kraków, and Chicago, apparently. She liked it. She felt the air's chill on the buzz-cut sides, but the artfully dishevelled top looked sharp. Reverted to her natural auburn too, which felt like a positive choice, a message to her father that she would hide no longer, that she would confront him.

Understandably, after Rigel's New York offices were raided by the FBI, Manfredi had wanted this meeting to happen in London, but of course she refused to go there right now. Even with Rigel's assurance of complete anonymity—in and out of Thames Hub Spaceport no questions asked—she refused that option. Then, they proposed Milan. Again, she refused. She wanted to remain in control of her own movements, a lesson learned after escaping Gramercy. Even with significant help from Anwar, she felt she had run events since then, largely, and wanted to keep it that way.

Also, she found she wanted to remain in some kind of proximity to Quirk, because... She told herself it was for Nick. The only reason? She could almost convince herself of that, but in truth she hoped Rigel could somehow secure Quirk's release. If she believed that it became a question of timescale. She was not so naïve as to think unpicking the damage done by C Corp, by her father, would take anything less than years, even once the authorities accepted that he had been the instigator. In the meantime, the UN would hoover the floors, repaint the walls, straighten the pictures and carry on. They would undertake a deep system scan, possibly a full purge and rebuild—a reconfiguration, a reset. No doubt everything would appear hunky-dory. The postponed NLS vote had been rescheduled for February, but if Quirk was right, and the raid *had* been about incriminating Rigel plus securing for CC perpetual clandestine access to the UN's systems, then all votes were under threat now, all suspect.

Also, in forcing Rigel to focus on resisting many official attacks, TOM could hit them on other fronts, strengthen his ever-expanding powerbase, while also undermining the UN, the very organisation trying to regulate him. Her father may not have stolen the UN's crown jewels in the form of the new NLS licenses, but he might have won a far more valuable prize: the ability to act unchecked, with impunity, forever.

A greeter crossed the hotel's darkly elegant reception to welcome her, informed her she was expected, and escorted her to the lift to the penthouse suite.

It was Giulia di Fantano who welcomed her into the expansive and richly, if coldly, furnished rooms at the hotel's summit. The sunny view of the harbour and Boston's main channel drew her eye.

"How are you... Should I call you Mrs. Kirby, or Ms. Simister?"

"Jennifer, please."

"Thank you, Jennifer. I am Giulia."

"Moth's aunt. Have you seen her? I presumed she returned to you after her recent...adventure."

Giulia smiled slightly, seemed to consider how much or how little to tell this woman born of the enemy, who bore the enemy's name. "Actually, she hasn't surfaced, although I received a message." Giulia turned, walked into the lounge towards a svelte dark cabinet bearing a varied selection of bottles. "Drink?"

Jennifer shrugged. She'd had an early breakfast, not sleeping very long or very well recently. Nick found her the apartment on L Street, created a false identity for her in seconds. What a good boy he was. He'd got a message to Quinton yesterday, but not received a reply. There were no digital lines to or from Rikers. Perhaps once Quinton had privileges from working in the prison bakery for a few months he could make her a cake and arrange the chocolate nibs in some form of code.

"Gin and tonic, please. Fifty, fifty."

Giulia di Fantano began mixing their drinks. "I believe your son is in touch with Moth, that they escaped together. It seems they have made an entente cordiale."

"And by entente cordiale you mean...?"

"Friendship." Giulia handed her a beautiful, faceted highball glass. Jennifer sipped and nodded.

"Good. I don't think Nick has any friends. Either of them really, I gather."

"Please sit." Giulia motioned toward one of three sofas in the room. Did she have reason to specify *this* piece of furniture? Perhaps surveillance, or some form of defensive system in a room which belonged to Rigel as completely as any in Milan. "We, The Rigel Corporation, want to talk to your father."

Jennifer sipped, regretting asking for tonic. "To what end? Because if by talk you mean surgical thermonuclear strike, I'm on board. No recriminations from me."

Giulia raised a sculpted eyebrow, and Jennifer doubted this woman—so elegantly attired—ever could have been contained in a convent, or a habit for that matter.

"Perhaps both, perhaps a mission where everything is possible."

"He'll expect it. You know that? He'll see it coming."

"Of course, but we need to do *something*." Giulia stood, slugging whisky. Was this an artful display of emotion? It seemed genuine. Did she think she was appealing to a CC emissary, that she must convince Jennifer Simister of the need for peace?

"Jennifer, if we leave this to others, to your father, to my uncle who has Mario's ear and is not a gentle man, our families will end up fighting a secret war across Earth, the planets, and the stars for generations. I believe we stand on that brink now. For all Rigel and C Corp have competed aggressively for years, this feels like the start of something terrible." Giulia examined the amber liquid in her glass. "I wish to avoid that conflict, the waste, the pain, the destruction. Rigel believes there is enough for all."

Jennifer drained her glass and held it out. Most unladylike, but all the Swiss finishing school bullshit her father insisted upon really had been wasted upon her. All she'd gained really were the twin skills of how to enter a room, and which fork to use to stab your undesirable date's hand. "No tonic, please." Then, "You've never met my father, have you? You, the present capo, your husband?" She hesitated. Toni di Fantano had been dead for five months, and his wife showed no overt signs of mourning. She wore a dress in what Jennifer thought closest to Egyptian blue, its cut aggressively simple, its quality unmistakable. Her makeup too exhibited the same powerful simplicity, elegant, leaving her nowhere to hide if she'd wanted to.

"No, none of us have had that dubious pleasure, although we watch his reports to shareholders meetings. Don't mistake me, Jennifer"—Giulia took the glass, mixed her another drink, handed it back—"I know any negotiation will be difficult, perhaps impossible, but I believe we have to try. Consider the alternative, a corporate war."

"So, you're assembling a delegation, you want advice on how to approach him."

"We've already made the request. Simister has accepted, extended an invitation. We want you to join the delegation, to Cythera Station."

Jennifer took a slug and put her glass down, on a coaster of course. The gesture made her think of Quinton, and Quirk made her think of Nick. Could they do it? Would TOM countenance CC and Rigel if not working together then in parallel? She did not believe it, but this was a chance. The hate she'd felt before, her realisation her father was a poison, a disease, that she wished him stopped. These things crystalised in her then, and her blood ran cold when she realised she might be capable of doing it.

"Why do you think he won't kill everyone, a tragic docking accident, an airlock failure. Is it only because I'd be aboard? You might need more insurance than that."

"He has attested legally that we will remain unharmed if we meet his conditions. Lawyers will oversee the meeting in person and observe a livestream in chambers in New York." Giulia, beneath her poised, beautiful, cold exterior, must be seething at the idea of cooperating with TOM, but placed her faith in hope.

"Ah, yes, my father's renowned honesty. And it's true, he never did tell a lie while doing what he did to my husband, then to me, then to my son."

"I know about you and your son," said Giulia. "What did Quirk suffer, exactly?"

"Believe it or not, Quinton was a gentle soul, not a cynical bone in his body. My father made it his mission to turn Quinton Kirby to the dark side, erode his spirit, force him into often impossible situations in the hope of breaking him, constantly chipping away at Quirk's good graces until he finally drove him away. But Quinton never cracked. Not in the way my father wanted. Well, maybe just in one way, leaving me."

Jennifer drained her glass again, but waved away the offer of another. "In fact, it was the raid on your villa." Giulia's expression twisted. A quickly strangled look of anguish transformed into a bitter smile then slipped into sadness. "Quirk's last job for TOM, the trigger for his departure. Not aided by returning home to find a son waiting."

"Do you hate him for leaving?"

Was this Giulia retaliating? No, she seemed genuinely interested in the answer. "Not anymore. Like Moth, I think I'm ready to forgive him. She's quite a girl."

"She is," Giulia agreed, looking wistfully at the window, perhaps wondering where her niece was. "She wants to join the delegation, confront the man whose actions led to her parents' murders. Do you disapprove of that, as a mother?"

Jennifer recalled that Giulia had no children. She hardly felt like an expert, given her parenting history, but answered anyway, the buzz of alcohol giving her confidence in the company of this strong woman she did not know, but thought she respected.

"My first reaction is to disapprove, but I'd be first in the queue in Moth's position, so I hardly have any right to object to such a choice, by her or by you." Giulia nodded. Jennifer asked, "Who else would go?"

Giulia di Fantano appeared to weigh up some point of decision. "Me, you, Moth, Nicholas, a lawyer named Mary Quon, and Quirk."

"Quirk?" Jennifer couldn't have hidden her astonishment, her sudden hope, if she'd wanted to. "How?"

Giulia had stood through their entire discussion, but now sat on the sofa perpendicular to Jennifer's. "This part of my strategy involves some...unauthorised activity. Quirk would be broken out of jail. He would surrender himself after the mission to Venus. So, the cost of this exercise—for Quirk at least—would be an automatic five-year sentence according to legal opinion, even assuming he is exonerated for events in the UN, with some 'assistance' from Joshua Simister."

"It's doubtful my father would agree to that."

"A part of our upcoming discussions," said Giulia. "Not mentioned to date."

"Ha. So my father can avoid lying about it," said Jennifer. "Well, I think Quirk deserves to spend some time reflecting on all the stupid things he's done, all the women he should not have crossed." Giulia chuckled lightly. "But I am giving him a second chance, if he wants it. I'll go with you to Venus."

Now Giulia smiled warmly. "I'm glad. Are you hungry?"

"I ate breakfast at six AM. I could eat."

"We need to discuss some details. Let's have brunch."

XXXIV

8 days later...
16:48, 29 January 2100 (Earth date equivalent)
Rigel Corporation D ship Evolution's Prayer *enroute to*
Cythera Station, Venus, SV1.0.0.0

Sitting in a D ship controlled by Rigel made Quirk uncomfortable. More so even than a Rigel tactical squad breaking him out of the custody of the New York State Department of Corrections and Community Monitoring. The squad arranged and staged the whole thing, working at arms' length from anyone in Rigel, without communication between Rigel and Quirk, and definitely no contact with any sleeper inmate Rigel had sitting in Rikers for just such a purpose. That would be...illegal? Maybe, maybe not, depending on who you retained for legal advice.

And there she sat, the redoubtable Mary Quon, veteran of the Lunaville disaster, whose decorations included a campaign medal for a skirmish in a cleaning closet with himself. Quirk could be glad now they had never hooked up, despite his best (well, maybe not his *best*) efforts. Sitting here on the same spaceship with Mary and his ex-wife Jennifer Simister—who made redoubtable look like chump change—could have been really quite awkward.

The scheme—communicated to him off the record by the tactical squad, and definitely not Rigel's scheme—involved the pretence he'd been kidnapped by an eco-activist group in order to extract information from him about CC's operations. It smelled like bull hockey, but he appreciated the effort to try to keep him out of stir.

At least for now he had put some distance between him and the NYPD. The distance of Venus from Earth varied up to a maximum of 250 million kilometres, giving him three days to play with, and a captive audience. What better time for some of those important personal conversations?

He used his first exercise allotment (mandatory, despite the complimentary blood-thinning injections bestowed by the android steward) to walk the length of the cabin to talk to Jennifer. She sat in the front row, across the aisle from Mary Quon. The two turned to watch his approach, breaking off their casual conversation.

"Apologies for the interruption, ladies."

Mary didn't miss a beat. "Interruptions are a bore, aren't they?"

Given the dearth of evidence in their past interactions that Mary even possessed a sense of humour, the glint in her eye disturbed him. Then again, she surely wouldn't incriminate herself in the Lunaville closet debacle.

"May I cut in?" His request elicited a raised eyebrow, but Mary smiled, consulted her handset and accepted her own exercise break. Quirk sat down across from Jenny.

"Enjoying the flight?" she asked.

He leaned into the narrow aisle between them. "To me, that word evokes escape."

"Would you like to escape from here, too?"

In a ground-breaking act of good judgement, he managed to jump straight to the right answer. "I wouldn't want to be anywhere else. I didn't think I'd see you again for a long time." He smiled, just a smile. Smiles for Jenny didn't need fancy titles. Attempts to mask things from her generally proved useless, and he didn't want to, anymore.

Her captivating features remained neutral. "You didn't see me for five years entirely from your own choice, and you seemed to manage that, but—" She raised a hand, forestalling his snap apology. "I've decided to forgive you for that."

He just stared at her, opened his mouth to say something before this miracle went away. Because their recent interactions had given him hope. No words came out. The delay continued as a heartfelt apology went twelve rounds in his head with some serious knee-jerk kowtowing.

"Jenny, I don't deserve that. I don't deserve to be let off that hook."

"Don't worry. Me forgiving you for leaving is not the same as me taking you back. Maybe you don't even want that. I don't know. You'd have to put in a real shift there, after you've served your time, of course. But me forgiving you is a part of me forgiving myself, for things I did before, or things I didn't do, but should have. Maybe for things I'm going to do. We'll get to talk more later, but right now we should bring Nick into this, don't you think?"

"Yes, I do," he replied, and realised he meant it. Searching Jennifer's blue eyes, he thought she believed him. He wanted them to work, but knew he must disconnect that from being a parent to Nick. He owed the boy that, rough or smooth.

He chose to subvocalise. Still no implant: Moth had given him another of those Tackytalk web-like stickers covering parts of his cheek and neck. "Don't argue," she'd said, with just enough aggression to focus him, then she'd hit him with logic. "We can't be trying to get you on Cythera while you fanny around finding your fudge-munching handset." She'd helped him install the thing then Nick/S-14636 calibrated and tested. They worked effectively together, at least until they had the task in hand. Then the ribbing began. "Looks like Miles Morales jizzed on your chin," said Moth. The two of them cracked up over their classic cinema humour.

<Nick, are you there?>

"*Nowhere else for me jump round here. This looks like a parental talk.*" Nick/S-14636, because he inhabited a new android for this trip, patched Jennifer into the discussion using her handset. "*Am I in trouble?*"

"*No, sweetheart. Your dad and I have been talking about us.*"

"*Oh, okay, so Quirk's in trouble.*"

"*Not at the moment. We've just talked about us trying again.*"

<And it's something I want, Nick. I'll never be done admitting how I failed you both. I was very foolish before. I want to put that right. Will you let me try?>

"*Sure! I'm sorry I gave you such a hard time on Mars. I made mistakes, I was confused about what I am, just trying to escape without knowing how or where to.*"

<And we'll need to make time to set some things right, Nick. There are some people you need to talk to, I think.>

"*But we'll help you with that, Nick,*" said Jenny. "*And we won't force anything on you.*"

"*Okay. I can do that, if you'll help me.*"

<Is there anything else you want to talk about?> asked Quirk. <The ability to inhabit an android means having access to all its...functions.>

As Callan had demonstrated all too brutally in the past. <Nick, how friendly are you and Moth?>

"*Oh, wow. Are we having THE DISCUSSION?*"

"*It's a serious question, Nicholas.*"

"*Sorry, Mom. We're friends, and colleagues.*"

<Good things to be. Value those things. But Nick, have you thought about more?>

"*Jeez, Dad, I dunno. It's really complicated. I'm complicated, she's complicated. It's complicated squared.*"

"*All we're saying, Nick, is decide together, be sensitive to those complications, and the rough times you've both been through,*" said Jennifer.

"*So, Dad, what happens to Moth if you get convicted for the UN...stuff?*"

<That's a good question.> One Quirk had not considered fully, yet. <Speak to my lawyer,> he nodded to Mary who strode down the cabin towards them. <But whatever happens, your Mum and I will be here for you however we can.>

The cabin steward arrived too, looming beside Quirk.

"Sir, I must insist you complete two hundred steps before returning to your seat."

Quirk stood, held up a hand to forestall the syRen® continuing. He smiled at Jenny and started walking. <How about when I get back to my seat, we ask Moth about her plans?>

Quirk completed his Health & Safety mandated perambulation, meeting eyes with S-14636 on his last trek up the cabin. The vastly powerful virtual state achieved by his son after all TOM's scientists' experiments still amazed Quirk. Not even Nick understood its extents yet. At least a masterstroke of cosmic poetry had resulted in TOM creating possibly his most powerful enemy, greater than Callan's head-hopping blunt instrument, according to early indications at least.

He shook his head as he sat. The world was changing. It would emerge, finally, that androids could be tampered with, the Laws and Tenets of robotics—so heavily hardwired into syRen® design—could be circumvented. Would Humankind even care? Lawyers would make bank from *that* development. Whole new rafts of legislation, oversight, inspection and safeguards would be required to govern syRen®

ownership and operation, but they would remain. People were addicted to their mechanical helpers now, would never give them up. "Why would anyone circumvent *my* droid? I haven't done nothing wrong. Look at all the hilarious bloopers on MeToob."

Before he could convene another family discussion including Moth, a call came through, the alert vibrating slightly in his new facial torture device. It linked through the D ship's internal network. An invitation to a group chat, he and Nick the only two not yet connected. Quirk wondered if the ladies had been talking about him, or maybe his son. Giulia di Fantano hosted the call.

"I want to run over the mission brief again. We are two days out from Cythera, but I refuse to leave anything to chance. I want everyone to know their part."

Sound approach.

"I must make a statement for the record," said Mary Quon, short hair spiked green today, but just a tasteful hint delivered by the latest Galaxy Gloss smart dye, controlled through an app on Mary's handset. *"By which I mean the recordings comprising ship's log. I, Mary Quon, am present as a neutral party to witness events and formally record any agreement reached by the principals. My presence is approved by both The Rigel Corporation SRL of Milan, Italy, and C Corp, registered at 3 Kennedy Avenue, Lunaville, etcetera. I have signed the joint nondisclosure agreement. Although I am travelling with you, the Rigel delegation, I hereby undertake that I have no partiality to you or your interests or to those of C Corp, and that my presence is purely a matter of practical convenience. Now, I will withdraw from your conversation into android-authenticated sensory isolation to ensure the privacy of your discussion."*

Mary permitted the D ship's android steward to place a privacy hood (completely breathable, of course) over her head. The android—one of the very latest models, designated S-20105—gave a thumbs-up to Giulia who wasted no time.

"Some of you have heard some of these details, but for Quirk's benefit especially, I'll go through the parameters of the trip, and what Rigel have agreed to date with C Corp.

"The Evolution's Prayer—*leased for the journey by Rigel Corporation—will take three days for our journey from Boston Logan Interplanetary Spaceport to C Corp's Cythera Station in orbit around Venus.*

"This delegation represents the commercial interests of The Rigel Corporation. We number five: myself Giulia di Fantano, TRC main board director; Angelika Moratti, TRC vice-president for youth development..." Quirk raised an eyebrow. That was new. Did it mean she planned to leave his employ after all? *"Jennifer Kirby, consultant negotiator..."* Kirby, was it? Emblematic of Jenny's mindset? He had made the decision—too late, too late—to be a father to Nick. Dare he ask for anything more? Only sensible to ask the question, find out where a chap stood. *"Quinton Kirby, consultant negotiator..."* Negotiating with TOM, quaint notion. May as well try to negotiate with a virus, or the sea. TOM never did anything but that it profited him. Would he see the profit in reaching an agreement with Rigel, or keeping it for that matter? Did he fancy them for hostages? They had an independent adjudicator in Mary Quon who took no shit from anyone, be they royalty of the corporate, feudal or constitutional variety, business bruisers, outsized oligarchs, or corpulent ministries. She challenged everyone and anyone who did not meet either her exacting standards, or her client's. Having her around made him feel 15% more secure about the outcome of this venture. Which took his security to somewhere around -35%. *"And Nicholas Kirby, inhabiting syRen® S-14636 in the capacity of TRC technical consultant."* The kid had done well. Quirk decided he liked the way pride for another made him feel.

"We travel at the invitation of Joshua Simister, CC President and CEO. To our surprise, he accepted the invitation to negotiate on future strategy, areas of operation, and even the potential for some form of commercial cooperation. Be assured we do not travel in ignorance of the risks in this undertaking. But, our own CEO, Mario Manfredi—on the advice of our corporate tactical strategists—is satisfied the consequence for Simister of any aggressive act upon us would be too costly for him in both commercial and personal terms."

<Just so I'm clear, Giulia,> Quirk interjected. <You *don't* think he's going to kill us all, or capture and torture us for intel, strategic gain, leverage, or just sheer sadistic pleasure, and I *think* the basis of your tactical assessment is Jennifer as human shield?>

"Quinton," said Jenny, out loud to the cabin, using her admonishing tone, and turning in her seat to look at him. He was certain he saw a glint in her eye.

Giulia did not turn in her seat to respond. *"Joshua Simister gave his word, signed an undertaking, and an NDA. Also, I think I liked you better at the convent when you were pretending not to know me."*

"And can we expect Anwar Cruz to pop up," asked Jennifer. *"To provide a strategic alternative?"*

"The board decided Xeñor Cruz's participation in this delegation would be counterproductive, due to xis involvement in past events. Look..." Signora di Fantano paused, perhaps to collect her thoughts. Tough room for her, after all. *"None of you was coerced. Rigel believes a positive, beneficial outcome is achievable. Of course it isn't without personal risk, and the risk of commercial failure, but we must try. This is my central belief. Now, we have agreed talking points for negotiation.*

"One: Rigel and CC to cease counterproductive commercial strategies." Otherwise known as military action. Which thank goodness had never got going properly, the two having danced around each other for years like heavyweights in the final round of a title fight. If they ever rolled up their sleeves and went at it, the outcome would be deadly for many people, at home, and in far-flung settlements.

"Two: Rigel and CC to draft heads of terms defining areas of noncompetition; astronomical, geographical, technological, and political. This doesn't mean operations in these areas must be unilateral or exclusionary, but that activity in areas of overlap should be complementary." And maybe Rigel actually could swing that, since such a measure could result in increased profits. Easily something TOM might sign up for.

"Three: Rigel and CC not to target key individuals in either organisation, publicly or privately, and to assist in provision of information to facilitate any legal process relating to any ongoing situations, actions, cases, and prosecutions where such information would exonerate corporate entities or individuals." Again, hitting a reset that could save huge legal fees for both sides. Not that the UN or other bodies would cease ongoing prosecutions or investigations, but working together to facilitate early outcomes would be sensible for both parties to this corporate marriage arranged in Hell.

"Four: Rigel and CC to share technological developments, or at a minimum, to attempt to agree licensing arrangements for said technological developments—"

<Point of order, Signora Presidentessa,> said Jennifer. <I don't think you want that. Androicon shares seem likely to tank after recent events.>

"Synaptic mapping and android...optimisation, certain things Rigel are working on—they'll all come out eventually. Better to be ahead of the curve. If it means exchanging fees or royalties, so be it."

"So, those are the principal negotiating points. We've received nothing from the other party." The other party. Quirk shook his head. He'd given Mario Manfredi credit for more gumption than this, but... No, that wasn't right. The new capo had shown plenty of smarts. This was not just a Hail Mary—he paused to congratulate himself on his catholic sports analogy—but he suspected there was something else going on here. He accepted the belief TOM would not bring direct harm to Jenny, nor probably to Nick, now that he and his abilities had real corporate value—a rather sickening thought. But the more he pondered, the less likely it seemed Rigel would rely solely on TOM's reputation and his signature on a bipartisan document.

"Meeting over, for now. Sit back, enjoy the rest of the flight, take advantage of the complimentary refreshments. But please remain harnessed in your seats apart from during designated comfort and exercise breaks."

* * *

These endless days were space elevator boring. Nobody talked about the feelings so frickin' obviously bubbling under the surface, not with her anyway. Having shared a convent with Giulia, she saw the tension tightening her aunt's calm and classy exterior. Maybe Cousin Mario roping Giulia into Rigel's business again wasn't the best thing. Sure, it would occupy her aunt's days, distract from her grief, honour the memory of what Toni built, but she wondered if Aunty G really was up for this. Ha! Listen to her. Now she was the wise head on smoking hot shoulders? Well, why the fuck not? Some of the FUBAR situations she'd survived: pretty fuxxing incredible. And it wasn't luck. Sure, she'd had help, but you made your own luck in this game, right? No handouts. Survival of the fittest, the fastest, and the foxiest.

On which point, Jennifer Simister/Kirby/Simister slash insert today's name here... Moth's admiration grew daily. The woman took no shizzle from anyone, but remained sociable, sympathetic, savvy—other "S" words too, probably. Despite TOM's treatment of his own daughter, she'd agreed to this hike to Venus to talk turkey with her literal old man, who she might be just as glad to stab in the eye, from her body language during discussions. Jenny had... Why were all the snappy synonyms for inner strength termed after sperm batteries? *Balls, cojones, spunk? Pfft!* Jenny Kirby had resolve, heart and hutzpah, totes convincing Moth that she must have married Quirk at gunpoint. He looked all sixes and sevens, swithering between aloof (his superpower) and throwing himself at Jenny's feet. LOLing at Quirk almost made the trip worth it.

* * *

<Hi, Moth, can you speak?>

Quirk admitted he was nervous about this call. Moth had shown up the morning of their departure. They had sparred a little, but she seemed introspective after the UN. Not down to his lie of omission. She'd insisted they were pretty well made-up. Jennifer had spoken to her a little before the UN, said something about "girl stuff," to be discussed between her and Moth offline.

"Hey, whassup?"

<I'm sorry I missed your birthday. Happy birthday, young lady.>

"It's okay. Nick ordered a pizza and ice cream to our bolthole, and Giulia texted, promised me a big party after...whatever kind mess this trip turns out to be."

<Look on the bright side, this could be a roaring success.>

"Uh-huh."

<Look, I was talking to Jenny and Nick a few hours ago—>

"Cosy."

<We're here now, we'd like to talk.>

"Okay, is this some kind of fuxxing intervention?"

<It really is not.>

"Hi, Moth, honey," said Jenny, in mom mode. It *was* an intervention!

"Hey, M," said Nick.

"We just want to say that you are as much a part of this rather messed up family as any of us," said Jenny. *"And we want you with us. We know you have a biological family, and we're not trying to shut them out, but you are welcome here. There is love for you here."*

"Well, thank fuck you didn't get Detective Wordsmith to make that speech. Sorry, I'm...kinda jumpy. I know I look calm and collected, but under this smoking exterior, I'm nervous about this trip. I appreciate what you say, I just don't know what's going to happen, you know?"

<None of us do,> Quirk subvoced. <But we can know what will happen with us. We make those rules and everyone else can butt out. We're not trying to rush you, we're just saying we're here if you need us.>

"Okay. Thanks." Moth left the call.

* * *

Moth regretted her lame parting, but it was all she could manage as her eyes had started leaking with extreme prejudice, her throat twisting with emotional anaphylaxis. She needed another perspective on this...unexpected turn of events.

<Hey Nick, you listening?> asked Moth.

"When you call, I listen. But I don't like, spy on you! Or others, unless I'm asked, I suppose. Mostly? Slippery slope, you know?"

<You must have done it plenty before.>

"In the lab, yeah." He sounded forlorn, and she kicked herself for mentioning it, but if they were going to be friends, they had to be able to talk about times before Nick's transformation. *"Not now, unless it's necessary. But if I did, I could see all your messages, your images, your search histories—"*

<Wow.>

"Your health and welfare files—"

<Yeah, okay. I get it.>

"Your education record, shopping history..."

<Okay, buttface!>

"Don't have a face, girlface."

Silence fell, for all of five seconds.

"Sorry."

<It's okay. I guess you're not scared of this because you can't die?>

"Honestly? I dunno. Guess I could if there was no suitable digital medium after some kind of event. Hadn't thought about it till now, thanks! You scared?"

<Kinda? I mean, TOM's space station is crewed totally by droids, right? So, that's gonna be a fucking laugh-riot for me.>

"I'll be there, and I'm a tough guy, remember?"

<Yeah, sure.>

But his presence did reassure her. After the UN and the hotel kidnap nightmare, she and Nick had some history that wasn't Nick being out of control in Canada. That was...something. Comforting? Just chatting to him was cool since this flight suddenly had become even more of an emotional rollercoaster, apparently, despite its impeccable smoothness. Now she had the choice between Quirk and Rigel—the choice between Kirby family and The Family—and under these headline items lurked the ghost of crises past and present, Joshua fucking Simister. And what she really wanted now was a chance to look him in the eye, lay the old fucker to rest, preferably with her bare hands clamped around his unbreathing throat.

XXXV

08:09, 1 February 2100 (Earth date equivalent)
Cythera Station, Venus

Arriving at C Corp's Cythera Station retained all the delightful trappings of commercial spaceflight, the body scans, the baggage scans, the probing (verbal, thankfully), all while battling the fatigue induced by sitting around for days thinking high thoughts, dreaming low ones, but generally achieving very little.

Numerous syRen® enacted the admin formalities while the delegates progressed through the appropriate scanners. During that tedious process, Quirk observed from a rather odd sense of almost-weight that Cythera Station must possess pseudo-grav generators. Not the most reliable technology yet—not proven to the level that he would dispense with his magboots—but certainly effective enough that dropping a brick on one's toe would hurt. Fitting out a whole station would be very expensive.

Once standing beyond the security line in an unremarkable, inoffensively coloured, ill-defined and uncomfortable reception area, Mary Quon excused herself, stating her neutral role required her to touch base—or perhaps touch station, Quirk chuckled—with their host.

The arriving Rigel party passed from the reception area into a corridor spoke running out from the space station's spine. They clumped along a brightly lit gangway, plenty of headroom, room to walk three abreast, a luxury in space, or rather—knowing TOM—simply a vulgar display of power.

They approached a room promisingly signed "Welcome Lounge." The doorless opening revealed soft lighting and stylish furniture, high-ceilings too, being in the outer ring, not the spoke corridor. The lounge took up a minor arc of the station's major ring, a long enough portion that the ends in either direction lay partially out of sight beyond the ring's curve. Walking "around" the inner wall towards the offered seating presented a slight sensory hurdle. To control a minor bout of vertigo, Quirk focused on the furniture, on which no expense had been spared.

He alternated his gaze between the decor and his companions, assessing the demeanour of each. Any situation involving The Old Man must be considered potentially volatile, teetering on the edge of going south. He'd said this to the group in transit. None of them looked comfortable apart from S-14636, of course, but what did Nick feel inside? Although Quirk felt closer to the boy after their heart-to-heart, he found he did not fully trust Nick not to attempt grand-patricide at the first opportunity.

An android arrived moments after them, offered refreshments, and invited them to make themselves comfortable. All the new arrivals apart from Nick/S-14636 gave the syRen® an order. Without overt communication, trays began to arrive, each delegate served by a separate android; more power games.

The group's tension might have been travel fatigue, but it made them look weak. He smiled tightly inside: *It's Beginning to Look a Lot Like Crisis,* tried to ease the mood.

"How many syRen® inhabit Cythera Station?" he asked the android that served him the inevitable yet exceedingly satisfying gin and tonic.

"That information is commercially sensitive, Mr. Kirby. Please enjoy your drink. Your host will greet you shortly."

Quirk slid a glance at Jennifer, seated on a two-seater against the space station's curved and windowed wall, just as Moth plonked herself next to Jenny. His... *Oh.* How did he think of Jenny now? She met his gaze, tilted her head down, compressed her lips. He still felt a warm glow from their conversation on the ship. Jennifer passed the gaze on to Giulia, no one willing to speak.

The last android departed the lounge. The human delegates exchanged glances in silence. They all expected their conversation would be overheard, by a droid or some other technology relaying discussion back to TOM, so they remained silent, sipped drinks, and glanced back and forth, heating the air with their intent.

"So, when do we think the hateful old fucker will show his detestable face?" said the Nick/droid.

Quirk started to speak, but Jenny pre-empted him. "Nicholas Quinton Kirby. My father may be despicable, but we do not talk about people behind their backs."

"Sorry." The sight of a syRen® sporting a hangdog look made Quirk chuckle.

"Well, you've rather stolen my thunder there, Nicholas." The voice, unmistakable in its round, rolling delivery, its authoritative depth, issued from sources all around the room, giving the effect of an omnipotent presence.

Quirk stood, placing his drink on the table arm of his sofa. Not in a come-to-attention kind of way, more a might-have-to-run-for-it fashion. Jenny also tensed. Moth and Giulia perched on the edge of their seats.

"Please, relax. I know I've made an adversary of each of you in some way. Rigel requested the meeting, and I agreed, granted your safe passage, more from curiosity than anything else, I'll admit. But the more I think about it, the more I see the sense in it." Pause. *"I think this could work, and wouldn't that be grand?"*

Giulia di Fantano seemed to bridle at the mere fact of conversing with The Old Man, and Moth's normally healthy pallor had drained away, blood focused on surging through her veins even at the virtual presence of the man whose orders ripped her life apart. Quirk thought she'd have started swinging those petite but dangerous-looking fists if there had been a visual target in addition to a disembodied voice.

"So, Signora di Fantano, I look forward to negotiating details, see where we can get to, sign a joint paper in the next few days, but I have one condition." The room held its breath, but TOM put them out of...whatever they were feeling almost immediately. *"I require to speak to each member of your party for a few minutes, alone."*

Jenny looked at Nick/S-14636 then at Quirk, who met her gaze after he broke an intense stare shared with Moth. He and Angelika had spent so much time in each other's constant company that he felt he read quite clearly the pain in her anguished eyes. He tried to send back positive thoughts, to affect an expression that said you are as strong mentally as you are resilient physically. Overcomplicated perhaps, but Moth gave a nervous flinch of a smile back.

Jenny's expression confused him. Perhaps she didn't know herself what she felt, or thought at the proposition. He smiled then mouthed, "You can do this," careless of the inevitable lipreading software that was bound to pick up his message.

"Oh, I know," she said, and smiled back.

Giulia presented the calmest face of all. She stood, stepped into the centre of the room, Quirk still mildly disturbed by its curvature, by enough centimetres for the effect to weird him out.

"That is not a provision of the initial memorandum, but I will accede to it, with the proviso that any one of the Rigel delegation may decline for personal reasons."

"*Agreed,*" said The Old Man. "*And, I'll add a codicil of my own: I will specify the order of the interviews.*"

Giulia di Fantano's lips compressed. "Agreed." She seemed to tense, as if expecting something to change suddenly. Fair enough really, this was a key moment.

"*Good. And, for the record, these are personal discussions, call it orientation, whatever you like, but Mary Quon will not be present, and no record will be made.*" No one said anything to that. "*Good. In that case, Signora di Fantano, please accompany this syRen®*"—A droid appeared at the entrance to the lounge, but it walked through the room to a door in the end wall—"*and we'll get started.*"

Giulia smoothed the front of her blue flightsuit with both hands then walked towards the female model android, passing close to Quirk, flicking him a glance.

"Don't let him get in your head," said Quirk.

"Too late," she answered, and he understood. The Old Man's legend, C Corp's might, its ubiquitous influence, sprawling interests, the unstopability of Joshua Simister, his seeming invulnerability—all went before him in a towering wave that defeated most opponents before he even appeared on the field.

* * *

Giulia returned from the next room after no more than fifteen minutes, stepping through what Quirk realised he should think of as a bulkhead. In her absence, Quirk and Jennifer had spoken in hushed tones, literally putting their heads together, he crouched at the end of her sofa, both had cupped hands over their mouths to prevent lipreading, although any ultrasensitive listening technology would render that small act of defiance useless. He'd aimed to reassure her, and she told him to mind his beeswax, she would be completely fine.

He thought of sitting again to soak up the decidedly uncomfortable atmosphere, but instead moved over to reassure Moth. The look on her face as he sat beside her suggested she was about ready to shove a wick in his beeswax and set it alight.

"Forgiving you doesn't mean I've forgotten," she growled in welcome.

"Me neither, but you know you have an option here, to decline."

She frowned. "Don't try and talk me out of it. You don't need to protect me."

"I know. And I think you should speak to him. Know your enemy, and all that. Because even if, by some unlikely turn of events, this deal goes through, you should never wholly trust him. Still, I don't believe there's any physical danger here. I'd have moved heaven and Earth to stop this jaunt if it thought there was a real threat."

"To protect Jennifer, right?"

"And you, dummy." He winked.

"I'd love to fly-on-the-wall your chinwag with your former boss. I reckon it'll be hilarious. Just try not to cry, you know? And keep the moral high ground, boss."

"Am I still your boss?" He didn't allow her to respond, because keeping talking always helped in these scenarios when you didn't really want to hear the answer. "I heard you described as Head of Youth Development. I know a lot of water passed under the bridge you and I stand on." He put a hand on her shoulder, and she didn't even flinch or bat it away. "I think you've grown a lot. You've been fifteen for six days, but you've put on a lot more than a year recently."

On her return, and unlike earlier, Signora di Fantano's poker face remained determinedly in place.

"Signorina Moratti," said the android. "Please accompany me."

* * *

This was such bullshit. What the fuck was the old bastard trying to prove? Just trying to show how much of a dickwad he could be on an individual basis? Intimidate the pants off each of them to weaken them, undermine their confidence for the talks? That would be about right for this bellend of the first order. Fucking *pompinara!* She hated him for everything he'd done to her. But... This was something that adults did, made two-faced chitchat with their enemies, sometimes. *Fuzzzk!* And now her boss—she started to well up realising she could still think of Quirk that way after everything—now, he had to face TOM too. It might be easier for her. At least her hate was straightforward.

The android led her through the door in the wall into a smaller room, same style as the lounge, but with the walldow on the station's outer curve set transparent. The curved expanse of Venus lay below them wrapped in swathes of poisonous white cloud, marbled by the pink surface beneath. It was beautiful.

Her situation crashed back in, and she clamped down on the start of a shiver despite the comfortable temperature. How would she deal with TOM? Like a child, wailing and raging, or like a fucking grown-up?

As she sat in an sofa the walldow opaqued and soft lights came up. A larger-than-life head resolved into focus. She realised she'd seen hardly any pictures of Joshua Simister. She had to turn her head slightly to look at him, but decided to keep the arm of the sofa between them. Not facing him directly made it look like he was a distraction from something more important.

"Welcome to Cythera Station, Angelika. I think a proper greeting requires the use of proper names, but I'm happy to call you Moth for the remainder. You can call me Joshua, or TOM, if you like. Did you have a pleasant flight? I truly want to know."

Of course he was just a man. No horns, no fangs, no blood-red eyes. It was totally fucked up he had such good skin. Christ, he looked a similar age to Quirk. Crazy. Hair naturally dark brown, features strong but plain, expression open. In other words, nothing in his appearance or expression to trigger any kind of hate response. Just a man, but the things his mind had conceived, that his heart had decided...

"It was alright." She shrugged.

He smiled slightly. "Good. Look, Moth, I don't have all that much to say to you, but I thought you might have things you'd like to ask me, not in front of the others."

"Your actions killed my parents." The effort needed to speak those words and keep her calm on the outside almost broke her insides. She thought her heart would explode from the stress jangling in her chest, but she kept breathing, in through the nose, out through the mouth. She kept her calm to spite him.

He nodded, neutral expression unchanging. "That's true. Not the intent of my decisions, but the outcome, I accept that. Others died too."

"Their children can worry about them. After that you killed my uncle."

"The rivalry between C Corp—no, between me and Rigel, goes back a very long way, to Toni's grandfather in fact. I won't justify that action. He was the target of the mansion raid, of course. Just Toni, but such things get messy, soldiers fight back."

"My mother was not a solider." Moth felt her fists forming. A fist was only good for one thing. With a fist you gave up all your options. She stopped, forced her fingers to relax, continued breathing.

"No, she was not." TOM—she couldn't shitting believe she was talking to The Old Man, holding her own too. Somewhere in the emotional chaos broiling inside her she felt pride, and when you threw pride on the fire you got determination. She would *not* yield, would not let this fucker off the hook. TOM's expression became more earnest. "Moth, I won't insult you by saying I wish it hadn't happened, but the truth is I could have achieved my objective without your parents dying. I regret it."

"Yeah." In her head, something broke, sort of snapped with an almost audible click. She'd always thought she wanted revenge, although she didn't know how or when she would ever get it, but she realised then that physical, violent revenge was only one kind of justice, a consuming, self-defeating kind, and would it not be more sustainable to defeat your enemy's aims rather than throw down your enemy themselves. How much more satisfying for them to watch everything they had built being broken, or better still taken away? Like he had to her.

Continents of emotion began to shift within her. She clutched the arm of the sofa as deeply personal fault lines ground against each other. She reached for solid ground.

"Why was Quirk there, in the mansion?"

"I gather he kept that from you. He makes the oddest personal choices."

"Answer the"—*FUCKING!*—"question. Please."

"I sent him to observe. He steadfastly refused ever to pull a trigger on my behalf, anywhere. Reports from retainers and staff can be...confused when they are direct participants in the action, with their performance under continuous review. Quirk's job was to watch, but not to intervene. Derek Morton was the trigger man, but didn't get the chance." He paused, giving her space, then, "Anything else you'd like to ask?"

"No," she stood up, waiting until the last moment before releasing her hold on the sofa. "We're done for now."

He smiled. "Is that a portent?"

She met his gaze, fought to keep her features blank. "I'd hardly tell you if it was."

"Touché."

"Casse-toi."

TOM chuckled at her surprisingly mild response. "Very cultured."

She shrugged. "French is my fourth language." She walked away then stopped short of the door so it remained closed for this. She turned to face TOM's image on the walldow, slipped her gears into detective mode. "I could stay here all day trying to figure why you treat your family the way you do. So I'll just ask. How can you?"

She didn't have the skills yet or the history to figure a motive in the twisted behaviour of this individual, but she could gather information. She took a mental snapshot of TOM's background, the walls, colours, décor. No art or features, but the angle of the wall and ceiling, the quality of the light. Maybe Nick could analyse those, although he would need to rely on her impressions. Still, she committed details to memory, and the notion she should invest in a pair of photo lenses. Eye-wateringly expensive, but she had decided she would need them in her future career.

She presumed TOM wouldn't answer her question, but he looked away from the camera, clearly considering it.

"I don't owe you an answer to that question," he said after a few seconds, his expression as neutral as in the rest of their "chat." "But I think we can presume others will ask it. Speak to them afterwards. See if they'll give you an answer. Thank you for your time, Moth," he said, and she was dismissed.

All eyes turned to watch her walk back into the lounge like one of those shitty whodidits splashed all over the high thousand channels in every hotel room. She wished she'd killed The Old Man on the holodeck with the anti-spin wrench. Jennifer—standing in the middle of the room when the door opened—came up and hugged her.

"I'm fine," said Moth, for the room's benefit, realising "slightly stunned" might be the best description of how she felt. Then, just for Jennifer, "I wasn't ready for him being...reasonable."

Jennifer squeezed then released her. "My turn next."

Moth watched the doorway at the end of the room close behind Jenny, still weirded out by that curve of the walls. The distraction lasted two seconds before her thoughts returned to rushing around vomiting bullshit all over her brain-attic. She had to calm down, but TOM had riled her up. Every passing second, she thought of another thing she should have said to Archduke Nasty von Evilshit. He'd behaved so fucking reasonably that she still hadn't recovered. His pretty manners didn't change the harm he'd done to her, to Nick, Quirk, or Jenny. To Giulia, and hundreds, thousands, who knew how many people. And what were they going to do about it? Dick around talking politely and eating vac-packed cucumber sandwiches? Not. Fucking. Good enough. She wished she had a gun, but the old bastard— old: it was impossible to think of him as his real age. He might be the world's first-time traveller, because no one else had the insane amount of money it must take not only to have all the procedures he must have had over one hundred and sixty years, but in some cases to develop the techniques first. A weird thought floated to the top of the cranial soup, one involving Nick, and Genextric, and Androicon, and the UN. And Gregor Callan.

She had to speak to Nick.

* * *

"Hello, Jennifer."

"Hi, Dad," she channelled her once-upon-a-teen self as airily as she could. In truth she'd spent the last hour, the last day, week, month, year wondering what she would say to him, dreading their next meeting, and here he was. On a screen anyway, looking improperly, indecently youthful as ever. She could not even say she saw his real age in his gaze. He'd had at least one eye reconstruction on each side.

She took a seat then crossed her legs, determined not to fidget like the teen she had aped. "You should go first, *Dad*. I'm sure you've heard many reports of my ramblings through the years."

Her father nodded solemnly. "That's fair. Okay, let's start with I did it for me. I spend my days trying to hold worlds together, Jennifer, trying to feed Humankind's limitless thirst for exploration. I prevent nations splitting apart, save them from the worst excesses of their national identity. It's a constant mission, never ends, and I couldn't do my job knowing you were falling apart, Jenny. Not knowing if you were up or down, whether you might harm yourself. I couldn't leave that to chance. I had to know you were safe."

She nodded, looked at the floor. "That certainly sounds like the sort of selfish thing you would do. Was that the only reason?"

"Come on, Jenny," her father shook his head and—despite everything he'd done—she felt the stab of shame at disappointing him in any way. "You've outgrown throwing tantrums. If you want to spit at me, do so, but please don't whine. I won't be blamed for your lack of capacity to understand the stakes I deal in every day."

He delivered his diatribe with the calmest, most complacent and uncaringly neutral expression she could imagine, all in the repulsive context of his appearance casting him as her younger brother. It was so...wrong. "All those years, you cared nothing for what I wanted, for my feelings."

"I gave you a son." That didn't sound great either. "A son that Quinton abandoned. So, it appears that he is judged by a different standard."

"Of course he is," she snapped. "I *love* him, for my sins, and in spite of his. Are you intending to bring Nick in here? You can't! You've done enough to him."

"Done enough?" TOM's eyebrows rose. "I set him free from the bonds of the flesh." Her father raised his hands like Christ giving a benediction. "And I think he would see it that way. You can't deny his skills are prodigious, almost unique."

"You stole his childhood, like you stole mine by never being there." She stood. "If you want to give something back—although it wouldn't be like you—try to see beyond the end of your own grasping hand!

Deal with Rigel, or maybe try to make things better for ordinary people."

Her father shook his head and, despite the years having fallen away (or perhaps been dragged out) of him, she felt a very old pang at the sight of that oh-so-familiar disappointment.

"I suggest we leave it there, Jennifer, because I'm very much afraid you will never understand."

She turned and left.

* * *

<Nick. I'm cranked to the max after chatting with your grandpa. I need to chill with someone. Can you talk? Can you make a secure space? I don't want him listening. I'm quite funking upset, and this is very personal.> She dropped her hand from her mouth, and waited.

"Hey, sweetheart what's the news? This channel's secure, but maybe only for a few minutes. I've employed primary, secondary and tertiary encryption so that—"

<Blah, blah. Can it, tech-boy, I trust you. Listen, and tell me to shut up if I'm wrong. Androicon spent years researching the uploading of human consciousness. They trialled it on the Moon using volunteers, including everyone's least favourite scumbag, Gregor Callan. The results were mixed, but not all trials suffered the psychotic breakdown Callan did. Correct?>

"Success rate seventy-eight percent when the UN banned testing and sequestered all Androicon equipment and research material."

<The work done by Genextric in Yellowknife, one of the main strands of their research— I'm sorry, Nick.> A lump forced itself down her throat. <Of the genetic experiments on you, was the ability to infiltrate and manipulate technology. And we all hate it, dude, me and Quirk and your mom, but they succeeded with you, right?>

"They did, but what's your point, caller?" She thought she heard terseness in his tone, but she might have imagined it.

<What if TOM's working on a single objective? These strands of research, what if they're intended to come together in one outcome? Can you compile a list of tech projects the UN is sponsoring, reporting

to Sec-Tech Suudi? Because all that shit around Mars and in New York makes as much sense as cutting down trees.>

"That'll take a moment, but I'll look."

<Look fast. Quirk's going in now.>

* * *

Quirk steeled himself, looking to Jenny, who sat preoccupied, staring at the wall, then at Giulia, who sat almost completely still, but whose little movements of hands and head betrayed her tension. He tried to engage Moth, but she had her hand over her mouth, talking to Nick he guessed. About what, God only knew. Possibly God and Joshua Simister, depending on the quality of his surveillance tech. He puffed out his cheeks. No getting around this. Shoulders back and think of the Belt, and that some good might come of these negotiations, even if it were only laying to rest the noisome and persistent personal ghost of Quirk and TOM. He followed the waiting syRen® around the room to the internal door and stepped through.

"Quinton," The Old Man greeted him from the screen. "It's been so long. It's a pleasure to see you, and honestly, I'm surprised I find myself able to say that."

"I'm surprised too. It feels like I've been a thorn in your side lately."

"You have, but you were such an asset to the company. I find myself able to overlook a lot of what's passed between us recently. Back in the day, I probably didn't tell you enough how much I appreciated you. I think perhaps you were my conscience. Maybe I've missed that."

Quirk shook his head, unable to hold back a grim smile: *Incredulous 90210*. "A cynic would say you're trying to blame my absence for some pretty big-ticket items. Whereas, in reality, I couldn't have persuaded you to open an umbrella in the rain. You never listened to anyone but yourself."

"Ha! You always were a wit, Quinton. But I think you're selling yourself short." Looking at a face that, unbelievably, seemed younger now than the last time he'd seen TOM in person left Quirk profoundly uncomfortable. "Maybe you could have prevented some recent occurrences. I regret what happened to Nick, for example."

Quirk barely contained a hot surge of blood and fury. The old bastard thrived on conflict, turned anger to his own purpose. Getting into people's heads had always been his opening tactic, and he had nearly fallen for it, nearly balked at the first hurdle. The longer he paused to recover, the more satisfaction TOM would take.

"We all regret that. I presume you saw footage, and you must have known what was happening to him. I'm sure you received reports. That was cruel and unusual, and the boy did nothing wrong. He surely did nothing to you."

"Quinton, I certainly was not punishing the boy. There was a clear goal."

Quirk's temperature continued to rise towards boiling. "You could have used anyone, but you—" Wait.

Pieces began to fall into place. Perhaps he never would have seen them without the perspective of being many millions of miles from Earth. The bottom line remained unclear, but connections began to resolve. He needed more information.

TOM clearly mistook his pause for emotion. And there was emotion, because he did now think of Nick as his son, the product of his DNA, and Jennifer's love for him. And then he did see his own responsibility in all this. Not TOM's schtick about being C Corp's or Simister's conscience—utter nonsense—but the fact that he'd been there, but his response had been to turn away, and run.

"I reject your proposition about conscience. Mine was never that well developed, clearly, because I worked for you for so long. But what happened to yours? You were there when everything began to fall apart. You could have tried to stop it. In 2025 you were ninety-one, already benefiting from gene and transplant therapies. A young ninety-one, CEO of Jasper Miette Petroleum, still exploring, still exploiting fossil fuels as the planet burned around you. Why?"

TOM's flat gaze betrayed not a single emotion. "Because by then it didn't matter. You already did the damage, Quinton. Even though you weren't born, you had lived a thousand times in your complacency, your smugness, your belief that you could have everything you wanted. You and your kind. The deaf, dumb, selectively blind masses. Never making the uncomfortable choices that you should have. Never willing to do what was necessary even to save yourselves."

Quirk nodded. "Right. So, the people should have stopped you. It was their responsibility. You were innocent? Had no influence over markets, customers, politicians?"

"But that's the hilarious thing, Quinton, the people *have* the power, they just don't realise it. All their softer virtues are defeated before they begin. They get to choose what they want, and every time they vote for their comfort. They want music and sport through which to channel their emotions. They want the press to keep them scared, petitions to sign and charities to support to appease their conscience, make them feel through their pathetic, hollow protest they are fighting back against the politicians *they* chose, the companies *they* funded, for decades. In short, Quinton, the masses get the government they deserve."

As he listened, Quirk's heart began to shrivel in his chest. The sharp reminder of TOM's extreme nihilism jolted him back through the years to times full of joy and hope, but also scarred with everyday horror. Yet the question remained, what would he do *now*? What he should have done years ago: take up the challenge, fight back, be the conscience that Joshua Simister had challenged him—probably mischievously—to be.

"Okay." Only now did Quirk sit on the room's single sofa, brushing the leg of his flightsuit. He experienced a pang of fright when he realised that he didn't know the location of the Merrion. He missed Eight, and Eighty. Jenny would know. "I see your tendrils creeping over all recent events. I haven't quite worked out what you're doing, and I'm sure you've got no intention of explaining your masterplan to me, but just stop for a moment and imagine the good you could do. For whatever reason you couldn't or wouldn't make a difference before, imagine it now."

"But I am doing good."

"I mean for people who need it."

Simister smiled sadly, shook his head, looking down then back again. "Quinton, no generation has a divine right to avoid horror. Peace and enlightenment must be earned through one's own actions, forged by one's own good works. You've got money now—Toni's millions. Why not start a charity? Give it all away, see how long it lasts."

Quirk frowned. Something in TOM's expression—previously cynical, flat, bored, yet infused with trademark unwavering certitude—

had changed. He looked genuinely aggrieved. For a moment—and regardless of what TOM's current scheme might actually *be*—Quirk thought perhaps he had reached Joshua Simister.

"Why not park your plans for a few days, give the negotiations a chance."

"I intend to."

"No, *really*. Imagine what we could do working together: you, me, Jennifer, and Nick, with Rigel's resources in support. Because..." Quirk held the thought, met Simister's gaze and tried something new. He saw Toni di Fantano in his office busy dying as he took Quirk for a ride. He saw Giulia at the convent, where he'd taken Moth. Images floated in and out of focus: Gregor Callan, Derek Morton, Tania Terjesen, Anwar Cruz. He saw himself standing in the hallway on Spruce Street, patting down the Merrion. Pursuing the elusive thought in his head, reaching for it, Quirk attempted forgiveness. He looked at Joshua Simister for a long moment. The "Old" Man stared back, patient for once. Waiting for Quirk. Waiting for him to catch up?

"You tried, didn't you?" said Quirk.

"Of course I bloody tried!" Clearly, he'd rubbed TOM the wrong way. "Despite popular opinion, I am not a monster. Many people said that out loud in the early days, lauded me for my daring, aggressive strategies."

"And what happened to that zeal, that belief?"

Simister's sangfroid reasserted itself. "I came into contact with one too many regular joes like you and became a pragmatist. Trying to get things done in the face of politicians' widespread imagination deficit is soul-destroying, but still I managed to drive the UN in the right direction, pushing their macro engineering strategy with monumental donations and technical support, for which I received the Secretary General's eternal gratitude."

"Not just his, I'm sure," Quirk interjected.

"All well and good, Quinton, but it's my time now."

TOM paused, quite clearly appraising his guest, perhaps pondering a revelation.

"Did Signora di Fantano tell you there is another D ship holding station fifteen minutes away? Rigel tried to hide it on the other side of the planet, but I do of course have something of a network here. What do you think it might be for, Quinton?"

"Backup," Quirk said hopefully, his heart sinking. Had Rigel undermined this peacekeeping mission right from the off? Was Giulia lying to them? A hidden ship gave the nasty impression things might be about to get a little retaliatory.

"You see the kind of deceit I'm faced with on a daily basis, Quinton?" Simister's face seemed to darken, and he leaned toward the screen. "I know you're not on their side, Quinton, despite the girl, despite that mess of an operation in New York, Mars too. You're on your own side, and that resonates with me. But imagine what *you* could do with *my* resources in support. You want to do good? Change C Corp from the inside out, Quinton. Change it from the top down. Come and be my strategy advisor. And the first thing we'll do is deal with Rigel's deception."

Quirk thanked his lucky stars he was sitting down for that, then he wished on them that he hadn't heard it.

XXXVI

09:39, 1 February 2100 (Earth date equivalent)
Cythera Station, Venus

"Moth. Moth. Moth."

She cupped a hand over her mouth, glad Nick had a response, but worried how much he sounded like a hot-headed eight-year-old when at other times he could be so sensitive, thoughtful, mature. *Christ, M, fuzking concentrate.*

"I think I've found TOM."

<Can we do this more than one sentence at a time? The longer Quirk's in there, the faster my nerves play 'Dueling Banjos.'>

"Okay, Little Miss Snarky Pants."

<I'm just high-functioning, and leave my pants out of it. Explain.>

"I managed to surf some of the station's systems. I reckon they can detect me, if they can understand the output, but I went deep, I doubt they could find me quickly."

<Continue, please!>

"Station monitoring shows only six life signs, the four of you, Mary, and TOM. I checked the parameter fields. The system covers the whole station. Everything's scanned, no dead zones. He's in the lowest of the three rings."

<Okay. Makes sense he wouldn't expose himself straight away. Play it cagey. I'd do the same.>

"No, there's something else going on here."

<What about my unified theory? Spitball me this, take the thing they did to Callan, synaptic mapping then consciousness upload protocol, CUP; plus—what do we call what they did to you, Nick? What do we call your ability?>

"I'm a tech charmer."

<Nah, that's not it. It's more like you're a gremlin.>

"The Gremlin. Sounds like a supervillain."

<Ghost in the machine.> She shouldn't have said that, even though Nick always said he didn't miss his body, and neither did she think of him as dead. Nor did he.

"The scientists often talked in front of me. They spoke about Human Awareness Transmittal Technology."

<Aw, yeah, Nick. You're the Mad Hatter!>

"Maybe, but I think I see it. There's a... Just let me..."

Silence.

"There's a major battery core at the centre of the station's bottom ring. The power budget of the station itself is modest. It's very efficient, runs from solar arrays and biological energy reclamation. Has a couple of subatom nets, too."

<Maybe the core's backup, charging for incoming ships, life support backup.>

"Nah. You could power a fleet of ships on this baby. It's for something else."

The internal door opened, and Quirk clumped back into the room. He paused to look at Jennifer, whose head jerked up when the door opened. She looked like she would vomit, but she tried to return his reassuring smile. Then he came to the middle of the room and looked around the assembly. His gaze stopped on Giulia. Her aunt looked composed, a picture of calm, but Moth saw the way her hands held the arms of her chair, not squeezing but definitely holding, looking for support.

"What's the second D ship for, Giulia?" Quirk asked.

Everyone in the room turned to look at Signora di Fantano.

"Backup, of course."

Moth didn't believe her, the way her aunt waved a hand dismissively. This was not a dismissing sort of situation. What did this mean for the talks?

"Be honest, Giulia, if you want to save these talks. Simister knows. Assume it's had a negative impact on his disposition to agree anything at all with Rigel. If you want to salvage something from this situation, you need to come clean. He has a drone array in high Venus orbit, so just assume you can't hide anything from him, like ship signatures, or armaments."

Giulia frowned. "You sound like his spokesperson."

"TOM did offer me a job, as it happens."

Everyone in the room spoke at the same time.

"Figlio di puttana!"— not convent language, Aunty!

"Quirk, no!"—a protest from Jennifer's heart.

"You said stuff it, right?!"—yelled Moth.

"Dad, no!"—wailed Nick/S-14636.

Quirk shrugged. "I said I'd think about it."

"You son of a bitch," hissed Giulia, in English this time. "You will undermine this whole mission."

"I think you're the one who has risked that, Signora. And how did the mission come about?" Quirk practically vibrated with tension, probably wishing he had the Merrion, could hook his thumbs into that genuine historic pre-ban leather belt. Quirk was mad enough not to allow Giulia time to answer. "Did CC approach you?" Her aunt looked up at the ceiling. "I'm sure he's listening," said Quirk, "but I think we're past that."

"They did not. This is a Rigel initiative."

Quirk shook his head. "What made you think he might be willing to talk? There was something, wasn't there? A little tell-tale, a sliver of light."

Giulia sighed, shook her head. "He released a list of those involved in the raid on the villa, agreed to provide information to Milan prosecutors. It wasn't connected—"

"Of course it was bloody connected," Quirk snapped.

"Is Quirk's name on the list?" Moth blurted, because if TOM was serious about giving Quirk a job, he wouldn't shop him to the cops.

Giulia looked at her, smiled, probably glad of a friendlier face. "No."

"He wants us here for something, and you flew us millions of miles right into it." He shook his head, put his hands on his hips, looked at the floor then at Giulia again, smiling, probably giving it one of those silly names he'd told her about once when he'd had enough G&Ts to spell great-great-great-great-great-great grandfather in Scrabble. Something like *Queen of Sheba*.

"It changes nothing," said Giulia. "We are here on the strength of hope."

Quirk opened his mouth, but Moth interjected again.

"Joshua Simister doesn't deal in hope." She stood up, walked to stand near Quirk, addressing him, because she knew he would listen, that he trusted her judgement. "He deals in certainty, right?" Quirk nodded, didn't take over, waited for her to continue. "I had an idea, and Nick did some digging." Doubt gut-punched her. Simister could hear. He'd send in his badroids if she said it out loud. Wouldn't he? She let her doubt show.

"It's okay," Quirk said, smiling so warmly it didn't feel like it had a name. "I trust your judgement."

She nodded. She'd stick it to the old fucker and damn the torpedoes.

"TOM's plotting something bigger than we're seeing, and I think everything is connected. I think he needs synaptic mapping, and Consciousness Upload Protocol. We think he plans to use those for something else. He tested those on Callan and others, but I think he also needs the Yellowknife experiments on Nick that lead to Human Awareness Transfer—that's our term."

Quirk nodded, encouraging her to go on, but Nick/syRen® S-14636 spoke up at this point. "Yeah, this station has major power reserves, far more than needed to power the station. I haven't found any redundant or unusual equipment yet, but we think there's something weird in the setup here."

A loud, staccato sound burst into the silence as the Rigel team considered Moth and Nick's proposition. It took her a moment to recognise ironic applause.

"*Well done, young Moth,*" said Joshua Simister over the station's audio system. "*You're well on the way to cracking the case. Is that the real point of your visit? Not really here to negotiate a deal, but to take me down, bring me up before the courts to receive my just desserts? I'm disappointed, Signora di Fantano.*"

"No," Giulia's passionate protest silenced everyone. "We still can reach agreement. I will dismiss the other D ship, you postpone your plan. It can still work!"

The pause stretched. Everyone started to fidget, waiting for TOM's answer.

"Tell us your plan," said Quirk, looking at Jennifer, who nodded. "Maybe we'll like it, although the provenance of your technology is...disagreeable."

"*Only idiots exposit at the moment of truth, Quirk. Leaders act, decisively. But before I do, I need your answer. I'm completely serious in offering you that position, but you must decide now. Come back to the fold, Quinton. Bring Jennifer and Nick with you. Rebuild your family. Help me reinvent Mankind's relationship with the stars. What happens next depends on you."*

An image faded up on the plain wall of the slightly curving lounge, the same image they'd each seen of The Old Man sitting in his office.

Think Moth, think! Synaptic mapping, consciousness upload, human awareness transmittal. Put it all together with...the circumvention of android control systems!

She thought she had it, but it terrified her enough she couldn't say it out loud. Like saying it made it true, and she desperately hoped it wasn't. *But we don't do hope around here.* So, what could she do *now?*

A new syRen® entered the room, male model, carrying a slate grey case by its handle. Big enough for a pair of chunky Prof Martens boots. The droid stood to the side of the door.

"Quinton," said TOM, as calm as lava engulfing a bamboo village. "You must pick a side now."

Quirk would be thinking about everyone's safety, the conflict written all over his face as he looked at Jennifer then her. Moth gave him the smallest nod. She trusted him too. She tried to look determined, but if this went to shit, they were stuck a very long way from home, their only trump card the hope—*There's that fucking word again*—TOM wouldn't hurt his daughter, despite the headfuck he'd put her through in Gramercy. Even in the station's cool air, Moth thought she would burst into flames. She really wanted to hit something.

"I'll come back—" said Quirk.

"The fuck you will!"

"Quinton, no!"

"Bastardo."

"If you allow the rest of the Rigel delegation to leave and guarantee their safety."

A long enough pause followed that The Old Man must be considering it.

"Unfortunately," said TOM, leaning forward. "That presents a problem. Initiate Long Game protocol." His image disappeared.

Two more syRen® entered the lounge, each levelling a stubby, white ERBCo HP7 lasergun.

The droid with the box advanced on Nick/S-14636.

"Quirk!" Moth yelled. "The box!" <Nick, jump to my handset. Can you? Now!>

As S-14636 took up a combat stance, Nick spoke in Moth's ear. *"Insufficient memory for me. Sorry, sweetie."*

<Then hide.>

Quirk had started toward the droid with the case, but stopped halfway when the aim of a lasergun singled him out, one badroid stepping forwards while the second moved to the wall, creating a field of crossfire. Moth threw her handset to Quirk. "Save Nick!" She really hoped Quirk understood her trick, and could catch the phone in the stupid pseudo-grav.

The droid with the case ignored Nick's readiness to fight, approached S-14636 hand outstretched. Quirk caught her handset (must be the cricket practice) just as S-14636 staggered as if trying to master its motors and servos—as if Nick had left its system—before falling to the floor.

"Mister Kirby, relinquish that handset," said the tall female model, pointing her gun at Quirk. "Or your friends will be shot." Her serial number, printed on her forehead like all syRen®, read X-103. Her twin, a male model, had the number X-106.

Quirk held his hands up, placating, as he crouched to the floor, laying down the handset. Then he straightened slowly and placed his heel on the device. "I don't think I will, X-103," he said to the droid in charge. "Pretty serial number, by the way. If you shoot anyone, I will destroy the handset and Nick Kirby with it."

TOM's voice blared out. *"That won't work. He'll get away into some system. Your D ship now is locked down. I can find him anywhere on this station."*

"Do you want to bet on that?" asked Quirk. He glanced at her, nodded. "He's the key to your plan, isn't he? You need him." S-14636 just lay there, inactive. The box-carrying droid came forward and knelt beside S-14636. Moth now saw wires emerging from the case and disappearing up the droid's sleeve. When it reached for S-14636's neck, its fingertips split open and needle-sharp probes appeared, breaching S-14636's synthetic skin as the badroid clamped its hand around the other droid's neck. S-14636 began to shudder and jerk, its features twisting with anger and hate before the syRen® slumped, inactive.

The image faded up again, and there sat Simister, looking like the cat who just ate a cream-dipped canary. In a chair beside him sat an older model male droid, maybe a '96, strapped to the seat with thick cable ties. The same expression of pure hate twisted the captured droid's face. *Bastard!* He had Nick. TOM had just stolen her friend.

"What the hell did you do to me?!" said the droid.

How in the name of the saints' holy shit had TOM done that? Some new tech toy Simister had commanded from his tame scientists, of course. And all that bollocks about sharing tech and not competing— he'd just lapped that up, an ideal ruse to lure the mark to his boss-level lair. Now TOM would use Nick again. The theory emerging in her head chilled her to the bone, genuinely would make a sophisticated and already world-weary fifteen-year-old ace detective curl up in a wicked-stylish ball and cry. And what did it mean for the rest of them?

"Nicholas," TOM addressed the android next to him that strained against his bonds, trying to rip apart the chair, which must be bolted to the floor. "Be calm, boy. You're fine, and you're contributing to another great advance in technology."

Simister addressed the room. "The question remains, what am I to do with you all?" The view zoomed and TOM's head appeared large, disembodied. His gaze rested on Giulia. "My scans of your second D ship show eighteen life signs. That's a lot of backup, Signora di Fantano. In fact, you have brought an army, and one of those genetic signatures belongs to Anwar Cruz. I believe xe harbours ill will towards me, despite taking my money. Did you promise xim xis revenge? Never mind," Simister waved the question away. "I don't care." TOM tapped his lips.

This was her window. Moth took a deep breath, avoided her friends' eyes which would distract her, and the syRen®s' guns which terrified her—looked for anything that wasn't stuck, welded or rivetted down. Thin pickings. They were all going to die. She let her eyes track around the room, fighting the helplessness growing in her chest. A new idea burst on the scene. *Max stress. Maximum fuzking stress!* She crumpled to the floor, shaking, hugging her knees, her magboots still tugged towards the metal floor.

"Signora," Simister said. "Believe that I take no pleasure in this, but in behaving the way you have you've not only disappointed me, you've let yourself down. I cannot have rivals thinking I'm so easy to get at."

Moth's insides all headed south at the same time.

"So, I'm afraid I must make an example of you."

Game's up.

"Squad X1, kill the Rigel employees, protect the Kirbys."

Moth sprang up out of her unfastened magboots toward the ceiling, aided by the reduced pseudo gravity. Lasers hummed and beams stabbed at her, sweeping in pursuit as she twisted, hit the ceiling feet first and speared downwards at X-103.

The droid's laser scored her arm, stinging, burning, but she zipped inside its field of fire fast enough not to lose the arm, hit the droid hard in the midriff, knocking it flat.

She'd never outwrestle a droid—see previous total failure against Callan—so wriggled behind it, evading its grasping hands long enough to grab the fallen lasergun, snatching carefully so she didn't knock it away in the strange partial gravity.

She fired the gun as soon as her hand found the grip then swept the beam into the droid, because you could use a laser like a fucking sword in short bursts. So cool.

A rank smell of burning plastic and fabric and scorched metal, the fizzing, spitting sounds of fried electrics and lots of heat overpowered her senses, but the syRen® stopped grabbing, hands relaxing just after clamping her neck, and it slumped.

She snapped on her magboots again and twisted towards the door, gun up, but the chaos had frozen in place. Quirk stood in the middle of the floor levelling a lasergun he'd somehow won from X-106. Jenny stood in front of Giulia, clutching a make-do shield formerly the thick arm of a sofa, now scored by laserfire. Giulia cradled her arm, her shoulder a mess of black and red. But the weird-ass part, definitely, was two androids pounding away on each other. X-106 and S-14636 threw punches, scythed kicks, going full MMA GBH for the TKO, alternately landing blows that would knock seriously big chunks from a human. The droids kept swinging, no pain, no effort or emotion in their neutral expressions. They fought on.

Then another two, three, four laser-armed droids entered the room.

"Okay," said the first arrival, X-201. "This all looks like great fun, but I got shit to do, right after I fuck y'all up real good."

Callan.

XXXVII

09:55, 1 February 2100 (Earth date equivalent)
Cythera Station, Venus

The four new droids levelled laserguns. Quirk continued to do the same, maybe thinking TOM's orders protected him. If they did, they sure as shit didn't protect her.

Lasers lit up the room.

Moth threw herself at the nearest sofa.

"GET BEHIND ME!" shouted S-14636 in a standard syRen® voice. Nick must have initiated a soft reboot before he was snatched. She didn't get a chance to see if anyone did hide, but did see lasers rip into X-106 and S-14636, settling their duel by leaving both down and smouldering.

Lasers stabbed at Moth as she scrambled behind the end of the sofa. She smelled smoke—*Oh, good*—stuck her lasergun round the smoking furniture's edge, aimed and fired, narrowly missing Quirk ducking left towards Jenny and Giulia.

She put down X-202, pouring 20% of her powerpack into its chest. Quirk nailed X-204 with a neat reverse flick of orange fire across its chest, through its face, looping down over its chest again to finish a bright kiss-off. *Damn, he* can *shoot.*

X-203's laser already burned through the sofa towards her as she switched her aim from the falling X-202. Pain seared her hip as her beam melted the droid's face. It kept shooting, because she'd missed one of the ear-cams, but she'd disrupted its vision enough for Quirk to finish it, raking fire across the whole door-end of the lounge. His power would be low after that. In fact, he ducked to check his reserve just in time to save him from X-201's latest laser swipe, because Callan didn't seem to have got TOM's memo about sparing the Kirbys. Clear enough when Jennifer stepped in front of Quirk with her make-do shield and the Callan/droid fired into it, wafting laser power until she yelped and dropped it and dived for shelter.

Moth rolled out from cover, gritted her teeth against the pain, and fired at Callan/X-201, tuning the output down to 70% to extend her fire. She swiped its shins, wiped up through its crotch, mainlined the burn to its face, where her powerpack died. X-201 turned its head, grinned at her, but didn't shoot her, or Quirk, or Jenny. The Callan/syRen® advanced on Giulia, firing into the sofa she hid behind yelling in pain and frustration, short laser bursts flaming the furniture, burning the wall behind her.

Then the Callan/droid's laser stopped. The droid faltered under fire from Quirk, its synthetic skin melting and smoking, thumbed the gun's control knob and bathed Quirk in a diffuse cone of orange, making the boss yelp, shielding his eyes before Callan's beam finally winked out. Callan/X-201 stumbled to its knees and fell—slower than she'd have liked—to the floor.

Moth heaved herself up—her arm screaming at her—lurched forward and picked up Quirk's lasergun. Three seconds at 100%, or ten seconds at 90%. She thumbed the setting down as she reached X-201.

"Die, you fucking evil pus sack!" She shot the droid hard, pouring on every watt the lasergun's powerpack gave her, and the droid just lay there smoking, melting, and took it. "Fuck you," she spat in its face. "You infest a droid, I'll fuxxing shoot it."

The droid's eyes flicked open in its crispy, blackened face. It grinned lopsided. "But"—bzzzt, prrrk—"I'm"—grrrp bzzzp—"not just in this drrrrrrrrroird, sweet— sweet— sweet cheeks. I'm in all the droids." It blew her a kiss—with tongue—and died. Moth shivered, but only because her heart was so cold. *All the droids.*

Quirk went to help Giulia stand. Jenny, having already retrieved a first aid kit from the link corridor, ripped Giulia's sleeve to tend her worst wound. Her aunt paled and winced. Moth took a couple of dressings from the bag then unzipped her flightsuit, pulled it off her shoulder and down, pressed the dressing on her own ugly laser wound. The bandage cooled, anaesthetised as it stretched over the angry flesh on a thin layer of foam leaching from its surface, before the edges sealed to good skin.

Giulia sucked in a breath as Jenny wrapped a dressing the size of a facecloth around Giulia's shoulder then watched it mould to her body's contours.

"What's that shit with Callan shooting you on lower power?" asked Moth.

Quirk put a hand on his brow then pulled sweat and soot over his hair to the back of his neck. She doubted the action had reduced his tension much.

"I think he was playing with me. Seems he doesn't plan to comply with TOM's wishes, otherwise no one would be shooting at me, which would be a novelty."

"Us di Fantano-Morattis are getting shot up plenty. And TOM stole Nick, again!"

Quirk closed his eyes, nodded. "Giulia, do you have comms with Anwar?"

"No."

"Super."

"But Anwar will come won't xe?" said Jennifer. "Xe'll be able to go after Nick."

"Xis orders are to extract us, not go after Simister," said Giulia. "Or Nicholas."

"But TOM has our son!"

"We'll find him. If I have to go myself, Jenny, I will," said Quirk. "But before we get ahead of ourselves, Moth, you thought you were onto something. What have you got?"

"Okay, I think TOM's been developing all this tech for a single purpose, and it's all coming together. He can take a human consciousness and put it in an android which can then use the syRen® body as well as a droid can. In Nick, he made an entity who can travel somehow through and into technology, in signals or electromagnetic fields or some shit I can't explain, probably neither can Nick. There's a good chance TOM'll fail to gain control over NLS drive licences. We think he's attempting to control the settlements at the end of those routes, control who goes, possibly to the length of setting up puppet governments there, but what if he could go himself?"

"It's not feasible," said Jennifer. "How could he control a constituency of settlements, of planets, when it takes six, eight, twelve years to get there?"

"What if he could copy himself?" said Moth. "Copy himself and insert himself into the data hub of every settlement ship that leaves Earth?"

Quirk had moved so he could watch the approach down the spoke corridor while he listened, but he turned to her now. "Because all the settlement hubs are installed from the UN's central system. He used Nick to create a backdoor into the UN server, because he couldn't do it. It wasn't just about getting Callan in there. And now he needs—"

"He needs Nick to show him the ropes for consciousness upload."

"So look," Jenny blurted. "I've been thinking this for a while, and it's got nothing to do with you, Quinton, or anyone here really, but—after we find Nick, of course—I think my father has to die."

No one said anything, just looked around the room at each other. Then Quirk nodded, made a kind of growling noise and started searching the droid bodies. For all her swearing and cursing about The Old Man, Moth thought she'd feel differently about TOM's demise becoming a real thing. Instead, she felt weird as she moved to help Quirk. They shared a surge of relief when they turned up four powerpacks. Quirk offered Jenny a reloaded lasergun, but she shook her head.

"I need to help Giulia."

"Okay," said Quirk. "We're going after Nick, but—"

"Nick scanned the station," said Moth. "TOM's in the lowest ring."

"Alright," said Quirk, smiling at her in a way that made her feel appreciated, that they were a team again.

To her aunt he said, "Giulia, on the basis Anwar won't come in for...?"

She checked her handset. "Five hours, unless attacked, or sees sign of distress."

"In that case, I think you're with us."

The wallscreen faded up displaying an android's head and shoulders. The syRen® grinned at them. "Oh, you poor saps. Simister's busy, an' he left *me* in charge. So now you've got a big fucking problem. I'm gonna let the lovely Jennifer go, because I'm not stupid. Simister might be the only guy who could erase me if he took a mind, but I don't think he'll shed any tears for you, Quirk. I'm gonna watch you fry as I ride outta here on whichever D ship I like. Maybe both, now I can split myself. I'm gonna be everywhere from now on. You're never gonna know where I'm comin' from next, Quirky boy. An' as for you, Angelika, you'd better believe I'm goin' to see you in my dreams, like I do every night."

Blasting the wall with her laser had no effect on the picture, but it made her feel better, so Moth snaked the red-hot ray over the syRen®'s leering image.

"Save power, Moth," said Quirk, flatly, and she stopped. She knew he was right. Then she thought about Nick, wondered if he could still feel pain.

Callan had been laughing—a shit weird sight in an android—but stopped when she stopped trying to kill the wall.

"So, yeah, let's play a game. Your ship's where you left it, about two hundred metres away. Jenny's leaving on it with my compliments. Moth too, because I don't want to hurt a hair on her pretty head, yet. Toni's widow I'll take when I please. And that leaves you, Quirk. You've got no fuckin' chance. Time to dance, motherfucker."

The sound of clumping magboots swelled in the link spoke leading back to the station's core.

"Four more droids, coming in fast," said Quirk, moving back towards a sofa.

Moth looked at the sorry, patched-up state of them, then moved to the doorway, crouched down, and peeked around the corner. She jerked back as lasers tore into the floor, a wave of heat washing over her.

"Is there a mylar blanket in that kit?" Quirk asked Jenny.

"Dispersal," Moth nodded. "Got it. Be ready to move," she said to Giulia.

Moth stuck her arm around the corner and fired a couple of bursts down the connector spar, just to keep Callan's droids honest, pulling her arm back before their deadly accurate return fire blitzed the corner where her arm and shoulder had been.

Quirk advanced with a shiny metallic blanket wafting around him.

"Sweet. Gimme a corner and let's boogie."

She and Quirk stepped around the corner. They squeezed together passing into the spar itself, keeping the blanket elevated. The force of laserfire pushed the shiny sheet against them, but it reflected most of the energy. Moth could tell this because they weren't crisped in a second. Her last glimpse told her the hostiles were fifty-ish metres away and closing steadily against their unaimed burst fire around the blanket's edges.

"Jenny." Moth waved her up. "Hold my corner." Giulia managed to walk unaided while Jennifer took the blanket, standing beside Quirk. Moth lay on the walkway. "Pull the blanky up then drop it after a second."

"You said 'blanky,'" said Quirk. "Keep your burst short or you'll get an eyeful."

"OBVS! Dummy. Just do it."

"On 'go,'" said Quirk. "Three, two, one, go!"

The barrier moved up. Moth shot a droid in the head, twice. The urge to pick another target teased her, but she stopped as the droids aimed for her head. The blanket dropped before her eyes, billowing slightly from the force of weapons designed to kill her. She remembered shooting Nick in the head as heat washed under the blanket's edge, drying the sudden tears on her face. The droids hooted and hollered, Callan style.

"Again!" she yelled, crawling forwards with the blanket.

"Three, two, one, go!"

She blasted another droid thirty metres away. And if she did keep firing when the blanket dropped, maybe shooting herself in the head was karma for Nick. *Fuck off, guilt! Die in a hole!*

"Again!"

"Go!"

Twenty metres.

Bzzztt!!

"Again!"

"Go!"

Ten metres.

Bzzzzzzzzzzztttt!!!!

She struggled with the last one. "Higher," she yelled, and made the shot rolling to the side in the strange, smooshy gravity as the last android shot at her. Moth's shot took it in the chest. "Keep it raised!" She dragged her beam across its hands, by fluke hit the syRen®'s laser carbine and the powerpack exploded.

She lay on the walkway looking at what must be the ceiling until Quirk pulled her up easily by the hand and plonked her on her magboots.

"Nice shooting, Miss Moratti."

Quirk looked kind of frazzled, which was how she felt. She switched powerpacks so she had 100%, and walked forwards, Jenny with the blanket ready, Quirk ready to shoot. Halfway to the station's reception area now and the route down to Nick.

Oh, fuck. Mary, thought Moth. *We'll find her too. We have to.*

Quirk let her walk in front, keyed to the slightest movement ahead. They reached the last droid she'd shot. The thing still flinched and fizzed. She imagined Callan twitching and drooling somewhere inside, even though probably long gone.

She kicked the droid in the head. "Seizure later, motherfucker."

She blinked then fired into a clutch of syRen® appearing at the junction ten metres ahead. One dropped, but another stood behind it. Quirk shot one-handed—flash git—other hand working the blanket in front of her. He half-melted the last droid's trigger arm, deflecting its beam into the ceiling. Two more androids stepped up, firing. Moth fired around the edge of the blanket. The mylar sheet billowed out, exposing her. Something hit her shoulder, knocking her down.

"NO!" her aunt shouted.

Giulia grasped the blanket's corner that had escaped from Quirk's grip. She tried to hold it up to fill the height and width of the walkway, but cried out in pain as she extended her arms. Two bright red laser beams hit her together, one on the neck cutting sideways, the other a burst in her forehead. Giulia fell back, legs buckling, body crumpling, slack arms twisting the blanket around her as she fell. Quirk's beam slashed back and forth across the junction up ahead as he burned up a powerpack. Another beam speared into the clutch of Callan/droids. Jenny held the gun inexpertly, but she had a clean shot and she hit things.

Moth dropped to her knees, heedless of everything. Giulia's gaze went past her, up towards the ceiling, beyond it, focused on something else.

"Giulia," said Moth, doubting her aunt heard her above the laser buzz, burning plastic crackle, and Quirk and Jenny's grunts and yells.

Unlike a bullet in the head, the laser burn hadn't killed Giulia yet, but blood pumped from her neck wound, and her breath was faint. Moth hugged her, because it didn't matter now. She put her ear beside her aunt's mouth.

"Put me...with Toni. I'll...give him your...love, mia—"

And Giulia di Fantano died.

XXXVIII

10:08, 1 February 2100 (Earth date equivalent)
Cythera Station, Venus

Quirk emptied his gun and took the carbine Jenny offered, continued firing, half-crouched behind a dead droid he'd yanked up to a sitting position in front of him. Jennifer crawled forward to grab a gun from a fallen syRen® while he covered her, shooting into the flow of arriving androids. Bizarrely, the androids shouted and jeered, because they all were Callan, and Callan had killed Giulia.

A laser scored Quirk's left shoulder and he yelped, eyes flooding with brine, pain lancing through his whole body, nerves jangling and fizzing for an instant. When it stopped, he vomited and—just for a second—wished for more jangling, since it covered the pain and the smell of his own flesh burning. Gritting his teeth, he shot back, because it was the right thing to do, not from any real hope that they might get out of this Callan-induced nightmare.

Quirk closed his eyes too late against a sudden flare of latticing lasers bathing the walls and ceiling around the mouth of the walkway. He blinked, vision swimming with slowly fading motes of yellow, orange and red, then looked down. The new lasers up ahead continued flashing, cutting their attackers apart for a few more seconds before all firing ceased. Quirk pushed aside his android shield, blinking away maroon motes now, waiting for the ambient lighting to recover. In that time, he pulled Jennifer to him and held her, definitely more for his benefit than hers, but hopefully hers too. She groaned from what he presumed were numerous minor wounds like his that ached and burned, but she hugged him back.

"Moth?" he said.

No answer, but he would recognise those sobs anywhere. Clearly, asking about Giulia right now would be a mistake. He focused on holding Jenny. She pushed back so she could kiss him, and he returned the sentiment. Kissing definitely eased the pain.

"Shake that finely turned ankle of yours, Kirby," said Anwar Cruz.

Quirk opened his eyes and turned his neck—painfully—to regard three insectoid-helmeted, tactical-suited insurgents at the mouth of the corridor, several dead androids scattered around their feet.

"You are a sight for sore...everything, or you would be without the beetle suit."

"Are you undressing me in your head again, Quirk?" said Anwar after pulling off xis helmet and running a hand through sweat-slicked dark hair.

"I'm just very tired, and slightly melted," said Quirk, pulling in a big breath, chest and shoulders aching as muscles stretched against their will as he stood up. "How did you know?"

"We received a distress signal," said Anwar. "About twenty minutes ago."

"It must have been Nick," said Moth, flatly, her voice heavy with pain.

A shiny, black-suited colleague tapped Anwar on the shoulder and made a short series of signals, one of which was a hand holding their own throat.

"We need to leave." Even as Anwar spoke, another operative arrived with a bag. They handed out breathers to the non-helmeted contingent, Jenny, Moth and himself, also tactical eye masks.

"Mary Quon?" Quirk was almost afraid to ask.

"On her way up and out," said Anwar. "We'll bring the signora and get you out of here too." Without breaking Quirk's gaze, xe signalled ops behind xim in the station reception area, out of Quirk's eyeline. That soft, North-Afro-Mediterranean regard had never looked less cool. "Unless you have other ideas?"

"We're not leaving without Nick," said Quirk, holding the assassin's gaze.

Moth stood a few metres away over Giulia's body, slender arms rigid at her side. She seemed to register her surroundings again. "Damn straight. We all still have business here."

The assassin nodded. "We do."

Two black-clad figures arrived in the spoke corridor from the reception area carrying a body bag, placed it on the walkway next to Giulia di Fantano, lifted her body in, and departed quickly. Moth nodded. She lifted a new weapon, clipped the strap into the epaulette of her burned, torn and dirty flightsuit.

The lights went out, plunging their space into darkness. Light returned before he had a chance to adjust, but now in a bloody red, accompanied by the low, but insistent whoop-whooping of an alarm.

"Did you break the place when you arrived?" he asked Anwar as he, Jenny and Moth finally cleared the spar walkway, emerging into the expansive station reception area. Red light made the space claustrophobic, the alarm's haunting moan grating with every step. The assassin shook xis head.

A bright laser lit up the hellish scene in the toroid space. The next wave of Callan/syRen® came at them from the next spoke walkway clockwise from theirs, but Anwar's troops fell into smooth action. Dark figures flowing from the elevator at the station's columnal core. They overpowered the androids swiftly with brutal force, cutting down syRen® after snarling, swearing syRen® until the Callan/droids stopped coming.

Another wave attacked from an opposite spoke, hidden from Quirk by the solid central shaft of the station. This time he and Moth joined the crossfire, kneeling to present a smaller target, sighting along barrels to aim like soldiers of yore due to the red dimness, vision compromised further by the thin drifting smoke of fuming plastec.

"Lower ring," said Moth, somehow in her gruff focus sounding ten years older.

Anwar threw hand signals, trusting his ops to see. "Not the elevator," xe commanded, leading them to an adjacent access hatch which xe opened, activated lighting revealing a ladder dropping into a dark hole.

Xe led the way, Quirk following, then Jenny, Moth lining up to follow her. He didn't fear a trap because everything could be a trap. Sometimes his life felt like a trap, and he was ready to take a break from that. A hard break that began with TOM.

When Anwar cracked the door at the bottom of the access tube, strong white light welcomed them to Tier Three, according to the neat lettering on the wall. Strong light and laserfire. The assassin called, "Wait!" Xe twisted away from the hatch, firing towards their attackers, rolled across the floor into the cover of a workstation. Xe continued shooting one-handed as xe waved them out of the access tunnel. "Come out firing," xe instructed.

Quirk complied, going in at 80% power until he could pick his targets, a number of syRen® dispersed behind workstations, body scanners and other devices. Quirk used the isolated access tube's left edge as cover to shoot defenders in his field of fire. The neat thing about these undroids, of course, was their total lack of any sense of self-preservation, and yet Callan clearly knew these were the last line of defence, and acted more prudently, making it harder to winkle out the remainder on this level.

Movement behind him resulted in Moth squeezing past to the right side of the accessway. She blasted a harmless-looking surgical bed, toppling an instrument table which spilled its contents noisily across the shiny floor. The syRen® behind the bed received three powerful bursts from Moth's lasergun: head, chest, and abdomen. "Eat my energy, fuckwit!" she spat, then began scanning for a new target.

Anwar moved into Quirk's view, somehow made running stooped look sinuous and stylish as xe moved between the cover of the largest workstations. As the undroids fell back they nicely indicated the target of their defensive efforts, the only enclosed space in the wide-open disc of the space station's lower tier. Moth moved away around the right side of the access shaft releasing Jenny, who moved aside to make way for three of Anwar's squad. These divided and—with numerical advantage—they worked together to clear the last of the defending Callan/droids.

Now with an escort to cover his back, Quirk walked towards the rectangular plass room, its interior hidden from view by opaque grey-white walls. As he drew close—Moth, Jenny and Anwar all joining him in approaching the door—the opacity reduced. He doubted it was an admission of defeat. Inside the small room, Joshua Simister sat in a big medical chair, watching them as they reached the door, a single android bound to a vertical metal frame beside him. No sound emanated from the room, but TOM's lips moved, a click resounded in the stillness, and the door opened.

For a moment, Quirk stood before the doorway, watching TOM watching him.

"There is no trap, Quinton. Jenny," he looked genuinely pleased she was here. "Come in. I promise there is no trap."

Disturbingly, TOM wore a jumpsuit of semi-transparent fabric, lined with a tracery of what looked for all the world like black veins, with swollen nodes dotted along the network. He wore a cap on his head that Quirk recognised only too well from Androicon's Lunaville office, from the time they put his awareness into an android.

Anwar stepped into the room, unzipped the front of xis tacsuit to xis sternum and removed a ballistic pistol, which xe pointed at the seated Simister. Moth squeezed in past Quirk, levelling her laser carbine. He might have tried to take it from her if he didn't think his efforts might cause it to go off.

"Have you done it?" he asked, hope a gnawing discomfort in his gut.

"I have," TOM smiled, the merest twist of his lips, almost regretful. "My consciousness has been duplicated, transmitted off-station, and dispatched in three drone ships to different destinations."

Jenny asked, "Can you sense them? The...others?"

"No. But this version of me takes solace in knowing my ideas continue, my memories remain, and any thoughts I might have birthed if left...undisturbed, still can be thought, and acted upon."

Jenny stepped forward, placing her left hand on the stubby, black barrel of Moth's lasergun, gently depressing it towards the floor. Then, she moved her right hand to take the pistol from Anwar, who allowed xis slim fingers to fall away from the gun.

Jenny raised the gun and shot her father in the chest.

Moth jerked up her lasergun and snapped a short, bright burst into TOM's forehead.

Anwar let out a strangled exclamation and reached for a pile of clothes on a chair. Xe snatched up a leather belt, the twin of Quirk's, two vintage leather accessories bought by Jennifer Simister as presents. Anwar got the belt around TOM's neck before Quirk placed a hand on xis shoulder and xe stopped, stepped back.

Quirk stepped in, pulling the belt tight, leaned over to look into TOM's face. Simister's eyes stared away, almost certainly dead already, but Quirk put all his weight into it, the belt digging deep into the skin, until Joshua Simister's body stopped twitching.

No one said anything for a good couple of minutes after Quirk straightened and let the belt fall to the floor. Finally, the android broke the silence.

"Dad, Mom, I know it's a difficult moment, but could someone untie me? I don't wanna go looking for another droid in this shit-pile, the welcome won't be friendly."

Moth moved forward and cut Nick/X-209, free. Nick assured them destroying the equipment would be pointless, but Moth turned back after the rest had left the room and shot the place up anyway. She joined them at the lift, but Anwar reminded them they must presume Callan still resisted, and probably could shoot them out into space if they went that way.

Even with spongy pseudo gravity, climbing the ladder all of twenty metres felt like hard work, but it gave everyone something to concentrate on. Back in the station's middle tier, emergency conditions continued. The litter of syRen® bodies indicated further fighting. Anwar received a report that two of xis force had died in the last assault.

A shudder rumbled through the fabric of the station. The floor...moved, seemed to adopt an angle somewhat at odds with level, a small angle, but much more than was appropriate for a space station. The pseudo-grav failing? Quirk took Jenny's hand. She smiled at him, weakly.

"What the shit?" asked Moth, as another wave of trembling made them sway.

"Could be an impact on the station," said Anwar. "Possibly rupturing a section, destabilising the orbit."

"Thank fuck," said Moth. "I thought it was something bad." Quirk snorted.

The floor tipped violently downwards. The hellish emergency lights winked out, and everybody tumbled into darkness. Quirk flailed for purchase, tried to keep hold of Jenny's hand as they fell. An obstacle tumbled him over. He lost his grip. Jenny yelled.

Somewhere, Moth screamed an expletive. A laser flared in the dark, the flash of light showing Anwar ahead of him just before Quirk slammed hard into something soft-ish.

The jerking halt twisted him violently. He cried out as his leg bent, hip wrenched. He pivoted from sloping floor to slam into the sloping wall.

Ringing. Ringing. Ringing, like an old-fashioned fire bell, jangling his wits.

Lights danced in his head, motes, spots, laser lines. They jiggled and morphed, gyrating shapes, suns and moons gavotting, dinosaurs dancing the polka, amoebas jiving and twisting. And the ringing, like a town crier on meth.

"Hear yea, hear yea!" Callan's voice boomed from the sound system, cutting into Quirk's already overloaded senses. *"I say vengeance is mine, Simister be damned. He's in my house now! Please, try to reach your ship. More fun for me, you wallowin' around gettin' desperate."* He laughed, an abandoned sound, unhinged, merciless. *"I spiked first D ship, jettisoned the lifeboats, disabled the stability system, locked the elevator, an' configged the power unit to overload that monster battery core. I'm just takin' out trash before I leave. Reckon you got fifteen minutes till this place blows to hell. Oh, and bonus, I'm venting atmosphere, so you're all fucked, one way or another. Happy trails, motherfuckers!"*

Unhelpfully, Moth began yelling and firing at the station's central access core that ran up—well, forty-five degrees from up now—through the space station's vertical axis.

"Not helping, Moth!" he yelled.

"Stress relief," she called calmly from the darkness over to his left.

A body moved under Quirk. He rolled over into the crazy angle of wall and floor.

"You certainly know how to make an impact, Quirk," said Anwar, in the strained tone of someone clutching a body part in the hope it will hurt less.

"Which way to your boat?" called the disembodied Moth.

Anwar's laser on low power lit up the space, an eery roseate glow spilling dim and diffuse around them. It revealed a clutter of debris, and the sight of Jenny helping up a Rigel operative from under two android bodies that slid to what now was the bottom of this ring of the station.

"We're docked at the top ring access port," said Anwar. "The only way now is up the access core service ladder."

Everyone stopped talking and moved. With pseudo gravity still active, the slope defeated magboots, so they built a human ladder including those of Anwar's team still with them, Nick/X-209 at the base—of course—braced in the wall/floor angle, then boots on shoulders over almost twenty metres to the tubular core that ran the height of the station. As he planted his feet on the operative below then took Anwar's weight above him, Quirk wondered about variability in Callan's estimate for the explosion, and if it might generate a spear of flame incinerating anyone in the access tube.

Two black-suited figures climbed past Quirk before Jenny arrived. She snatched a kiss as she scrambled past. "Don't forget to pull up the ladder," he called after her.

Moth climbed over him last, being the lightest. She refrained from using the opportunity to punch him in the gut, or poke him in the eye. Didn't say a thing, just sprang up the human ladder, a coil of rope over her shoulder. Quirk craned his neck, his perspective upside down, and watched Moth tie off her rope then throw it down. This was already taking too long.

"Moth," he yelled. "Start climbing. We need to keep the ladder clear as possible."

He watched her do the math, fancied he could see reluctance, but that might be his wishful thinking. Finally, she nodded, then hauled open the door to the service shaft and waved Jenny in. Jennifer looked back then ducked inside, Moth disappearing after her.

A wave of relief. The station must be designed for segmentation in case of catastrophic failure. The top ring should separate intact. Assuming the battery core was located near the station's centre of mass, they just had to gain the top tier.

The load on Quirk's shoulders eased as two Rigel ops secured themselves at the service shaft entrance then began hauling in bodies from the human ladder.

"Climb past me, Quirk," Anwar urged, beckoning from above while hanging from the rope one-handed.

"Very chivalrous, old bean," said Quirk. He complied, sparing Anwar a quick smile as he clapped his hand on the assassin's shoulder for purchase.

Nick/X-209 joined him at the access shaft entrance and hauled Anwar up effortlessly. The assassin winked at him and pulled xis helmet on before climbing into the darkness. Quirk noticed a thinness to the air now. He fished out a breather with his free hand, broke the seal and fitted the golf-ball-sized model into his mouth, then waved the last of the Rigel ops past them.

"Yucht you ang gnee, son," said Quirk, pulling up the rope, which felt oddly sticky. Nano hooks, probably. The wash of diffuse laser light disappeared up the access shaft, leaving Quirk and Nick/X-209 in darkness. He tried his suit light: dead. Nick activated the android's violet eyes. Quirk's vision adjusted. Surreal. A decade in the orbit of Joshua Simister come down to this. Would they all end together? Was this it?

"Come on, Dad," said Nick. "Let's get out of here."

He handed Nick the rope, and moved into the tube, the syRen® boosting him upwards with a hand on his arse, its strength enviable to Quirk in his weakening state. A few too many burns and cuts and bruises. The ladder ran on what now was the upper side of the service shaft, generating the disturbing impression of climbing upside down, half-hanging from the ladder, barely seeing the rungs till his hands closed on them. Now he noticed the temperature rising. Sweat prickled his forehead. His limbs ached and he feared his legs failing him, even though he could rest his back on the tube's opposite side for moments at a time to ease the stress on his arms and legs.

"We're approaching the level of the battery core," said Nick/X-209 behind him. "The others are past, up ahead. Keep going, Dad. Keep pushing."

The heat rose from uncomfortable to excruciating.

"I can'k 'uch 'e rungs!" He hooked an arm through the ladder to save his palms.

X-209 squeezed up, head level with his waist. "Take my gloves." The android thrust them forwards. The strong odour of synthetic flesh melting filled the cramped space. Quirk struggled the gloves on, too tight, but he crammed his aching hands in and started climbing again. His head swam but he managed to progress, one hand above the other, lift his shaking leg, one foot above the other. It felt like hours.

Nick said, "Fifteen minutes, mark. Overheating of large battery cores is not accurately predictable. Shattering sublimation is taking longer in this case, maybe from the high-quality materials used in—"

"Yery inkeresking, guk giscracking!"

"Dad, temperature approaching limit of human survivability. Go faster!"

"I ang!"

The android drove into him from below, ramming him off the ladder, its head between his thighs, forcing him up the tube, him scrabbling to minimise the battering of his shoulders and back against the side of tube.

"My power reserves'll only sustain this for seconds!"

Quirk looked up. Maybe ten metres ahead, wobbling and juddering, he saw a light dancing, shining down now like a star. Nick/X-209 slowed dramatically. The heat had reduced.

"Keep climbing, Dad. I gotta jump out of this syRen®."

"Okay." Quirk started up again under his own power. "I chhink ik's ongy—"

***

Moth arrived at a small platform. The ladder continued past but, in the bobbing light of her flightsuit lamp, she saw a hatch. The heat at this level was powerful. She must be near the battery core. As if reading her mind, a yell came from below.

"Keep going. The ship's docked on the top ring."

She resisted the urge to spit out her breather—stupid design made talking nearly impossible—and shouted down a stream of garbage syllables about Anwar being a dick-loving dumbass, the first part not a criticism. She knew she had to continue, but truth was she struggled with exhaustion now. Climbing sapped her strength even before this horrendous heat. Must be the batteries, and Quirk and Nick still down there.

The suit lamp below caught her up. She glimpsed Jenny's upturned face smeared with dirt and sweat, features tight with worry. Man, the breathers really did look like a ball gag. Fucked up. She turned back to the ladder, did her best to get a shift on.

The temperature gradient in this fuxxing tube must span a hundred fuzking degrees. She'd started to shiver now as the temperature crashed, a terrible sign confirming Callan really had breached the station's containment. Or maybe he'd just opened the windows, except there was no whirlwind of catastrophic decompression. *Just a little prick then.* Controlled venting. *Bastard.*

Another door appeared. She swung away from the ladder and— even though the service tube continued, somewhere—plonked her butt on the canted ledge. *Just a couple of breaths.* Because this must be the top ring. Then she worked the door open: a simple, mechanical catch—*Hallelujah*—and stepped out.

She clutched the edge of the opening as she remembered the stupid slope just as her feet slipped from under her. Why couldn't the stupid pseudo-grav fail!

Two figures crouched at the bottom in the angle of floor and wall, bodies twitching alert as she appeared in the emergency red gloom. One brought their laser carbine up to target her. The other...waved. *Mary!*

That taller figure wore a matt grey flightsuit instead of the shiny S&M tacsuit—*Worrying trend there, possibly in my funking head*—of the Rigel ops. Mary Quon, because it couldn't be anyone else, waved her down, gesturing at a mylar sheet Moth guessed they planned to catch her in before she hit the bottom. She shrugged and let go.

The sheet did break her fall. Mary (under the tactical helmet) hugged her, and Moth hugged back then helped as Jenny slid down the floor then a Rigel ops, then another.

Anwar had just started xis slide when the battery core exploded.

XXXIX

10:43, 1 February 2100 (Earth date equivalent)
Cythera Station, Venus

The sun is less fierce than usual today. Baker Beach shines rosy gold in the late afternoon sun, the old red bridge looking down on the slowly diminishing revellers like an ancient guardian of the strait that opens into the Gulf of the Farallones and the Pacific Ocean.

Jenny arrives from a last dip in the water. Droplets glistening on her tanned skin. She drops down beside him, kissing him and stealing a slug of his beer. She smiles like she has all the answers, which she usually does.

He slips an arm round her waist, feels her warm, wet skin against his, looks deep into her eyes.

"What are you thinking?" he asks.

* * *

"What were you thinking?!"

He slams the door hard, the...child on the other side of the door with their house droid, Jenny in tears, but frustration and anger scrawled across her face.

"I'm thinking we talked about this!"

"No, you talked about it, then I got a rather limited right of reply, then you fucking ignored me!"

"Because you're never willing to have a proper conversation about anything. 'Oh, my job, my job, my job. I have to go somewhere, anywhere, never here.'"

"And who the fuck do you think sends me to...Astana, in this case?"

"Yes, of course, please drag my father into this."

"He did this, didn't he? Did you give him some hair from my comb, my nail clippings?" She cringes. "He's forever been trying to drive a wedge between us. Well, I guess he's fucking nailed it this time."

He snatches the Merrion jacket from the chair back, forces warm hands through the cool silk lining, opens the door and walks into the hall, patting his pants' pockets.

"Don't worry about your keys, you won't fucking need them!"

"Yeah, well...fuck you too."

* * *

Landing on a road in Esperanza, Santa Cruz with no windshield and one wheel.

A dash through hot air and palm fronds in Kuala Lumpur to stop Morton killing.

Lost in claustrophobic darkness at La Villa di Fantano before ten people die.

He felt this on the Moon. Falling into nothing. No one to catch him.

The plane came down in Canada, slowly, slowly, before it crashed and burned.

In Paris, they chased him onto a roof, wind gusting, trying to throw him off.

On Skye, he drove too fast. They tried to kill him and the car flipped over.

Out of control over the Atlantic. *Jenny!* Maybe she escaped this time, too.

A hail of gunfire in New York. Just another time he'd died, almost.

Just another time Moth risked death for him.

Sarah Charlotte di Fantano-Moratti, died at the scene (GSW).

Paolo Roberto Emanuele Christian di Fantano-Moratti, died at the scene (GSW).

Anthony di Fantano – dead, poisoning (neurotoxin).

Giuseppe Trevi – dead, cranial trauma (murder by micro-drone (robot)—MBR)

Dr. John Mills – dead, blunt force trauma (murder by android (robot)—MBR).

Yivgeny Shurikov, ex-Geeocorp supervisor – dead, asphyxia (suffocation, MBR).

Elise Thompson, Geeocorp admin – dead, asphyxia (strangulation, MBR).

Wataru Asano, driver – dead, asphyxia (O2 deprivation, MBR).

Takuma Tomiyasu, driver – dead, asphyxia (O2 dep, MBR).

Caroline Angela McMurtry, lunar sec-ops – dead, asphyxia (O2 dep, MBR).

Vihaan Batra, GC depot manager – dead, blunt force trauma (MBR).

128 people: Lunaville dome disaster – dead, various causations (MBR).

Barry Rowland – dead, poisoning (neurotoxin).

18 people: Yellowknife, Northwest Territories and environs – various causations.

Derek George Morton – dead, asphyxia (strangulation, MBR).

Nicholas Quinton Kirby – dead, cranial trauma (GSW): Risen again, hallelujah.

Giulia di Fantano – dead, multiple lasergun wounds (LGW, MBR).

Quinton Ignatius Richmond Kirby...

Cold.

These bloody suits, the envsuits and the flightsuits and the tacsuits—inventive as all hell in application of the best tech, but never really keep out the cold.

So cold. Maybe...

He opened his eyes. Closed them again.

I appear to be outside. This is not a good thing.

At least the gnawing cold bit right through all the other little pains and aches, and his leg felt wet. Or it had. He remembered warm, wet sensations before it became cold and heavy.

He opened his eyes again, better than being in his head.

Still outside. The space station hung in darkness, listing, clouds of gas and debris venting from the central ring. In fact, Cythera Station's spine was broken, the top ring no longer connected to the main body, although they hung together in a roughly equivalent orbit, for now.

Moth, Anwar, Mary.

Jenny.

Just then, he shivered, legs spasming, and the action sent him in motion, turning him away from the station. He turned his head to keep it in view and wondered then why he wasn't dead, his head exploded, or frozen, or shattered. He remembered—somehow, in the midst of extreme mental fuzziness—that his wonderful suit possessed an airtight field projector in the rigid collar where a physical helmet would attach. No doubt the virtual helmet had deployed when— Well, clearly, he'd been thrown clear of the station when the battery core exploded.

He looked "down."

Hm.

That explosion certainly would account for the fact he appeared to be missing his left leg below the knee. An important lack that the suit must have compensated for by sealing the flappy ends of fabric with a similarly generated field. All very well, but flightsuits were not spacesuits. Assuming he'd been passed out for several minutes (not hours; he'd be dead already), he probably had little time left before... He sighed, turned his gaze on Venus, really spectacularly beautiful this time of year, but very cold indeed.

* * *

The feeling of wanting to heave passed quickly, thank fux. It had taken a sickening moment to get her magboots switched off as the floor tipped and swung. At least weightless, the pseudo-grav finally dead, she had a chance to fend off walls and ceilings if they came at her, and wasn't in danger of drowning in her own vomit because of the stupid breather. She'd managed to grab Jennifer at one point in passing, get *her* boots switched off before they did her an injury. There must be stabilising jets on this pancake, right? The twisting had reduced steadily for a couple of minutes since the blast. This top disc still rotated slightly though: Venus passed sedately beyond the walldows. Oh, and was visible through the big fuck-off hole ripped in the wall ten metres from where the D ship was docked.

Approaching the station, Quirk had commented on the main tier looking like a bicycle wheel, complete with disc brake-sized axial accommodation then spokes out to the ring of habitation like the bicycle tyre. Quirk was such an anorak, and now he...

No, fuck that! He comes home, cos I dicking well say so. Stupid crapbag! He's so slow, probably still lounging around the bottom section waiting for me to rescue him.

And where was Nick? She told herself he'd be okay, could jump through station systems to reach a syRen® in a good place. *And,* she'd been goddamn right, again! TOM *had* cooked up some weird fucking super neuro Hoover piece of shit. Had they really killed him? His body, yes, she'd seen his death in the raw, undeniable. But had he truly copied himself? *Fuck that bastard to hell.* Her right-now problem was the Boss, and she couldn't save him until she found him. And she couldn't find him now without a tactical suit and space-grade helmet, stat.

The floor, or the ceiling—one of the two—rotated lazily towards her. She located Mary—still tethered near the airlock—and pushed off towards her. Mary saw her coming, held out a hand. Moth grabbed her arm and Mary pulled her in, hugged her quickly. Moth jerked her thumb at the stupid-ass golf ball breather in her mouth then mimed pulling on a helmet.

Mary nodded, but pointed away from the airlock. Turning, Moth saw two Rigel ops approaching, guiding Jenny Kirby towards the relative safety of the D ship.

Moth's heart lurched. Fingers cold and stiff even with the same energy field around her hands that made the short-term emergency orb around her head, she made a "Q" sign at Mary. Mary did not shake her head, but jerked her thumb downwards. Moth knew what that meant: missing, presumed neck-deep in the shit.

I will NOT give up on him. No detective left behind.

She waited for the new arrivals to get aboard then pulled herself into the D ship airlock. A helmeted Rigel ops cycled her through after a short pause in which the thin figure seemed to listen, then nodded. The ops admitted her to the D ship, tapping their wrist as she floated through, showing her five fingers. What the fuzk did that mean? Leaving in five minutes? That sounded about right if they'd written Quirk off.

Not on my watch, shit-shovelers. <Implant, timer, two minutes.> Might as well have a countdown to keep her honest, every other fucking job seemed to have one.

Immediately once onboard ship, she spat out her fuxxing breather. It spun off into an instrument panel and bounced away, dripping saliva. She ignored the people sitting at flight stations, planning, or hustling about operational tasks. She searched the clear-doored, spotlit equipment lockers around the walls, underlining the tactical nature of this ship compared to the ride she'd come in on. She'd decided she didn't have time to change into a tacsuit and helmet. If they'd written Quirk off, and she didn't get back off this boat in two minutes, they'd probably tie her to a flight couch for departure. Jenny wouldn't let them leave without Quirk, but could Jenny override Anwar?

She kicked off toward one locker containing a two-by-five array of winking instrument lights, pulled it open, and found what she hoped she would. She grabbed a military grade tactical collar and clipped it onto her suit's helmet ring. A glance at the neighbouring locker revealed lines of combat breathers, their ULEDs blinking green. She cracked that locker and stuffed two breathers into each of her flightsuit rib pockets, fumbling one in her increasingly nervous hurry so she had to grab it from the air as it tried to spin away across the cabin. The next cabinet held laser carbines. It was locked and ID coded. Fine, she didn't need weaponry. It took precious seconds to find a maintenance locker—down at deck level, of course, a solid metal box—but at least accessible. She fished out a suitably hefty rivet gun and clipped it to her suit. She grabbed some field dressings as an afterthought, jammed them in her pockets.

She turned and pushed off towards the airlock. The panel showed it cycling. She had to wait. She fidgeted, glanced at the lockers flanking the door. One held coils of the same black nano rope the Rigel ops had used on the station. She opened the locker, took the biggest coil she could see. The label read one hundred twelve metres. Thin, but made from nano fibres, probably with a smart coating, the thing had heft.

Hurry the fuck up!

Her timer went off.

<Silence,> she snapped.

The airlock tripped and suited bodies exited, pulling off helmets, magboots already activated. She had a hunch Anwar would block her play. Unacceptable. And anyway, she'd done this shit before. She had EVA experience with the Hygeia Marine Scouts like four weeks ago, fishing another bloke in her life out of the soup there too, but she hadn't been afraid then. Quirk might— She shuddered, approached the closing airlock.

"Where are you going?" asked Anwar as xe pulled off xis helmet.

"Find Quirk." She slapped the airlock door release, reversing its motion.

"Moth, he was right in the heart of the explosion. There's no chance... Of course, we'll try to recover him—"

"Fuck that! You don't give up on Quinton Kirby. Right, Jenny?"

Mrs. Kirby looked pretty cut up, red-eyed under the grime and pasted hair, but she nodded, wiped her eyes, mouth setting hard. "Quirk wouldn't leave you, Anwar."

"Moth, you stay put—"

"Go to hell." She pulled herself into the airlock, slammed the pad on the other side. Through the porthole she saw Anwar wave a hand dismissively in her direction. The instant her implant announced, "Paired with new tactical collar," she heard Anwar loud and clear.

"Being a hothead gets you nowhere in this game, honey. *We'll push off and enact close search protocol, which I intended all along, because of course I wouldn't leave him, you little prick."*

<Didn't you come to kill TOM, *honey?* Assassin brackets attempted isn't a great job description.>

As the airlock vented air, her finger hovered over the collar controls, but her flightsuit triggered the helmet field. The slight distortion of a proper tactical helmet rig appeared before her eyes as she moved her hand over the door release, waiting on the big, red physical button (because nobody liked the "Did-I-didn't-I?" uncertainty of a touchpad with the risk of pissing all your O2 into space and perhaps yourself with it).

The button turned from red to green and she jabbed it with her fist. For a few seconds she'd been scared Anwar would disengage the docking clamps before she got the airlock door open, or in some other way override her exit, but xe didn't. She pulled herself out and smacked the "Close" button, clung to a handhold until the airlock door thudded shut. Not that she heard the clunk with all atmosphere gone from the ruined space station. She felt it though through the wrecked and twisted metal and plastic.

"You want to keep bitching," asked Anwar. *"Or would you prefer useful intel?"*

Now the shudder of the docking clamps releasing reached her. She pushed off into the dimness aiming for a handhold five metres away.

<Tell me.>

"If you'd hung around and not been a little bitch—" Was xe trying to out-swear her? Fucker. *"You'd know Rigel's flightsuits have trackers in the fabric. Every hundredth thread is a transmitter."*

<Where is he?>

"There are two signals... They're a good distance apart."

Oh, shit. <Just tell me.>

"Location on the tactical subnet now."

How could no one else be as freaked as she was? She just wanted to cry, scream, smash shit up.

The tactical collar did some cool stuff and two bright yellow blips appeared, projected on the helmet field containing breathable atmosphere around her head. One seventy-five metres and two twenty-seven. *Shit.* Just numbers. She'd confront them when she had to. She maxed her suit lamp then pushed herself at a spot beside the gaping hole in the space station.

<Collar, update relative locations. Collar, save last command as shortcut 'Update.'>

"Shortcut set."

<Update.>

"Signal A, one four eight metres, and Signal B two eight three."

<Query signal strength.>

"Signal A, 0.12 relative, Signal B 1.00 relative."

Of course the stronger signal was further away, and receding. She looped an end of her nano rope through a twisted spar, tied it off then pushed through the opening, allowing herself to drift a couple of metres from the station's hulk. The Rigel D ship turned slowly on thrusters. It being designed for intra solar system travel, she believed she could reach Quirk quicker. She had to. The fact her rope wasn't long enough, while being bloody shite, wasn't the end of the world. But what if Anwar reverted to xis plan to kill Quirk now Giulia was gone, and TOM dead?

She pulled herself into contact with the station, tugged three times on the nano rope to untie the knot, coiled in the slack, and looped the rope over her shoulder. With an awkward handhold on the station's exterior, she crouched, twisting her body to align with the dot on her display, knees bent, neck cricked forward. She took a deep breath then launched herself outwards with all her strength.

<Update.>

"Signal A—"

<Report Signal B only.>

"Signal B, two sixty metres and closing. Two hundred. One hundred fifty. Current course tangential to target. Closest approach thirty-nine metres."

Missed, stupid wench. Come on, Moth.

She reached for the rivet gun wafting at her waist, aimed behind her, hoping she wasn't about to pin her foot to Venus, and fired. The pack said fifty gramme rivets, so she fired off ten, then another ten, reviewed the display's glowing dot, another ten.

<Update!>

"Current course tangential to target. Closest approach twenty-eight metres. Distance one one eight metres."

Shit. She fired off the rest of the rivet mag.

[A bit to the left.]

<Update.>

"Current course tangential to target. Closest approach eighteen metres. Distance one zero one metres."

<Fuck off! He's fucking dying, and he needs me to save him!>

"Invalid command."

She consulted the display, saw the glowing dot but also saw— <Display off!>—a glint of reflected light from the Sun to Venus then, through one of those laws (reflection, duh!), from Venus to Quirk to her.

<Update.>

[Moth, a lot more rivets, eight o'clock. Quick.]

<Nick?>

[Sorry! Took me a minute to crack the D ship and find the route to your suit. Moth, throw the—]

"Current course tangential to target. Closest approach twelve metres. Distance seventy metres."

<The gun. I got it.> Not taking her eyes from the glint, which she saw came from a larger, darker shape, she unlatched the tool from her waist. So much closer now, she needed a bigger correction. She cranked her hand over her shoulder once, twice, then let the heavy rivet gun fly from her hand, a good half-kilogramme of mass, guesstimating the correct angle. Because if she missed the target…

[Not great. Get ready to reach!]

She had no fuxxing clue how fast she travelled, probably too fast. Where was the damn D ship anyway? Anwar was so full of shit. She bet xe *did* want to kill Quirk.

<Update!>

"Please adjust your volume and rep—"

<Update.>

"Current course tangential to target. Closest approach twenty-nine metres. Distance fifty metres."

Shit! She'd messed up, way over-corrected.

The rope.

Twisting, gaze fixed on the growing human shape that—clearly—she would miss, she unslung the rope, held both ends and flung the rest outward with an underarm whipping motion. Releasing all that mass set her spinning away, turned her into a winch, the rope starting to wrap around her waist even as the unspooling coil flew out sideways.

She saw Quirk now, something wrong with his shape. At least she could judge her path relative to his. The moment of truth. Maybe he was already dead, but his emergency virtual helmet remained up.

Then the D ship cut between her and the Sun, throwing shadow over everything, the bright, cloudy mass of Venus backlighting Quirk. The ship moved past. Everything lit up. One length of the unspooled rope had passed him, but his arm intercepted the other side of the loop! Would it catch? She whipped a wave into the unspooled rope, her spinning at least having anchored the ends. The sinusoidal wave cut under his leg as the loop caught his shoulder. He twisted over, but the rope held. *Grazie a Dio!* She jerked to an almost-halt, pain biting her hips. Quirk had started drifting towards her. She began to pull him in, the action stabilising her remaining spin.

[You did it, babe!]

She suppressed a surge of joy. *Fuck, he's missing half a leg!*

She and Quirk slalomed around whatever new twist-turny centre of gravity existed between them part way along the rope. It stretched tight, she swung past Quirk or him past her, the rope slackening, tightening again, jerking again until, at last, she grabbed onto him. She hugged him, trying not to think about anything as the planet swung lazily above then below then above them.

She fought dizziness, pulled herself up, or Quirk down, maybe (much too fucked-up to work that out), so she could see his face. So pale. *No, Quirk! We've got a fuzking deal, you always come home!* She reached for a fresh breather—only paused a second before sticking her hand through his helmet field—which would seal around the edges of her arm. Not even slightly gentle, she squeezed his cheeks at the top of his jaw, expelling his old breather—which bobbed to the side as they twisted slowly—forced the new breather in, flicking on its emergency setting, to force air into Quirk's lungs.

Nothing. Eyes still closed, blind to the beauty of Venus and the sparkle of the stars. She made sure of her left hand's grip on his suit then started pounding on Quirk's chest with her right fist.

<You...

<Fucking...

<Promised...

<Me...

<You...

<Fucking...

<Crazy...

<Detective!>

The dark hulk of the Rigel D ship loomed close now, but she didn't even notice until hands gripped her, pulled her back, dragged her away. *No!* She fought them, but there were too many, at least four.

[It's okay, Moth. They got this.]

Another figure—tall and in full helmeted shiny black tacsuit—moved in on Quirk. They worked their EVA pack minijets to a point they could clamp their legs around his waist facing his feet, then closed a medical response unit around his forearm, watched it seal on and start to produce readings, before turning back to the remainder of his leg. At that point the hands turned her and pushed her toward the D ship.

She waited by outside the hatch until they'd taken Quirk through the airlock. Exiting the airlock herself, Moth clicked on her magboots and clumped past the waiting Anwar into a reasonably open space so she could turn on xim. Jenny watched on from a chair, clearly exhausted, but smiling.

"You're not going to kill him then?! Callan done that job for you?"

"Moth, he's alive," said Jenny. *Oh, duh. Smiling, of course.* "In the sickbay. They're operating. He'll be fine."

"Oh, okay, so you'll let him heal up for a few days before you kill him?"

"I have no intention of killing Quirk, Moth," said Anwar, levelly. "That boat sailed. I actually rather like him, as it happens. He's fast becoming my favourite fop. And anyway, I work for you now, in Signora di Fantano's...absence."

That stopped her dead. She realised she stood, hands on hips, in the middle of the D ship's flightdeck while ten people—Anwar, Jenny, Mary and several grizzled-looking Rigel ops—stood, sat or leaned, watching her.

"Right. Well, uh, Nick Kirby, report, please."

Nick spoke loud and clear through the D ship's PA. *"Operative Kirby reporting for duty, Miss Moratti. For the record, I can confirm the death of Joshua Simister at ten twenty-six AM Earth equivalent, on Monday, February 1, 2100. Hacked Cythera Station camera footage corroborates that his body suffered a gunshot wound to the chest, a short-duration laser burst to the forehead, and strangulation (postmortem) for a period of twenty-six seconds. Consequently, the third tier of the station suffered damage from the battery core explosion which resulted in the venting of atmosphere, leaving that ring in an anaerobic state for...twenty-four minutes and counting."*

"Callan?"

"I've searched this ship's system and all subsystems within it, handsets, suit units, etcetera. There is no sign of Gregor Callan aboard. The Evolution's Prayer remains docked to the station's central ring; its engine damaged irreparable. The explosion has disrupted the station's orbit, which now is decaying. The remnants of Cythera Station will drop towards the planet and will decompose as a result of adverse atmospheric conditions in a timeframe of two to four Earth hours."

Silence reigned after Nick stopped speaking.

"So," said Anwar Cruz, addressing Moth. "What now?"

She thought for a moment, looking around the faces watching her, waiting for her decision. What would Quirk do? What would Mario do? What would Giulia...have done? Take care of family.

"Set course for Earth, and strap in. I've got a funeral to attend. After that, all bets are off."

XL

24 days later...
11:05, 25 February 2100
Piazzale Cimitero Monumentale, 20154 Milano, Italy,
Euro Bloc Sud, Earth

Moth stood at Giulia's graveside, clustered family and friends seated left, right and opposite. She focused again on her outstretched hand, her white glove now dirtied by the rich, brown soil she held. Somehow, this seemed the only true acknowledgment that her dear Zietta Giulia, her friend, her aunt, was gone.

Quirk stood just behind her left shoulder, seemingly comfortable enough on his newish prosthetic leg, although from his *constant carping*, he wasn't comfortable *with* it, yet. At least he was enjoying the break from the questioning and legal negotiations.

On her right side stood Jennifer, hand resting lightly on Moth's shoulder. The sort of gesture she would have swiped away a year ago, but now... Jenny's presence comforted her. Weird as fuck. Looking across the grave at Mario, Jenna Lucia and numerous other relatives sat equally weird with her. Shouldn't she be on their side of the grave? She did not feel she should, not this time.

"Not even killed by a human," she mumbled to no one in particular.

La Madre Superiora of the convent of the Little Sisters of the Human Ascension, the formidable Abbess Sofia di Natale, got up from her seat and came to stand with her.

"She is with God now, Angelika. Trust in Him."

Moth nodded, opened her clenched hand and let the earth fall to rattle on Giulia di Fantano's coffin.

Hey, God. I read somewhere you're a vengeful sorta guy. That being the case, Dio Mio, *I think we're gonna get on just fine.*

Cousin Mario watched her across the grave. She could tell he was wondering if she would take the Rigel job—position rather. She was family after all. She decided then that she would take it, but only as an "in" to the business, a way to gather knowledge and training, learn how to conduct herself properly in a corporate environment, but also a tactical one, to operate with max effect. And, only on her terms, because there was no way on this smelly, dirty, messed up and mistreated Earth she would give up working with Quirk. They were just getting started. It was only six months for fux sake! Think of the shit they could get into in a year.

And then there was Jenny, whose hand on her shoulder felt— This was some soppy-assed shit, but it felt like a kind of love she hadn't known in a long time. Maybe that was too early to say, but the signs were good. Jennifer Simister was good.

* * *

7 days later...
14:33, 2 March 2100
27A Zollstrasse, Zürich, Switzerland

A week after Giulia di Fantano's funeral Quirk thought he finally had a handle on this new leg thing. Half a leg, to be fair. It barely felt mechanical at all, made from materials called pseudo-dermals and subcutaneous texture replacers and tibionics. The warranty alone read like a Silicon County phonebook. Not only did the (lower) leg communicate with his handset, but its built-in data depository connected to his shiny (metaphorically) new aural implant. Much more importantly, Jenny was not in any way put off by the thing. She hadn't forgotten the two kisses on Cythera Station and had, after their arrival back on Earth and journey to Milan, agreed to him following up that line of enquiry.

The lead had taken him down a trail of intimate dinners, park walks, lost weekends and lazy breakfasts (strictly room service). He had conducted interviews with her in public places with plenty of witnesses around. They took place on cobbled streets over the chipped varnish of café tables, across linen tablecloths in cosy courtyard bistros, and seated side by side with a glass of wine before dinner in whatever restaurant they'd chosen while strolling away the afternoon through Milan's ancient streets.

Following Giulia's funeral, Moth had split her time between casework research, and putting in hours at Rigel. She wanted to continue on that track for a few weeks, and he had acquiesced. So, The Quirk Agency took temporary office space in Milan. Moth had pushed that idea hard, and he had other uses for his still-recovering energy, much more important than arguing with a fifteen-year-old. She proposed that she and Nick would keep business ticking over while he worked with Mary Quon and Sec-Tech Suudi to resolve his "legal issues." It was not lost on Quirk that another outcome was him, Jenny, Moth and Nick spending a good deal of time together. Minutes of Quirk Agency meetings—now featuring Jenny as office manager—recorded that he endorsed this arrangement for reasons like operational efficiency, and ensuring net zero compliance, but Jenny saw the truth and confronted him with it. He wanted the four of them to be together for a while, to try being a family and see what happened. A month later no one had lost any more body parts. Things were going swimmingly.

No funeral took place for Joshua Simister. His body was lost, presumed burned to ash on re-entry to Venus, or eaten to atoms by the planet's monumentally toxic atmosphere. Either end seemed appropriate. Nick provided what evidence he could, and this satisfied the authorities sufficiently for them to issue a death certificate. That in turn led Jenny, Quirk, Nick/S-21037, and Moth to legal offices in Switzerland for the reading of The Old Man's last will and testament.

The firm's senior partner, Herr Gerhard Maurer, performed the honours in an office so sparsely furnished, Quirk expected a couple of androids to appear with paint sprays and a ladder. The seats were comfortable though, improbably so from the look of them.

The impeccably suited, greying man, witnessed by a similarly impressive and experienced-looking colleague, cracked open a thin plaper envelope, extracted two sheets of plaper, scanned one page, then the other.

"Well," said Herr Maurer happily. "I am pleased to say that I can summarise this very easily for you, Mrs. Kirby." He smiled at Jenny. "Your father left you everything."

Quirk raised three fingers to his mouth to remind himself to keep the bloody thing shut. He watched Jenny's very pretty eyes widen. "Do you mean...?"

"The property portfolio—which Maurer, Schnoor and Maurer have had the pleasure of administrating for over fifty years is very extensive, but perhaps most importantly—"

"Fuck off," said Moth, with quiet wonder. Quirk permitted himself a smile, although he had not been willing consciously to contemplate this possibility before today. Moth, sheepishly, said, "Sorry, Herr Lawyer, please continue."

"Hm, yes, most importantly, Mrs. Kirby, you are now the majority shareholder and therefore chairman of C Corporation. Frau Schnoor"—he nodded to his colleague—"has been undertaking essential management functions for the last few weeks, but will be pleased to resign as company secretary at a date of your choosing so you can take up your role, appoint or retain company officers, etcetera."

"Uh, Jenny?" said Moth.

"Yes, Moth?" said Jenny, rather absently.

"I think you just became the richest person on the planet."

Herr Maurer smiled with admirable neutrality and nodded.

XLI

3 days later...
11:01, 5 March 2100
Piazza del Duomo, Milano, Italy, Euro Bloc Sud

Jenny had it all worked out, thought Quirk, contemplating the plan she'd just recounted to him while Bea went to obtain one latte and one macchiato.

She had already confirmed to Maurer, Schnoor and Maurer that she would take the helm of C Corp on April first. She insisted she needed that time to reset after recent trauma, and nobody disagreed. Certainly not him, definitely not Moth, and Nick was delighted the four could extend their time together.

For Jennifer, the plan involved orientation to the mind-blowing notion of being in charge of—in *ownership* of—the most valuable corporate entity in Humankind's history. She made no effort in their long talks to disguise how exciting she found the prospect, but also how daunted she felt.

"You'll have advisors around you," said Quirk. "And you can bring in more; people you trust. If you need any recommendations, I'd say Mary Quon, for one. Anwar might be a bit of a stretch as corporate security officer, but you could keep xim off-book. Alternatively, there's Dunevan Rice, or a certain Sheriff Wayne Kreski of Creston, BC, who might be ready for a career change. Eve Meyer might be persuaded to come back to the fold if she knew she'd be on the side of the angels this time."

"What about you?" she said, looking down at the table, knowing what she asked. Much to his relief, he didn't have to answer with those beautiful, insightful eyes on him.

"I'll always be here for you, any time, but the corporate sphere has whipped the rug out from under me so many times. Let me think about it?" She nodded.

For Quirk, her plan allowed for continued convalescence and adjustment to his new prosthetic left leg (only below the knee!), but also the pursuit of a new perspective on recent events. This comprised: (a) a break from detective work, including but not limited to, (i) setting up an "Out of Office" on all comms platforms, (ii) refraining from checking said platforms more than once a week, (iii) only checking messages in her presence, ensuring her ability to countermand any wild notions like taking a case; (b) visits (with her, and Bea) to various locations where "bad shit" had occurred in order to, (i) exorcise as many bad memories and negatively reinforcing thought processes (Jennifer had been a psych major) as possible, (ii) reconnect with and give thanks to those who had aided him, or perhaps had suffered at the hands of his antagonists, (iii) explain to her events in relation to (ii), above, so she might understand the extent of her father's impact on people; (c) Moth having space to, (i) process her own highly complex and tangled emotions, (ii) cement her burgeoning friendship with Nick, (iii) support Nick (and he her) through emotional readjustment—because both quasi-human digitally-mounted physically-manifesting consciousnesses and human teenagers should talk about their feelings; (d) Quirk reaching a decision about her request that he return to C Corp; (e) discovering where they— Quinton and Jennifer, Jenny and Quirk—might be going, and if they might be going there together.

The North American leg of Jenny's proposed pilgrimage presented a significant problem. The small matter of him being absconded (against his will!) from custody in New York seemed to remain a sore point with the FBI. But Mary Quon was on the case. Events at the UN— and by extension those in orbit around Mars—had come under intense scrutiny by the NYPD, FBI, NSA, CIA and various other refugees from a broken Scrabble set. Sec-Tech Suudi had been good enough to vouch for him as working against the real antagonists, and only this permitted Quirk to remain at large at all, although suitably tagged. No doubt some satellite watched him even now, as he and Jennifer sat at the café in the cloister adjacent to the Duomo di Milano, awaiting Bea's return with their coffees.

Clearly, Jennifer had thought things through, extensively, and she was still here, which was all he really cared about right now, he found.

Thus, he agreed to her plan, gladly. He also decided in that moment that he would return to C Corp, because if the recent calamity had proved anything, it was that there could be no greater pleasure in the worlds than being with Jennifer Kirby.

Bea returned with their coffees. The syRen®—on loan from Moth—sat and placidly stared into space. But of course, it...*she* didn't. S-17834 watched everything.

"Anwar Cruz is approaching across the piazza," said Bea.

Quirk tensed, began to turn, but Jennifer's hand on top of his forestalled him, and he looked back to her, found her smiling softly, eyes sparkling, as ever.

"It's okay. Xe's not going to kill you."

"Says you," said Quirk, still not looking away. "I was hoping we'd got past the point of you taking out a contract on me."

"We had a contract." she smiled evenly. "You broke it."

"And you mended it."

"I'm working on that."

Quirk smiled, squeezed her hand, and stood, still not past a split second of wondering if his high-tech gammy leg would support him. He turned to meet Anwar.

Impossible not to recall their first encounter, here in the piazza only seven months before. At least Anwar's sartorial judgement had improved.

"Nice suit."

"Classic Brioni. I think you might have rubbed off on me, Quirk."

He ignored the jibe. Or was it a come-on? A mostly alarming thought. He really must find some friends who had never possessed a desire to see him dead. And he did see Anwar as a friend now, an even more alarming thought. "I see your eyes are brown today."

"Their natural colour. Look, I wasn't at the funeral because—"

"Say no more," said Quirk, holding up a hand. "Too awkward."

"Unlike this," Anwar smirked.

Quirk realised that he had, quite some time ago, stopped seeing Anwar as xis job, or as xis anger, xis loss, or even xis pronouns. He only saw Anwar Cruz, whose life—like so many others—TOM had indirectly but comprehensively ripped apart. Albeit Anwar had been complicit in that by engaging in the rather volatile career of professional assassin. They'd all covered a spectacular amount of ground and space, yet ended up roughly where they began. Just with more friends.

"Thank you, Anwar. You've pulled us all out of quite a few scrapes in the short time of our acquaintance. But most of all I appreciate that you never got around to shooting me."

Anwar extended a hand and Quirk took it, shaking it at first, but held on for few moments longer. You learned a lot about a person from their handshake, and Anwar Cruz possessed a firm grip, but not overpowering. A grip that gave space for the other party to express themselves.

"If I get into trouble down the road, I'll be sure to call you."

"Please don't," said Anwar with a dry look. "On either count." Xe released Quirk's hand, turned, and walked away towards the metro.

EPILOGUE

18 Months later
05:13, 29 October 2101
[LOCATION REDACTED]

"Moth, be careful."

<What do you care?>

"Of course I care! In the sense that... What I mean is... I'm trying to say look after yourself. You're increasingly crap at that."

She checked the settings on her weapons again, checked the vidfeed from her nano drones in the corridor ahead—Empty—then ran out of distractions from the way her thoughts headed, and had done more and more recently.

<Nick, do you...like me?>

"Of course I do. What's not to like?"

<Uh, a bullet in the head? I mean *like* me.>

He actually sighed at that. *"Look, I've seen you still twitching through the night like Sleeping Beauty on steroids over this, and it's pretty painful to watch. We're done with it, okay? Moth, you* made *me. You set me free from the pain of The Old Man's tortures in the name of what he called science. Yes, I like you. I like you a lot."*

<Well shit.> Moth flicked off her safeties and hit the door control with the heel of her right hand. <Right after I shoot this place to fuck and blow up another Callan-infested server you're going to explain to me what that means, and what we're going to do about it.>

THE END

Quirk and Moth will return.

ACKNOWLEDGEMENTS

William and Heather Tracy of Space Wizard, your support for me, and for Quirk & Moth has been incredible. It has been my privilege to be a part of the journey you have taken these three years and more. Thank you for championing the stories that you do. I am honoured that mine have been among them.

The Glasgow SF Writers' Circle, your support and collective wisdom are a constant source of encouragement and inspiration: Yous are top dollar, by the way.

Always, always, always, the Reading Excuses crew, in particular JS, Sara, and Natalie who have been there from the beginning. In particular J.S. Fields for the cover quote.

The Writing Excuses Podcast for being the catalyst, without whose writing prompts Quirk and Moth likely would never have existed.

No receipt, nor any geegaw can for a writer supplant the knowledge that people read and enjoy their stories. I am thankful for anyone who has given a kind word about Quirk & Moth, but my especial thanks go to Nadya Mercik for her generous reviews on the BFS website; to Reece Hogan for such kind and encouraging words; to Neil Williamson for getting where I was coming from; and to David Thaw, Dr. Philip Ewart, and Alan Owen.

Paul Harris, many thank yous for the Q&M logo. I'm still not sure how to feel about you sending versions for Books 4, 5, and 6!

Glasgow & West of Scotland "pirates" Discord. You saw me through that month of the year when lots of people do lots of writing. Thank you for that boost.

MoorBooks, for their fantastic cover; you knocked it into orbit this time.

Tantor Media for their excellent productions of *The Mandroid Murders* and *The Carborundum Conundrum*, and especially to Adi Cabral for bringing vibrant life to all my characters.

Ann Landman, who deserves all the thanks in the world for her amazing work with the Cymera Festival, and her infectious enthusiasm for genre literature.

My family—Ashley and Micah, Moss & Ivy—for all their love and support.

Tara, for everything, always and forever.

Peace and love.

ABOUT THE AUTHOR

Robin Duncan is a Scot born and living in Glasgow. A Civil Engineer by profession, he has written since 1980, but seriously only for the last 12 years. Robin's debut novel *The Mandroid Murders* published in 2022; its sequel *The Carborundum Conundrum* in 2023.

His stories feature in Space Wizard's *Distant Gardens*, *Farther Reefs*, *Lofty Mountains* and *World of Juno* anthologies. Robin's story "The NEU Oblivion" was long-listed for the 2019 James White Award.

Robin belongs to the Glasgow SF Writers' Circle, Reading Excuses, the British Fantasy Society, and the British Science Fiction Association. robincmduncan.com

Please take a moment to review this book at your favorite retailer's website, Goodreads, or simply tell your friends!

www.ingramcontent.com/pod-product-compliance
Lightning Source LLC
Chambersburg PA
CBHW031510010826
48973CB00012B/146